Mikael Lundt

COLD SEED
Beneath the Ice

MIKAEL LUNDT
AUTOR & SELFPUBLISHER

Imprint:
© Mikael Lundt 2024
Editing & Proofreading: Cecilia Rydberg
Cover design: Michael Gückel
Photo credits: Mike McGee

Publisher:
Mikael Lundt c/o Michael Gückel
Gartenstr. 15, 95191 Leupoldsgrün, GERMANY

Contact: mikael@mikael-lundt.de
On the net: www.mikael-lundt.de

Print: Amazon KDP
ISBN: 9798333381453

1

U.S. base " Camp Century", Greenland
August 2, 1967

Paul Memphis' heavy boots crunched on the hard-packed ice of the tunnel floor as he hurried along the narrow shaft. The ground was so hard due to the severe frost that it sounded as if he was walking over coarse gravel with every step. What's more, the sound echoed unnaturally loudly from the smooth walls that bordered the tunnel on all sides: twelve meters of ice upwards, a few kilometers downwards, and, depending on the direction, 80 to 800 kilometers to the sides.

Before he was stationed on Greenland, Memphis had never imagined how immense the ice masses were here, how huge the dimensions of the glacier were - and how enormous the problems were that the ice caused every day down here in the tunnels.

The frosty air gradually burned in Memphis' lungs, forcing him to slow down a little. The vapor from his breath poured out of his mouth in thick white clouds and condensed instantly. It was 25 degrees below zero in the tunnel, making it only slightly warmer than on the surface. As he had run most of the way, he was sweating under his thick polar gear. After so many months, he hardly cared about the cold anyway.

The lights in the corridor flickered for a moment and then went out completely for a brief second. Memphis stopped abruptly and imagined with growing unease what would happen if the lights failed forever. He hated the thought! Impenetrable darkness met unrelenting cold that wanted to suck the life out of him. The light promptly returned, and Memphis called himself to order. He had to keep going!

The incessant crunching of his boots was increasingly mixed with cracking and roaring. He knew that the surface above him was a hive of activity. Up there, the numerous Caterpillar vehicles that were to take the equipment and crew away from here forever were being loaded on a piecework basis.

This had been happening since this morning when he and his Danish colleague Erik Jansson brought the first load of equipment to the surface. The soldiers' unusual haste had been ordered from the very top. And Memphis himself was also clear: they had to hurry.

He would have preferred to go with Jansson, who was surely already halfway home. But he had had to stay because some stubborn fellow scientists were still reluctant to leave this gigantic block of ice on the edge of civilization. Unfortunately, despite the commander's warnings, one of these scientists was his boss, who had sent him out to collect samples shortly before his departure. He had no idea why. There was no time left for them to analyze anything!

At the end of the tunnel, one of the many isolated huts that the military had built into the shafts in the glacier over the last few years appeared. Memphis climbed the few steps and entered the hut, which was still several degrees below zero. He burst into the middle of an argument between his superior scientist, Dr. Stirling, and the base commander, Major Wurlitz.

"I'll ask you one last time: What are you still doing here? Why aren't you finished? We're moving out!" Wurlitz shouted around the laboratory, where Dr. Frank Stirling continued to pack ice cores unperturbed.

"We're going as fast as we can," he explained coolly.

"Leave that junk," Wurlitz said sharply.

"And all the results? The equipment, we have to..." Dr. Stirling started and then waved it off.

Memphis, meanwhile, walked around the large experiment table and stood next to Stirling. He placed the case with the samples he had collected on the table.

"I don't think you heard me right, Dr. Stirling!" Wurlitz yelled. "We're moving out now! This base is history! We'll leave everything here, fill in this goddamn hole and never come back, got it? You said yourself that the situation can't be controlled effectively!"

"With all due respect, don't you see the unprecedented opportunities..." Stirling tried to object, but Wurlitz cut him off.

"That's enough! Pack up your things and let's get out of here. You have half an hour; after that, the last entrances will be closed. And I'm beginning not to care if you're still here by then." The major turned around and addressed one of his soldiers, standing silently in a corner. "You make sure those eggheads are on the surface in 30 minutes at the latest!"

"Understood, sir! 30 minutes to departure," the soldier reported and nodded.

Then Wurlitz left the room with jagged steps.

"You know he's right," Paul Memphis now said, giving Dr. Stirling a worried look. "If we don't leave, the ice will swallow us up."

Stirling smiled mildly. "Hornochs like Wurlitz are great at shouting, but not very good at listening," he commented, switching off a series of measuring devices on the table.

"Yes, maybe ....," Memphis continued. "But we can't stay. They're loading the reactor right now, and in a few hours, the batteries will run out. Then we'll be in the dark! Under meters of ice. Well, for my part ..."

"I got it!" Stirling roared but immediately calmed down again. "I want to wait for these final results; it could be crucial that we find out what we're dealing with."

"We'd better leave it; they already know what they're doing," said Memphis.

"They don't know anything! They're evacuating and covering everything up, hoping it will stay buried forever. But what if that's not enough? What if it finds a way out? We should be prepared for that. And the best way to do that is to find out as much as we can about this phenomenon."

"We don't have time. And even if we did, I don't think there's anything we can do," Memphis said resignedly, shaking his head. "Do you think they'd leave even one of the missiles here if there was the slightest chance of saving the situation?"

Stirling let out an agonized sigh. "No. You're right, of course. But it would be a once-in-a-lifetime opportunity."

"It's not worth the risk. As much as I hate to agree with Wurlitz, but after all the incidents and the recent affair with Benjamin Sattler, I don't think anyone can blame him for pulling the ripcord."

For a moment, there was silence in the room; only the muffled rumbling and cracking from the surface prevented an eerie silence from settling in.

Then Stirling took the floor again. "These cores could still win us the Nobel Prize one day," he said without the slightest hint of modesty in his voice. At the same time, he shook his head, as if he could hardly believe his own words.

"Maybe ... At some point. But not if we don't make it out of here alive," Memphis interjected.

"Then we'll finish packing and take as much as we can with us."

The two scientists set about packing the collected samples and ice cores as safely as they could in the rush. After about 15 minutes, the most important items were stowed away in boxes and suitcases.

"Corporal!" Stirling called out to the soldier waiting next to the door with a cigarette in the corner of his mouth. "Help us with the luggage."

The soldier let out an unwilling grunt, threw his cigarette on the ground and grabbed some suitcases to carry outside.

Stirling and Memphis also grabbed as much as they could with both hands. After one last look back to check whether they had forgotten anything important, the two of them left the hut that had been their laboratory for the past year and a half.

"It's strange. First, you think this godforsaken place could never feel like home, and now that you have to leave it forever, it doesn't feel right either," commented Memphis, putting his suitcases on the back of a snowmobile that was parked next to the cabin.

The vehicle and the sled attached to it were already loaded to the maximum, but Stirling squeezed in two more crates. "Don't worry about it. For people like us, the place where we work is irrelevant. What's important is what we achieve with what we do," he said.

"We're leaving now!" the corporal interrupted the conversation and climbed onto the snowmobile. "The doctors will have to walk," he added, only half-heartedly suppressing a grin. "The sleigh is too full and there's no time to drive twice." He lit a new cigarette and started the engine.

"Drive off! And don't you dare lose a single piece of luggage," Stirling ordered him. "We're good on foot."

The soldier shrugged his shoulders, stepped on the gas and left the two scientists alone in the ice tunnel.

"Don't panic," Stirling now said to Memphis. "Wurlitz won't leave us behind. These guys always allow for a buffer."

They set off and walked through the deserted tunnel towards the exit. Barely two minutes later, they heard a rumble and a muffled scream. They instinctively stopped.

"What was that?" asked Memphis.

Instead of a reply, he heard a shot, then a second, followed by a screech.

"That's coming from over there, from the parallel tunnel!" Stirling shouted, pointing to a narrow passageway that led across.

Another shot rang out. Then a furious scream, just a single word, a name. "Sattler!"

"Did you hear that?" Memphis asked.

"Come on, we have to go and see," said Stirling.

"Are you crazy? Those were gunshots!"

"If it was Sattler, we have to take care of him; he's one of our people. The military will shoot him."

"And maybe us too, if we get in their way!" protested Memphis.

"Nonsense! I'm sure it won't come to that," Stirling defended himself and pulled open the door to the connecting corridor.

"That's the stupidest idea in a long time," Memphis commented, following Stirling through the door.

They ran along the narrow corridor to the second large tunnel that ran the length of the underground base. Here were mainly the military supply depots, the reactor room, the infirmary and access to a separate area where secret missile silos were housed. As scientists on a semi-civilian project, Memphis and Stirling only had access to the infirmary and were basically not even supposed to know that there were dozens of missiles stuck in the ice over there. But it was a small base and people were talking.

They pushed open the door to the parallel tunnel and immediately saw a dark red trail of blood on the ice. They hurriedly followed it and found a soldier a few meters further on, leaning against the wall, wounded and holding his radio in front of his mouth with trembling hands.

When he recognized the two, he lowered it and explained: "It's Sattler, the son of a bitch. Somehow he got out of the infirmary!"

"But how can that be?" asked Stirling incredulously. "He was unconscious, the doctors told me they wanted to wait until the last moment to see if he was even fit to be transferred."

"I don't know!", the soldier gasped and then had a coughing fit. He spat blood onto the floor. "He's armed, I couldn't stop it," he gasped.

"Where is he going?" Memphis asked.

At that moment, a shrill alarm sounded, echoing in the smooth tunnel and piercing the ear canal.

"What does that mean?" asked Stirling, looking around frantically.

"The missile silo," the soldier replied. "Sattler must have tried to get in."

Memphis felt himself getting hotter and hotter under his

jacket despite the cold around him. What was Sattler doing in the missile silo? Could he even manage to get in there? The guy had been out for days with a fever of over 40 degrees. Had he run off in a frenzy and was now doing some fatal nonsense?

"We have to stop him," Stirling said firmly.

"What?" Memphis blurted out. "Not the two of us?"

"I've already radioed for reinforcements, they're on their way, but there's only one open access at the far end ..." The soldier coughed again. "We're alone down here."

"This is taking too long," Stirling explained. "Who knows what he's up to!"

The door to the connecting corridor through which Memphis and Stirling had just stepped was pushed open, and the corporal in charge of transporting the equipment came running to them. "What happened?"

"Sattler! He wants to go into the missile silo," said the wounded soldier curtly.

"Hang on, someone will be here to help you in a minute," the corporal explained and wheeled around. He immediately pressed a pistol into Memphis' hand and pulled a second one from a holster on his belt. "Come on!" he barked at him and Stirling. "Now we're going to kill the madman! You can shoot, can't you?"

Before Memphis could protest, the corporal shoved him towards the far end of the tunnel.

The three of them ran through the icy corridor and reached an airlock area that concealed the secret missile silos. For Memphis, this part of the base had previously been absolutely off-limits. At least two heavily armed guards normally secured the entrance, but now the heavy steel gate stood wide open. There was not a guard to be seen for miles around.

"Bloody hell, how did he get in there? It should have been locked long ago!" said the corporal, stopping right in front of the gate. He cautiously peered into the dark corridor behind it.

The next moment, his head burst into a storm of blood, brain matter, and bone splinters.

"Fuck!" Memphis gasped and threw himself to the ground.

"Sattler! Don't shoot, it's us, Stirling and Memphis!" Stirling shouted into the darkness. "Can we come in and talk?"

"Are you crazy?" Memphis breathlessly breathed. His whole body was trembling.

"He knows us; he trusts us," said Stirling calmly.

"I don't give a shit!" hissed Memphis. "The Sattler I knew didn't just shoot a soldier in the head like that."

"Right, that's why we have to talk some sense into him. You know what's down there?"

"Yes, the damn rockets," Memphis replied a little more calmly.

"Yes, nuclear-capable missiles. At least a dozen," Stirling clarified.

"What? But..."

"Stirling!" shouted Sattler from the missile silo. "You and Memphis can come, but if I see anyone else, I'll shoot!"

"Shit," Memphis commented. "Now we have to get down to that lunatic."

Stirling pulled Memphis to his feet. "It's either that or..." He left the sentence unfinished and stepped towards the gate instead.

Memphis shook his head. Nuclear missiles! He had always feared that but had suppressed the thought as best he could. He came to his senses and scraped together the last of his courage. They had to do something before a catastrophe happened here.

They walked through the airlock together and found a wide steel staircase less than ten meters behind it, which led down a good 20 meters. There were three tunnels at the bottom, just high enough to walk upright in.

The lighting had failed, and only a pitiful remnant of light shone from above. Nevertheless, it was not completely dark. At the end of the right-hand of the three shafts, a diffuse glow could be made out that shimmered between violet and pink.

"What the hell is that?" Memphis asked in a whisper, as if speaking too loudly could set a catastrophe in motion.

"You know what that is," said Stirling succinctly. "The reason we have to leave."

"Back here!" shouted Sattler from the very tunnel where they saw the glow. "Hurry up!"

"Please, let's get out of here and let the soldiers handle this!" Memphis tried one last time to talk some sense into his colleague.

But Stirling set off unmoved.

Memphis reluctantly followed him. Despite the ever-increasing fear that was spreading through his body, he felt the scientific curiosity within him. He hated having to give up on this discovery - without any real clarity about what exactly they had found here.

He hid the pistol in his jacket pocket and entered the tunnel with deliberate steps behind Stirling.

This ended after about 50 meters on a kind of platform on which a control console stood. There were five more narrow shafts around it, which led to the actual rocket launch ramps. There was no sign of Sattler. But it was now clear where the glow was coming from. It shimmered directly out of the ice, like pulsating veins under thin skin. They seemed to come from deep below and ran up the walls and into the corridors that led to the rockets.

"What on earth is going on here?" Memphis breathed.

"That's them," explained Sattler, stepping out of the darkness with his gun drawn. Thick beads of sweat stood out on his forehead, his skin was unnaturally pale and his veins were bulging out as if his blood pressure was beyond the measurable range.

"Sattler, why aren't you in the infirmary, you look terrible," said Stirling.

"What I look like is completely irrelevant. I'm beyond help. They're already inside me. I have to end this before I lose control," explained Sattler and stepped up to the missile console.

"What are you up to?" asked Memphis.

"Well, what is it? I'm going to save you all and die a hero's death in the process. Me of all people! What a fucking irony."

"Heroes..." Memphis began and immediately broke off again. "You're not going to set off the rockets, are you?"

"We don't have time to discuss it. Save yourselves! Get the soldiers off my back, get everyone out of here. It's going to get very uncomfortable here soon."

"What did you mean when you said they were inside you?" Stirling wanted to know.

"Those damn things! Look around you. They're coming up from the depths. We drilled these holes and woke them up. Then they somehow got into the reactor's radioactive cooling water. That changed them, I don't know how ... You can see the glow! And I was stupid enough to touch them." Sattler rolled up the sleeve of his shirt on his left arm and turned it so that the underside could be seen. The veins were not only distended here, but seemed to glow pinkish-purple under the milky skin, just like the ice around them.

Startled, Memphis took a step back.

"I told you, I'm beyond help," Sattler repeated.

"What happened over there in the reactor?" asked Stirling.

"Overheating. The temperature under the base rises as they spread."

"Still? They've already taken the reactor away," said Stirling.

"That's not enough. All the radioactive waste is still there. They seem to be feeding on it. I don't have time to explain everything to you. You have to leave. I'll ignite the rockets but won't release the holding clamps. That will cause a massive meltdown. Everything will sink."

"Then we have to get out of here," said Stirling. "This will have a devastating effect on the stability of the base. They've already filled in the openings of the missile silos above!"

"What good does it do us to set off the missiles?" Memphis interjected. "You say they destroy radioactive radiation. How could nuclear missiles, of all things, help us?"

"Trust me, I'm convinced that it will work. The missiles are not equipped. I can feel this alien presence inside me and now

I know how to get them. The rocket fuel is our salvation, not the bombs."

"You talk like these things think," said Stirling.

"You have no idea!" Sattler roared. "Now get out of here!"

"Come with us, we'll find another way," Memphis asked.

"There is no other way, aren't you listening to me? They are inside me! I'm part of the problem." He waved the pistol in the air. "Get out!" he then shouted and put his free hand on the control console. "I have to stay here and lock the retaining clamps manually. I'll give you ten minutes. And make sure the soldiers stay outside, otherwise ..." He didn't finish the sentence, but just shook his head briefly. Then he pressed the launch buttons of all five missiles stationed in this silo one after the other. "The clock is ticking!"

Memphis turned on his heel and pulled Stirling with him. He pushed him ahead through the narrow corridor and up the stairs. The pink-purple mesh still pulsed and glowed beneath the surface of the ice.

They had barely stepped out of the large gate when three soldiers came running towards them.

Memphis stepped forward and waved his arms in the air. "We have to get out. He's firing the rockets!" he shouted.

But the soldiers made no move to slow down or even turn around.

"It's too late, turn around!" he shouted again.

The men were barely ten meters away. One of them raised his rifle.

"What are you doing?" he shouted in amazement and turned around.

Then he saw that Stirling had stayed behind and was pulling the heavy steel gate shut from the inside.

"Stirling, no!" shouted Memphis.

In the next moment, bullets rattled against the gate, which was now locked. They did not cause any damage, but only ricocheted off as sparks.

The soldiers continued to fire, although they must have

known that it was absolutely pointless to try to open the entrance in this way.

Memphis didn't waste another second. He ran off, straight towards the exit. The lights flickered and went out again and again, but he no longer cared. Darkness was the least of his problems. If he didn't get out of here as quickly as possible, he wouldn't have any more problems. Because he would be dead, first consumed by a fireball and then buried by thousands of tons of ice.

Memphis switched to the parallel tunnel, the end of which would lead to freedom. He found the snowmobile parked by the corporal halfway down the tunnel and sent a prayer of thanks to heaven. He hastily mounted it and sped off. Half the load fell off during the breakneck ride, but Memphis couldn't be bothered. It was probably better if it all stayed buried here.

At last he reached the ramp that led to the last open exit. The large gates had already been closed except for a narrow gap. He struggled out and landed directly in a veritable snowstorm. The sharp wind blew ice crystals into his eyes. Memphis was as good as blind and staggered towards a noise that sounded like the engine of a large snowcat. He stumbled and went down, still completely disoriented without his goggles.

He felt someone pulling him to his feet and pushing him into the vehicle cabin.

"What the hell is going on down there? Where's Stirling?" they shouted at him.

Memphis blinked and realized that it was Wurlitz, sitting opposite him with a bright red head and glaring angrily at him.

"No time, drive!" shouted Memphis. "Everything's about to go off. Sattler's firing the rockets!" He thought he saw sheer terror in Major Wurlitz's eyes for a moment, but the commander immediately regained his composure.

"Off you go!" he ordered the driver. "Go!"

He didn't hesitate and pressed the gas pedal to the metal. The caterpillar started to move, roaring but still agonizingly slowly, before picking up speed.

"God have mercy on you if you lied to me!" Wurlitz said sharply and poked Memphis in the chest with his index finger.

"God have mercy on us if Sattler's plan doesn't work," Memphis replied wanly and slumped back in his seat, completely exhausted.

A few minutes later, the top-secret Camp Century in eastern Greenland was history. The rockets' engines unleashed their devastating power and caused the ice to collapse over a funnel that had melted into the glacier. Underneath it buried Sattler, Stirling, half a dozen brave soldiers and a tremendous secret that would never see the light of day again - or so they thought.

2

PRIN outpost "Snowbird", East Greenland
September 8, 2023

Nora Grimm let her gaze wander over the endless expanse of the Greenland ice sheet, watching the gently gliding cloud formations above the brilliant white that stretched to the horizon in every direction. She did not do this to enjoy the wild, majestic landscape, but for purely practical reasons. Like everyone who worked in the harsh Arctic, she knew how important it was to keep an eye on the weather. In no time at all, it could change and turn the idyllic tranquillity of the far north into a raging inferno of snow and ice.

She had experienced this several times in the past two and a half months of her stay here and was prepared for anything: thick polar suit, lined boots and gloves, goggles, two hats on top of each other, the hood over the top and several hand warmers in the jacket pockets just in case.

But the weather was still looking good; the clouds were inconspicuous, and the wind was almost imperceptible. She and her colleague Steven Dryer would certainly make it back to the research station in one piece after working on the borehole - if the drill played along today and didn't start bitching again.

Judging by the sound the drill had made so far, everything was running smoothly today. The steady hum had accompanied her since the start of the shift a good three hours ago. She could only hear it muffled out here, but as soon as she was back in the steel tunnel tube, which was meters deep in the ice, the unnerving hum would increase many times over.

Nora turned around and made her way back. She had already stayed upstairs longer than necessary and could picture her colleague's reproachful face. Steven Dryer was the epitome of a curmudgeon: humorless, stiff as a stick, but also meticulous beyond measure. What's more, the Englishman looked like a disgruntled version of an oversized Harry Potter - even the glasses model was right.

But you couldn't choose your colleagues in a place like this. Nora knew it was a privilege to be allowed to do research here. She had had to fight for the PRIN scholarship for a long time - but now, at 25, she was the youngest scholarship holder the project had ever had. She certainly wasn't going to let a stinker like Dryer spoil her mood.

She walked down the flat ramp to the tunnel entrance. They regularly had to clear it of snow in order to be able to start work. The drifts kept blowing whole mountains in front of the entrance. The ramp led down into the heart of this outpost of the international PRIN mission "Snowbird", where Nora was collecting data for her doctoral thesis.

She pulled the massive handle of the steel door with both hands. Behind it was a small vestibule with another, less bulky door at the end. The room served as a kind of airlock to prevent too much snow being carried in during bad weather. Nora crossed the chamber and got inside through the door. The floor here was partially covered with wooden planks, which gave the interior of the station, which was still minus five degrees, at least a visual hint of warmth. Nora kept her thick jacket on and only took off the hood and the second hat. She brushed some of her blonde strands back and tucked them under the side of the remaining hat.

Dryer stood in the center of the six-meter-long tube, stone-faced at the drilling rig, keeping an eye on the speed. Nora knew that he took this task very seriously and did well to do so, as unreliable as the system had been in the last few days. But that was the way it was up here, you either tried to fix things and come up with creative solutions, or you were allowed to pack up. You couldn't make a quick trip to the nearest DIY store or electronics store when an appliance gave up the ghost.

"Nice to see you making an effort again," said Dryer sarcastically.

"Did you have a longing?" Nora asked back just as sarcastically.

"Not me, but the drill head missed you."

Nora sighed. She and Dryer had come to terms with the fact that they didn't particularly like each other and, interestingly, had both chosen sarcasm as a tried and tested means of getting along better.

"What's the weather like?" Dryer asked.

"Everything is calm. I think we'll get back to base tonight without any problems."

"I should hope so. I don't have the slightest desire to spend the night here again," Dryer replied.

Nora knew very well that this allusion was meant for her. Two weeks ago, she had insisted on staying longer to complete a drill. Unfortunately, the weather had taken such a turn for the worse that they had actually had to stay overnight in this uncomfortable outpost.

She decided not to respond, but remained diplomatic. "That's why I check so often," she explained succinctly and then stepped closer to the drill's controls to check the displays. "It's going like clockwork, we're already at 2,480 meters. We'll be down soon. Maybe we can still make it today?"

"Hardly," Dryer rebutted. "I won't stay a second longer than necessary. The plan is for the drill to hit bottom tomorrow. And we're not going to increase the speed again just because impatience trumps any professional expertise."

"It's okay, it's okay," said Nora, who could hardly bear to wait any longer for the longed-for breakthrough.

This was especially true after a rival research group had already succeeded in a similar experiment three weeks ago. Nora's feeling of being too late had become even worse since then. They had an advantage in terms of drilling technology, as the new prototype they were using here was more error-prone than expected but 20 times faster than conventional drilling equipment. This meant that, given the thickness of the ice here, they did not need three to four years to hit bottom, but a few weeks at best. In return, they had to act as beta testers for the company that provided the equipment and generously contributed to the funding of the research.

A shrill resonance snapped Nora out of her thoughts. It was the kind of noise that caused unforeseen problems.

"Looks like we finished early today," said Dryer and consistently reduced the speed until the drill came to a standstill.

"What happened?" Nora wanted to know.

"How should I know that?" Dryer replied, turning to the display that showed the telemetry of the drill head, which was now more than two and a half kilometers below them. "That's weird," he said suddenly.

"Show me!" Nora demanded, pushing herself next to him so that she could also look at the displays. "The..." she began and immediately fell silent again.

"Yes, that's right. The drill head is blunt," Dryer confirmed.

"Can't be!" Nora protested, "We changed it yesterday. That could only be the case if..." She pushed her colleague completely to one side and made a few entries on the keyboard.

"Now I'm curious," Dryer said tonelessly.

"He must have run aground," Nora reported.

"Nonsense," Dryer rebutted.

"Yes, look at this. The data clearly shows that it hit something hard. I can't say whether it was rock, but it was certainly something much harder than ice."

"These readings can't be right, we're still 200 meters from the bottom."

"Maybe the thickness measurement was faulty in the first place," said Nora, looking at Dryer questioningly.

She knew that it was his job and that she was probably offending him badly by raising the possibility that he might have made a mistake. But at that moment, she didn't really care. If Dryer could harp on about her failings for days on end, she was entitled to doubt his infallibility for once.

Dryer's expression darkened. "I think that's absurd," he commented curtly, but then set about re-examining the mapping data he had created about four weeks ago. "There's a margin of error of less than 20 meters, which is unfortunately unavoidable, but if there was bedrock down there, the deviation would have to be ten times higher, which I can't imagine."

"If it wasn't a rock ... maybe there's a foreign body in the ice?" Nora wondered aloud, earning a skeptical look from Dryer.

"Foreign body? Ridiculous! What's that supposed to be? Surely, you know that the ice at this depth is 400,000 years old. What could possibly be there? A shock-frozen mammoth skull?"

"Steven, of course I know how old the ice is," Nora replied calmly. "I admit it was a stupid idea, okay? But then what do you think happened?"

Dryer swayed his head back and forth. "Maybe a sensor error. The device is not fully developed."

"And the noise? The drill head must be broken, the way it sounded. Do you remember the failure two weeks ago during the first drilling attempt, when it failed after just 25 meters? What if we drilled into a foreign body there too?"

Dryer grimaced. "That's even less likely. No, no, it was probably a sensor error. Or the spare parts we used were faulty and wore out too quickly."

"We'd best get it out and have a look," Nora said firmly.

"It takes hours!" complained Dryer.

"We have to do this anyway, because we can hardly go on like this, can we?"

Dryer gave an unwilling snort but nodded.

"You don't like it up here much, do you?" Nora asked.

Dryer made a dismissive gesture with his hand. "What do you care?"

"Hey, listen, I have nothing against you. And I think we could perhaps work together more efficiently if we tried to understand each other better. We've got a good two hours before the drill head is up, so we can have a chat."

"No need," Dryer defended himself and started the retrieval process on the drill head control. Then he turned away. "I'll go and check the weather."

Nora was left shaking her head. This guy was really difficult.

She watched the displays for a while, which showed the current depth and ambient temperature. She called up the data for the last half hour and took a close look at the graphs with the recorded values. As expected, the depth measurement showed an almost linear progression. The displays had also looked like this over the last few days. Dryer must have kept the speed very constant, and they hadn't encountered any obstacles so far - because the disgruntled colleague was right about that. What could possibly be down there?

The temperature curve was even more boring to read at first, because there were hardly any fluctuations in the readings this deep in the ice. Until today. Now there was a clear deflection. The curve had clearly jumped just before the drill head failed. This fueled Nora's suspicion that he had hit something hard and that the sudden increase in friction had also caused the temperature to rise significantly. She zoomed in and read the values. First, once, then a second time. And finally a third time.

She shook her head. The measurement reported a rise to 47 degrees above zero. That was practically impossible. In the short time between the sound appearing and the shutdown, the drill could not have warmed up that much through friction alone.

Had the internal motor burned out? Or the ultrasound generator? She hoped it wasn't because they didn't have any spare parts. Such damage could mean the end of their project. And Nora didn't want to think about flying home just yet - and empty-handed at that!

She left the displays and walked over to a low workbench where the workshop equipment, some simple analytical instruments and her thermos flask of hot Darjeeling stood. She poured herself a cupful and enjoyed the steam and fruity, tangy aroma spreading around her. There was nothing better than a hot cup of tea in the Arctic cold.

***

About two hours after the start of the retrieval procedure, the drill head reached the surface. Nora Grimm and Steven Dryer disconnected the supply cables and ropes and lifted the 50 kilogram structure over to a container on wheels. They drove it to the work table so that they could take a closer look at the device.

"Looks pretty strange," said Nora on her first external inspection.

"As usual, highly scientific language," Dryer commented, leaning down.

"Please, enlighten me with your elaborate expert opinion," Nora countered.

"There seems to be a deposit on the surface," said Dryer and tried to scrape some of the silver-grey traces from the dark drill head casing with his fingernail. But he didn't succeed, because the layer looked as if it had been burned into the metal casing. "It doesn't seem to be sediment anyway; it's too hard for that; I can't get any of it off. Maybe with a tool."

"Hang on. I want to have a look at the drill core first. It's possible that this material is also inside," Nora replied, grabbing a special wrench to open the outer casing.

She used it to loosen the veneer in two places and flipped it open. To her astonishment, there was no solid ice core inside, but a half-frozen mixture of pieces of ice and cloudy water, some of which poured out onto the workshop table.

Nora quickly turned the drill head with the opening facing upwards so that the flow stopped. "What the hell? How can that be?"

Dryer also seemed so perplexed that he couldn't think of a snappy comment.

"Give me a hand," Nora asked, pointing to a polystyrene container in which they usually stored extracted ice cores. "Number 18 is empty, we'll tip the contents in there!"

Dryer grabbed the white box and set it down in front of the table, then helped Nora pull the heavy drill head forward and empty out the contents. "It's freezing down there, how can it be liquid?" he asked, puzzled.

"I have no idea. But I noticed earlier when I was studying the data that there was a sudden rise in temperature before the drill head failed. The measurement showed 47 degrees at the peak."

"Completely impossible, even if the engine was through..." He broke off and examined the drill head, which was now empty.

He removed a diagnostic device that looked like an overly thick, clunky tablet from a dark gray case and connected it to an interface inside the drill head. The device began to beep and flash and stopped after about five seconds.

Dryer looked at the readings on the display. "The motor and ultrasound are working, but one of the sensor boards is broken," he explained.

"The temperature gauge?"

"No, he seems fine - which makes it even stranger. Nevertheless, Olofsson is going to rip our heads off."

"Come on, he knows the conditions we're working under here. Let's take the samples and the drill head back to the station. Let Macmillan have a look at it, he'll get it back on track before Olofsson even notices."

"That's not possible. You can't always play up your chick bonus with the old man. I'll have to write a report."

"Sure you do," Nora replied coolly and shook her head. She really didn't need that last reference to her young age. In her mind, she added: You can make your own problems, you grump.

Now she picked up the lid of the polystyrene container. Before she closed it, she took another look inside. The mixture gradually began to solidify. "In case you're interested: I'm going to analyze the meltwater today. Or the ice - depending on what state it's in then."

"My interest is limited, but go ahead," Dryer replied and set about reassembling the casing of the drill head.

3

PRIN research station "Amarok II",
17 kilometers south of the borehole

After just under half an hour on the snowmobiles, Nora Grimm and Steven Dryer arrived at the Amarok II research station, where they were accommodated with a dozen other scientists.

The current station was the successor to its predecessor, "Amarok I", which was abandoned 18 months ago and was built as a tubular structure under the ice. However, after several years, the force of the glacier had bent and compressed the tubes to such an extent that it no longer seemed possible to continue operating them safely. The international research network PRIN decided to replace them with an above-ground base on high stilts, virtually floating above the ice.

The eccentrically designed building was immediately given a fitting nickname: the UFO. The association could not be dismissed, as the futuristic construction resembled a bloated, circular soup bowl with a diameter of just over 20 meters. The station, including its five feet, towered a good 15 meters into the air. The large, transparent dome, which rested on top of the bulbous bowl like a lid, gave the Amarok II an additional UFO character. The astrophysicists and atmospheric researchers stationed here took their measurements and observations through this glass dome.

Nora had often imagined how breathtaking the sight of the clear starry sky or the Northern Lights must be in winter. So far, Nora had only spent her time here in daylight, as the midnight sun was known to never set in summer this far north. Now, in September, there was something of a day-night rhythm again, even if the transitions took some getting used to.

In a few weeks' time, however, persistent darkness would descend on the north and banish the sun from the sky for several months. The Northern Lights would then be the only source of light unless the clouds intervened. On the one hand, Nora could hardly wait to experience this spectacle for herself, but on the other hand, she also felt a slight sense of unease when she thought of the leaden darkness that lay ahead of her during the last few weeks of her planned stay. But her days here were numbered as soon as the polar night reigned. At the end of October, she would have to make room for new scholarship holders who were eagerly awaiting their chance. Until then, she urgently needed tangible results.

As an interdisciplinary station, the UFO offered space for a whole range of different disciplines: geologists, glaciologists, physicists, biologists, doctors - there was even a philosopher on board, who Nora had been wondering what he was doing here since she arrived. But it wasn't her job to question the selection process of the committees and sponsors.

Nora and Steven drove down a wide ramp into a garage built directly beneath the station. It was an ice cave milled into the glacier and reinforced with steel struts, in which two snow groomers were parked alongside numerous snowmobiles. They headed for free spaces and parked their vehicles.

Nora took the polystyrene box with her samples from the luggage rack and walked towards a steel door on her right.

Meanwhile, Steven worked on the drill head and cleared his throat loudly.

Nora turned around and noticed that he was giving her a reproachful look. "Do you want me to carry it up alone?" he asked.

"Why don't you write your report first? I've got my hands full," she said curtly, turned around again and went through the door that led to the west staircase.

From the garage, spiral staircases wound through two of the station's tubular legs into the residential and research complex. The other three legs were covered with supply lines, cables and narrow emergency ladders.

Once upstairs, Nora removed her thick polar gear and hung it in her locker. Then she entered the actual core area of the station through another isolated door. The atmosphere in the Amarok was in stark contrast to the small Snowbird outpost where she worked most of the time.

Everything was modern, if not extravagantly designed. This began with the layout of the station, which consisted of three floors full of rings.

On the lowest level, a circular corridor curved around the rooms with all the technical systems as well as the supply and equipment stores. Nevertheless, nothing here was reminiscent of an engine room. The floors, walls and ceilings were white, but had accents in soft shades of beige and gray. There was also diffuse, warm lighting and glass doors with matt gray fittings. This image was continued one floor further up, where two concentric circles connected the living and laboratory areas due to the larger size of the UFO. In between, there were six corridors radiating from the center. The floor plan therefore looked more like an antiquated wagon wheel on a carriage.

The center contained a meeting room and the canteen, surrounded by the workrooms and laboratories. The quarters, fitness area, and various other common rooms were outside.

On floor number three, on the other hand, there was no circular corridor, as almost the entire area was taken up by the glass observatory and a communal viewing area. There were also a few offices in the northern section, including that of the station manager Per Olofsson.

Nora climbed up to the second floor and met some of her colleagues, who greeted her in a friendly but cursory manner. As usual, they were all busy with their own tasks. No one asked why Nora had returned two hours early, and she didn't tell anyone. Dryer would take care of the formalities and the repairs and would be sure to tell everyone that the malfunction of the drill head could certainly not have been his fault.

The chief machinist Ian Macmillan would inevitably follow

up with her, but she didn't care much about that at the moment. She had other things to do than deal with technical malfunctions. Even if Dryer had immediately dismissed it as nonsense, she was sure the drill had hit something unexpected today. Not sediment or bedrock - as had been the plan for tomorrow - but something completely different that had triggered a violent reaction. She was probably holding the proof of this in her hands right now. She was dying to find out what it might have been.

She hurriedly brought the box with the sample taken from the drill to her assigned laboratory 2-B-09. She immediately placed the contents of the transport box in a special cooling compartment, which was intended to preserve ice cores and was set to minus 35 degrees Celsius. She then began to power up a whole series of measuring devices that she had originally planned to use over the next few days to examine the sediment samples and which she now had to reprogram for the analysis of ice.

Nora did not conduct research directly on the perpetual ice of the Arctic, as there were already enough colleagues doing this. These glaciologists usually analyzed the composition of the air bubbles trapped in the ice and drew conclusions about the atmospheric conditions 100,000 or more years ago. Nora, on the other hand, was a biologist and was interested in what lay beneath, namely the layer between the bedrock and the glacier. This was the remnant of what had once lived on Greenland - a good 400,000 years ago, when the world's largest island had been largely ice-free, according to the findings. Apparently, a tundra landscape had covered the land at that time. And Nora wanted to uncover the secrets of this former vegetation.

Nora knew from analyzing decades-old soil samples that Greenland had lived up to its name during a previously unexplained warm phase much more than it does today. Almost two and a half years ago, she had read enthusiastically in a specialist journal about an ice core that had been lost since the

1960s and was only rediscovered in Denmark in 2017. The core originally came from the northwest of the island - in other words, from the very area where she was now drilling. Of course, this was no coincidence.

Immediately after reading the report on the organic remains found beneath the ice sheet, Nora decided that this should be the subject of her doctoral thesis. This was followed by laborious weeks in which she had to deal with university bureaucracy, opaque funding regulations, masses of unsuccessful applications, and finally, the highly demanding application to the PRIN. She had thought she had the least chance of success with this one in particular, but contrary to expectations, she was accepted.

And now - after two and a half years - she followed in the footsteps of those researchers who were the first to reach the bottom of this glacier in 1967 and whose work had disappeared into oblivion for unknown reasons.

After all the measuring devices and computers had been booted up and reconfigured, Nora took a sample of the collected ice-sediment mixture from the cooling chamber and divided it into three pieces. One she placed in an evaporator to separate the solid particles from the water, another in a prepared vacuum chamber where the gas released during melting was extracted and analyzed, and the third cut into wafer-thin layers for visual inspection under the microscope. The ice, now completely solidified again, clearly contained gray streaks that indicated solid particles.

No sooner had the first layer been placed on the microscope slide than there was a knock on her lab door and Alex Corbinian poked his head in. As always, the American geologist had a mischievous smile on his lips. "Hey, are you all right?" he greeted her.

She gave a cursory nod and immediately turned back to her microscope. She wanted to gain as many impressions as possible before the sample melted. She heard Alex close the door and come over to her.

Nora hated it when someone looked over her shoulder while she was working - even if it was the always friendly Corbinian, whom she probably liked best of everyone on the ward.

But she wasn't going to let that distract her now. She changed the magnification factor on the microscope and moved closer. Now the melting ice clearly revealed finely distributed particles that varied in size and shape, but still gave the impression of a pattern. Nora saw how the sample melted on the slide and the particles shifted. But they did not do so completely at random.

Nora stumbled. "That's..." she began and fell silent again.

"That's what?" Alex asked.

"Um... Nothing. I have ice samples here with strange particles inside, and I just felt as if they had moved. Surely a reaction to the melting process. What else could it be?" Nora shrugged her shoulders instinctively.

"May I have a look?"

"Please." Nora made room in front of the microscope.

Alex slid closer and looked through the eyepiece. As he examined the sample, he made a long, low humming sound and kept moving the slide back and forth. "Well, I can't tell visually what this is, but it seems to me to have some kind of crystal structure. Where did you get that from, did you say?"

"From an ice core. I was just able to save the sample before it melted. Our drill malfunctioned, possibly because of that!" She pointed to the microscope.

"Very strange. The material seems to reassemble as soon as the water evaporates."

"Do crystals do that? And anyway, could the material be so hard that it ruins our drill head?"

Alex tilted his head. "In theory ... Well, diamonds are also crystals after all and are one of the hardest things we find in nature."

"Oh, how nice. I've stumbled across diamonds! So I'm all set then, am I?" joked Nora, putting on a smile.

"Hmm... you're rather out of sorts, aren't you?" Alex nodded towards the door.

"Oh," Nora said curtly. "So that's why you're here."
"Yes, unfortunately."
Nora sighed. "What did Dryer say again?"
"Nothing to me, but Olofsson wants to see you."
"That was obvious. And now I'm supposed to drop everything?"
"That's up to you. But I'd rather go up sooner than later."
"All right then. The other measurements will take at least half an hour anyway. And these crystals probably won't run away from me." Nora stood up and pushed the chair up to the table.

"I can stay here and take a few detailed photos of your samples," Alex offered. "I've got nothing better to do today anyway."

"Nothing to do? You?" She paused. "Wait, today is Friday. Are you trying to avoid the communal cooking event again?"

"Never! It's just that my heart beats for science," Alex replied unconvincingly.

"Yeah, sure! But okay, if you like, you can have a look at the crystals. I'll be back soon." She turned towards the door and left Alex alone in the lab.

4

A few minutes later, Nora entered the office of station manager Per Olofsson, a jovial Swede in his early 60s who was not easily flustered. However, he tended to always explain his point of view in great detail. And that's exactly what Nora was expecting now, because her colleague Dryer certainly hadn't waited a second to tell the boss about her mishap today.

Olofsson sat with his back to the door on his black office chair covered in genuine leather and gazed out through the large panoramic window into the vastness of the Greenlandic ice desert.

Nora cleared her throat to announce her appearance.

"Be so good as to close the door and sit with me," Olofsson asked, without turning away from the view.

As instructed, Nora closed the office door and then took one of the visitor's chairs in front of Olofsson's desk. She pushed it about a meter away next to Olofsson and sat down.

"Breathtaking, again and again, isn't it?" the station manager began. "What sensational insights we can gain here!"

Nora knew that Olofsson didn't really want to hear an answer or confirmation, he just liked to lecture - probably a remnant of his many years as a professor at various universities and private colleges.

"Up here in this hostile world, it is extremely important that we all pull together and know how difficult it is to carry out research in such a place. We must understand that we must make the best possible use of the resources available to us and not waste them carelessly."

Nora still said nothing. She knew that this was the introduction to a very elegantly delivered rebuke.

"Our station is the best facility that has ever existed on

Greenland - and this is only the case because we have public and private donors from over 18 nations behind us. But they expect us to handle their investments wisely." Now Olofsson turned to her and looked directly at her.

This scolding was hard for Nora to bear. She felt like a father scolding his daughter because she had taken the car for a spin without permission and now had a nasty scratch on her expensive car.

Olofsson was simply a father type. And that's how he treated her, which was completely inappropriate. Nora was a grown woman, had an honors degree in biology and was now doing her doctorate at one of Germany's most prestigious universities. Just because she had a youthful appearance and liked to be a bit silly around her colleagues didn't mean she had to be mothered - or in this case, fathered.

The worst thing was that she liked Olofsson and couldn't really blame him for his behavior. She knew that he had a daughter back home in Sweden who was only slightly older than her. If she wasn't mistaken, her name was Agnetha. Macmillan had once said that Olofsson had named her after the ABBA singer Agnetha Fältskog. Just thinking about the pop music of the 70s and 80s sent shivers down Nora's spine. Just like Olofsson's speech, which just didn't end and still didn't get to the point.

Nora cleared her throat loudly once again, then raised her hand to stop Olofsson. "Please, I know how difficult and important our work here is," she continued. "Whatever Dryer said, you should be fair enough to listen to a second opinion."

"Very well," replied Olofsson. "That's why you're here, isn't it? We have to tell the Swiss something if we're requesting spare parts for their drill again."

"Well, firstly, it's a prototype that nobody can expect to run flawlessly. And secondly, we adhered exactly to the specifications in terms of speed and feed rate. Dryer will certainly have mentioned this; after all, it was his job to check this."

"Yes, he emphasized that," said Olofsson, smiling. "Several times."

"Who can blame us then?" Nora wanted to know.

"Nobody does that. I just want our projects to run as efficiently and smoothly as possible. Most of the scientists are only here for a short time and we have to make sure that we achieve the best possible results despite the limited framework. And the equipment we are given should be usable by everyone for as long as possible."

"Yes, of course. I'm aware of that. I also know that we broke the rules last time. I apologized profusely for that. But this time it was different. And it may still have been worth it. I won some very interesting samples."

"You mean ice samples? Or rock already? I thought you wouldn't hit bottom for a few days," Olofsson asked.

"Right, we haven't come across any rock yet. It must have been something else. I want to find out what it was."

"Then I don't want to keep you unnecessarily. But be on time for Friday dinner in the canteen. I'm far less lenient than I am with defective drill heads."

"Thank you. I'll be there to do the dishes as punishment." She grinned briefly, but immediately became serious again. "Can we get a replacement for the drill?"

"I've already sorted everything out. Dryer is ordering a new sensor board. It could be here in two or three days." Olofsson smiled at Nora. "And now back to your science! I don't want it to be said that the old man kept you from your work with his long-winded lectures."

"Who could spread such infamous lies?" Nora said ironically and stood up.

Halfway back to her lab, Nora ran into Alex Corbinian. She was just descending the stairs that connected the two upper floors not far from the canteen when she spotted him.

At the same moment, she heard a woman's voice calling from the kitchen: "Hey, Alex! Are you coming at last? You have to cut the onions." It was Melissa Warden's scratchy voice.

However, Alex completely ignored her and continued to

walk towards Nora. He took her by the arm and pulled her with him.

Nora was more than irritated by this, but put up with it and just asked: "What's going on?"

"Come with me to the lab," he whispered to her and led the way back to room 2-B-09, which was just a few steps away around the next corner.

Once inside, he headed straight for the work area where the microscope was located. He pointed to a laptop that he had placed to the right of it. "I took pictures as we discussed and uploaded them to the computer."

"Yes, okay. But why are you so excited?" Nora wanted to know.

"Because..." Alex faltered. "... something like that is actually impossible."

"Like what?"

"Look for yourself." He opened a first photo of the fine crystal structure that Nora had already seen when looking directly through the eyepiece.

Then he clicked one image at a time. The structure changed. Only very minimally and only in individual areas. If Alex hadn't accidentally created a kind of time-lapse recording, the process might not even have been noticed.

"Oha!" Nora exclaimed as Alex continued to go through the pictures. "How many did you take?"

"200 shots for sure," he explained. "Wait, here it comes."

Nora gazed spellbound at the monitor of the notebook. After three more photos of the slowly forming structure, one suddenly appeared in which a flash of pinkish-purple light lit up. It took up most of the image and outshone the crystals behind it. The next image showed the usual structure again, but with a knot in the middle in which the particles seemed to have condensed. The following images showed no further change.

Nora reached forward and tapped the cursor keys on the keyboard to return to the shot with the flash of light. Then she went back a few frames and finally let the sequence run forward again. She jumped back and forth several times between the images around the light phenomenon.

"Okay, now I understand why that got you so excited," she said.

"Sorry, excited might be the wrong word," Alex complained. "I may be a geologist, but ..."

"Oh, come on, you know what I mean," she hastened to say. "What do you think it could be? A camera malfunction? A reflection?"

"I've already checked everything," Alex replied. "You can see that the behavior of this sample has changed completely since then. The structure is different too."

"But what can that mean?"

"Well, that's the big question!" said Alex. "The best I could do is speculate."

"Please, go on then!"

"Well, it looks to me as if an energy discharge has been released. These crystals - or whatever they really are - have come together to a critical point. A reaction was then triggered at this point, which we perceived as a light pulse."

"And then suddenly it was quiet."

"Yes, strange. It's hard to say why that is. Perhaps it's because we're only dealing with a relatively small amount of material whose potential is now exhausted. Or perhaps this substance strives to reach a certain state where it remains stable. Your drill may have broken the material out of its usual structure and now it wants to return to its original state. There is such a thing as shape memory, even with metals."

"It wants to return to a certain state?" Nora asked skeptically, emphasizing the word wants. "That almost sounds like..."

"Nonsense! Nothing like that," Alex quickly interrupted her. "Don't take that literally. I'm just musing aloud about what we've seen. You know, there are very interesting phenomena with crystals. Jacques and Pierre Curie discovered back in 1880 during experiments with tourmaline crystals that mechanical deformation generates electrical charges on the crystal surface. The same effect is still used today in the igniters in hand lighters."

"Hm, okay. But we didn't mechanically deform these samples." Nora looked at the microscope. "Whereas..."

"Right, your drill may have triggered a similar reaction and that's why it burned out," Alex said. "Now we might be seeing the reverse process."

"A steep thesis." Nora sat down on the chair and was silent for a moment.

"You might have stumbled across something really big!" Alex blurted out.

Nora just nodded, but didn't say anything back. Only after what felt like an eternity did she speak up again. "It's all still too mysterious for me. My gut feeling tells me that there might actually be something to it, but..." She looked Alex straight in the eye. "Can we please keep this to ourselves for now? At least until we have solid proof. I don't want to make a fool of myself with a rash theory that my colleagues will blow up in their faces. You know how some people are!"

Alex sighed. "You know that all the data automatically goes to the backup? There can't be very much secrecy here."

"Oh no, secrecy! I mean restraint. I just want to rule out the possibility that it's a mistake. And the first thing I want to do is collect more data to come up with a useful theory."

"I understand. That's a good plan. Maybe I can give you a hand tomorrow? My project is as good as finished."

"That would be great, because to be honest, that's not my specialty. I didn't want to study crystals, but organic residues."

"Well, the ways of science are sometimes unfathomable. How many sensations have been discovered by chance?"

"You really think this is a sensation?" Nora asked.

Alex grinned. "Maybe not yet, but eventually?"

"Let's wait and see," said Nora, feeling the excitement about this find growing inside.

What if Alex was right? What if this was a completely new

discovery? She liked the thought. At last she had the chance to prove to everyone what she was capable of. But she couldn't rush things. She had to make a plan, proceed meticulously and not make any mistakes. Tomorrow she would approach the matter with fresh ideas.

Only now did she realize that she had been sitting there in silence for quite a while and quickly put on a smile. "Come on, let's go over to the canteen, I promised Olofsson we'd be there on time."

"Really bad number," Alex complained.

"That's the price you have to pay if you want to be part of my sensation," she said jokingly and stood up.

Alex let out an agonized groan and stood up as well. "So that's the thanks I get for my expertise."

"Now stop complaining. I'll help you chop the onions too."

5

Greaves Ranch, Idaho, not far from the Nevada border, USA,
Morning of September 12

"Hooooo!" shouted Robert Greaves reassuringly, raising his left arm in the air while clutching a thick rope with his right. It looped around a post of the gate and ended at the neck of a young brown mustang horse that wouldn't stop running and jumping wildly.

Greaves had been struggling with the new arrival on his ranch for around two hours and could feel his arms gradually becoming tired. In the meantime, he had christened the horse "Bumper" in his mind because it kept throwing itself suddenly against the fence, as if it wanted to break through it with its head. Bumper was certainly a tough nut to crack, even for the experienced horse expert Greaves.

"That I should see something like that again!" he suddenly heard a familiar voice behind him, but it didn't fit here. He hadn't heard the sound of it for a long time, but he could never forget it. Robert knew immediately that the voice belonged to Linda Shoemaker.

He still avoided turning around too quickly. Instead, he calmly tied the rope around another pillar and then left the horse to its own devices.

"Robert?" asked Linda.

"Hello," he said curtly and finally turned around.

He climbed over the fence and approached Linda, who had stopped a few steps away. Her black curls hung down over her shoulders, her gray-blue eyes shone as brightly as ever. She looked damn good and hardly seemed any older than the last time he had seen her on that gray November day. Could it really have been eight years ago?

"What are you doing here?" he asked. "Do you want to buy a horse?"

Linda furrowed her brow. "Do I have to if I want to talk to you?"

"Would be a good start," Robert replied and fetched a water bottle from the shade of a hut next to the horse gate. He took a big gulp. At 24 degrees, it was quite warm for this mid-September morning, and the sun had been shining relentlessly from the sky since the early morning. There was no rain in sight, as had been the case most days in recent weeks. He knocked the dust off his clothes and came back to Linda.

"So, Robert, what is this?" she inquired.

"A ranch," he said succinctly. "It belonged to my uncle. He's been dead for a while, but Aunt Mary still lives here."

"Pretty," Linda replied, putting on her winning smile, which could just as easily indicate a compliment as a sneaky one. "Yes, I mean, this neighborhood here..."

"... is almost as remote and uninhabited as Mars, is that what you're saying?" he interrupted her. "Well, you just have your peace and quiet here, which I really appreciate."

"Funny you should mention Mars," said Linda. "But you're right. It almost looks like that here too. I looked at the satellite images before I came here. The Nevada desert begins three miles beyond your green oasis. Endless, bone-dry wasteland, you have to like that."

"Well, and yet there's life there too. Fascinating, isn't it?"

"Sure. You've always had a penchant for extremes."

"Once upon a time," Robert rebutted and saw Linda's gaze slide to the bumper at the gate behind him, which was bucking again. "I see, and that's why you've made it your business to tame wild horses?"

"From a biological point of view, mustangs are not wild horses. Their ancestors were domestic horses that were brought to the so-called New World by the Spanish conquistadors. Today's mustangs are therefore the descendants of captive refugees. Apparently they liked it here so much that they had spread across large parts of North America by the end of the 18th century," explained Robert.

"I see, and because there's no more room out on the prairie, you have to lock them up here?"

Robert sighed. "As is so often the case, bureaucracy throws a spanner in the works. The mustangs fall under the jurisdiction of the Bureau of Land Management and they think there are too many of them. So they capture them."

"And then?"

"In short: if no one can be found to adopt them and they are older than ten years, they can be sold. And that means: off to the slaughterhouse. The meat is exported to France or Japan."

Linda grimaced in disgust. "And because there's no one else willing to save the animals, good Robert had to step in? Is that your new vocation?"

"Yes, that's all right. Let's leave it. You wanted to know what I was doing here, so I told you. But now tell me why you've come all the way to this wasteland."

Linda nodded. "You're right, of course. I need to talk to you - about something other than horses."

"That hardly surprises me," Robert pointed to a spot directly behind Linda. Come on, I'll make us some coffee," he offered and walked toward the house. If you're lucky, there'll be some of Mary's apple pie left."

Fifteen minutes later, they were sitting with a cup of coffee on the wide veranda of the old farmhouse, which Robert had renovated with great attention to detail in recent years.

Aunt Mary had just brought two plates of apple pie from inside. She was in her late 60s and had snow-white hair, which she had pinned up in an old-fashioned tower hairstyle. She wore a simple dress with a floral pattern and a white apron with a wooden spoon stuck in the breast pocket.

Mary stopped next to the table and looked at Robert and Linda for a moment before she spoke. "Are you sure you don't want me to make you something healthy? Perhaps the lovely young lady would like to stay for lunch too?" She looked at Linda questioningly.

"Oh, no, no. Don't go to any trouble. I don't have that much time anyway. Besides, the cake looks fantastic."

Mary smiled. "Well, you can take it. Not an ounce of fat on your body! Whereas good Robert here ..."

"Give me a break, Mary, I'm in top form!"

"Don't always let yourself get annoyed, you'll never learn," Mary joked and put the plates down on the table. "If you need anything else, just shout. I'll be in the kitchen."

With that, she turned around and went back into the house.

"Your aunt is sweet as sugar," said Linda. "Almost too authentic, if you can put it that way."

"She is a kind-hearted person and old school, so to speak."

"Hm, yes ... I like to think so. And there's no other woman in your life?"

Robert furrowed his brow. "That's a question that can easily be misinterpreted. But no. I'm probably going to die single."

Linda nodded thoughtfully and took another look around the ranch. "There's something about the peace and quiet. Life here is certainly very different in a city."

"Mountain View isn't a metropolis either," Robert replied.

"Oh, I haven't been there for a while. I've been working at the Goddard Space Flight Center for the last few years."

"It was obvious that you would make a career at NASA at some point," Robert said without the slightest reproach in his voice.

"You could have done it," Linda replied diplomatically. "But maybe it's not too late for that." She picked up a thin black briefcase that had just been sitting next to her chair.

"That's not a good idea," said Robert. "You know I'm out!"

"Everything has been approved from the top," said Linda. "I'm just asking you to take a look."

"But what if I don't want that at all?" asked Robert.

She looked at him insistently and then put on her beguiling smile again.

But Robert resisted. "No," he said firmly and demonstratively placed his hand flat on the folder so that Linda couldn't open it.

"Robert, please," she insisted, "it's important, do you think I would have come here otherwise? And this is certainly a great thing ..." she gestured with her outstretched hand over the surrounding ranch land, "... but is this what you've always wanted in your life?"

Robert grimaced at this mean low blow. "It's really nice to see you, Linda. In a purely private way. But professionally, I don't see a future for either of us."

"I know I should have sided with you back then. I'm sorry, you have to believe me."

"You're right, you should have done that. But that's all history. Let's forget about it and leave the past in the past."

"You're right to be angry. They practically threw you out. But you also overstepped your authority and made a lot of enemies."

"As if I didn't know that!" Robert said much more sharply than he had intended.

"The point is: you could have been right back then."

Now Robert looked back and forth between Linda and the folder a few times. He hesitated to ask the next question because that would mean that he might get involved again with the people who had played him pretty badly during his time at NASA. But there was probably no way around it, just as he was already plagued by curiosity. "Okay, what's in there?"

"Just two pictures. Microscopic images."

"From what?"

"Let's say a crystalline structure that you know quite well," Linda explained.

"New pictures? From the Perseverance mission?" Robert asked in astonishment.

Linda shrugged her shoulders innocently. "I'm happy to

leave them here for you. You can study them. But if you want to know more, you'll have to come out of your hermit's cave - figuratively speaking, of course."

Robert ignored the side blow and just asked, "Where do you want me to go?"

"First to Washington, D.C."

"Why is that?"

"This investigation will be conducted off the record."

"Investigation? Unofficially?" Robert asked in irritation. "That sounds very mysterious, I don't know you like that."

Linda opened the folder and pulled out two printouts. She pushed the plate with the half-eaten apple pie to one side and placed the pictures on the table before Robert.

He leaned forward and looked at the images with a growing tingling sensation in his stomach. He tried not to let his inner excitement show and inquired matter-of-factly: "So, please tell me: Where did they come from?"

"I'm sorry. That's all I can tell you now. You'll find out the rest when you've agreed to investigate."

"Oho, gentle blackmail! But why are you even coming to me? Surely you must have 100 other qualified people for something like this."

Linda tilted her head. "You know that's nonsense. You're probably the only one who really believes in that theory - or at least almost the only one. Besides, the project is extremely well paid, you could use the money to finance your project here for years. You get all the freedom and the chance to rehabilitate yourself." Linda put on her winning smile again. "And if that's not enough of an incentive, I'll tell you that these pictures weren't taken on Mars. The origin is much closer."

Robert shook his head instinctively. His gut told him that it was madness to go back on this old and ultimately very painful track. But at the same time he knew that he practically couldn't do anything else. And Linda knew that too. She had him on the hook - again.

"You're really good at convincing people," he noted.

"It wasn't that difficult in this case," Linda replied kindly but firmly. "Do you want to go packing now?"

"This morning I still thought that Bumper would be my biggest challenge of the day. But who knew that you, of all people, would turn up here?" Robert stood up.

"Bumper is the horse, I presume?" Linda asked. "He seems to have calmed down, anyway." She pointed to the gate, where the young mustang was standing at the fence without jumping. "You see, sometimes it's good to give things time to work out."

"Of course," said Robert. "But eight years?" He made a dismissive gesture with his hand. "Forget it. I'll talk to Aunt Mary and get my things."

***

Nora sat at her workstation in laboratory 2-B-09 and studied the results of the analyses she had prepared. She had done this several times in the past few days, but had never come to a satisfactory conclusion. And it didn't look like she would now either.

The initial euphoria that she and Alex had felt after observing the effects under the microscope had almost completely evaporated. Nora was glad that she hadn't rushed to tell anyone about the strange behavior of the crystals. Because this phenomenon could obviously not be reproduced, not by melting more samples, not by heating, refreezing or any other treatment. The remaining results also puzzled her. The only thing that had been reasonably clear was the dating of the ice that they had retrieved from inside the drill. Comparisons with other samples had confirmed that the ice was around 400,000 to 430,000 years old. The composition of the trapped air had also been exactly as expected.

None of this helped Nora in her attempt to explain the malfunction of the drill and the subsequent light emission and restructuring of the sample. The solid residues that she had removed from the vaporizer did not help either. Although an examination of the substances showed that they also contained crystal fragments, they did not react in any way.

"That's obvious," Nora scolded loudly and slammed a hand on the tabletop. "They're bloody crystals! Why would they move?"

There was no one else in the lab who could have noticed her outburst. Alex had been busy with his project again since yesterday and seemed to have lost interest in her samples. She couldn't blame him. Steven Dryer, on the other hand, continued to avoid her. He had only been assigned to her as support on the drill because he had experience with such equipment. However, she didn't really feel like spending any more time here in the lab with the sourpuss.

The weather had been lousy over the past few days, a snowstorm had persistently prevented any outdoor mission and had also thwarted the planned supply delivery. The delivery that was supposed to bring the replacement part for the drill head. But it had finally been announced for today.

Nora was on pins and needles because, firstly, she wanted to make another drilling attempt to bring up fresh samples and, secondly, she was waiting for the material she had already obtained to be sent to her university in Munich for in-depth molecular analysis. There, much better possibilities were available to determine the exact composition of the microscopic particles she had found in the ice.

Perhaps this explained why the samples had behaved so strangely at first - and why they no longer did so. Nora realized how she kept doubting what she and Alex had seen. If it weren't for the image sequence that had been created as clear proof...

There was a knock on Nora's lab door and she turned around. "Come in!" she called out as she recognized chief machinist Ian Macmillan through the glass pane.

The somewhat cranky but lovable Scotsman could confidently be described as a veteran. His age was difficult to estimate due to his weather-beaten skin and countless wrinkles, but he had to be well past 50. He had been looking after the technology here since the station was commissioned and had previously worked at the old Amarok I station, which had been decommissioned a year and a half ago.

"Jo, how's it going?" he asked in his deep, smoky voice.

"That's fine. And yourself? How's the drill?" Nora asked.

"You owe me one," Macmillan said. "That was quite a bit of tinkering. I don't know what these engineers are thinking these days, but there's no such thing as easy maintenance!"

"What did you have in mind as compensation? You know I don't have any whisky."

"Listen to me! Just because I'm Scottish doesn't mean I can be bribed with whisky." He put on a conspiratorial smile. "Okay, actually that works quite well, but I'll take cigars if necessary."

"Smoking is everywhere here ..." She fell silent. "That was a joke, wasn't it?"

"You're really funny," Macmillan said, shaking his head. "You and your weird colleague can pick up your drill downstairs. But I guess you won't be able to get to the drilling site until tomorrow afternoon, it's still whistling like crazy out there."

Then he turned around and left the lab at a stroll.

"Thank you! I'll think of something nice for you!" she called after him before the door closed behind the engineer.

Nora turned back to her devices and the laptop. She nodded with satisfaction. Things were finally looking up, the drill had been repaired and there was a gradual prospect of an improvement in the weather. The latter, in particular, could really cheer up the bad mood that had taken hold of her. She would be able to hold out until tomorrow, but then she had to get to the bottom of this phenomenon!

She opened a chat window on her laptop and wrote to Alex Corbinian. Perhaps the colleague had time to accompany her and contribute his expertise? In any case, she would prefer that a thousand times over standing alone at the borehole with Dryer for hours again.

6

Underground base of the U.S. Air Force near Washington, D.C.,
Evening of September 12

"This is definitely not a NASA site," Robert Greaves stated matter-of-factly as Linda Shoemaker led him deeper and deeper into the gray, bunker-like building on the outskirts of Washington, D.C. "Upstairs I thought it might be a particularly sensitive laboratory, but no scientist would volunteer to work down here. This is a military facility, right?"

Linda nodded. "Yes, there's no denying it, you're right. That's because the Air Force is in charge of the operation." She paused and then added: "So am I, in a way."

"Air Force, Linda! When did you start working ..."

Robert was abruptly interrupted when a soldier jumped up briskly from his guard post and shouted: "Can you prove your identity?"

"Here's your ID card," said Linda, holding out to Robert a visual ID card dangling from a ribbon. It was printed with his name, date of birth, and a rather old picture of him with longer hair. The card also had several shimmering green holograms on it to make it forgery-proof.

Robert took the plastic card, looked at it for a moment and then held it out to the soldier. He placed it on an electronic reader and checked its validity on a screen next to it.

"These things have a radio chip inside," Linda explained.

"Thank you, sir," said the soldier, handing Robert his I.D. back. "Keep it visible on your person at all times."

Robert hung his I.D. around his neck as ordered.

After the guard had also checked Linda's access authorization, he cleared the way and they passed a metal turnstile, behind which a barren corridor led about 20 meters further into the building. To the left and right, dark gray doors had been built into the light gray walls. Apart from cryptic room numbers, they were not labeled in any way that would have revealed what was hidden behind them.

They headed for the end of the corridor, where there was a slightly larger double door with another soldier posted in front of it. He took a quick look at the I.D. cards and then opened the door. "The general is already expecting you."

"General?" Robert asked quietly in Linda's direction.

"Frank Sattler, also known as ‚The Eagle'. But come on now, we'll sort everything out inside," Linda replied and led the way.

Behind the door, a conference room of sorts awaited them, bathed in twilight that was far too dramatic for Robert's taste. Perhaps it was the dark brown wood paneling that covered all the walls and the ceiling. There was also an equally brown oval meeting table, which could seat a good two dozen people, and a dark gray carpet underneath. The light, which came from small spotlights on the ceiling, really struggled in this room, which was almost as empty as it was dark. This may have been intentional, as it created a kind of opaque interrogation atmosphere that Robert was already uncomfortable with.

Now he heard the soldier close the heavy door behind them, and an eerie silence fell. Surely this conference room was soundproofed and bug-proof.

At the other end of the table, and therefore as far away from the entrance as possible, sat a man in a dark blue uniform under two of the spotlights. Judging by the medals and insignia on his chest, he was a long-serving and highly decorated officer. Four stars were emblazoned on his shoulders, making it clear that this general had gone as far as he could in the hierarchy. Robert guessed that he was in his late 60s or perhaps even over 70, although it was always difficult for him to make an accurate assessment of steel-hard military men.

Now the man, who had thick gray hair and an equally gray moustache, stood up and pointed to the chairs. "I'm glad you could come, Dr. Greaves. You too, of course, Dr. Shoemaker. Please come in and sit down. Then we can discuss what this is all about in peace and quiet."

Robert and Linda took their seats and the general sat down again before continuing. "I still owe it to you to introduce myself. General Frank D. Sattler, Special Representative of the President for ..." He fell silent. "Wait, maybe we should clear up the formalities first." He turned and looked behind him.

Another person stepped out of the shadows. It was a woman in her mid-30s in a black trouser suit with short, straight hair - also black - and a stony expression on her face.

"That's spooky," said Robert, who had just thought they were alone with the general because of the spotty lighting.

"I'm sorry, I didn't mean to startle you, Dr. Greaves," the woman said coolly, placing a thin black folder in front of him. "I'm Sandra Gillie. In the folder you'll find a confidentiality agreement, which I'd like you to sign immediately." She placed a classy-looking fountain pen with a gold rim in front of Robert.

Robert looked questioningly at Linda.

She just nodded. "It's all right, I signed it too."

"Why doesn't that reassure me?" Robert replied, turning back to Gillie and the general. "I don't suppose you'll wait until I've read through everything?"

"No, we don't need to discuss the clauses either. It's a standard form," explained Gillie. "Just sign it. Otherwise I'm afraid I'll have to ask you to leave."

"Please, Miss Gillie," General Sattler now intervened. "All due respect to the formalities, but we're counting on the cooperation of Dr. Greaves." He gave Robert a half-questioning, half-asking look.

He opened the folder, which contained two sheets stapled together. They were printed on both sides with legal gobbledygook that would have taken Robert hours to understand. He skimmed the text to see if he could find the word "death penalty" anywhere, and when he didn't, he pulled out his pen and signed the document.

"Thank you very much," said Gillie and took the folder. Then she sat down at the table to Sattler's left.

"Okay, General," Robert now took the floor. "This is all pretty weirdly staged. But be that as it may. You were just about to tell me what special assignment the President gave you. And I have to admit that I would actually be very interested to know."

"Your colleague, Dr. Shoemaker, has probably already explained to you that we don't want to make a proverbial big deal out of the project you're supposed to be involved in, I assume."

"That's right," Robert replied. "And the thing with the nondisclosure agreement also reinforced that impression a little."

General Sattler smiled indulgently, but his eyes remained hard. Robert suspected that he didn't think much of his easygoing manner.

"Good, good, Dr. Greaves. Then let's talk straight. I've been assigned to investigate the possibility of extraterrestrial infiltration on Earth. And please, spare me any comments about lizard creatures with rubber masks or other nonsense!"

Robert raised his hands apologetically. "I'm a scientist. And I also know very well what it feels like to express unconventional ideas."

"Yes, your career at NASA didn't go quite so smoothly. But perhaps that's a good thing in view of current developments," said Sattler. "In any case, I've asked Dr. Shoemaker to contact you because I think your very special view of things is needed here."

"The pictures she showed me?" Robert asked. "They're actually from Earth?"

Sattler nodded. "Greenland. A young scientist from Germany called Nora Grimm took them. She's there as part of an international research mission that we've been supporting financially for some time."

"I see, so that's how you got the data. Did you try to contact the woman?"

"No," Gillie now intervened. "That will be our job."

"Our ..." Robert faltered and looked at the general again. He promptly turned to Linda. "Thank you for your efforts, Dr. Shoemaker; we'll take care of the rest."

Linda looked at him perplexed, opened her mouth as if she wanted to say something back, then nodded and got up from her seat.

Robert looked on irritated at first, but then stood up to protest.

But Linda raised her hands placatingly. "It's all right, please sit down again." She left the room without another word.

When she was out the door, Sattler continued. "Shoemaker would not have been suitable for this mission, she is a pure theorist, unlike you, Dr. Greaves. Instead, Miss Gillie will accompany you to Greenland and provide you with active support. Don't worry, she's well trained."

"For what, please?" Robert wanted to know.

"For whatever it takes," commented Gillie.

"So, Dr. Greaves. Your mission is very simple: you fly to Greenland, check the data and samples of this Nora Grimm, secure any material, seal the borehole if necessary and ensure that no further samples are taken. We have already compiled all the research data from her time at NASA and transferred it to an encrypted laptop, which Miss Gillie will then hand over to you."

"You're telling me to secure everything there and close down the site? On what grounds? What right do you have? The scientists on site could refuse and ask questions. And what about the local authorities?" said Robert.

"Let us worry about that," the general assured him. "According to your record, you are an extremely intelligent and pragmatic person. I'm sure that you and Miss Gillie will find the best possible solution."

Robert shook his head silently.

"Come on! You know that we cannot allow such a discovery - if it turns out to be true - to fall into the wrong hands. You make sure that doesn't happen, and in return I promise you that you can lead the subsequent investigations. What would you have said if someone had predicted eight years ago that you would one day be able to back up your theory with solid evidence? Especially here on Earth. I don't need to tell you what a unique opportunity this is, do I?"

"No, you don't have to," Robert confirmed.

"Well, you see. Then we're in agreement."

"All right. But I can put together my own team."

"Sure, but only after the thing on Greenland. You only go there in pairs, as inconspicuously as possible. As scientists."

"When does it start?"

"They fly out of Andrews Base in two hours," replied Sattler.

"In two hours! That's something ..."

"Are you going to let this opportunity pass you by?" asked Sattler in a dramatic tone.

Robert felt surprised and at the same time overwhelmed by what had just been revealed to him. Of course, he couldn't let this opportunity pass him by! As much as he disliked Sattler and Gillie's manner.

"That's what I thought. Then everything has been discussed," said Sattler. "Oh, and Dr. Greaves, I'm sure I don't have to remind you about confidentiality. The same goes for Dr. Shoemaker. You're welcome to bring her on board later. But only once everything is under control, do you understand?"

Gritting his teeth, Robert nodded and stood up. "I'd better settle a few things before I set off into the eternal ice."

"I'm delighted that you're on board. You can arrange everything else with Miss Gillie. I'll send her to your hotel to pick her up." The general then gestured towards the door.

Linda was waiting outside with a look on her face like seven days of rain. "Son of a bitch," she cursed, "First, he sent me to the desert to lure you here, and now he's throwing me out of the project."

Robert sighed. "Yeah, I guess that doesn't bode well for all the promises he just made me."

They walked back down the corridor together and through the security barrier.

When they had left the building and were a few meters away, Linda stopped and took Robert by the arm. She now looked him straight in the eye. "Promise me you'll be careful over there! And keep an eye on that, Sandra Gillie. That woman is unpredictable."

"Who is she? Certainly not a scientist. And she doesn't look like a soldier either."

"I don't know exactly where she comes from. She's only been on Sattler's staff for a few weeks. I certainly don't trust her - and neither should you."

Robert nodded. "I'll be careful," he assured her. "Shall we go for a proper coffee before I go to the ice desert?"

"As tempting as that sounds, we'd better postpone it. They won't let you out of their sight and I don't want to be targeted. When you're back and everything's sorted, we'll catch up on the coffee, okay?"

"I'm looking forward to it," Robert said and smiled. "It was nice to see you, even if only for a short time. I'm off to buy some thick hats and thermal underwear. That's not what we wear in Idaho."

Linda smiled. "Sounds sexy, send me a photo." Then she hugged Robert and turned to leave.

***

Meanwhile, the general gave Sandra Gillie final instructions in Sattler's secure briefing room, two floors below ground. "Miss Gillie, I'm sure I don't need to emphasize how important the success of this mission is. I'm doing it anyway, because it's not just a matter for the armed forces, but also a very personal one for me." He looked penetratingly at Gillie to get some feedback that she had grasped the magnitude of the undertaking, but could read nothing in her usual emotionless expression. "Well?" he followed up.

"As you said, you don't need to emphasize that. And with all due respect, General, your personal reasons are none of my business. And they don't affect my work either. I have a mission to fulfill and I will."

As usual, Sattler didn't particularly like the way Gillie expressed herself, but he had to appreciate her professionalism. "That's all I wanted to hear," he lied. "Then I won't bore you any further with the back story - for now. It may not actually be relevant to the work at hand. The main thing is that you on Greenland ensure everything is done to our complete satisfaction. You will give Greaves all the support he needs to carry out his investigation, but you will not dance to his tune; you will follow my instructions; is that clear? If he is successful, you will take all necessary steps to secure the region in question. We will then take care of the rest."

"Understood," Gillie commented curtly. "And what do I do if Greaves doesn't stick to the plan? His file reads as if he acts quite stubbornly from time to time."

"First of all, we give him as much freedom as possible. Scientists don't like it when you put a gun to their head. But you keep me informed and keep him in check. If he seriously wants to contravene our objectives, we will take appropriate measures."

Gillie nodded. "All right. Anything else?"

"Yes, one thing: please make an effort to gain his trust instead of seeking confrontation. I know by now your sometimes gruff way of dealing with people. It won't lead to success with Greaves, but will encourage his rejection. Why don't you try to be a bit like Dr. Shoemaker? You'll achieve more." Sattler thought he saw a hint of disgust on Gillie's face - but he was probably mistaken, as this impression vanished the very next moment.

Instead, Gillie put on a pained smile. "If it serves the mission objective, I'll be as sugary sweet and hand-tame as Greaves likes. But he shouldn't get the wrong idea, I always have a loaded P229 under my pillow."

Sattler tilted his head. "I'll take your word for it. Get the equipment now and collect Greaves. The plane takes off as planned at 21:00. Report back when you've landed."

"Very well," Gillie replied coolly and rose to head for the exit.

7

PRIN research station "Amarok II", Greenland
Morning of September 13

On the lowest level of the Amarok II station, where the main technical and storage areas were located, Nora and Alex were busy packing the newly repaired drill head and other equipment for today's shift at the borehole. It was only just after 8:00 in the morning, but as the weather forecast was already very good, Nora had decided to set off as early as possible. This would hopefully allow them to gain new insights before the evening - and she was really looking forward to it.

Steven Dryer suddenly burst into the middle of their preparations. "Well, that's interesting!" he snapped at Nora. "When were you going to tell me that we were resuming work on the borehole today? Before or after you set off there?"

Nora raised her hands placatingly. "Steven, we're just getting everything ready. I wanted to come up and see you in a minute."

"Yeah, sure! You wanted to boot me out. And anyway, since when has Corbinian been part of this project?" He gave Alex a dark look. "As far as I know, it's just the two of us. And now that the tedious, dirty work is done, he suddenly comes along and takes the credit, or how am I to understand this?" Dryer gave Nora a reproachful look and, at the same time, pointed with his left hand at Alex, who was visibly irritated by Dryer's flare-up.

"It's not like that!" Alex defended himself. "I only offered Nora help because it's at least partly about geological issues. Nobody wants to boot you out."

"Oh, then why don't I know about the results you've achieved?"

Nora tilted her head and looked at Steven for a moment. Then she said calmly: "You obviously know about it. Besides, the data is available to everyone. And while we're on the subject of being open and honest about our opinions, listen carefully: you've shown absolutely no interest in my research goal over the last few weeks and months! I even had the impression that you found it downright dull and irrelevant. But so be it. The deal is that you support my research in the first phase of the project and in return I support yours in the second half. So what are you actually complaining about? You've obviously realized that my project is interesting, albeit in a completely different way than originally thought. That makes me happy. You're welcome to continue contributing, but don't forget that I'm still in charge."

During her presentation, Nora had noticed how she had become louder and more upset, but at the same time more confident and convinced. She had bottled up her displeasure at her colleague's behavior for so long that it was now really good to let it all out. And the effect was immense.

Dryer's arrogant, angry expression changed to astonishment and then became more and more thoughtful. He let a moment pass after the end of Nora's outburst before he replied. "All right, I'm sorry. I was frustrated, I have to admit. And I was jealous." He stroked his chin over his close-cropped beard. "You're right. It's your project, and I'll support you."

"It really was about time you two had a word," Alex commented and smiled. "So, of course I'm happy to continue supporting you. Without any ulterior motives."

"Okay, what's the plan?" Dryer now asked in a downright friendly manner.

"We'll finish packing, load up the snowmobiles and then we can leave in 30 minutes," Nora explained. "I want to try to get to the bottom today."

Dryer nodded. "Okay, that should be doable if the drill progresses as expected."

"Great, colleague!" Nora was pleased, "Always stay positive; I like you a lot better this way."

"We'll see how long the harmony lasts, won't we?" Dryer said dryly, but then turned up the corners of his mouth to hint at a smile.

***

A hole in the air woke Robert Greaves from his sleep. He pushed his sleep mask up from his eyes to his forehead and took out his earplugs. He immediately remembered why he had stuffed them into his ears shortly after take-off. Without them, it was almost unbearably loud inside the military transport plane they had boarded at Andrews Air Base. It was a Boeing C-17 Globemaster III, Gillie had explained. The Air Force had used these robust and reliable aircraft for decades for supply flights. And he and Gillie were on one, along with a handful of other passengers and dozens of tons of cargo.

Robert's bottom ached from sitting for so long on the uncomfortable folding seats along the outside wall of the plane. He turned to his left, where Sandra Gillie had been sitting two seats away. He could now see her in the front of the plane, where the transition to the cockpit must be.

She saw that he was awake and came back to him. She stopped right in front of him and gave him an unusually amused look. "I thought this sort of thing was only for beauty queens," she said sarcastically.

It took Robert a moment to realize what she meant, but then he plucked the sleep mask from his forehead. "What's good enough for Miss America should be good enough for me," he replied. He wasn't a fan of such accessories, but he was still grateful that he had the mask. He had been exhausted after yesterday and had slept like a baby despite the noise and the uncomfortable seats on the plane. But he wouldn't mention that to Gillie. Instead, he asked: "How much longer do we need?"

Gillie took a seat next to him. "We're almost on our approach. It'll take about three quarters of an hour. If we factor in an hour's time difference, it will be just before 8:00 a.m. local time when we arrive."

"Local time ... Where exactly are we landing, I assume on a base?"

"At Pituffik Space Base, formerly better known as Thule Air Base, which has been in existence since the 1950s."

"And then?"

"We will change to a helicopter and fly about an hour inland until we reach the researchers' station. The borehole that Nora Grimm is working on is only a few kilometers away."

"Perhaps we shouldn't land the military helicopter right outside the front door, that could give the wrong impression," said Robert.

"Or just the right one," Gillie disagreed.

"No, no. If we want to gain the scientists' trust, we have to be a bit more sensitive. We'll land away from them and walk the rest - preferably straight to the borehole. I assume there's suitable equipment on this military base?"

"That can be arranged. We need thermal clothing, but also weapons."

"Weapons, why is that?"

"Polar bears," Gillie replied. "If we go on foot, we might come across one. And such encounters often end fatally. Believe me, I've prepared well for this mission."

Robert nodded approvingly. "That's good, I can see that you're quite ahead of me. But we should also brush up on your knowledge in other respects."

Gillie gave him a skeptical look as if she didn't think there could be anything she hadn't already thought of. "In what way?" she asked diplomatically.

Now Robert took his laptop bag from under the seat and pulled out the computer. He started it up and promptly received a black screen with an unadorned gray window in the middle asking him to enter a password. He looked questioningly at Gillie.

She pulled a dark red envelope out of her jacket pocket and handed it to Robert. "You need the code. Please memorize it and destroy it."

Robert opened the envelope, entered the numbers and then crumpled up the paper. He looked at Gillie. "What should I do with it? I can't very well burn it here on board, can I?"

Gillie tilted her head.

"I'm not going to eat it either, if that's what you're suggesting," Robert added.

"Give me that!" Gillie demanded. "We'll put it in the shredder at the base."

"Good, now would be a good time to get to know each other. I don't suppose you want to tell me too much about yourself, but as my assistant you should at least know a little about our work to be credible."

"A sensible suggestion," confirmed Gillie. "But please understand, I'm not a fan of technical jargon."

"Even if the word technical jargon is not necessarily politically correct, I understand what you mean." Robert opened the file browser on the computer and got an overview. You actually pulled all my work from the NASA server. How did you get it?"

Gillie shrugged her shoulders. "I'd say that falls under what's known as a trade secret."

"Well, fine. I probably don't even want to know." He navigated to a folder containing a compilation of images and data sets from the Mars rover Curiosity. According to the time stamps, these were collected between 2012 and 2015.

He then opened two images as examples and displayed them side by side on the screen. They showed images of rock samples and boreholes taken by the rover. "As you probably know, I was one of the scientific directors at NASA in the early years of the Mars Science Laboratory mission, or Curiosity for short. And this is what most of my work looked like. As a biologist, an exobiologist to be precise, I looked for signs of life on the planet and tried to find out whether there could be any at all under the prevailing conditions - or whether there ever was any."

"It's all in your file," Gillie interjected, obviously wanting to get to the point.

"That's right. What is not in my official file at least, but Sattler is probably aware of, is that I found life there." Robert paused. "And if you're wondering why this hasn't become a worldwide sensation, I should add that I was pretty much the only one who supported this theory. It wasn't believed and after a very unpleasant argument, I was asked to resign. So much for the short version. But there seems to have been something to it, otherwise we wouldn't be sitting here now."

"How did you try to prove that?" Gillie asked, and Robert had the impression that she was showing genuine interest for the first time.

"Good point!" he replied and scrolled down through the file list. Right to the end. He frowned, searched through a few other folders and couldn't find anything there either.

Sattler and Gillie had obviously not obtained all the data after all - something crucial was missing. Either these particular data records had been deleted after he left or they hadn't been copied. If Robert was completely honest, he had almost expected something like this - and had taken precautions. He reached into the inside pocket of his jacket and pulled out a silver USB stick shaped like a horse's head. "Better safe than sorry, Aunt Mary always says."

Gillie gave him a skeptical look.

"Parts are missing from your copy," he explained curtly and inserted the USB stick into a free port on the laptop. A new window immediately appeared on the screen, prompting him to enter the security code Gillie had given him.

He entered this and another file browser opened. "Here are the missing pieces of the puzzle," he explained. "Someone probably didn't want them to be in the official results."

"Interesting," Gillie replied curtly.

"Well, you should also know that the Curiosity rover is not a moving robot with a camera but an entire laboratory with various instruments for geological, chemical and physical investigations. It's pure high-tech in a very small space."

"You don't say," Gillie stated.

"Be that as it may. Two of these measuring instruments are particularly suitable for detecting life: the so-called CheMin module and the SAM. They analyze the samples that the rover collects for organic traces or the effects of water, among other things."

"And you found something that indicates life?"

"This is where it gets tricky," Robert said, grimacing. "What was found was basically nothing organic but a kind of crystal lattice. However, under very specific conditions, it was stimulated to behave in a way that suggests it was a form of life." He opened some images that showed the crystalline structure mentioned. "Unfortunately, I was unable to reproduce the effect, the sample was destroyed in an accident. To this day, I don't know exactly what went wrong. But I was blamed for it."

"Strange, I thought only freaks who wanted to meet aliens worked at NASA," said Gillie.

Robert shook his head. "That's only about 50 percent. And the further up the management ladder you go, the fewer there are. Someone didn't like my theory, and neither did the vehemence with which I pushed for publication. At a certain point, the pressure simply became unbearable."

"So you took your hat and moved to Idaho to raise horses?"

"I don't breed them, there are too many of them anyway. But let's not go into that. I just wanted you to know the back story."

Gillie looked at her watch. "Twenty minutes to landing. It'll be best if we go through our cover."

"Camouflage?"

"Yes, of course. We have to tell the researchers there is something credible, as you said yourself. That's why we've created two new identities, or rather positions. We are MIT scientists who will be responsible for this mission. Congratulations, Professor Greaves, you now have a chair at one of the most prestigious universities in the country."

"And you?"

"I've been your research assistant for two years, Dr. Sandra Gillie. One day, of course, I would like to follow in your footsteps. For the sake of simplicity, we'll keep our real names."

Robert raised his eyebrows. "I suppose you're used to working with cover identities?"

Gillie left the question unanswered and pointed to the laptop. "Copy the data from the stick to the internal hard disk and you'd better switch the thing off for landing."

"Of course, I always do what my loyal assistant tells me," Robert replied sarcastically and shook his head. Then, he started the copying process.

8

"Snowbird" drilling project,
17 kilometers north of the Amarok II

Even though it had still looked like there was plenty of potential for conflict in the morning, Nora was glad that she had two men at her side in, Alex and Steven. The access to the outpost where they had driven their borehole into the ice had been covered by a snow bank several meters high during the three days of stormy weather.

The three of them had now been digging their way out for a good half hour and were slowly approaching the actual lock that sealed off the underground structure. Nora hoped that the storm had only left traces on the outside and that everything inside had remained as they had left it. She really didn't feel like shoveling snow off the equipment and technical devices. Not to mention the damage it might have caused. Her need for downtime and delays was covered.

"I'm through, the door's back there!" Alex announced. "A few more minutes and we can warm up inside with a cup of tea."

"That's a nice view," Nora replied.

Steven only let out a disgruntled grumble. He was obviously not at all enthusiastic about the extensive physical activity.

They cleared away the remaining snow and then took the equipment from the snowmobiles. The airlock had thankfully held tight, so there was no snow inside the outpost. Once they had carried everything inside, Steven set about unpacking the drill head.

Nora booted up the technology while Alex went over to the workshop area to fetch two thermo mugs of tea.

"Tell me, did you spill solvent or hot water here?" Alex called over to Nora and Steven.

Nora looked up from the computer screen and frowned. "What do you mean?" she asked.

"There's a dent in the floor here in front of the table that looks like it's melted into it."

"Yes, that could have happened when we opened the drill head. Some of the contents were liquid and sloshed out. We hadn't expected that when we dismantled the cladding."

"But..." Alex didn't finish the sentence.

Nora saw that he was brooding. Then he tipped the contents of his recently filled mug of tea onto the floor and watched what happened.

At first, Nora was irritated, but then she understood the point of the experiment and went over it to Alex.

Steven also let go of the drilling equipment and joined them. "Very scientific," he commented, looking at the reddish stain on the ice floor.

"But effective," Alex replied impassively. "The tea is probably 50 to 60 degrees and still freezes almost instantly on the icy floor, whereas your half-frozen sample has left a deep dent. At best, it could only have been a few degrees warm."

"That doesn't make much sense, you're right," Nora admitted. "It's also strange that the temperature sensor on the drill head was reading almost 50 degrees above zero before it malfunctioned. Maybe there's a connection?"

"The last measurement could only have been a mistake," Steven interjected. "We now know that the sensor board is burnt out. That must have produced false readings."

"And that one?" Alex asked, pointing to the floor. "What's your theory on that?"

"Probably a chemical reaction," Steven said.

Nora swayed her head back and forth. "Yes, it could be. There were solids in the ice, after all. Some kind of physical or chemical process may have taken place. My analyses didn't reveal anything that could explain this phenomenon, but I sent samples to Munich yesterday and hope to receive the first results soon. I'm very interested in finding out exactly what it is. Until then, we'll try to find out more here." She pointed to the borehole and then looked questioningly at Steven.

"The drill head is already on its way down. No error messages or complications for the time being. Everything seems to be going according to plan."

"How much longer will he need?" Nora wanted to know.

"It goes faster downhill. In about an hour, he should be at the position where we left off."

"Very good," said Alex and poured himself and Nora a new cup of tea. "Then we can warm up in peace. Do you want one too, Steven?"

"All right, then. We have nothing else to do," he replied and took a cup from a plastic box on the table.

It turned out that Steven's estimate was quite accurate, because after a good 55 minutes the depth indicator reported 2,400 meters. Steven slowed down the rate of descent and waved Nora over to him. "We're almost there, but..." He paused. "Take a look at this."

Nora and Alex joined him at the controls and looked at the displays. "Please stop it completely," Nora asked and called up some of the stored data as a graphic. "There, look!" she said to Alex. "Another temperature spike, not that extreme, but still."

Alex shook his head. "Plus degrees? Down there?"

Steven shrugged his shoulders. "I have to admit, it's starting to seem very strange to me too. Either the electronics have major damage or ..."

"Or?" Nora repeated.

"To be honest, I have no idea," Steven admitted.

"Welcome to the club," she replied briefly and gradually checked all the values collected by the drill head again. "That doesn't look like a measurement error. The values seem to increase exponentially the further the drill has penetrated into the depths."

"Where are we now?" Alex wanted to know.

"9.5 degrees Celsius."

"I don't understand," said Alex. "Then the drill would have to float in the water."

"Good point," said Steven. "That doesn't seem to be the case here. However, the freezing point of water is not a fixed value. There have been experiments in which water has been cooled to minus 40 degrees without freezing. This can be controlled using electric fields, for example."

"You mean we're dealing with a similar phenomenon here, only possibly the other way around? So there's ice down there that remains solid at plus temperatures?" Nora inquired.

"Just a hypothesis based on our observations so far," said Steven. "Maybe it matches the strangely melted floor over in the workshop area. There seems to be something in the ice there that is shifting the usual physical framework in relation to water."

"If your hypothesis is correct, it could have an electrical charge. I assume you've seen the pictures I took of the first sample?" Alex asked in Steven's direction.

"Yes, I did. It looked like some kind of crystal to me."

"Exactly. It is known that crystals emit electricity under certain conditions, such as high pressure. We have observed an effect that could represent such a process. It is possible that the kilometer-thick ice sheet generates such high pressure that these crystals release energy, which in turn affects the ice."

"That's a bit much speculation for me," said Nora.

"Me too," Steven agreed with her. "There's no clear evidence."

"Well, then we need to generate more data. And for that we need new samples," Alex replied calmly.

Nora nodded. "Yes, we couldn't get anything more out of the last remnants. We couldn't repeat the process."

"Will the drill work under these conditions?" asked Alex.

"It's hard to say," Steven replied. "Actually, there shouldn't be a problem with the temperature. This device is built for the most extreme conditions. Whether it's minus 50 or plus 50 degrees, the machine shouldn't really care."

"Actually," Nora repeated, "Olofsson made it very clear that we shouldn't provoke another failure."

"Well, I don't see any alternative," Steven replied.

"Me neither," Nora confirmed. "Then we lower it to the edge and drill like this ..."

Then she was interrupted by a voice that clearly didn't belong here. "Please wait! Can we talk to each other first?"

Surprised, they turned around. At the door stood a 40-year-old man with tanned skin and a woman ten years younger with a much paler complexion and jet-black hair.

Nora was quite perplexed. They had obviously been so engrossed in the discussion that they hadn't heard them come through the door. Besides, the chance of suddenly having an unexpected visitor up here in the middle of the glacier was about as small as winning the lottery. She cleared her throat and stepped out from behind the technical desk. "Uh, hello, you really surprised us," she began. "What ... I mean, who are you?"

The man pushed back his hood and approached Nora. He pulled off his glove and held out his hand. "Dr. Robert Greaves is my name. And this is my associate, Sandra Gillie. We'd like to talk to you about your work here. You are Nora Grimm, aren't you?"

Nora shook her head in amazement, then nodded. "Yes, sure. That's me. But what makes you think I am? Besides, we're in the middle of a critical phase of a project here!"

Only now did she realize how absurd this situation was. How could someone know about her research? And then he came here in person? According to the man's dialect, he was from the USA, which made it all the stranger.

"I know it's unusual for us to ambush you like this. But you've come across something..." He paused for a moment as if thinking about what to say next. "Well, it's very important that we proceed very cautiously."

"What do you mean, we?" Steven blurted out. "This is still our project. What do you think you're doing? Typical American arrogance!"

Nora saw Alex, who was also from the USA, give him a skeptical look but didn't say anything else.

Instead, Nora took the floor again. "This really isn't the right time to discuss - and certainly not to argue. I don't know who you are or where you come from, Dr. Greaves, but I would be very grateful if you would let us continue our work in peace."

"You have to stop the drilling!" Sandra Gillie intervened and stepped forward.

Dr. Greaves grimaced and turned to his assistant. "Let me handle this, please." Then he looked at Nora again. "We're from the Massachusetts Institute of Technology in Cambridge, I'm a professor there. Please, believe me; it's better if you stop drilling until we've had a quiet chat."

"I think your weird act has gone on long enough," Steven took the floor again. "This is a PRIN research mission, and as the scientists in charge, we decide what we do and don't do. If we want to keep drilling, we will."

Sandra Gillie took another step forward, but was held back by Greaves. "Of course, you're right," he said. "That's why I'm asking you politely."

Nora shook her head. "No, that's not how it works. You can't show up here and demand that of us without giving us valid reasons."

"I will do that. Maybe we can talk somewhere undisturbed?" asked Greaves.

"We can all hear what you have to say, can't we?" Alex said in a sarcastic tone.

Greaves looked at Alex for a moment. "If you wish."

"No, that wouldn't be a good idea," Gillie interjected. "We should keep the circle as small as possible."

"You're starting to make rules again!" Steven got upset. "The best thing is to get out now."

Gillie gave him an icy look. "Fine, but we'll be back."

"Is that a threat? It almost sounds like it," said Steven.

"Hey, it's okay," Nora intervened. "Let's calm down."

Dr. Greaves reached into his jacket pocket and pulled out a business card. He handed it to Nora and looked at her urgently. "Please get in touch when you have time." He looked at Alex and Steven. "We shouldn't have surprised you like that, I'm sorry. We were in a hurry. But I'll ask you again to stop drilling for the time being."

"We'll think about it," Nora replied, "but it's better if you leave now." She gestured towards the door.

Greaves nodded, slipped his gloves and hood back on and turned around.

Sandra Gillie cast a dissatisfied glance around the room, then turned around and followed the professor out.

Nora waited a while longer to make sure that they had gone through the outside door and were out of earshot. Then she turned her attention back to her two colleagues. "What was that, please?"

"I have absolutely no idea," said Alex. "The woman in particular was really unpleasant. It's good that Steven stood up to her. His uncharming manner was good for something." He laughed.

Steven grimaced. "I just made it clear to them that they have no say here. What do they think they're doing? Professor at MIT, so what? I'll take the guy's word for it, but that Gillie hardly seemed like a scientist."

Nora nodded. "There's something fishy about this. And how the heck did they know what we were doing here? He even knew my name!"

"Yes, that would mean they were explicitly looking for us. So we've actually made a sensational find?" asked Alex.

"I'll talk to the guy. But first I'll check his story and ask Olofsson if he knows anything about the matter," Nora said firmly.

"And what do we do with the drill?" Steven wanted to know.

Nora looked back and forth between Steven, Alex and the borehole. "Put it on stand-by. We'll continue tomorrow."

"You believe this guy?" Steven asked.

"I don't know," Nora admitted. "He hasn't told us anything, so there's not much to believe. But we've seen enough oddities ourselves to be a little more cautious."

"You're right," Alex agreed with her. "If someone goes to the trouble of looking you up in person in the Greenlandic ice desert, they're probably very serious."

"All right, let's go back," said Steven. "But we should lock the airlock and secure all the equipment. Just in case they come back while we're gone."

"The world has really come to an end," said Alex, shaking his head. "If you have to worry about burglars in the middle of an Arctic glacier now."

"True," Nora replied, "but still a good measure. We'll do as Steven suggested. And we'll take all the data carriers back to the station."

9

Robert and Gillie had spent almost the entire way back to the helicopter in silence. Only the crunching of snow and ice under their boots and the occasional whistle of a gust of wind had punctuated their walk. Robert was annoyed because the conversation with Nora Grimm and her colleagues had not gone as he had hoped. But he understood her reaction only too well. The whole thing had been rushed.

If someone had burst into his laboratory and asked him to drop everything without explaining exactly why, he would probably have reacted even more irritably than these three. Sandra Gillie had certainly played a part in the suboptimal course of events. Robert had only known the woman for a short time, but by now, he was pretty sure that most people had found her to be completely unappealing. Was that calculated? Did she want to appear hard-boiled and tough? Something like that didn't go down well with scientists - and not with him either. He would have to talk to her and make it clear to her that diplomatic skills were needed now. They had to convince her with facts and not give orders. Robert stopped just before the helicopter landed.

It took a moment before Gillie stopped and turned to him. "What's on your mind?" she asked soberly.

"That didn't go well," Robert said curtly. "You pushed her too hard."

"Nonsense. I was just making it clear that we're serious," Gillie replied. "They'll stick to it."

Robert shook his head. "We have to convince these people, get them on our side, otherwise we won't achieve anything here. And if you don't learn to keep your grumpy military demeanor in check, you'll jeopardize our success."

Gillie puffed contemptuously. "We'll see about that."

"No," Robert said sharply. "I know the researcher type very well. They'll put up a stubborn front if we put them under pressure."

"We have to apply pressure, our mission ..."

"Our mission?" Robert intervened. "We were at the same meeting, weren't we?" He fixed his gaze on Gillie. "Sattler asked me to look into this. I want you to support me. Ergo, I decide how it goes. And I say it's not going to work the hard way."

Gillie gave him a look almost as frosty as the icy desert around them, but said nothing.

Despite this, Robert even adopted a more conciliatory tone. "We need Grimm, we need to have access to their samples and data."

"We might be able to get them without having to beg and plead."

"Oh, I'm sure you'll think of something, but that could cause an international conflict. Greenland is an independent country. Even if we Americans like to presume that, we can't just call the shots here and ignore all the rules. We don't have permission to conduct any investigations here, but the PRIN people do."

"Then we'll put pressure on the research community. The general will sort it out," replied Gillie.

"Maybe we will do that. But let's try the gentle way first. That's much more promising, in my opinion."

"Here you go. I'll still report to the general as soon as we get back to the base. Then we'll see what he says. And now let's get on the helicopter before our fingers freeze off."

Robert pointed to the helicopter with his outstretched hand. "After you, my colleague."

She turned around and walked towards the door at the side to pull it open. "We're flying back!" she shouted inside.

The pilot promptly started the engine and the rotor blades began to turn, first slowly and then faster and faster.

Robert also climbed inside and took a seat. He sincerely hoped that he had been convincing enough to Nora Grimm earlier. If he was lucky, she would interrupt her drilling and get back to him. If not, they could always increase the pressure.

***

On her return to the Amarok II station, Nora's first stop was on the third floor in the office of station manager Per Olofsson. She was upset. It was only after Dr. Greaves and his unsympathetic companion had left her that she had really realized how brazen their visit had been. The whole way back, she had wondered how they could have known where to find her and what she was researching. Nora was not a famous scientist whose projects caused a sensation in the scientific community while they were still being carried out. She was at the beginning of her career. Of course, she knew that people tended to underestimate her because of her young age and thought she could be bossed around, but being young didn't mean being stupid. And if there was one thing Nora knew, it was that she wasn't stupid. But someone was obviously trying to sell her for stupid, which really went against the grain.

Olofsson seemed to have been waiting for her, because the door was open and as soon as he saw her coming, he immediately pointed to one of the chairs in front of the desk without saying a word.

But Nora didn't want to sit down, she was too excited. Instead, she stood in the middle of the room and crossed her arms demonstratively in front of her chest.

Olofsson frowned and sighed. "Please close the door," he said curtly. "Not everyone needs to hear that."

Nora reluctantly followed her superior's instructions and returned to her position in the office. "We had a strange visitor at the borehole today," she began, "and somehow I have a feeling you know something about it."

Olofsson nodded. "Don't you want to sit down? That's silly!"

Nora reluctantly threw her hands up in the air. She felt like being silly, but realized that would be pointless and counterproductive. "Yes, you're right. I was just getting so excited." She took a seat, after all. "That guy from MIT who came to visit us, how did he know what we were working on? How did he find us?"

"Well, I can only answer that in part. But I can tell you that I had a phone call fifteen minutes ago informing me of this."

"About what exactly?" Nora asked.

"Not about as much as I would like." Olofsson turned to the large window and looked out for a moment in silence. "I don't know what hornet's nest you've stirred up, but it's been made unmistakably clear to me that cooperation with Dr. Greaves is desired."

"From whom? Who decides that?"

"I don't really know myself. In any case, the instructions come from the very top." After a short pause, he added: "I hate politics."

"Politics," Nora repeated, trying to figure out exactly what that meant. "And now what?" she asked. "Some people turn up here and influence our organization and we're already dancing to their tune?"

"No," Olofsson replied emphatically. "We don't do that. As I said, I hate this kind of influence, but we can't resist it completely."

"What does that mean in concrete terms?"

"The good news is that you can continue and remain in charge of the project. Alex Corbinian can support you, but Steven Dryer will be assigned to another project. Dr. Greaves is on board as an external consultant."

"What? I should bring someone from outside into the team and leave an experienced colleague out, just when I'm getting on a bit better with Steven?"

"That's nice to hear, but unfortunately, completely irrelevant now. Believe me, that's the best I could do. The alternative is that you pack your bags and someone else takes over the project."

"But that's not fair!"

"Fair? What's fair?" asked Olofsson, obviously not expecting an answer, because he continued immediately. "Nora, you know I like you and I think you're exceptionally talented, but I have superiors too." Now his expression became more somber. "And I have to say, I'm a little disappointed in you. Why didn't you tell me about these groundbreaking results? Did you want to keep them secret?"

"Not in the slightest. The analyses were contradictory, I wanted to confirm them first before I drove everyone crazy."

"That probably didn't work - on the contrary."

"A good point!" Nora interjected. "If you've just received the call that we have to cooperate, then that means they've already found out about what I've discovered in other ways. Even before I was fully aware of how sensational this discovery might be, they already knew about it. How?"

"I can't answer that for you. But all our data is made directly available to the research network. PRIN's principle of transparency applies. Nevertheless, this data should not go to external bodies. You need to ask Dr. Greaves these questions."

Nora screwed up her face. "Is he even who he says he is?"

"They emailed me a dossier. According to it, he is a highly decorated researcher in the field of exobiology. Before he started at MIT, he also worked for NASA."

"Exobiology," Nora repeated as if automatically and began to ponder.

"That's what it says here," Olofsson confirmed. "Now make the best of the situation and keep me informed. I'll see if I can find out more about Greaves' background."

Nora stood up. She didn't know what she had hoped to gain from this conversation, but the outcome only partly convinced her. The fact that she was now being forced to work with someone she didn't know and whose motives she couldn't fathom made her feel more than a little uneasy. Nevertheless, she was sure that Olofsson was behind her and had her back - and she was glad of it.

"Thank you, Per," she said and headed for the exit. Then she turned around again. "Can you please forward me this dossier on Greaves? I'd like to know who I'm dealing with."

"It's already happened. It's in your emails."

"Well then, let me do my homework now."

She left the office and went down to her lab, where she opened her laptop and immediately checked her e-mails. In addition to the message mentioned by Olofsson with the attached dossier on Robert Greaves, there were several others in her inbox. Most of them were uninteresting chats with colleagues or annoying administrative notifications from the intranet. One email, however, immediately caught her attention. She ignored Robert's dossier and opened the message from her professor in Munich, Katja Westerhoff.

"Hello Nora, The results of the sample analysis are enclosed. I looked at them personally after Dietmar Rödel started quite a discussion about them earlier. Tell me, did you want to test us? It's best if we make a video call. I'm at the university until 6 p.m."

Nora frowned. What could her colleagues have found that had confused her so much? She looked at her watch: 2:45 pm. That meant it would be three hours later in Munich. If she wanted to speak to Westerhoff today, she had to do it now and couldn't wait to work through the results. So she opened a video chat window and rang her professor.

After a few seconds, Westerhoff's friendly face appeared on the screen. The shoulder-length blonde hair played around the 60-year-old's unusually wrinkle-free face. She had a mysterious smile that always reminded Nora of Mona Lisa.

"Hello, nice of you to get in touch, Nora," she greeted her.

"I'm impatient by nature, you should know that by now. I've just read your email, but I haven't been able to check the results yet. What did you find?"

"Yes, well, that's tricky. I've already written that it's triggered quite a few discussions. You know Dietmar, he's from the old school. To cut a long story short, He thinks your samples were contaminated."

"Contaminated? With what?"

"With some kind of microscopic high-tech product. Maybe it comes from your drilling equipment? Residues from a surface treatment would be conceivable."

"I don't think that's likely. What makes him think that?" Nora wanted to know.

"He has discovered a kind of nanostructure on the particles that he thinks is unusual. Although we know of several examples in nature where similar surfaces have formed on plants, Dietmar thinks it looks more like the remnants of an artificial nanocoating."

"As far as I know, the drill doesn't have anything like that. I can't think what it would be good for either. But I can ask the manufacturer."

Westerhoff nodded. "You should definitely do that. Even if it's just to rule out the possibility."

"You don't agree with Dietmar?" Nora asked.

"I don't know. Something about this material is very unusual, it ..." Westerhoff interrupted herself and tilted her head. "Well, you'll have to find out exactly what it is. Even if it doesn't really fit in with your research. I mean, from what I can see here, it's inorganic."

"Right, I suspected that too. And we're biologists after all." Nora suddenly thought of Greaves. Olofsson had described him as an exobiologist, which meant that he was interested in the possibility of life on other planets. She wasn't quite sure yet what his appearance here meant in concrete terms, but gradually a suspicion began to manifest itself in her mind. She just wasn't ready to say it out loud yet.

"Well, it still seems to be an incredibly exciting puzzle if this material was actually found under kilometers of ice," Westerhoff said and at the same time warned: "But please don't lose your focus." She smiled.

"No, no. Don't worry, I won't miss out on my doctoral thesis."

"I'm glad to hear that, Nora. I wish you all the best. Get in touch if you need anything. We might even try a few more things."

"Thanks, I'll let you hear from me." Nora ended the video call and stared for a moment at the screen, which now showed the background image she had set: a lush green spring meadow with islands of daisies. How she missed the living green in this often colorless desert of snow and ice.

She came to her senses and pulled out Dr. Greaves' business card. This guy was here for a reason. He might even know more than she did. So there was no way around contacting him. She had also received official instructions to cooperate with him. And she would take that literally. Cooperation meant complementing each other. If she was given a new research partner unplanned, then he also had to do his bit. And that was exactly what she would demand! But first of all, she wanted to know what had brought the exobiologist to her.

She typed the e-mail address from the card into the recipient line of a new message and began to write.

10

                              Pituffik Space Base, West Greenland,
                                        Evening of September 13

Robert Greaves sat alone in his assigned quarters on the Pituffik Space Base, which was relatively sheltered in a bay at the westernmost tip of Greenland. The room could be described as functional at best and hardly exuded any coziness. Simple gray furniture against white walls - a bed, a wardrobe, a table, two chairs. This could just as easily be a prison cell in the middle of nowhere. Only the bars on the windows were missing. But if this really were a cell, the lack of bars wouldn't do the prisoners much good either. Because beyond the pane of triple insulating glass was nothing but snow and ice - and perhaps hungry polar bears that could put a quick end to the escape.

    Why was he even thinking about something like this? Did he feel lonely? The thought seemed strange and unusual to Robert. He had always been enough for himself. The company of other people was not an absolute necessity in his life. In recent years, Aunt Mary and the horses had provided plenty of social contact. But then Linda had appeared and catapulted him back years, to a time he had actually wanted to forget and bury.

    Now he was sitting here on Greenland and everything seemed quite unreal to him. By that he didn't just mean the surroundings, but the whole mission. He thought of Sandra Gillie, who was still acting opaque and who he suspected was hiding things from him in order to play her own game. Gillie had taken him to this accommodation as soon as she returned and then disappeared without further explanation. He hoped she wasn't fooling around and turning the scientists against them even more. They needed her cooperation if he was to do his job properly - and that was what he was going to do!

Robert grabbed the map of the base that Gillie had laid out for him. He saw barracks, hangars, fuel silos, supply buildings, radar facilities, the runway and various buildings labeled with abbreviations he didn't know.

Where was the canteen? Was he even hungry or was he just trying to distract himself?

His gaze slid out of the window again, where darkness was gradually descending over the land. The clock on his cell phone showed 18:30 local time. He noted with satisfaction that there was cell phone reception and Internet via WLAN at the base.

The fact made it all the more clear that this was a real enclave in the wilderness, a grain of civilization in the eternal ice that stretched all the way to the horizon.

Robert shouldn't mind; he is used to seclusion. At home, near the desert, it was also lonely, but nowhere near as cold. The thought of the red-orange desert landscape at home brought back associations with Mars, the planet that had been the center of his professional interest for years. It was really cold there too. People often thought the red planet was hot because it looked that way, but in reality it was much icier than here. The average temperature of Mars was around minus 63 degrees Celsius, almost 80 degrees below that of Earth. During the day, the thermometer at the equator of Mars could rise to over 20 degrees plus, but at night it sometimes plummeted to below minus 80 degrees. The planet was therefore a hostile lump of ice with no atmosphere worth mentioning. They were still a long way from that here on Greenland, although not as far as Robert would have liked. Here on the base, which was relatively sheltered and right next to the water, the current temperatures were only just below freezing.

And there was something else Robert wanted to sort out in his head first: the reason why he was here. There had to be a connection with his research, with his theory about the finds on Mars. But how likely was that actually? He had no answer to this question. But the evidence suggested that it was very possible. Otherwise, Sattler wouldn't have gone through all this trouble to send him here. Did the general know more than he was saying? Probably. This suspicion bothered him enormously, but there was nothing he could do about it for the time being - apart from finding out more himself.

Robert shook off the uncomfortable thoughts about the US military's supposed intentions, got up from the bed and stepped to the table. He took the laptop out of his bag and opened it.

He found a message in the fake mailbox with an MIT address that had been set up especially for this mission. It was from the scientist Nora Grimm. His face brightened. She had taken the first step and contacted him, that was good! Gillie's uncharming appearance today had probably not done as much damage as he had initially feared.

***

Sandra Gillie had just returned from a rather mixed conversation with the base commander of Pituffik, Gordon Hastings, when her smartphone rang in her pocket. She pulled it out and answered it. "General?"

"Are the PRIN people playing along?" Sattler inquired, without wasting time with a friendly greeting.

"I think I've made sure of that."

"I see, and do I want to know how?"

"Quite diplomatically," Gillie assured him. "Well, since that's not my strong point, I've sought professional help."

"That means?" Sattler asked.

"Our former colleagues in Langley have put on a nice show for the head of the local PRIN station. It looks to him as if our presence here has been approved watertight by the highest authorities. We should have done it like this straight away."

"Gillie, you work for me now and no longer for the CIA. I wanted you and Greaves to sail under the radar for a reason."

"That's what we do. And now it's even easier than before. These scientists have to cooperate!"

"We agree on that point," agreed the general. "But for God's sake, in the future, you'd better get my permission before you involve outside agencies."

"Very well, sir," Gillie replied with only a little emphasis in her voice. "But I didn't let anyone in on it. They're used to it at Langley. They basically know nothing."

"What's the plan now?"

"I've seen that Nora Grimm has sent an email to Greaves in which she holds out the prospect of a collaboration. Tomorrow I'll make sure that it goes our way."

"You stay in the background," ordered Sattler.

"I should keep an eye on her."

"You'll do the same, but don't interfere. Let Greaves do his job. Then we'll see."

"One more thing," Gillie continued. "Since you want to be fully in the picture: When we were at Grimm's research outpost today, I infected one of the laptops with a Trojan, which should now spread unnoticed throughout the station. That's how I know that Grimm has sent samples to Munich for analysis and contacted her professor."

"Is this going to be a problem?"

"I don't think so, apparently the samples were largely inactive and they don't seem to have any idea what it's about. But as a precaution, we could send someone to Germany to secure the samples."

"Not for the time being," said Sattler. "That's kicking up too much dust. We can deal with it later if we need to."

"Understood. So I'll take Greaves to the research station tomorrow and have a look around without attracting attention? It's quite a long drive, but we'd better take the snowmobiles, because the helicopter could blow our cover."

"Very good, do that! I expect a full progress report every evening from now on, is that clear?"

"Of course," Gillie replied. "And could you please talk to Gordon Hastings, the base commander here, again? He's asking far too many questions for my liking."

"Okay, I'll call him," said the general and then hung up. Gillie put the cell phone away and continued on her way to the accommodations.

***

Steven Dryer was boiling with rage. He had been tossing and turning in his bed for two hours trying to fall asleep. But he couldn't. His thoughts circled around the same point: he had been thrown out of the project team - just when things were getting exciting. It was an impertinence, an outrage! He had put up with the grueling dirty work for months and now others were supposed to take the credit? Dryer was most furious about the appearance of Robert Greaves and Sandra Gillie. It wasn't hard to imagine that these two were responsible for his expulsion. He had stood up to them and this was the reaction.

Dryer had complained to Olofsson and inquired about the reasons, but only received flimsy excuses. "Instructions from the top," the station manager's words echoed in his mind. What nonsense! PRIN had always been an open and transparently organized research community. It was completely unusual for such decisions to be made from the top down - and so quickly and rashly at that. There had to be something wrong with it! His thoughts drifted back to Sandra Gillie's visit. The woman was never a scientist in her life, not even an employee of a university professor. If Robert Greaves was one at all. Dryer doubted that too.

Annoyed, he threw aside his comforter and switched on the light. Then he sat down at the desk in his quarters and grabbed his tablet. Now he would investigate these two strange fellows. He would dissect their story and present the evidence to Olofsson on a silver platter. Then they would see who had the last laugh. He would also lodge an official complaint with the PRIN network today and demand to be reinstated to Nora's project team.

The angry helplessness had now completely fizzled out. Dryer felt new courage, he had a plan. And he was convinced that he would succeed!

11

PRIN research station "Amarok II", Greenland
September 14

Nora looked out of the panoramic window on the third floor of the station and followed the path of the two snowmobiles outside, which were heading straight for her location. She knew they were Greaves and Gillie and estimated they would be here in ten minutes at the latest.

The visit had already been announced in Greaves' email reply, which she had fished out of her inbox this morning. Nora wondered where they had come from on the snowmobiles - judging by the direction, pretty much from the west. However, apart from a few tiny settlements on the coast, there was nothing there but the large US base at Pituffik. Greaves and Gillie were Americans, so it seemed most likely to Nora that they had spent the night there. It was also already midday, which suggested that they had had a long journey.

However, an Air Force base was not a hotel where you could just stay. You certainly needed permission to get in at all. Had US government circles been involved in making this possible? Nora didn't trust the whole thing and decided to get to the bottom of Greaves - who she thought was the more affable of the two - as soon as they were undisturbed.

The snowmobiles had now come within a few hundred meters of the station, and Nora turned away from the window to receive the visitors below and escort them inside.

On the way, she bumped into Alex Corbinian. "Will you come down and say hello to our new colleagues?"

Alex twisted the corners of his mouth. "Sure, it's always nice to meet fellow countrymen," he said in a clearly ironic tone.

Nora left the point uncommented on because she had long known that Alex was a rather atypical American who was quite critical of the pompous whims of many of his fellow citizens. "Go on then," she said instead, putting on a smile. "Let's make the best of it!"

They continued on their way together.

"Is Steven coming too?" asked Alex.

"Oh, I thought you already knew he was out."

Alex shook his head. "No one's told me yet. I haven't seen him since we got back yesterday. But that explains it, of course. He's probably squatting in his quarters writing nasty letters."

"That would be understandable. I don't agree with the decision at all. But that's just another item on the list of inconsistencies. Nevertheless, we should strive for productive cooperation. This Dr. Greaves knows more than we do, I'm convinced of that."

They reached the lowest level and put on their thick jackets and boots. Then they descended the stairs to the underground garage where the station crew's vehicles were parked. Nora activated the opening mechanism for the entrance, and less than two minutes later, the snowmobile with Greaves and Gillie came down the ramp. She assigned them free parking spaces and waited until they had dismounted.

"Have a good trip?" she asked Greaves, who was now taking off his mirrored goggles.

"Really wonderful, thank you," he said and added with a smile: "Without this thing, I'd probably be blind now. I've never seen so much white in my whole life."

Nora nodded. "Snow blindness can occur after just a few hours if the sun is really strong. Have you been out that long? Where did you start from?"

Greaves was about to reply, but Gillie beat him to it. "To the west," she replied curtly. "Can we go up now? As beautiful as this ice cellar is."

"I would be grateful for some warmth," Greaves added.

"Of course. Follow me," Nora urged her. She led the way

back to the stairwell and up through the service level to the second floor, where Nora's laboratory was located.

Alex turned off in the direction of the kitchen shortly before that - saying that he was going to make tea.

"So that's my humble kingdom," Nora said and sat down on a chair in front of the measuring devices. "What happens now?"

Robert put down his bag and also took a seat, while Gillie leaned against the wall a little to one side. "First of all, I'd like to apologize for the unfortunate start yesterday. We should have handled it differently. But I didn't want you to go rushing ahead. You didn't do that, did you?"

"No," said Nora, tilting her head. "Can we maybe stop this awkward banter? I'm Nora."

"I'd love to. Robert."

Gillie let out an almost inaudible moan, which Nora deliberately ignored.

"Okay, now tell me why we shouldn't keep drilling? And what's down there," Nora demanded.

"I don't know exactly what's under the ice - not yet. But we'll find out soon if we work together."

"Nevertheless, there is a suspicion. Otherwise you wouldn't have come all the way here. After all, it's an enormous effort."

Robert pulled the laptop out of his pocket and flipped it open. "I want to be completely open and honest now, but I expect us to maintain a certain level of confidentiality."

"You don't want me to tell anyone?" Nora asked in a joking tone.

At that moment, Alex came in with a steaming teapot and four cups on a tray. He set everything down on the table. "Help yourselves!" Then he poured himself a cup and sat down next to Nora on an empty chair.

Robert also took a sip of tea and began to talk. "Okay, let's start from the beginning. About eight years ago, I was heavily involved in analyzing data from NASA's Curiosity rover mission. We learned a lot about the planet and its composition with the help of the measuring instruments on board. As an exobiologist, it was my job to examine Mars for potential sources of life - or even to detect extraterrestrial life. Let me make a long story short: I succeeded. Although, to my regret, this information never found its way to the public."

"Why not?" Alex asked. "That's a sensation."

"Because there were major differences about how the results should be interpreted and I was ultimately alone in my opinion."

"To be more precise," Nora said, "you found signs of life there, but no one believed you?"

Robert nodded. "Something like that. I left NASA then. The details aren't really relevant now. This back story is just to explain why I'm here."

"There are similarities," Nora interjected.

Robert opened a folder on the laptop with the collected Curiosity data, loaded a few images side by side and then turned the computer so that Nora and Alex could see the screen. "This crystal structure should look familiar to you. And so does this spectrographic analysis of the composition."

"Holy sh...," Nora gasped, and she slapped her hand over her mouth. "Sorry. But that's..." She broke off again and shook her head. "Are you sure?"

"My goodness," Gillie intervened. "You said it yourself! Would we be here otherwise? Do you understand the importance of this?"

"I understand very well," Nora said coolly. "Certainly better than you." This woman had such an unsympathetic manner that she could drive her up the wall in seconds.

"Why don't you take a look at the station and let us eggheads talk about the boring details?" suggested Robert.

Gillie narrowed her eyes, but remained silent at first. "Maybe not a bad idea," she replied and turned towards the door.

"There's a panorama lounge upstairs," Alex explained, pointing to the ceiling. "It has a really nice view."

"Thank you," Gillie replied dryly and left the lab.

Robert turned back to Nora and Alex. "Well, I don't know what it means at the moment, but there's obviously something under the Greenland ice that looks extremely similar to what we found on Mars. That alone might not be a sensation, as some many substances and compounds occur on both planets, but this material is different. We agree on that, don't we?"

Nora and Alex nodded almost in sync.

The geologist now took the floor. "It showed clear activity, it reacted to an external influence yet to be determined. It modified its structure independently and released energy in the process - that was amazing!" he reported.

"And this was also observed in a very similar way on Mars. My conclusion from this was that we were dealing with a type of life that was previously completely unknown to us. Unfortunately, the process could only be observed once and could not be reproduced. What's more, my attempts to learn more about it almost destroyed an irreplaceable measuring instrument costing millions. My superiors were not exactly thrilled about that."

"We also scrapped the drill head when we came across this material. Seems to be a tradition in this respect."

Robert laughed. "Where there's serious research, there's collateral damage - that's especially true at the extremes. But seriously, we have a unique opportunity here to find an answer to the question of whether Earth is the only living planet in the universe."

"I can understand your enthusiasm, but we don't have any real evidence of it yet," Nora interjected.

"That was precisely the problem with the Mars mission. We were limited to the procedures and measurements that the rover could provide. There was no way to get a sample of the material to Earth for further investigation. Now, of course, the situation is completely different."

"I've already had special analyses done at the university in Munich," said Nora and turned to her notebook, where she was now loading the results onto the screen. "Whatever it is exactly, you can't call it organic. What's more, one of the laboratory experts suspected that it was man-made. The material has an unusual nanostructure that is not found on Earth, at least not in this form."

Robert nodded slowly and thoughtfully. "I understand. But that doesn't necessarily contradict our theory. Just because the nature and composition differ from those we find in organisms on Earth doesn't mean that there can't be completely different life forms."

"Good point," Nora agreed. "Although I still can't quite believe it."

"Of course, I'm a bit ahead of the game," Robert admitted. "But from what I've seen so far, I'm pretty sure you've already come to a similar hypothesis on your own."

"Only when I heard you were an exobiologist. From then on, it was clear what direction this was going to take," Nora explained.

"Wait a minute, I'm just a geologist," Alex interjected. "But did I just get it right that you're talking about aliens?"

"Question of definition," Robert replied. "If by that you mean the popular idea of little green men in flying saucers, then no. But this could still be an alien life form - although obviously not a particularly advanced one. So the big mystery is, how did it get here? Why are there traces of it on Mars and Earth?"

"And of course the most important question: is it dangerous?" added Alex.

Robert looked at him, frowning.

"Come on, we've all seen enough science fiction movies!" said Alex jokingly.

"I don't think it poses any danger," Robert replied and looked at Nora.

She shrugged her shoulders. "I don't know, you're the expert on this. But based on the findings so far, I don't see any particular risks. The material is non-toxic, non-pathogenic and doesn't emit any radiation. Or rather, at least it doesn't now. We have not carried out any measurements while it was restructuring under the microscope. Therefore, it cannot be ruled out that it could give off potentially harmful emissions."

"We have to get new samples and examine it more closely," Robert said.

"That was our plan yesterday. We were going to use new samples to recreate the effect and capture the electromagnetic radiation emitted," Nora explained. "Then you showed up and we didn't continue."

"Once again, I would like to apologize, that must have seemed rather strange."

"It did," Alex confirmed. "But never mind, you still seem to know your stuff."

"Thank you," said Robert. "And you're already much further along than I thought - and on the right track, too. Okay, shall we try again?"

Nora shook her head. "Not today. It's not worth going to the borehole now. We wouldn't be back before nightfall. We'll have to postpone the sampling until tomorrow. But I can show you the telemetry data we collected yesterday, which is also very interesting. If it's not a blatant measurement error, it's actually plus degrees down there. And I can't think of any other reason for this than this strange substance."

Robert raised his eyebrows in astonishment. "Show me, please," he demanded.

12

One floor up, Sandra Gillie looked around the large glassed-in viewing room. She had already walked through all the rooms on this and the other floors and had memorized their exact location and function. She had encountered surprisingly few people. Apparently all the scientists were busy with their projects. That was just fine with Gillie, because it meant she didn't have to answer any annoying questions.

She had finally found the office of station manager Per Olofsson up here and was now considering whether she should seek a conversation with him to see if he had any doubts about her cover. She could also use this opportunity to fit his office with a hidden bug to discreetly eavesdrop on him.

But Gillie dismissed the idea. The Trojan that she had smuggled into the system yesterday should soon have infected all the computers, and then she could tap into the laptops' built-in microphones and cameras without risk. And she could tap into the internal systems to monitor and, if necessary, control communication with the outside world. Access to sophisticated spy software was just one of the perks of having a CIA background, like Gillie.

She hadn't been keen on the job with Sattler, but had agreed to it because it meant she could avert an unpleasant career setback. At least that was what she had been promised if she carried out the assignment to everyone's satisfaction. Sattler couldn't know that she was still committed to the CIA, even though she was now officially part of his staff. But she wasn't fooling herself either. The general probably knew that long ago, or at least suspected it. Sattler was highly intelligent, even if you couldn't tell that from looking at such a greying, uniformed paper pusher like him. That was another reason why she kept all her options open.

Now Gillie heard footsteps behind her, coming quickly up the stairs. She turned around slowly and recognized Steven Dryer, who was hurrying to the upper level with a determined expression.

When he saw Gillie, he stopped abruptly and put on a half frightened, half angry expression. "You, of all people!" he snapped at her. "I should have guessed you wouldn't waste any time!"

"Time is a valuable resource, isn't it?" Gillie confirmed.

Dryer narrowed his eyes. "Yes, but your time is almost up. Convenient that I find you here. Because I've figured you out. And now I'm going to tell Olofsson about it. Then he'll throw you out in a wide arc."

"I don't think you know too much," Gillie replied calmly. "And before we drive everyone here crazy, you'd better calm down. I'll be happy to explain the connections." She gestured to a row of chairs closer to the western picture window.

Steven shook his head. "What are you doing? Shall we go and see the countryside together? I can think of more pleasant company!"

"Don't make a fool of yourself, Steven. I would like to involve you. But you have to understand how important this project is. Let's talk calmly, please." Gillie pointed to the chairs again.

Hesitantly, Steven took a step in the direction indicated and then looked towards Olofsson's office door.

"Come on, I want to show you something. If it doesn't convince you, we can go to your supervisor together," said Gillie, taking another look at the empty lounge.

"All right, five minutes," Steven replied grumpily.

Gillie led him to the window, behind which the sky was gradually turning a yellow-orange hue. "You know, Steven, I didn't want you on the project team for a good reason," she began to explain while inconspicuously fiddling with her right jacket pocket.

Steven looked at her questioningly. "Oh yeah? I'm very curious about that explanation."

Gillie quietly flicked the cap of a pen that was stowed in her bag and pulled it out, invisible to Steven. "Yes, but of course I'll explain it to you. That's what I promised."

"Then do it at last, or I'll waste ..."

He didn't get any further because, at that moment, Gillie pricked him in the neck with a fine needle that had previously been hidden inside the pen.

Steven barely managed an astonished gasp, then staggered to the side.

Gillie grabbed his arm and maneuvered him onto one of the waiting chairs before he could fall over. "The reason you're not on the team is because you ask too many questions - uncomfortable questions." She waited a moment for the effects of the drug she had administered to take full effect, then patted Steven on the shoulder as he stared apathetically out of the window. "But everything will be fine now," Gillie promised, turning and leaving Steven alone at the window.

To anyone who happened to be passing by, it looked as if they were simply enjoying the view. Gillie was pleased to see that no one had seen her sort out the Steven Dryer problem, and calmly made her way back down to the lab.

***

General Frank Sattler sat in the semi-darkness created by his old-fashioned desk lamp. It was one of those iconic banker's lamps with a green glass shade and brass base that appeared in countless films. But this was no cheap copy or prop, it was the original in top condition that Sattler had inherited from his grandfather. This example was over 100 years old and had been made in 1911 according to the original design by Harrison D. McFaddin. The lamp bore the illustrious name Emeralite, a reference to the emerald green glass, which consisted of two layers - colored on the outside and white on the inside. This lamp created the subdued, unobtrusive light in the room that Sattler appreciated so much, while the desk itself had enough white light to be able to read and write meaningfully.

On the table in front of him was a thick brown file folder with five decades' worth of confidentiality notices. The file was correspondingly old, first created in 1967 by one of his unofficial predecessors. But he had never shown the same level of interest in it as Sattler did.

The file contained a treasure - and it was a bomb. It just depended on how you read its contents. For Sattler, it also meant pain, because it also dealt with the fate of his father, who had never returned from his posting in Greenland. No one had explained to the family at the time what had happened or how exactly Benjamin Sattler had died. That a snowcat had accidentally run over him had been an obvious excuse. But despite many inquiries, nothing more had ever been given.

It had taken Sattler decades to get to a position where he could inspect this file. It had not been as revealing as he had hoped, but it was still a big step towards clarification. It said in black and white that his father had initially been the victim of an extremely strange accident and had even gone on a killing spree in the end. And not only that, but he had set off half a dozen medium-range missiles, virtually melting the entire facility where he had been stationed.

It read too fantastic to be true, but also too absurd and strange to be a military invention. The so-called Camp Century, which his father had destroyed in a kind of madness, had already been evacuated at lightning speed. The base commander had known that a catastrophe was imminent and had tried to get the crew out of there. He had succeeded with almost all of them - except for his father and a handful of others who were buried there. And something else lay there in his icy grave: the cause of it all. This was described very vaguely at best in the file in front of him. None of the experts at the time could make any sense of it and they were probably glad that grass was growing over the matter and no one was asking uncomfortable questions. But Sattler wanted to ask questions. And he demanded answers, no matter how much grass - or in this case ice - lay over the truth. It had long since become clear to him that his father and the others at Camp Century had had contact with an unknown life form, a potentially extraterrestrial life form. Sattler would find it and then ...

A noise brought him out of his thoughts. He saw Linda Shoemaker standing in the doorway.

"Excuse me, I knocked," she said hastily. "There was still a light on, so ... I wanted to..."

"That's all right!" replied Sattler hastily, slamming the lid of the file shut and letting it disappear into his desk drawer. He looked at Shoemaker again. He wondered if she had seen anything. Probably not at this distance. "What is it, Dr. Shoemaker?"

"I just wanted to know if Robert Greaves has reported in. Has he arrived safely in Greenland?"

"Of course he is! He'll get back to you when he has time. After all, I sent him there to work!"

"Of course, excuse me. I'll finish work a little early today, if that's all right with you."

Sattler nodded and waved Shoemaker out. "Yes, yes, do that!"

***

Nora and Robert were so engrossed in analyzing the data that they only noticed in passing when Sandra Gillie came back into the lab and sat down at the table.

Nora was glad that she was able to discuss the data and hypotheses with Robert undisturbed and on an equal footing. Her reservations about her initially unloved project partner visibly faded as she realized that he was not only genuinely interested in the phenomenon, but also knew a great deal about his subject. She was sure that she could learn a lot from him. Sandra Gillie, on the other hand, was a completely different story. This woman puzzled her. She still had great doubts that she was Robert's assistant and decided to put her to the test when she got the chance.

"Are you making progress?" Gillie now asked, looking over at them with interest.

"You could say that," Robert replied. "But I don't want to bore you with it."

"What about the samples, have you had a look at them yet?" Gillie asked.

Robert shook his head. "No, we have to get new ones, fresh from the borehole."

"But that won't be possible until tomorrow," Nora added, taking a considered pause. She wasn't at all sure it would be a good idea, but she continued: "Maybe I can arrange for you two to spend the night here. There should be a few rooms available because the astrophysicists won't be arriving until next week. But we'll have to discuss it with Olofsson."

"He won't mind," said Gillie.

Nora had almost expected something like this and gave her a skeptical look. She still secretly wondered why this woman - or her employers - were able to exert such influence. But apparently, that was the way it was, and she had to play along, which really got on her nerves. "Okay, let's do this as soon as we've finished with the last ..."

Nora was interrupted by commotion and loud shouts from beyond the lab door. She recognized the scratchy voice of Melissa Warden, who was almost doubled over with excitement.

"Where the hell is Keller! Can someone go and find him? Now!" she screamed as she rushed through the corridor outside.

"Who's Keller?" Robert asked, rising to his feet curiously.

"The ward doctor," Nora replied and jumped up from her chair. "Something must have happened!"

She hurried through the door, followed by the others, and then in the direction Melissa had come from.

A small crowd of people had formed on the stairs to the top floor, all talking excitedly to each other.

"What happened?" Nora wanted to know.

"Steven ... he is," Macmillan said haltingly. "I don't know what's wrong with him." He pointed upwards.

Nora pushed past the mechanic and stormed up the stairs.

Olofsson bent over Steven Dryer, who lay twitching on the floor. Foam ran from his mouth.

"What about him?" Nora asked breathlessly.

Olofsson looked at her helplessly. "I don't know! It looks like a seizure, maybe he has epilepsy?" He turned Steven into the recovery position.

"He would have mentioned that, wouldn't he?" Nora turned to Steven and put her hand on his forehead, which was covered in cold sweat. His eyes were expressionless, as if he wasn't even aware of what was happening around him "Steven! Can you hear me? What happened?"

She only received a choke in response.

Finally, Dr. Keller came sprinting up the stairs. "Make way!" shouted the experienced doctor in a commanding tone and knelt down next to Steven.

Nora and Olofsson stood up and stepped back while the ward doctor examined Steven. "He has to go down to the infirmary. Get the stretcher!" he ordered.

Nora ran to the stairs. "Bring the stretcher from downstairs!" she shouted and saw Macmillan and Alex running straight away.

When she returned to Dryer, he had stopped twitching and closed his eyes. He was breathing more calmly now. "What about him?"

"I can't possibly say that," Keller replied. "I've given him a sedative to dampen down the seizure. We'll have to sort out the rest downstairs."

Macmillan and Alex came up the stairs with the stretcher and helped to place Steven on it. Then, together with Dr. Keller, they carried him down towards the infirmary.

Nora followed them down the stairs and met Robert and Gillie there. The biologist had worry written all over his face, while his companion had her usual indifferent expression.

"Please wait for me in the lab, I need to talk to Olofsson," Nora said, leaving the two of them in the hallway.

After Nora and the other scientists had left, Robert pulled Gillie aside and looked at her penetratingly for a moment. He hesitated to ask the question that was burning on his tongue, but there was probably no way around it. As quietly as possible, he whispered to her: "Tell me you had nothing to do with this."

Gillie's eyes widened and she demonstrated surprise. "I had nothing to do with it," she said.

Robert was unsure whether he should believe her. "You had a problem with the man. He provoked and questioned you. And I can imagine that you like to get obstacles out of the way."

"He was no longer an obstacle. I had already made sure that he was removed from the project team. So your suspicions are pretty absurd! Dryer probably had an epileptic seizure."

Robert tilted his head. He didn't know what to believe about this woman. But it still sounded plausible. Why would she take such a risk? Maybe he was seeing ghosts. Gillie was probably right, it made little sense. "Okay, I'm sorry," he said. "It's been a long day, and I guess I'm a little too upset about the discovery."

"It can happen to anyone," Gillie replied succinctly. "But to convince you completely, I can try to get help for Dryer from the base. They have a hospital there where he can be treated if necessary if his condition doesn't improve."

"But then we'd have to put our cards on the table," said Robert.

Gillie swayed her head back and forth. "Not necessarily. I'll think of something. Up here, you have to provide unbureaucratic help in emergencies, I think we can sort that out."

"Let's wait a little longer, maybe he'll feel better soon," Robert suggested.

"Sure, whatever you say," Gillie replied and started to move.

Robert watched her for a few seconds, still not completely convinced that his suspicions were unfounded, then he followed her back to Nora's lab.

13

Linda Shoemaker's apartment, Washington, D.C.
Evening of September 14

Linda Shoemaker placed a glass of red wine on the rustic wooden table in the middle of the otherwise modern living and dining room. She loved the combination of old and new and was always boldly placing the odd refurbished antique right next to futuristic-looking furniture and electronic devices. Contrasts made life interesting, Linda thought. This applied to people, professional tasks, pieces of furniture, and food. She placed a bowl of finely chopped vegetable sticks - carrots, peppers, celery - next to the red wine.

While she sipped her wine and nibbled on vegetables, she started to browse the internet on her smartphone. She had actually wanted to distract herself by going to one of the usual trading platforms for second-hand furniture and accessories, but after just a few minutes, she lost interest. She couldn't get the irritated look on General Sattler's face out of her mind when he had seen her standing in the doorway. She had knocked, twice in fact. Nevertheless, the general seemed downright surprised. That was unusual, as he was usually always alert and never distracted. But at that moment he had been, because something had caught his attention.

It must have had something to do with the file he had hurriedly made disappear. Linda had only caught a glimpse of the cover page. But she was pretty sure she had read the word "Century" on it.

There had been more there, but the general had let the file slide into his drawer so quickly that she couldn't read anything else. That alone was puzzling, even if it hadn't been for the many red "Top Secret" notes on the cover.

Linda had to find out what it was all about, even if she already suspected that this could cause difficulties. But where should she start? Century was a pretty arbitrary name, she wouldn't get far with that alone.

The most likely scenario was that it was the code name of a military operation. So she tried several combinations of search terms and looked at the results of the online search - they were as numerous as they were inappropriate. None of them seemed to be related to Sattler or her project until Linda finally tried the combination of "Century," "Greenland," and "US military." The first entry was a direct hit. The search engine's summary described the former Camp Century on Greenland, a secret US base from the Cold War.

She opened the Wikipedia entry and learned a lot about the history, purpose, and many problems of this station that was once built under the ice.

As the first step towards the larger Project Iceworm, in which nuclear missiles were to be stationed under the ice sheet, Camp Century should have represented a milestone in the defense of the United States against the Soviet Union. At least that was the view of those responsible at the time, until the base was abandoned and filled in in 1967.

Nevertheless, long-term plans and an enormous effort had been made to disguise the station as a scientific project. They had even drilled ice cores in order to have something solid to show for it. Some old black and white pictures showing the researchers at a drilling rig sent a shiver down Linda's spine and confirmed her suspicions that she was on the right track.

The parallels to the current project of the PRIN researchers led by Nora Grimm were striking. Very deep boreholes in the ice, unforeseen difficulties and even the approximate area was correct, as Linda found out when she displayed the position of the former Camp Century on an online map. The coordinates of the PRIN drilling site were only about five kilometers away as the crow flies. That had to be more than a coincidence.

A thought occurred to her: Did Robert know about the connection? Had Sattler let him in on the story? Probably not. Because Sattler was always careful to maintain secrecy, only giving out information when it was absolutely necessary.

For a brief moment, she thought about accessing the internal databases from her computer, but immediately dismissed the idea. If it was confidential material, she wouldn't be able to access it from here anyway. But it would probably be even more disastrous if the access attempt was logged and saved together with her IP address. That would earn her a very unpleasant conversation with Sattler, during which she would have to admit that she had taken a look at his file and then tracked it down. She wanted to avoid this confrontation.

Linda picked up her cell phone and dialed Robert's number. She knew that there wasn't much chance of reaching him, but she didn't want to leave it untried. But, as expected, it remained an attempt. Robert's voicemail went through almost immediately. Either he was outside the base, where there was no reception, or he had switched off his cell phone. She left a short message asking how he was and asked that he call her back. She deliberately didn't mention Camp Century and her suspicions - just in case he wasn't alone when he checked the voicemail.

She thought of Sandra Gillie, and immediately Linda had the uneasy feeling that this woman was likely to cause a lot of trouble. Linda reproached herself that she might have been wrong to persuade Robert to take part in the affair.

But she also knew why it had happened. Because she had secretly hoped to work on it with him - and perhaps get a little closer again. And now? He was there with Gillie, a snake of a woman who she didn't trust an inch. As if the place he was in wasn't already dangerous enough and full of unpredictable risks!

Robert could have done with someone he could rely on there. Instead, he was at the mercy of numerous imponderables, to which another had now been added.

The way Sattler had handled the secret file on Camp Century fueled her suspicions: What if there had been a catastrophe back then that had led to the camp being abandoned? What if it hadn't just been a million-dollar grave? It was still nothing more than a bad guess, but Linda could usually trust her instincts. There was something fishy about this.

She turned back to her smartphone and started digging deeper - but only in public sources for the time being.

***

The morning after Steven Dryer's collapse, the mood on the Amarok II station was strangely subdued. Nobody knew exactly why he collapsed, but all kinds of rumors were circulating, each one sounding more unrealistic than the last.

Nora preferred not to participate in the speculation, but the possibility that it could be the result of a contagious infection worried her, too. Something like that would be a disaster on a remote ward like this, where everyone worked together in a comparatively confined space. If it was a case of illness, only one of the two new arrivals, Dr. Greaves and Sandra Gillie, could be the carrier.

Ward doctor Winfried Keller had already tried hard to argue against this at last night's meeting. There was no evidence to support this suspicion, especially as no one else - including the two recently arrived guests - showed any symptoms. However, he could not give the all-clear either, as his diagnostic options were severely limited. Face masks had been issued as a temporary precautionary measure. In addition, everyone was instructed to keep their distance and avoid unnecessary gatherings. Nora, therefore, also had breakfast in her quarters.

Steven Dryer, on the other hand, was unchanged. He had not yet woken up from the acute sedation initiated by Dr. Keller, but remained in an unconscious, almost comatose state. He did not react to any stimuli, but also showed no more signs of a seizure. Olofsson had ordered Steven to be flown out by helicopter if his condition did not improve in the next 24 hours - provided no one else fell ill. Olofsson hadn't said the conclusion out loud, but Nora knew what that would mean: he would have to quarantine the station.

She found it correspondingly difficult to concentrate on work that morning. Even though she knew she didn't have time for excessive musing. They didn't help Steven either. She had to let Dr. Keller do his work and do hers in return. After all, Olofsson hadn't forbidden that. As long as they were well, they could drive to the borehole and continue their research.

After breakfast, she packed her things and set off to pick up Alex, Robert, and Gillie. Despite all the worries about Steven, something else had to take priority now. Today, they would take samples and finally take a big step closer to unraveling the mystery that lay beneath the ice.

About an hour later, the four of them reached the outpost with the borehole, and Alex set about clearing the entrance. "We're lucky; the weather has held," he explained, grabbing one of the snow shovels.

In fact, there were only minimal snowdrifts, which made it difficult to get in. Robert lent a hand and together the snow was quickly cleared away.

Meanwhile, the two women unloaded the equipment they had brought with them from the snowmobiles and made it inside through the now open entrance.

Nora pushed back her hood and took off her hat. She turned to Alex, who was putting down a heavy transport crate behind her. "Is it me, or is it not as cold in here as it was yesterday?"

Alex also took off his cap and paused momentarily in the underground ice cave. He shrugged his shoulders. "Well, to be honest..." he began. "I still think it's fucking freezing. Just like everywhere else in Greenland." He smiled at her.

"Yes, you're probably right. Can't really be. Let's set up the technology and get started."

"How can we help?" Robert asked.

"It would be best if you got the microscope and the measuring devices ready for use." Nora pointed to the heavy box Alex had just put down and another one standing right next to it. "I've brought as much technology as possible. There's no point in going back to the station until we've obtained new samples. Who knows, maybe the material will become inactive too quickly."

"Very sensible," said Robert.

"Besides, there's already enough unrest on the ward after what happened with Steven." Nora glanced at Gillie. "Even without your presence there."

Gillie didn't comment on this and instead grabbed the box next to Alex. "Over there on the table?" she asked matter-of-factly.

Nora nodded and then waved Alex over. "Come on, let's get the technology up and set up the drill head."

"Okay, Steven was the expert on this, but we'll manage," Alex replied confidently.

"Of course we can do it," Nora said firmly and stepped up to the drill's control panel to activate its systems. She followed the exact procedure that she and Steven had carried out so many times before, and there were no difficulties today.

After a few minutes, the individual components reported that they were ready for operation. "Mission Control, all systems G.O.!" she called over to Robert.

He couldn't help but smile at the allusion to his NASA days. Gillie, on the other hand, rolled her eyes slightly and turned away.

"Okay, everything looks good here too," said Robert. "I just don't know how long the lab equipment will last in this weather." Now, he came over to Nora and Alex at the drilling control and examined the readings on the displays. He tapped on the current temperature that the drill head was transmitting. "This is what you meant when you were talking about inconsistencies, right?"

"Yes, because it should be well below freezing down there. There shouldn't be any fluctuations at that depth. And a temperature above zero? That should be physically impossible. But I no longer believe in a measurement error." Nora called up the previous day's data again. "Yesterday we were at 9.5 degrees plus. Now it's 12.8 degrees. It's getting warmer down there. And I'd love to know how that can be."

"Me too," Robert agreed. "Let's gently drive the drill a little deeper, just far enough so that we can get a sample up."

"Alex, please take over and keep the speed constant?" Nora asked. "We don't know what condition the material is in down there and whether there could be another malfunction."

"Sure, I'll do it," Alex replied and took his place at the controls. "Off you go." He pressed the start button and a low hum could be heard as the machine revved up.

"We then immediately pack the sample into an insulated container and only take as much as we need," Robert suggested.

Nora nodded. "Good plan. First we'll do the microscopic analysis and try to reproduce the crystallization effect."

"This time, we're not just recording optically but also capturing all potential electromagnetic vibrations," added Robert. "So we kill two birds with one stone."

"Now it's almost time, the drill head should hit the ground," Alex explained.

Everyone watched the displays spellbound and followed the drilling progress. All of a sudden, the humming sound of the drill became much more aggressive.

"Already 17 degrees!" Nora exclaimed. "There can't be any more ice down there."

"But it's certainly not water either. Look at the resistance coefficient, the drill is running at the stop."

"That's not good. If we carry on, something will break again," said Nora. "How much have we done?"

"28 centimeters," Alex replied.

"That'll have to do, shut it down and get it up as quickly as possible!" Nora ordered.

Alex reduced the speed and then immediately started the retrieval procedure.

"The temperature was almost 42 degrees," said Robert, shaking his head.

"Then we stopped just in time. The first time, the circuit board failed at 47 degrees," explained Nora.

The next hour and a half passed agonizingly slowly as Nora and the others were condemned to inactivity while the drill head made its long return journey from the depths. Alex had found a way to shorten the process by 25 percent, but it was still a long time to kill in the freezing environment.

Nora had hoped for a while that Sandra Gillie might leave her alone again so that she could talk to Robert in private, but today she was glued to him, watching every detail. She seemed to be trying hard to hide it by standing apart and not seeming to care much about the scientific details Robert and she were discussing, but Nora didn't buy it for a moment. Gillie's indifference seemed too rehearsed. She knew this put-on coolness too well from her school days.

Finally, they were able to lift the drill head out of the shaft with their combined strength and place it on the workshop table. Alex prepared an insulating container underneath the workstation and Nora began to dismantle the casing.

Just like the first time, there was a mixture of ice and water inside, but this time it seemed to be a little firmer. Only a little condensation had formed around the frozen core.

With Robert's help, Nora carefully removed the core and positioned it on a precision saw, which she used to cut off a thin slice. She carried this to the microscope, while the rest of the ice went back into the insulated container.

"Now it's getting exciting," she said, setting up the slide and adjusting the focus. "Start recording as soon as you're ready," she added, turning to Robert.

He immediately complied with the request and entered a few commands on the laptop.

"So, is anything happening yet?" Alex asked.

Nora shook her head. "No, nothing so far. But the structure looks almost like it did in the first rehearsal, before it took on a life of its own. See for yourself!"

Alex stepped up to the microscope and looked through the double eyepiece, while the others looked at the digitized version of the live image transmitted to the laptop.

"Let me think about it," Alex said. "Have we activated it somehow?"

"I wasn't there," Nora replied with a shrug. "What exactly did you do?"

"Nothing. It started on its own."

"Then it's the conditions," Robert said. "It's much colder here than in your lab."

"That's right. It can only be because of that. Maybe it needs liquid water," Nora speculated and took a few steps over to the drill head, in which a small amount of ice-water mixture was still floating. She filled this into a transparent plastic container and then placed it under the microscope. "Let's try this," she said.

At first, nothing happened for a few seconds, but then the mixture began to react. The fine crystal fragments scattered in the liquid clumped together and formed a larger structure.

"Watch out, it should be happening now," Alex announced, and he was right.

The next moment, a pinkish-purple glimmer of light, visible even to the naked eye, swelled and then suddenly went out.

"Did you record that?" Nora asked Robert.

"Yes, it's all there," he said enthusiastically. "It was, as I suspected, not just an optical phenomenon. This crystal was emitting electrical energy in the form of radio waves, or more precisely as oscillations in the gigahertz spectrum."

"Gigahertz, you mean like Wi-Fi or mobile telephony?" Alex asked. "That seems pretty far-fetched to me."

"Maybe a malfunction? Is someone on their cell phone?" Nora asked, looking at one person after another.

"What for? There's no reception here," said Gillie curtly.

"There could still have been interference that disturbed our measurement," Nora insisted.

"No, no," said Robert. "Look at that. There was only a relatively short pulse at the exact moment when the glow was visible. Nothing before and nothing after. If it had been a cell phone, we'd probably have to pick up more signals."

"That's true," Alex admitted, "but still ... that ... I mean, how could ..."

"Let me take a closer look, please," Robert interrupted him and set about analyzing the recorded data. "The signal is quite broadband and covers a frequency range from 8.3 to 12.6 gigahertz. But it's not simple noise, it has an uneven distribution. That ..." He paused and switched to another view of the analysis program. "I think I'm crazy," Robert said now. "It wasn't a random pulse. The signal looks modulated."

"Modulated? That's nonsense!" Alex objected.

"Yes, look at it. There seems to be a carrier wave to which a second layer has been applied that contains the actual information."

Nora stared at the screen and was slow to grasp Robert's words. Did he mean to say that these crystals had communicated when they merged? And in what she saw as a highly technological way? She absent-mindedly raised her hand and soon felt rather stupid, as she now looked like a pupil who wanted to ask the class teacher something.

"What is it, Nora?" Robert asked when he noticed.

"I ... was just wondering whether we were dealing with a life form or a microscopic machine."

"That's what we're here to find out, isn't it?" said Sandra Gillie coolly.

Nora turned to her and gave her an irritated look. "I know what I'm here for. I can figure it out with Robert, but with you..." She left the sentence unfinished and waited for Gillie's reaction.

None came.

"Let's concentrate on the work," Robert said diplomatically and made a few more entries on the laptop. "In any case, this is clearly a complex wave pattern that should be analyzed. If we can do that, we'll be a big step closer."

"Agreed," Nora replied.

"Okay, but theoretically, we can also do that on the station, where it's not so icy," Alex suggested. "I also think Robert was right when he said that the equipment is resilient."

"I agree," Gillie agreed, a comment that caused astonishment - both in Nora and in Robert, who turned to her and looked at her questioningly.

"We don't want valuable instruments to be damaged. Besides, we still have an appointment, Professor," said Gillie, looking Robert straight in the eye. "You haven't forgotten that, have you?"

Robert scratched his chin and Nora was pretty sure that Gillie had surprised him with this hint. "Yes, okay. Then I'll get a copy of the data and try to analyze it later," he said, pulling out his laptop.

Gillie turned to Nora and Alex. "You two go back to the Amarok. We'll be in touch tomorrow."

"But..." Alex started. "That's a bit sudden. And since when have you actually determined our schedule?"

"I'm not doing that. You can stay here and freeze, of course. But since you yourself suggested that you continue working in the warmth, I just didn't want to stop you," Gillie explained calmly.

Alex grimaced and then walked wordlessly to the workshop area to pack.

Robert handed Nora his USB stick. "Can you copy the telemetry from the drill and the recorded signals onto this, please?"

Nora nodded and plugged the stick into her computer. A file browser opened automatically, displaying the folders it contained. The names all began with "Curiosity", "Mars" or "Exobiology". She looked at the folders for a moment and remembered Robert's previous history at NASA. "Should I create a new folder?"

Robert's reply was drowned out by a rumble followed by a pain-filled scream.

Everyone turned to Alex, who was just pushing the insulating box with the drill core off his foot. "Damn it!" he grumbled and tried to straighten the lid. Curiously, the half-melted contents spilled out and poured over his boots and gloves.

Nora and Robert rushed to his aid and put the box to one side.

"My gloves are soaking wet," grumbled Alex, taking them off and throwing them to the floor. "It's going to be a nice ride back."

"It's not so wild. I've always got a spare," Nora said calmly and pulled dry gloves out of her jacket pocket. She handed them to Alex. "Has anything else happened to you?"

"No, it'll just give you a nice bruise on your shin. But the sample is half destroyed! What a bummer," he grumbled.

"We still have enough material," Nora reassured him, "but it's strange that the ice had already melted again. Just like the first time."

"These crystals somehow make the ice structure unstable," Robert speculated. "Maybe it's the pressure down there. It's probably much higher than here on the surface. I think we still have a lot to investigate."

"Yes, we'll still transport the mixture to the station, even if it's just water by then. Who knows how many more opportunities we'll get to take samples."

"I think that's a good idea," Robert agreed.

"Then we'd better set off while there's still something left," Nora decided and looked hesitantly at Robert. "So you're not coming with us?"

Robert shook his head. "We've got things to do and we'll be in touch tomorrow."

The look on his face clearly told Nora that it was a white lie and that he didn't feel at all comfortable with it. Nevertheless, she didn't probe any further, because as long as Gillie was around, Robert obviously couldn't talk as freely as he would have liked. But the opportunity would present itself.

14

Robert waited until they were a few hundred meters away from the drilling site with the snowmobiles, then he slowed down and stopped in the middle of the open ice field.

It took a moment for Gillie, who had been driving ahead, to realize that he was no longer behind her. She turned around and came back to him. "What's the matter? Do you have a problem with the engine?"

"Not with the engine, no," Robert said angrily. "So, what was that all about earlier? What's so urgent that we have to leave in the middle of the investigation? Should we drive about three hours back to the airbase now?"

"Not at all. I've requested a helicopter. We'll just drive out of sight, and then we'll transfer," explained Gillie.

Robert looked at her, shaking his head. She hadn't answered his most important question. "But you know that must have seemed pretty suspicious. You took me by surprise. And at a inopportune moment. Nora will think for herself."

"We have a conversation with General Sattler," Gillie replied impassively. "And we can't have it at this borehole or on the station. Besides, you now have the proof you were supposed to bring - even more. You must explain this to him in person immediately."

"I don't know anything yet!" protested Robert. "Is that how you think research is done? Collecting a few superficial clues and then immediately drawing a conclusion?"

"Didn't you do that before?" Gillie countered.

"Ha! That's enough now." Robert was furious. His gaze fixed on Gillie, but she remained completely unmoved. "It was a mistake back then. But you know what? Everyone makes mistakes. I'm looking forward to when you do."

Gillie waved him off. "You always take everything personally, Dr. Greaves. This lack of professional detachment is the reason why your career isn't where it could be. And I'm telling you this in good faith."

"Oh, thank you," Robert replied sarcastically. "But I'm still not going to take your grotesque callousness as an example."

Gillie just shrugged her shoulders at this point too. "You don't have to, as long as you stick to the rules. You have voluntarily agreed to take part in this operation. And as I want to emphasize again: this is a confidential military matter."

"I'm aware of that. I'm just starting to wonder ..." He didn't finish his sentence, but crossed his arms in front of his chest and looked into the distance for a moment. He found it difficult to find the right words to make his point to Gillie. For a moment, he looked at the horizon, where dark clouds heralded the arrival of a new bad weather front.

"Oh, it's fruitless," he said resignedly, turning back to Gillie. "So if we absolutely have to talk to Sattler today, then let's do it. I've got a few things to sort out with him, too."

Robert revved the engine of his snowmobile and sped off.

***

Alex Corbinian felt sick as a dog when he entered his quarters on the Amarok II station. The journey back from the drilling site had already been an ordeal and had seemed three times longer than usual. They had made it here in time before the blizzard had broken out, but the icy wind had still tugged at him and gradually stiffened his limbs. The cold had first crept through his hands and feet and then spread further and further throughout his body. All the more reason for Alex to look forward to a long, hot shower.

He entered the cramped bathroom of his quarters and stripped off his clothes. His fingers and toes were so white that Alex almost thought he might actually have contracted frostbite. But that was nonsense. The boots, like the rest of the equipment, were absolutely suitable for the Arctic and kept his body at the perfect temperature.

Alex stood under the shower and turned the water up from lukewarm until it was so hot that he could barely stand it. It was a complete waste of resources, but he needed it then. The heat revived him, but only briefly. As soon as he stepped out of the shower and dried himself off, he felt exhausted and tired again. Looking in the mirror didn't help either. He had dark circles under his eyes and a glazed look.

As Alex looked at himself, a worrying thought popped into his head. Was he getting seriously ill? Like Steven?

What if the rumor that an epidemic had broken out on the ward turned out to be true? He thought of Steven's seizure, his twitching body, the foam at his mouth. The coldness had suddenly left Alex's body and he felt downright hot at the thought that he could be in the same situation. Should he pay Dr. Keller a visit and have himself examined? Just to be on the safe side?

"Oh, what! You're driving yourself crazy!" he said to his reflection and shuffled back into the living and sleeping area. There he dropped onto the bed and was asleep within seconds.

***

By 6:30 p.m., Robert and Gillie had landed at the Air Force base in Pituffik, grabbed a snack from the officers' mess, and were escorted by a soldier to a small meeting room in an outlying building in the northern part of the base.

As soon as they had taken their seats, General Sattler's face appeared on a large monitor on the wall. "Good to see you both well," he greeted them, "I hear you're making progress."

"I could be further along by now," Robert said sullenly. "But Miss Gillie here has stalled the research to get me back here. To be honest, I'm anything but happy with the way things are going here. They had assured me that I would be allowed to research the phenomenon unhindered!"

"And I stand by that," replied Sattler. "But we have to provide the right framework conditions and make sure that we stay in control. You understand that, don't you?"

Robert sighed. He was reluctant to agree with the general, but there was something to the argument. "I'm not questioning the fundamental explosiveness of this project, I'm dissatisfied with the approach. Nevertheless, I admit that caution is in order. Because Nora Grimm seems to have made a sensational find here."

"How is the collaboration with her going? Is she cooperating in our interests?"

Robert pondered for a moment whether he could answer this question honestly, because basically Nora was simply acting according to her convictions and the usual conventions of science. It couldn't be said that she was working in Sattler's interests. How could she? He himself didn't know exactly what Sattler was up to. And he wouldn't be able to put up with this for much longer.

Nevertheless, he was diplomatic. "I think things are going as well as they can under the circumstances. Nora is very talented and has the necessary research instinct."

"I like to hear that. And now to the real reason for our conversation. What did you find out? Is it the same material as on Mars?"

"As I said at the beginning, I can't say that with one hundred percent certainty yet because we were interrupted." He cast a grim sideways glance at Gillie. "But it appears to be almost identical in terms of chemical composition and structure. Logically, we can't get a sample from Mars here to make a one-to-one comparison, so we'll have to make do otherwise."

"And the effect?" Sattler asked.

"It has reappeared. The crystal fragments have reorganized themselves and given off emissions - light and other radiation. But I haven't gotten around to analyzing the signals yet."

"That all sounds very pleasing, keep at it, Dr. Greaves," Sattler praised him. "Let me know as soon as you have any news. By the way, I've already arranged for the first half of your fee to be transferred to your account."

Robert was surprised by this remark. Did Sattler think he could motivate him in such a crude way? "Yes, thank you," he said hesitantly. "But that's not so important to me at the moment. I'm concerned with the cause and for that ... well..." Robert interrupted himself before continuing in a firm tone. "Maybe it would be good if I went on alone with the PRIN people. No offense to Gillie, but she simply lacks tact when dealing with scientists. It makes for unproductive irritation."

Sattler tilted his head. "I don't think that's a good idea, but I'll think about it. Now, please leave me alone with Miss Gillie, and we'll discuss this in peace."

Robert didn't particularly like the fact that the discussion was to continue without his presence. Because it was just another sign that they didn't want to put him fully in the picture. But at the moment he saw no way of changing that. So he stood up, took the rest of his sandwich and left the room without saying a word.

When he had gone, Sattler looked at Gillie urgently. "What's happened?"

"Nothing worth mentioning. These researchers are just a bit sensitive. I'll stay in the background, as discussed."

"Apparently only you see it that way. Greaves will have mentioned it for a reason. I don't want avoidable problems to pile up here."

"Well, one thing couldn't be avoided. But I doubt that a connection will be made."

"What in three devils' names is going on now?" Sattler roared.

"I had to put Steven Dryer - Nora Grimm's former project partner - out of action."

"Surely you didn't kill him, for God's sake!"

"No, just made sure he didn't cause us any more trouble. He wanted to blow our cover. I couldn't risk that. He's now in a state where he can't talk to anyone. But don't worry, it all seemed like an epileptic seizure."

"And such a drastic measure was really necessary?"

"Unfortunately, yes. Do you think I'm doing something like this just to pass the time?"

"I still hope it's not like that," said Sattler, leaving open how convinced he was.

"And now what?" Gillie wanted to know. "Should we let Greaves go back to Nora Grimm and Alex Corbinian on his own? We would lose a lot of control and direct influence."

"I'm aware of that," replied Sattler. "But I want Greaves to find out as much as possible in the shortest possible time. If he thinks he can work more productively without you, then we'll try that. But you monitor his laptop and report any potential difficulties."

"That at least seems like a compromise to me."

"Oh, and Gillie ... No more actions like the one with Steven Dryer."

"Understood," said Gillie curtly.

"Good, then report back to me tomorrow!" Sattler demanded and ended the video chat.

***

Meanwhile, Robert had arrived in his quarters and threw his clothes on the bed. Then he put his laptop bag down on the small desk and sat down on the wooden chair in front of it, which was far too uncomfortable for his taste. He was still annoyed. Even more so than before the conversation with Sattler. He had made every effort to hide it from the general, but there was nothing he could do about it. The way they were ruling over this project and the people involved was atrocious. Robert detested the underlying arrogance and the illusion of total control that Sattler seemed to be indulging in. He hardly believed that he would now keep his watchdog Gillie out of the matter, even if the general had promised him a little more freedom. And now he was also stuck in this base, from which he certainly couldn't get out without permission.

Shaking his head, Robert went to the window and looked out, where thick snowflakes were floating down and gradually forming a layer of slush on the ground. A snowplough was already clearing the streets between the buildings. It was certainly a never-ending task in this place.

Perhaps he should never have agreed to help. But he had once again succumbed to Linda's charm. And he had probably imagined that they would work together, which he would have found very pleasant. He had had a bad feeling from the start when he heard that the military was involved. But he had also been curious; too eager to finally prove his theory. And now he was so close!

If he did it right, this could be his breakthrough - it could even change humanity's perspective if the structures he found did point to extraterrestrial life. But at the same time, a dark thought crept in. What if Sattler had no intention of letting him and Nora take the credit for this success? All this secrecy didn't reflect well on the matter. And Gillie was playing a convoluted game. Linda had warned him.

The two wanted to protect themselves - and Robert was well advised to do the same. He had to take precautions in case the military secretly wanted the whole project to disappear into oblivion. But to do this, he had to stretch the rules imposed on him quite a bit.

At that moment, his cell phone, which had been without reception for the last two days and had apparently reconnected to the base network, vibrated in his pocket. He pulled it out and saw on the display that someone had left a voicemail.

Pressing speed dial connected him directly to the voicemail and he was told by a computer that two messages had been left. He listened carefully to the first recording, which was from Linda and had been recorded the previous evening. Robert was pleased to hear her voice, even if her tone sounded rather mysterious.

"Robert, it's me. I hope you're okay up there and haven't frozen your toes off. Listen, I really need to talk to you. It's about the project. But we should talk in confidence first. Get in touch!"

A beep announced the end of the message, and the artificial voice now listed the date, time and number of the second caller. It was Linda again, shortly after 7:00 this morning. "Robert, please call me. It's important. And I need to know if you're okay."

It beeped again and the computer asked if it wanted to be connected to the caller.

Robert pressed the number 3 to confirm this.

It clicked, and then the call sign rang out. It rang three times until Linda answered. "Robert, thank God. Is everything all right?"

"Take it easy, Linda. I'm all right. There's just no reception out on the glacier."

"I thought so. I'm really pleased to hear about it, I had already imagined the worst."

"Come on, you're not usually so anxious. Besides, Sattler would certainly have told you if something had happened."

"Well ... I don't know. He's been extremely taciturn lately. Actually, he's been doing that ever since that Sandra Gillie turned up. Something's up. And I think I'm on the right track."

"Oh, Linda, your tone sounds more like I should be worried," Robert said.

"Can we talk openly?" asked Linda.

"Yes, why not? It's my private cell phone and I'm alone in the room."

"Okay, pay attention. Last night, I went to Sattler's office to tell him I was going to leave early. I apparently surprised him by studying a classified file. He tried to act like nothing was wrong, but I could tell he was uncomfortable."

"And it has to do with this project? I mean, have you been able to recognize anything?"

"Not much. Just one word, actually. Century. But I didn't fall on my head. After a little research, I now know that it was a base built in the middle of the Cold War called Camp Century. And now guess where it was."

"Greenland," Robert said as if shot from a pistol.

"Hit! But it wasn't that hard either."

"Yes, otherwise you wouldn't be calling me about it."

"That's right. And the trickier question is why Sattler is making such a secret of it when there is even a public Wikipedia entry."

"I strongly suspect that the contents of an online encyclopedia are very different from those in a secret file," Robert said and then added: "Can we get hold of the file somehow?"

"Not without breaking open Sattler's desk," Linda replied. "And that would probably have unpleasant consequences. That's why I pulled an all-nighter and emptied half a bottle of wine to find out more on the Internet. But unfortunately, there's not much about the camp."

"Maybe not on the Internet," said Robert.

"I've already told you that we can't get hold of the file," Linda insisted.

"That's not what I mean either. But I'm on Greenland. There must be records here too."

"Not a bad idea. But Greenland belonged to Denmark back then, it still does - at least more or less. From what I've found out, Denmark is still keeping quiet about whether they knew about the construction of the facility at the time. But that is to be assumed; after all, it was about the stationing of nuclear missiles."

Robert sucked in his breath in amazement. "Nuclear missiles? Oh, man. I should have guessed."

"Don't worry, they obviously never got that far - at least officially. Otherwise I'd be worried too if I were you. The remains of Camp Century are only a few kilometers away from your drilling site."

"Phew. That's really exciting news. I'll see if I can find out anything discreetly. Can you send me the coordinates, please?"

"The emphasis should be on inconspicuous. Sattler might get nervous and fire you."

"I won't let that happen. Not now, when I'm so close."

"Is that so, Robert? I'd really like you to, but to be honest, it scares me a little," Linda admitted.

"It's incredible what we've discovered. And I have to ask you to do something about it."

"Do I want to hear that? The way you say that doesn't mean anything good."

"You owe it to me," Robert replied curtly.

"I know. And I'll do what I can. So what is it?"

"You're still in touch with some of the NASA guys, aren't you?"

"I was afraid of that."

"I have a recording here that needs to be analyzed. But I don't have the means or the know-how to do it myself."

"Does Sattler know about this?" Linda asked.

"Not in detail. I just told him that we had picked up signals and that I wanted to analyze them."

"Oh, Robert, that's not possible. Sattler will freak out if he finds out I'm involving unauthorized experts."

Robert didn't answer immediately. He first considered the consequences of handing over the data. Then he remembered that Linda had signed the same confidentiality agreement as he had and could, therefore, legally obtain the data in principle.

He cleared his throat. "Let Ted Cummings and Peter Ristle give you their A.I. tool for pattern recognition. I reckon they've probably perfected it by now. We can probably use it to analyze the signals ourselves."

"And what do I tell them we need it for?"

"A research project. Come on now! It's not a task that you haven't completed in no time at all with your persuasive skills. Cummings has always had his eye on you."

Linda let out an agonized sigh. "I just hope the guy doesn't want anything inappropriate in return."

"Cummings? If you look at him too hard, he'll faint," Robert joked.

"All right, I'll get the program, but what do we do with Sattler?"

"Nothing. We present the results to him when we have them. And before that, we make sure there is a backup copy. There's nothing illegal about that."

"That doesn't make us any safer. But I still agree with you."

"Great, then I'll send you the data. Please see what you can decode. You have more experience than I do."

"I just hope it goes well," Linda replied.

"We'll just have to see to it. I'll be in touch," Robert promised and said goodbye.

The dissatisfaction that had built up in him over the last few hours had been blown away. It had given way to a new feeling of confidence. He had a plan - a very good plan, in fact! And it finally gave him the opportunity to determine the course of this project himself. What Gillie and Sattler thought of it didn't matter to him at the moment.

15

PRIN research station "Amarok II", Greenland
Morning of September 16

The muffled roar of a helicopter flying over the station made Nora sit up and take notice. It was only 7:00 a.m. and she had just gotten up to freshen up and get dressed. She knew the helicopter was coming for Steven, but hadn't expected it so early. Yesterday evening, Olofsson had informed everyone that the condition of his still unconscious colleague was not improving and that Dr. Keller no longer saw any possibility of treatment on site. Nora hastily put the hairbrush away, threw on a sweatshirt jacket and put on her shoes. Then she ran out into the corridor and towards the infirmary. She at least owed it to Steven to say goodbye in person. A few others were already waiting in the corridor in front of the closed door. Looking at their faces, Nora realized that she had forgotten to put on her face mask in her haste. She quickly pulled it out of her trouser pocket and put it on. Although she didn't believe in the possibility of a serious infectious disease, she didn't want to start a discussion about it right now. And as long as a potential spread could not be completely ruled out, it was certainly a sensible precaution. After a few minutes, two paramedics in protective clothing approached the waiting staff. They carried a stretcher that had been converted into an isolation cabin to the infirmary and disappeared inside. "That's a bit of an exaggeration," muttered mechanic Macmillan, shaking his head. "They're acting like he's got Ebola." He made a dismissive gesture and turned around. "I've had enough," he grumbled and disappeared. Nora realized that it was hardly possible to say goodbye to Steven in a sensible way. Nevertheless, she stayed until the paramedics had taken the sick man out. People began to disperse and Nora turned to leave. She was a little surprised that Alex wasn't there, but explained it by saying that he and Steven didn't like each other very much anyway. Or was it because Alex had been so exhausted yesterday and was still asleep? That wasn't like him, especially not when there was so much to do. She decided to visit him in his quarters. She knocked on the door and waited. When no one answered, she knocked again and listened in. After a while, she heard moaning and footsteps from inside. The door was opened a crack, and Alex looked at her sleepily and with reddened eyes. "Oh, sorry!" she said instinctively. "I thought..." "What's the matter? I've just been lying down." Nora flinched in irritation. "Alex, that was more than 14 hours ago, it's already morning."

"What? But that can ..." He grabbed his head and squinted. "You look terrible," said Nora. "Yes, I have a splitting headache. I must have caught a cold somehow yesterday." "Surely you know that the cold doesn't give you a cold. There's always a pathogen involved."

"Anyway, I'm totally gobsmacked."

"It's best to have Dr. Keller examine you," Nora advised him. "They just flew Steven out. And I ..."

"You think ... I could have caught it?" Alex asked hesitantly.

"I don't know. But you shouldn't take any chances." Alex nodded silently.

"You'd best wait here, I'll get Keller here, okay?"

"Yes, you're right. I'll go back to bed." Alex closed the door, and Nora hurried backreturned to the infirmary to call the doctor.

**

"I don't want our program to be used for any espionage crap, Linda," Peter Ristle said in a tone that made it clear he was deadly serious. Then there was a moment of silence on the phone line. "Peter, how long have we known each other now?"

Linda asked as kindly and firmly as she could. Shortly before, she had already tried the more sociable ex-colleague Ted Cummings, but he had apparently just taken his entire annual vacation and was hanging around at some kind of live role-playing game where everyone dressed up like aliens or mutants. So she had to make do with Ristle, who was much more critical of Linda's new employer. Nevertheless, she had to somehow convince him to hand over the AI-based analysis tool to her. "So, what is it? I promise you that your program won't leave my computer. I'll delete it when the project is finished, all right?"

Ristle sighed audibly, then replied: "All right, for old times' sake - and because Robert asks for it." Linda remembered that a good eight years ago, Ristle had been pretty much the only one who had backed Robert - until he had been blatantly threatened with expulsion and told to distance himself from Robert. "I'll send you an encrypted download link for the basic program. But you'll need an internet connection to use it properly. The A.I.A.I. will fetch the latest pattern definitions from our server." "Thank you, Peter. We owe you one." "Yes, that's all right. I'll think of a way to make it up to you." "Do that, please," Linda replied and ended the conversation. Less than five minutes later, the aforementioned download link fluttered into her mailbox. Linda clicked on it, entered the password sent to her by Peter Ristle and downloaded the file from the server. It was much smaller than Linda would have expected from such a powerful tool, but this was probably due to the online connection mentioned above, which was used to download data as required. Fortunately, the installation on Linda's laptop went quickly, so she still had about an hour and a half until she had to be at her desk. Officially, she had taken the morning off for a dentist's appointment so that she could work on the analysis at home. Sattler wasn't supposed to find out ahead of time that she was working on the project without his knowledge. As she had already worked with a previous version of this software at NASA a few years ago, Linda found her way around relatively quickly. Although Cummings and Ristle had optimized a lot of the interface and added one or two functions, the essential elements were still all in the same place.

She then loaded the data set sent by Robert into the program and waited until it was fully processed. A pop-up asked whether the software should perform an automatic analysis - and if so, whether it should be "typical", "extended" or "full". Linda thought for a moment. This function was new, but she was quite sure that due to the completely unknown nature of the signal, a full analysis would probably have the best chance of success. She clicked on the corresponding option and the program began to calculate an estimated analysis time. It then pulled various data from the web. Finally, the software presented a time that Linda didn't particularly like: 3 hours and 18 minutes. This meant she had to leave the computer running in her absence and could only check the results tonight. Nevertheless, she realized that this was the best solution. After all, if a superficial search, which was probably quicker, didn't produce anything, she would have to start all over again anyway and waste even more time. She got up, grabbed her cell phone and car keys and threw on a jacket. There was nothing more to do here, so she might as well go to work now. She paused briefly at the door, picked up her cell phone, and wrote a message to Robert: "Analysis is running,; I might know more tonight."

Then she left her apartment and set off.

***

It was justJust before 10 a.m. when., Robert was on his way to the drilling site by helicopter. He had arranged to meet Nora Grimm there last night at 11 o'clock. He was still amazed that he had actually been let off the leash. Or rather, Sattler had given his guard dog Gillie leave, as Robert had requested. He found that remarkable, to say the least, but still didn't trust it. He felt that he wouldn't be rid of Gillie for very long. But until then, he would make the most of his new freedom. The pilot had been instructed to drop him off at the exact spot where they had left the snowmobiles yesterday. There were two canisters of fuel in the hold, which Robert was to use to refill the tanks before driving to the outpost. He wondered whether he should stick to the route he had been given. He had the coordinates of the former Camp Century with him, just in case. Even if there probably wasn't much to see there, he wanted to take a look at the place. Should he squeeze it in on the way to the borehole or should he take Nora with him? He felt uncomfortable that he was still hiding important background information from her and keeping her in the dark about who he was working for. On the other hand, the information about Camp Century was not a secret. The location was even found in online map services. It would neither be a breach of any confidentiality agreements nor a breach of trust towards Sattler. The general wouldn't find out about this little detour anyway. Robert made a decision. He should at least be completely open and honest with Nora in this respect, even if he didn't know whether they could even find a clue there. He wouldn't be able to fool a young woman as intelligent as Nora for long. She was probably already having second thoughts anyway. After a while, the helicopter began to descend and Robert could already see the two black dots in the shelter of a large snow bank. The vehicles were only covered by a very thin layer of fresh snow. Now Robert checked his equipment and fumbled for the satellite phone that Gillie had given him before his departure. He could use it to call for help if necessary and hope that it would arrive in time. Until then, he was on his own - alone in the white wilderness, where polar bears and unpredictable changes in the weather lurked. There was nothing he could do about the weather. He had been given a pistol for the polar bears. Robert was not afraid to use it in an emergency. Since his time at the ranch, he had been pretty good at shooting when it mattered. But he hated the thought of having to kill a polar bear just because it stupidly saw him as lunch. These animals had already been hit hard enough by climate change.

The helicopter touched down gently on an open area of ice not far from the snowmobiles. The co-pilot got out together with Robert to help him with the canisters and freeing the vehicles. After a few minutes, everything was done and the helicopter took off. Robert was now also able to set off. He selected the coordinates of the borehole that had already been saved on the outdoor GPS and stepped on the gas.

***

Nora's thoughts were jumping in a triangle today - from Steven to Alex to Robert and then back again. Since the discovery of the alien material, the events on this research mission, which had been rather leisurely and almost boring in the months before, had come thick and fast. Those days were definitely over, but she would deal with that. She just wanted more clarity. In every respect. It was still a mystery why Steven had fallen ill so suddenly, and it was still unclear what Alex was suffering from. But above all, she wondered: what kind of devilish game had Robert Greaves got himself into? Was it all connected? Could it really be the same thing? Her gut said yes, because so many coincidences were unlikely. Still, she had no real evidence to connect the dots. However, she clearly sensed that Robert had not told her everything. This situation was becoming increasingly unbearable and she was determined to talk to him straight up today - even if it meant Sandra Gillie turning herself inside out.

Nora parked her snowmobile not far from the entrance to the borehole and saw that there was already another one on the other side - but only a single one. That boded well. At the bottom of the ramp, she found Robert waiting in front of the locked gate. He had already cleared away the snow and greeted her in a friendly manner. "Hello, colleague! I hope you're not disappointed that I've come alone today." Then he looked behind Nora in surprise. "Are you alone, too? What about Alex?"

"Morning, Robert! Alex is unfortunately ill. A fever of over 39 degrees. It started all of a sudden last night."

"Oh, damn. I hope he gets back on his feet soon." He paused for a moment and then asked: "And Steven? Is he feeling any better?"

"They flew him out early this morning. But now let's go inside. We need to have a serious talk." Nora walked past Robert, unlocked the door and entered the outpost. Robert followed her inside. "Why should we actually meet here?" he asked inside. "You took all the instruments and samples back to the station, didn't you?" "Firstly, because I was hoping that we could talk here undisturbed - and believe me, I'm really glad that you came without Sandra Gillie! And secondly, the rehearsal is still here. I had serious doubts about whether it would be a good idea to bring the material to the station." Robert frowned. "Why is that?"

"You can imagine that. After you left, I thought it all over again. What we found down there is either an alien life form or a completely unknown technology. And you have to ask yourself how carelessly you handle it."

"You think it's dangerous?" Robert asked. "No ... well ... maybe," Nora said haltingly. "The point is that we don't know. But I do know that people have suddenly fallen ill on the ward. Two colleagues who were directly involved in this project. Doesn't that ring alarm bells for you?" Robert nodded. "I understand what you're getting at. But the other three people who are also working on the case are in perfect health. It could be a coincidence."

"I'm aware of that. But forgive my concerns, the way you and Gillie behaved didn't exactly inspire confidence."

"I know that, of course," Robert admitted. "If it had been up to me ..."

"Who's it all about?" Nora interrupted him. "Don't tell me that as a university professor you follow your assistant's orders."

Robert made a rather pained expression that spoke volumes.

"So?" Nora insisted.

"It's complicated," Robert began. "I'm not officially allowed to tell you anything. They made me sign a pretty nasty non-disclosure agreement."

"That rules out the possibility that you're really here as part of a research project at your university," Nora noted.

Robert nodded. "There probably wasn't such a watertight cover. It had to be quick. But everything else is true. I'm an exobiologist and I worked for NASA on a Mars project that produced the data I showed you. And I have a genuine interest in investigating this phenomenon. At the same time, I also have other interests, but I have been kept as much in the dark about them as you have. I can only ask you to believe me."

"And Gillie?"

"She works for the USU.S. government,; that's all I know."

Nora looked at Robert scrutinizingly for a moment, trying to figure out what to make of his explanations. Her instinct told her that it was the truth, at least as far as he could reveal it to her. "Okay. Let's start again. But no more secrets from now on."

"All right," Robert promised and put on a smile. "I just hope I don't regret it."

"Definitely not," Robert assured her and then asked, "Would you like to go on a little excursion before we continue here?"

16

PRIN research station "Amarok II", Greenland
September 16

"Is he feeling better?" asked Per Olofsson, addressing the ward physician Dr. Keller.

The 60-year-old doctor tilted his head and replied: "I think you actually want to know if he's suffering from the same thing as Steven Dryer and should be flown out, don't you?"

"You're right about that. I have to admit that I'm seriously worried."

"That's understandable. But the way it looks now, Alex just has the flu. No seizures, no comatose states, no palpitations. Just a fever and leaden tiredness."

"I guess that's good news. You'll get a handle on it?"

"There's not much I can do. If it's the flu, the only thing that helps is to lower the temperature and wait. No antibiotic works for a viral infection anyway."

"I understand. But the flu is highly contagious, isn't it?"

"I've checked the records. Everyone on the ward has been properly vaccinated - including Alex. But a vaccination never offers one hundred percent protection. It's possible that his immune system didn't react to the active ingredient or that it was a different strain of virus. In any case, I assume that we will hardly see any more cases. He will remain isolated in his quarters until he gets better. That should make any potential spread even more difficult."

"Can we take the masks off again then?"

"Yes, I think it's enough that I wear one when I check on Alex. We don't really need them in the rest of the ward."

Olofsson nodded and felt a clear sense of relief. "That's good, also for the mood. We've had a lot more unrest in the last few days than I would have liked." He paused and looked around the empty infirmary. "Have you heard anything from Steven Dryer?"

Dr. Keller shook his head. "It's too early for any real news. All I know is that he's arrived at the clinic in London. They'll probably run through the full range of diagnostics over the next few hours and days. We'll see what comes out of it. The whole thing is still a mystery to me."

"You did everything you could. I know that we are only equipped to treat emergencies and standard infections here."

"Of course, but I would still have liked to have done more. On the one hand, it looked like an epileptic seizure, but at the same time it looked like poisoning. I went through Steven's medical records carefully, he has no pre-existing conditions that could be linked to this. And you don't suddenly become epileptic unless you suffer a serious head injury or something like that."

"Then all we can do is wait and see what the clinic finds out. In any case, I'm reasonably reassured that there's no threat of an epidemic on the ward."

"Yes, at least that seems to have been averted," agreed Keller. "This is not a good place for large-scale medical operations."

"Please keep me informed if there is any news from Steven," Olofsson asked.

Dr. Keller nodded. "Of course. I'll go and check on Alex now, maybe he's already showing signs of improvement."

The two left the infirmary and parted company. While Olofsson went upstairs to his office, Dr. Keller approached Alex's quarters.

***

It took Nora and Robert less than ten minutes on their snowmobiles to get from the PRIN drilling site to the former U.S. military Camp Century. In principle, this place was no different from the rest of the surroundings; everything was white and deserted as far as the eye could see. There were a few snowdrifts or gentle elevations all around, but that was all in terms of variety.

Robert checked the coordinates on the navigation device once more and then parked his snowmobile.

Nora did the same. She took off her safety goggles and looked at Robert questioningly. "And now what? I mean, I don't mind a little drive, but ..."

"You're wondering what we're doing here," Robert finished the sentence. "I don't really know myself. Still, I had to come here. It ... well ... might have something to do with what you've discovered."

"But there's nothing here," Nora contradicted.

Robert pointed to the frozen ground. "Not up here. But there was something down there - and I think there's still quite a bit there."

Nora frowned, but didn't ask, instead waiting for Robert to continue on his own initiative.

"Does the name Camp Century mean anything to you?"

"Not that I know of," Nora replied.

"No wonder, that was long before you were born and also before mine. I recently heard from a colleague that the U.S. military wanted to station nuclear missiles here during the Cold War. And they went to incredible lengths to build an entire base under the ice that was virtually invisible from above. The project was even disguised as a scientific expedition, although I can't imagine that the Russians believed that for very long."

"Wait a minute," Nora interjected. "Something's ringing now. When exactly was that?"

"It was probably in operation from 1959 to 1967."

"That fits."

"What does it fit in with?" Robert asked.

"It's no coincidence that I'm drilling in this exact area. The impetus came from an article about a Greenland ice core that was accidentally rediscovered in Denmark in 2017. It had been drilled in 1967 but was lost due to strange circumstances."

"I'm pretty sure it's from Camp Century," Robert said. "They actually did research to make the camouflage look as authentic as possible."

"You never read much about the results. I looked for it, but apart from this old ice core, there doesn't seem to be anything."

"The military keeps a lot of things under wraps," said Robert.

"Is that a guess or do you know more?"

Robert sighed. "All right, I don't think there's any point in telling you any more fairy tales anyway. I was assigned to investigate by an Air Force general. Sandra Gillie is on his staff, so I had to take her with me." He put on an apologetic smile. "But this general didn't tell me everything either. The connection with this camp was made by a colleague who happened to see him studying a secret file about it. That's pretty much all I know. We'll have to find out the rest ourselves."

"Thank you, Robert," Nora replied, "I'm glad you're talking to me openly now."

"As I said, I don't think there's any point in keeping this from you. But please keep the information to yourself. I have no desire to end up in prison."

Nora nodded. "I'm silent as an arctic grave."

"It's quite possible that we're already standing on one," said Robert, looking around the area. "Have you noticed that this area forms a kind of hollow? It looks to me like we're standing in the middle of it."

Nora now also looked at her surroundings. "You're right. It could be due to certain wind conditions that prevent as much snow from accumulating here as in the surrounding area. But to be honest, it would have to be a pretty blatant phenomenon if there was a difference of several meters."

The rattling of a snowmobile interrupted their conversation.

"Oh, damn!" Nora rolled her eyes in annoyance. "Please don't let it be that unspeakable Sandra Gillie."

They both peered in the direction from which the noise had come and spotted a bright orange snowmobile.

"She certainly isn't," Robert said. "It's hard to imagine her using anything in a color other than black."

The orange vehicle pulled up directly towards them and parked a few meters away. A young woman got out, pushed up her glasses and looked at the two of them. Judging by her appearance, she was a genuine Greenlander - barely older than 20.

"I didn't expect to meet anyone here," she said.

"Neither do we," Robert replied. "But there are the strangest coincidences, aren't there?"

"Hardly," the woman replied. "I am Nanouk Bruun."

"Robert Greaves," he introduced himself.

"I am Nora Grimm. We are biologists."

"Ah, so you're researching the environmental impact here?"

"You could say that," said Robert.

"It's a real mess what those damn Americans have done here!" Nanouk roared and then fell silent. She looked at Robert. "You're American, aren't you? Sorry, but your countrymen ... well, at least the military, they're the last straw! They can't even clean up their garbage, and they're poisoning the environment," she continued.

"Okay, slow down," Nora asked, "are you talking about the camp?"

"Camp? Toxic waste dump is probably more appropriate. Did you know that they left everything behind when they left? Not only large parts of the equipment, but also 200,000 liters of diesel, highly toxic PCBs, radioactive waste, millions of liters of untreated wastewater, garbage of all kinds! It's all down there in the ice, waiting for climate change to bring it to the surface."

Robert nodded. "That would be a real environmental disaster - and in a sensitive ecosystem."

"That's right! That's why we've been demanding for years that the Americans get rid of their legacy, but they're being stubborn."

"And what are you doing here?" Nora asked.

"Please, can we be on first-name terms? Otherwise I feel like I'm 70 years old," said the Greenlander.

"Okay, Nanouk. What are you doing here?"

"I am part of a Greenlandic environmental protection organization that works to protect our homeland from harm. Today I wanted to take samples to see if there are any toxins on the surface, if radiation is leaking and so on." She pointed to a transport case on the back of her snowmobile. "I've got everything with me."

"Could such a release have already occurred?" Robert asked.

"In principle, yes. Nobody knows how deep down the garbage is or how much it might be pushed upwards by the ice movements. But it is clear that the ice is melting - climate change is hitting harder and harder here. Calculated over the entire Greenland ice sheet, the result is a negative balance year after year. New snowfall has not compensated for the melting for a long time. Over a hundred gigatons are missing every year!"

"I wasn't aware that the situation was already so extreme," Robert admitted.

"You're just an American," Nanouk said sarcastically. "You're not so good with climate change."

Then she set about getting the sample containers and measuring instruments out of her transport box.

"Shall we help you?" Nora asked.

"No, I'm fine. I'm used to working alone. Surely you have something to do yourself? Or did you just come out here for fun?"

"No, not directly," Nora said. "We come from a station of the PRIN research network, I'm drilling a few kilometers away from here."

"Is it about climate data?" Nanouk asked.

"Also. First and foremost, I want to find out what the vegetation was like on Greenland a good 400,000 years ago. According to the latest findings, almost the entire island was ice-free back then."

Nanouk nodded. "I know the studies too, yes. Imagine what that must have meant for the sea level. It must have been several meters above today's level. Only back then, there were no towns anywhere on the coast. If you now imagine what would happen today ..."

"Fortunately, we should be decades away from that," said Robert, earning a dissatisfied look from Nanouk.

"However, we must draw the right conclusions from this realization now and take action, even if the ice sheet will of course not disappear overnight."

"You're absolutely right," Robert agreed.

Nanouk packed the snow and ice samples she had collected into the box and then picked up a device the size of an oversized cell phone. She watched the display, which showed sporadic deflections and made a soft rattling sound.

"A Geiger counter?" Nora asked.

"That's right. Nobody knows exactly how much nuclear waste they've left behind or how much it radiates. I want to establish facts." She walked a few steps and drew a circle around the parked snowmobiles. At one point, the rattling of the measuring device increased significantly. "Can you hear that? When I look at the readings like that, it's pretty clear that a disaster is inevitable."

Robert reached into his jacket pocket and pulled out one of his business cards. "I'd be very interested in your results. Maybe I can pass them on to the right people?"

Nanouk came over to Robert, first examined his card suspiciously and then looked him straight in the face. "I'll take your word for it! But I don't want any complaints later that I'm nagging you with questions." She grabbed the card and pocketed it.

"It was nice to meet you, Nanouk," said Nora.

"Yes, it was definitely more entertaining than usual. I wish you every success with your project."

Robert and Nora got back on their snowmobiles and made their way back to the outpost.

17

Pituffik Space Base, West Greenland
September 16th

Sandra Gillie had retreated to one of the secret service offices at Pituffik Space Base to analyze the data from her secretly installed spy tools. She enjoyed the peace and quiet in these offices, which didn't officially exist here, and found it all very fitting - secret offices with a cover designation for a double-bottomed covert operation.

In fact, she no longer knew how many floors this venture had. There were definitely more than two. In addition to Sattler's level, on which she herself also operated to some extent, there was her own, on which she supplied the CIA with information - or rather was supposed to.

At the very other end of confidentiality, there was the façade they had put up for the PRIN people, which might have started to crack as a result of the incident with Steven Dryer. But despite Sattler's misgivings, she was still sure that it had been right to intervene. What she wasn't sure about was whether it was necessary to seal these cracks further.

Between these two extremes, there was the level on which Robert Greaves was wandering around half-haphazardly, and he also wanted to pull up the scientist Nora Grimm without permission. Given his psychological profile, this was to be expected sooner or later, but Gillie still disapproved. Especially after he had also contacted Linda Shoemaker and provided her with the data he had obtained. The latter was operating on another, potentially dangerous level, which she now had to take care of. But perhaps they could ultimately involve Linda in a beneficial way?

All of this forced Gillie to constantly look at the operation from different angles and weigh up which scenarios were most likely. This determined what needed to be done and in what order. Although she knew that everything could never be planned, because reality did not always adhere to hypotheses and theories, she trusted in her ability to keep all the threads in the best possible hands. She liked to see this as a welcome challenge that would allow her to make a name for herself and then rise through the ranks.

The critical factor in everything she did was time. Timing was crucial for overall success - and she would keep a meticulous eye on this.

The fact that Greaves had passed on confidential information to Nora Grimm was not dramatic. She just had to continue to ensure that the young researcher remained under control. One positive side effect was that her colleague Alex Corbinian had been absent due to illness. There was a good chance that he would not have recovered by the time the project moved on to the next phase. Then there would be one less imponderable.

Gillie checked the status of Linda Shoemaker's laptop, which had been running a computationally intensive analysis for hours. She didn't have access to the program itself, but it was very likely that it was an analysis of the data sent by Greaves. She would love to know what the results were, but would have to be patient until Shoemaker checked them and, if necessary, sent them to Greaves. As soon as that happened, she would make a copy of it and then render the computer unusable with some nasty hacking software. A slight smirk crept onto Gillie's lips as she imagined the helpless expression on Shoemaker's far-too-handsome face when she realized that all her supposed brilliance wasn't going to help her here.

***

"You wouldn't want to have this Nanouk as an enemy," Robert said after he and Nora had returned to the borehole.

"I can understand why she's so dogged," Nora replied and unlocked the door.

"Me too. This is her home. And she has to watch how the legacy of a completely insane arms race could now poison the environment."

"That's right. She rightly demands that you Americans take responsibility."

Robert spared himself an answer, because he knew that much of what his country's governments had done in the last 100 years could hardly be justified. And this absurd idea of stationing nuclear weapons under the Greenland ice was undoubtedly one of them - not to mention the audacity of leaving all this garbage behind. Perhaps there was a reason for this. From what he had learned, Camp Century had been abandoned rather hastily. The connection with the current finds in the area was almost obvious.

Robert would love to take a look at Sattler's secret file to get some clarity. After all, if similar discoveries had been made back then, why had the cloak of silence been kept over them for decades? Were people afraid to investigate the phenomenon further? Or were there serious complications?

"What's wrong with you? Don't you want to come in?" asked Nora, who was standing at the inner door of the airlock, waiting impatiently.

"Sorry, I was thinking."

"You can see."

Robert set off and entered the interior of the site together with Nora. It immediately seemed to him that the temperature had risen again compared to the surface. "Am I that frozen through, or is it getting warmer here?"

Nora took off her hood and hat and tried to feel if there was any warming. She swayed her head back and forth. "I had the same feeling the other day but dismissed it as my imagination. If you can feel a warming now, too, there might be something to it. Still, I'm not quite sure how that's possible."

Robert pointed to the borehole. "It's about as unusual as the plus degrees down there, huh?"

"Point taken," she said. "Do you think that radiates all the way up here?"

At Nora's last sentence, a strange thought popped into Robert's mind. He didn't know exactly from which corner of his subconscious it came, but the word "radiate" curiously connected with the image of the Geiger counter that Nanouk had used earlier.

"You look so broody again, what's going on?" Nora asked.

Robert cleared his throat. "I ... well, this is going to sound far-fetched, but do you think these crystals could be emitting radioactive radiation as well as electromagnetic emissions? Yes, I know, I have no evidence ... It's just a spontaneous thought."

"No, it's not completely far-fetched - even if I haven't found any known radioactive elements in the material I've collected. I admit that I don't particularly like this possibility, but we should look into it. Unfortunately, we don't have anything here to measure potential radiation."

"We should get a Geiger counter, just to be on the safe side. If only for our own protection."

"That's what I meant by saying that I don't like the theory. But I like the fact that it might explain the rise in temperature."

A knock on the lock door interrupted their conversation. They both turned and saw Nanouk Bruun come in. "Sorry to barge in like this, but you've lost something." She held up the satellite phone that Robert had been given. "This was over on the ice, and it can only belong to you. These things are expensive, so I thought I'd better bring it back."

"Oh," Robert said. "That's mine. It must have fallen out of my pocket when I was looking for the business cards. Thank you, Nanouk." He stepped up to her and took the device, which seemed undamaged thanks to its robust outdoor casing.

"I've made a few long-distance calls, you don't mind, do you?" She grinned mischievously.

"Even if I did, I wouldn't really care, I'm not paying the bill." Robert laughed.

"How did you find us?" Nora wanted to know.

"Piece of cake. The weather is calm today, all I had to do was follow your tracks." She looked around the room. "What exactly are you doing here? Or is that a secret?"

Robert looked at Nora meaningfully. "Only partly secret," he said truthfully.

"As I mentioned earlier, I'm drilling down to the bedrock," Nora explained. "It's almost two and a half kilometers under the ice at this point. I'm interested to see what organic remains can still be found there."

Nanouk nodded. "And have you had any success?"

"How to take it. There were difficulties with the drill. It's a completely new prototype that we're beta testing."

"Tell me, Nanouk," Robert now intervened. "You don't have your Geiger counter with you, do you?"

Nanouk gave him a skeptical look. "Yes, of course. Outside with the equipment. Why do you ask that?"

"Can I borrow it for a moment?" Robert asked back.

"All right," Nanouk replied. "But I want to know what for." Then she went outside to get the measuring device.

"And what do you want to tell her when she gets back?" Nora asked.

"I don't know, but I do know that we can't waste any more time."

Nanouk promptly returned and pressed the Geiger counter into Robert's hand. "Well, I'll be interested to see."

Robert switched on the device and began to walk around the room. According to the readings, the radiation was at the usual level. Then he approached the borehole and registered the first, very slight increase. The rattling of the device became slightly more intense. Now he turned around and walked towards the workshop area, where the half-dismantled drill head was still lying. When he pointed the Geiger counter at it, there was another, this time more pronounced increase in radiation. When Robert finally opened the lid of the container with the sample, the meter began to beep rather shrilly. Robert snapped the lid shut again and returned to the others.

He took a notebook and wrote down the measured values of the borehole, drill and sample. Then he handed the Geiger counter back to Nanouk.

She pocketed it and frowned. "What's in the box? And don't you dare fuck me up!"

"A drill core," Nora said, pointing to the hole behind Nanouk. "From down there."

Nanouk nodded. "I was afraid of that. Is it rock? There are many places on Greenland where you can find radiant ore."

Nora shook her head. "It was ice, just ice and water." She didn't mention that there was also a strange crystalline structure in the sample.

"Just ice, all right, if you say so. I'll be on my way." She turned to go.

"One more thing, Nanouk," Robert asked. "You ..."

"Yes, I'm not supposed to tell anyone about it," she interrupted him.

"At least until we find out what it's all about. Okay?"

"What's it all about? I already have a theory. It must be from the camp. Apparently, the movement of the glacier has shifted the garbage here. You drilled right through it."

"That far?" Nora asked incredulously.

"Like I said, just my amateur theory. Let me know if I was right." She turned and left the facility without another word.

"I still think it's unlikely, but I still have a bad feeling about it," Nora mumbled.

"Yes, me too. The radiation levels were elevated, but not harmful, at least as long as we don't plan to sit on the sample for days."

Nora nodded. "No, we certainly don't intend to do that, but I wonder if Alex might have had less luck the other day. He did have direct contact with the sample. The meltwater was even in his gloves. What if he got too high a dose? He's been pretty sick since yesterday."

"It's possible, yes. It should definitely be investigated," Robert agreed. He hesitated for a moment before continuing, then suggested: "Let's go to the station. I'm sure one of your colleagues has a Geiger counter." Robert knew that he was breaking the agreement to return to the U.S. base and report back when the work was done, but for the moment he was happy to accept a reprimand from Sattler.

"They have everything we need in the geology department. And I'd like to ask Dr. Keller to examine it for radiation exposure."

"And us too, just to be on the safe side," added Robert.

"Do you mean..." Nora started and didn't finish the sentence.

"Purely as a precaution. As I said, I don't think this dose of radiation could cause any real harm. But better safe than sorry, as they say."

"Then we'd better get going right away," Nora decided and turned towards the door.

18

Linda Shoemaker's apartment, Washington, D.C.
Evening of September 16

Linda Shoemaker did without her usual glass of red wine that evening. Although she could have used it for her frayed nerves, she wanted to keep as clear a head as possible when she looked at the results of the signal analysis. It had taken her former NASA colleagues' AI-based tool a total of four hours and three minutes to process all the material and compare it with the stored spectrum of potential patterns.

The sobering figure came right at the beginning: only 0.3 percent of the data contained decipherable information. After the initial disappointment, Linda tried to look on the bright side. Because 0.3 percent was more than nothing. And that in turn meant a small sensation, considering that the signal came from a microscopically small crystal structure. Linda was eager to find out what kind of information the A.I. had discovered in the signal.

The program first listed a list of numbers that it had extracted. Linda skimmed through them and tried in vain to find anything that looked familiar. Below the first list was another table in which all the previously listed values were assigned another number in brackets. And these numbers again looked very familiar to Linda. She sucked in a hissing breath and then breathed in disbelief: "Oh, shit!"

The list of bracketed values included the number 137.035999046. As a physicist, Linda knew that this was the reciprocal of the fine structure constant - a physical constant that described the strength of the electromagnetic interaction. In quantum electrodynamics, the fine structure constant also stood for the strength with which photons coupled to electrically charged elementary particles.

Next, she found the number 6.62607015 times 10 to the power of minus 34, which in turn corresponded almost exactly to Planck's quantum of action, a fundamental natural constant in quantum physics that expresses the relationship between the energy and frequency of a photon.

The list included countless other constants from physics and mathematics, such as the circle number P.I. with 3.14159265359.

Linda looked over at the bottle of wine from last night, which was still half full on the table. Maybe she should pour herself a glass after all? These results were too crazy. They had used the program at NASA to analyze all sorts of signals from space and never got anything close to such a clear result. She still couldn't believe it and scrolled down the results page.

There was an explanation of the relationship between the columns with the bracketed values and those originally contained in the data. The numbers did not appear directly in the signal, but could be extrapolated and converted by the A.I. based on their relationship to each other.

Apparently, it was based on a mathematical system that was not based on the number 10, but on 6. Accordingly, the constants it contained all had completely different values, but could easily be converted into the decimal system. They all matched the values calculated or measured on Earth to at least five decimal places.

Linda recalled the photographs of the crystals that Nora Grimm had taken and also those that Robert had discovered on Mars. The structures had all been hexagonal. Just a strange coincidence? Linda suspected it was more than that.

Robert had been right all these years. It was a life form—but not an exotic alien microbe or the Martian equivalent of a simple plant. The presence of these values was clear evidence of intelligence. They must have been deliberately placed in the signal to prove exactly that.

Mankind had made very similar attempts, even as early as the 19th century, when mathematician Carl Friedrich Gauss, for example, suggested planting plants according to the Pythagorean theorem that could be seen from the moon. There was also the idea of setting up mirrors in Europe to communicate with possible inhabitants of Mars. NASA later placed plaques on space probes such as Pioneer 10 and Pioneer 11 or the famous "Golden Record" on the Voyager 1 and Voyager 2 space probes, on which image and audio information was stored. In addition, dozens of radio messages were aimed at targets in space, the most famous of which was the Arecibo message, which was sent in the direction of the globular star cluster M13 as early as 1974. Logically, there has been no reply or other response to date, as the potential recipients were thousands of light years away.

But now Linda had something in front of her that could be interpreted as a very similar signal from an extraterrestrial intelligence. The main difference here was that the source was on Earth and not in the unreachable distance.

What should she do with this sensitive information? Who could it be entrusted to? The thought of Sattler's secrecy over the last few days and weeks made her uneasy.

Now Linda grabbed the bottle of wine and poured her glass more than half full. She looked at the contents for a moment and let the wine breathe. Then she took a big sip and made a decision.

***

When Robert and Nora returned to the Amarok II station in the late afternoon, the mood had improved noticeably compared to the previous day. The protective masks had disappeared, people were working on their projects and even joking around again. There was only a warning notice on Alex Corbinian's door stating that he was still in quarantine for the time being and that contact was only permitted after consultation with Dr. Keller and medical clearance.

While Robert went to Nora's lab to investigate the connection with Camp Century, Nora paid a visit to the ward doctor.

She wanted to talk to him as soon as possible about her concerns about potential radiation poisoning.

The door to the infirmary was half open, as usual, and Nora saw the doctor's short gray curls peeking out from behind the monitor on his desk. Keller was writing something on the keyboard.

"Am I interrupting?" Nora asked and stepped inside.

Keller looked up from the monitor and smiled. "No, no. I'm more than grateful for any distraction from this pesky paperwork. What is it?"

"I wanted to talk to you about the latest cases of illness."

"Ah, yes. I see. There's not much news. Steven has arrived in London and is being examined. I haven't heard anything yet about whether they've been able to find a reason for his collapse. And Alex, well... he's sleeping most of the day. I don't think it's anything serious. In consultation with Olofsson, I've ordered isolation as a precaution."

"But what caused his illness? Is it the flu?"

"I can't say for sure, we don't have a test facility to determine that. But I think it's likely."

Nora thought for a moment, then inquired: "Is it possible that something completely different is the cause? I mean ... I'm not asking that for no reason, of course."

"What exactly are you thinking of?"

"I took some very worrying measurements at our borehole today. The drill core we were working with is emitting significant radiation."

"What kind of radiation?" Keller wanted to know.

"Radioactive radiation. Alex came into direct contact with it."

The doctor frowned. "Well, I think it's rather unlikely that Alex could have been exposed to a dose that would cause serious radiation sickness. Naturally occurring elements emit relatively weak radiation, so he must have been in contact with them for a very long time. Acute symptoms only occur at high doses in a short period of time."

"But would the symptoms even fit?" Nora asked.

"Partially. That doesn't necessarily mean anything because the signs of radiation sickness are extremely varied and, at the same time, unspecific: nausea, vomiting, headaches, dizziness, tiredness, and fever. Almost everything also matches the flu. Alex, however, has none of the common dermatological symptoms such as reddening of the skin, blisters, ulcers or even hair loss - although the latter only occurs at very high doses."

"That reassures me a little," Nora admitted. "But maybe we can examine him anyway? And while we're at it, me and my colleague Greaves too?"

"Sure, why not? I can hardly imagine it, but there should be some residue if there has been significant radiation. Why don't you accompany me to Alex? I wanted to examine him again tonight anyway."

"Excellent! I'll go to Alex's geology lab and get a Geiger counter."

After a short detour, they set off and soon reached Alex Corbinian's quarters.

Keller handed Nora a face mask and put one on himself. Then he knocked on the door.

It only took a few seconds for Alex to open the door and smile at her. "Hey, good to see you, Nora."

She was quite perplexed. Alex looked dazzling, healthy and vital - the complete opposite of his appearance yesterday. "What ... you ..." She broke off.

Dr. Keller obviously didn't quite know what to make of his patient's apparent flash recovery either. "Can we come in for a moment, please?" he asked.

Alex nodded and waved them in. "I've just tidied up the quarters, it looked terrible here! Have a seat."

"Alex, what happened? Yesterday you had a high temperature and we thought you had to go to hospital. And now?" Nora asked, still puzzled.

"I know it's strange. But I feel great, not sick at all anymore."

Dr. Keller pulled a digital infrared thermometer out of his doctor's coat and approached Alex. "May I?"

Alex nodded, and Keller placed the device on his forehead. "36.8 degrees, perfect temperature," Keller stated shortly afterward.

"That's great! Then I can finally get out of this room again; it's getting a bit too cramped for me."

Nora exchanged glances with Keller and then looked back at Alex. "Um, don't think I'm crazy, but I've borrowed something from your lab that I'd like to try out." She pulled out the Geiger counter and held it up.

"What do you want with it?" Alex wanted to know.

"Testing you." Nora activated the Geiger counter and checked various parts of Alex's body, including his hands, which had been in direct contact with the sample. There was no increased radioactivity anywhere.

"You're clean," she said with relief and put on an apologetic smile.

"What was that about?" Alex asked, irritated.

"Purely a precautionary measure. We found radiation on the drill core, which is clearly measurable radioactivity. And then I thought you might have been exposed to too much of it, and that's why you fell ill."

"Seriously? Radiation from the ice? That's curious in the extreme! I can hardly wait to get involved again. I'll get to work tomorrow!" said Alex excitedly.

"Slowly," said Dr. Keller. "You should take it easy so that you don't have a relapse."

"I feel wonderful. It was just a short, severe bout of flu. Now I'm feeling great!"

"Yes, I can see that. But I'm still amazed. The course of events is more than unusual."

"I slept off the illness and my fabulous immune system did the rest," Alex replied.

"The medical advice is still for you to rest for at least another day. Of course, I can't forbid you from going back to work if you no longer have any symptoms of illness," Keller clarified. "But I am appealing to your common sense."

"I'll be careful," Alex promised. "But I still need to know what this material is all about. Even more so now!"

"I'm glad you're fit again, Alex," Nora said. "Let's have a quiet chat tomorrow about how we're going to tackle the rest of the investigation, okay?"

"All right," Alex agreed, "I can hardly wait."

Nora and Dr. Keller said goodbye and left his quarters.

"That's really strange," Keller muttered outside. "But I'm also glad that he's well again."

"Yes, and I'm relieved that my fears have been allayed," Nora replied, taking off her mask. "Thank you for your time. Let me know if there's any news from Steven."

"Will do."

They parted, and Nora made her way to her lab.

Robert was there organizing his research on the former Camp Century. When Nora came in, he looked up and gave her a smile. "Thank you for your trust," he said. "It's not a matter of course that you let me use your computer all by myself."

Nora frowned. "I think we're past that point. You also showed confidence today and let me in on it. And as far as I'm concerned, everything's fine for now - as long as Sandra Gillie isn't around." She paused and looked at Robert questioningly.

"I can't promise that we'll be rid of them for long. But I have to admit that I wouldn't mind the idea. You know, I would much rather have worked on it with Linda Shoemaker, an old colleague from NASA days. You can trust her."

"They probably didn't want you to come together as a team?" Nora said.

"Apparently. I can't think why, but there must have been a reason why I was supposed to travel here with Gillie instead. I certainly didn't choose it that way." Robert now put on a mischievous grin. "There's bound to be trouble, but I brought Linda on board anyway."

"How so?"

"We recorded these signals yesterday, which I wanted to analyze. The point is, I can't do it effectively myself. I don't have the resources, and I'm not an expert in the field."

"You sent her data! And what came out of it?" Nora asked impatiently.

"Unfortunately, nothing yet. I had hoped that she might have already emailed me the first results, but apparently the analysis is more complex than I thought - or it doesn't lead to any usable results."

"Then I guess we'll have to be patient. But I have some news. Alex is perfectly healthy again. Don't ask me how that's possible, but it is. He wants to look into the phenomenon of radioactive radiation tomorrow. As a geologist, he's far better qualified than we are."

"That's good news. I'm glad that it was probably just a harmless infection."

"Yes, me too. How I hate those face masks!"

"Absolutely, you can't properly assess people's facial expressions with these things."

Nora nodded and pointed to the screen in front of Robert. "Have you found out anything new?"

"I don't know yet. You mentioned that a study about a drill core from the 60s gave you the idea to drill here. So I looked for it and skimmed the paper. I wanted to know if there was anything in it that could help us."

"I've read through it so many times, I don't think that's the case."

"Right, there is no mention of electromagnetic radiation or radioactivity, nor do you read anything about crystal structures or anything else out of the ordinary."

"Well, it's not very surprising. They weren't looking for anything like that. And even if they had stumbled across it, they might have deliberately left it out because it had nothing to do with the actual aim of the research."

"Or maybe they just couldn't explain it and didn't want to compromise their work?" added Robert.

Nora shrugged her shoulders. "Pure speculation, I'd say."

"You're right about that. But I did find one thing interesting. The footnotes mention a certain Erik Jansson, who rediscovered the drill core and gave it to the researchers to analyze. I was just about to find out a bit more about him. But that turned out to be quite difficult. He is apparently Danish, but not a scientist."

"Strange, show me what you've got," Nora asked and sat down next to Robert at the table.

"Here, that's everything," he said, pointing at the screen.

"That's strange. I mean, ice cores like that aren't necessarily something you keep in your freezer at home. How could he even have got hold of it if he wasn't a scientist?"

"That's exactly what I was wondering. It seems really strange to me, especially when you consider where this ice presumably comes from."

Nora opened a few scientific databases and searched for Erik Jansson and various variations of the name. There was not a single hit anywhere. "Not a single publication, not in Denmark and not internationally. It would be very unusual for a researcher to have access to such a sample."

"We should contact him and ask where the core came from," Robert suggested.

"And how do we do that when there's virtually nothing about him on the net? Do you think he's in the phone book?"

"It's hard to say," said Robert. "It would be worth a try."

"I don't know. Even if I did, Jansson is a very common name in Denmark, not to mention Erik. There must be dozens ..." She fell silent. "But maybe..." Nora tapped on the keyboard and searched the address directory of the research network. "There it is!" she exclaimed happily.

"What?" Robert asked.

"Two of the scientists who analyzed Jansson's ice core are in our database. I was in contact with them last year about my research. It's just a guess, but if Jansson gave them the samples, they could very well have his email address or phone number."

"Yes, that's a really good idea. Can you ask them to make the contact? I'm pretty sure that man might know something."

"I'll write to them straight away and ask for it. And then we'll go and eat something urgently. My stomach is growling louder than a polar bear's," said Nora and set about composing the emails.

19

PRIN research station "Amarok II", Greenland
Night of September 17

When Alex Corbinian woke up from bed, it was pitch black outside the window of his quarters. The ice outside lay dead still in the arctic night, which seemed to have no end in sight.

Alex felt his heart pounding in his chest and his breathing was rapid and intermittent, as if he had just woken up from a horrific nightmare. And although he couldn't remember anything at all, his body's reaction told him that it must have been sheer horror. Only very gradually did his pulse slow down, and Alex stopped shaking.

He looked down at his hands and winced. The veins under his skin seemed to glow softly.

That was completely impossible! He must still be dreaming. A dream within a dream! How could he force himself to wake up? It was stupid, but Alex pinched his arm to wake himself up. But it didn't have the desired effect. Instead, the glow was now pulsing slightly, and Alex let out a startled groan. He threw off the covers, rolled over the bed, and switched on the lamp on the table next to it. The room was immediately bathed in warm white, diffuse light.

Alex looked skeptically at his forearms. They looked completely normal, no glowing, no pulsing. His hectic breathing finally normalized. It must have been a fever dream! Perhaps he hadn't quite got over the infection after all? Should he see Dr. Keller again tomorrow morning? Perhaps that would be a good precaution. He'd rather not tell anyone about the strange glow. God knows he had no desire to be locked up in his quarters again just because he was talking crazy. No, he would keep his mouth shut.

"I'm fine!" he said aloud, as if he could convince himself better that way. Surprisingly, it even had a certain effect. Alex managed to convince himself that he had beaten the illness and would be at work on time tomorrow. He switched off the light and slipped back into bed.

***

"What's the situation, Gillie?" asked General Frank Sattler impatiently, looking at the video image projected by a projector onto the narrow front wall of his bug-proof conference room. It was only 7:00 in the morning, but Sattler had already been in his office for almost two hours, waiting for the latest update from Greenland.

Sandra Gillie grimaced and rocked her head back and forth. "Suboptimal. It turned out as I suspected. Dr. Greaves didn't return to base last night. Instead, he went to Amarok Station with Nora Grimm. The two of them continued their work there. The surveillance is spotty, just as I feared."

"Do we have reason to believe that he is trying to hide something from us?" Sattler asked.

"I think there are several reasons to be concerned. He drove from the landing site to the borehole, but set off again shortly afterwards together with Grimm."

"Where to?" Sattler interjected.

"I don't know. I don't have access to the GPS device on the snowmobile. He took it with him to the Amarok. All I know is that they were gone for three-quarters of an hour. It doesn't necessarily mean anything. But it could also be that he met someone secretly."

Sattler nodded silently. He secretly suspected what the real explanation might be. Greaves was highly intelligent and good at research, he could make connections and draw the right conclusions. That was why he had brought him on board. Sattler was pretty sure that Greaves had paid a visit to the former

Camp Century. He didn't know why, but Gillie's second objection reinforced his suspicions.

"I must also inform you that Greaves involved Linda Shoemaker without authorization. To make matters worse, he sent her a copy of the data collected on Greenland so that she could analyze it. We should take urgent action in this regard."

"Hm..." Sattler grumbled, wondering what to make of this development. Shoemaker had been on his team for two years and had never disappointed him. She was highly professional and had always behaved loyally. However, he didn't want people working behind his back. He would probably have to have a serious word with her.

"So, what should we do with her?" Gillie asked.

"Nothing," replied Sattler. "We're not doing anything for now, we're letting them work with the data. I'll take care of the rest myself. Has she found out anything yet?"

"Well, it looks like it. I've just sent you a copy. I'm not an expert, but the results seem pretty conclusive."

Sattler turned to the laptop in front of him on the conference table and opened his mail program. He downloaded the data sent by Gillie and unpacked the archive. He stared at the results for a while, reading the lines over and over again.

"Sir?" asked Gillie.

Sattler looked at the video image on the wall. "Good work. That's just the confirmation we needed to move on to the next phase. Prepare everything and make sure there are no unforeseen difficulties."

"And Greaves? He could very well cause problems."

"Let him carry on for now, his progress speaks for itself."

"Whatever you say," said Gillie with audible displeasure in her voice.

"Yes, as I say!" Sattler repeated sharply.

"Anything else?"

"No. Let me know everything tomorrow."

Sattler ended the video call and turned back to the results on the laptop. There was the confirmation he had been looking for for so long. The key to the secret that had plagued him for over 50 years - ever since the day a sergeant came to the door and told his mother that his father would never return from Greenland. He was only 16 then, but had always known that such bad news could arrive one day. But he could never understand it. The Air Force had no credible explanation as to how his father had died. There wasn't even a body for them to bury.

Sattler couldn't remember exactly when he had made the absurd decision to join the army when it had brought his father nothing but a far too early and mysterious death. It could only have been because he wanted to know more. But even when he had risen quite quickly in the hierarchy, everyone involved in the project had continued to stonewall him. It was not until 1997 - 30 years after his father's death - that he learned some of the background. And they were fascinating and frightening at the same time. It took another 15 years before he was finally in a position to find out the whole truth. Sattler knew that this was selfish in the extreme and that he had had to lie to so many people that it could hardly ever be justified, but he had had to do it. He wanted to know what had happened and who was to blame for the catastrophe of 1967. And now he was about to find out, with the help of Greaves, Shoemaker and Grimm. As for Gillie, he was sure his authority was enough to keep her in check long enough.

Sattler reached for the phone next to his seat at the conference table and pressed a speed dial button that connected him to the site's administrative assistant. "Megan, please check the scheduled supply flights from Andrews to Pituffik for the next three days and reserve a seat on each of the planes."

He did not wait for the assistant to confirm the instruction, but hung up again immediately. Sooner or later, he would have to see for himself, even if he still secretly had qualms about traveling to the place that held his father's cold grave.

***

Linda Shoemaker felt quite silly as she made her way to the Woodridge Library in Washington, D.C., early one morning. This was one of 28 public libraries in the city. Woodridge wasn't the closest one from her point of view, but it was the one where she knew someone.

As she maneuvered her car through the morning rush hour, she kept having doubts. Were these precautions really necessary? After all, she wasn't a spy and shouldn't have to hide her findings. But that was normally the case - her gut feeling told her that she was currently quite far from it. The public library in Woodridge was the ideal place to store a backup copy of the analyses. Finally, the infertile dates of the last few years were paying off, because she had met Mike, one of the librarians there, on one of them. Mike was a quiet, pleasant person who was a pleasure to talk to, but a little too boring for Linda's taste to seriously consider a relationship with him. But they had kept in touch and occasionally had a drink together. Nothing more had ever happened, and Linda was glad about that.

But now she needed Mike's help to let her in before the official opening time of 9 a.m. so that she could stow an old-fashioned CD-R in the archives. Linda had deliberately chosen this medium because nobody would be interested in such a data carrier today, when downloads and streams were the means of choice.

But Linda not only wanted to hide the copy, she also wanted to send the results to Robert's private e-mail address from a public computer so that he would be aware of what she had found out. This was to be done as secretly as possible, as she was still not sure what Sattler and Gillie were really after - and whether they should be trusted with this data.

Linda parked her car a few streets away from the library and walked the rest of the way. She headed for the modern building's wide, glass front door, which looked a bit like a dozen concrete cubes glued together at an angle. An overhanging, semi-transparent roof stretched around the building. Behind the glass at the entrance, she recognized Mike, who was obviously waiting for her.

A quick glance at the clock told her that it was 8:10 and that she had a good three quarters of an hour to get everything done and have a coffee with Mike. She just hoped he wouldn't ask too many questions.

Mike opened the door and invited her in. "The early bird catches the worm," he said and locked the door behind her.

She found his quirk of constantly throwing around proverbs rather annoying, but had finally accepted it. "The early bird catches the worm," she replied and Mike smiled as expected. "Thank you for making this possible," she continued. "It's really important."

"No problem, I'm always here an hour early anyway to sort books and process pre-orders. But of course, I'm still curious as to what could be so urgent that you have to come to the library so early."

"I need you to keep something for me."

"These are sentences that nobody wants to hear. You inevitably think of drugs, weapons or top-secret documents."

"You read too many thrillers," Linda replied.

"That's right. But still. If you have something to hide, there must be a reason, right?"

"There is one. I don't want anyone to secretly make this data disappear before I've had a chance to fully analyze it. It is possible that they will lead to explosive developments."

"Why would ..."

"Mike, please," Linda interrupted him. "It's nothing criminal. Just a backup copy of scientific analysis. I'd be happy if that could suffice as an explanation." She pulled out the CD case and held it out to Mike. "Here, that's all. Can you put it somewhere in your stocks where no one will find it?"

"Yes, of course. We have a whole shelf full of old computer programs and educational videos that hardly anyone ever borrows."

"Perfect, then we'll just put them on the shelf there inconspicuously." She looked at Mike encouragingly.

"Okay, let's go." He led her through the aisles to the back of the library, which was still in semi-darkness. The automatic lighting was switched on and bathed the rows of shelves in a pleasant, slightly golden light.

"Here we are," Mike announced and grabbed a cover from the top shelf. Judging by the design of the cover, it had to be the long outdated version of a graphics program. He took out the CD and held the cover out to Linda.

She inserted her self-burned data CD and Mike placed the original program CD over it. "Thank you, Mike. I'll return the favor."

"I hope so. Dinner at Pepe's?"

Linda nodded. "Agreed, I'll invite you." She paused for a moment, then added: "Can I use one of your computers?"

Mike frowned. "Well ... I actually thought you'd earn enough to be able to afford your own, but ..."

"It'll be very quick," she promised, without responding to the objection. "I just need to send someone an email. Nothing illegal!"

"That's the second time I've heard that today. It somehow doesn't seem very credible when it's always emphasized like that."

Linda smiled and shrugged her shoulders sheepishly.

"Well, come along then. They're at the front." Mike showed Linda the computers and started booting them up one by one. "Do you have time for a coffee?"

"Sure, I always make time for coffee."

Mike left to get two cups, and Linda pulled a USB stick out of her jacket pocket. She plugged it into the computer and loaded a password-protected ZIP archive into the attachment of an email to Robert Greaves. She wrote a few brief lines and pressed "Send." As soon as the webmail page confirmed the dispatch, Mike was standing next to her with the coffee.

"With milk, no sugar," he said, handing Linda a cup. "Will you be longer? I need to organize a few things in the front."

"No, I'm done." She pulled the memory stick out of the USB port and stood up. "Come on, I'll help you. As a little something in return."

Linda and Mike worked through the orders together for about ten minutes, then all the day's preparations were done for the time being.

"If you ever get tired of research, I'm sure I can get you a job here," joked Mike.

"Yes, we'll see. You never know how career paths will develop." Linda hadn't meant it seriously, but even as she spoke these words, she realized how quickly they could come true. She was currently treading a dangerous path by withholding information from Sattler. But she was convinced that it had to be done. "Okay, Mike, thanks again. Now I have to go. We'll talk about dinner when we get a chance, all right?"

"By all means, I'll nail you on it." He took her back to the door, where several visitors were already waiting for the library to open. "I guess today is International Early Bird Day," Mike remarked and unlocked the door. "Well, I'll let the reading-hungry crowd in then. Take care, Linda. It was good to see you."

"I thought so, too. See you soon!"

While the first visitors streamed in, Linda left the library and made her way back to her car. She looked at her watch again. It was quarter to nine. She would definitely be at work early enough not to arouse suspicion. Then, she would try to find out whether Sattler already knew anything about her research.

She had almost reached her car when a man stepped out from between the parked cars and stood in her way. He was wearing a black suit and a light blue tie. "Miss Shoemaker, do you have a moment?" the man inquired.

"That doesn't mean anything good," Linda was still able to say when she heard the screeching of tires. A black limousine with tinted windows stopped abruptly on the road.

Linda panicked and rushed away, back towards the library,

but after just a few meters she bumped into a second man in a black suit who grabbed her by the arm.

"Stop it, you bastard," she snapped at him and kicked him hard in the shin.

But the man did not loosen his iron grip one bit. Then she felt her free arm being grabbed from behind.

"Don't make such a scene, we just want to talk to you undisturbed," the man explained calmly but firmly. "Get in the car. Please."

"What if I don't feel like getting in the car with you agents?"

"Then we may have to use force," explained the second man, who was still squeezing her wrist.

Meanwhile, the limousine had driven a few meters further up to their level.

"The sooner you realize that it's pointless to resist, the better," said the first of the black-clad agents, pointing to the rear right-hand door of the car. It was opened from the inside at that moment.

The agents no longer waited for Linda to make a decision, but gently pushed her towards the car and forced her inside.

The door was slammed shut from the outside. One of the agents got into the front, and then the limousine sped off.

20

PRIN research station "Amarok II", Greenland
September 17

The light of the new day struggled against the gloomy, stormy gray that seemed to be approaching the Amarok station from all sides. The endless icy expanse of the Greenland glacier shrank more and more into a compact knot, in the middle of which the research station appeared to be constricted.

Nora Grimm and Robert Greaves had just sat down to breakfast in the canteen with station manager Olofsson. They had to plan the day ahead. Alex Corbinian had actually wanted to join them, but he was probably still in his quarters.

Nora decided to give him a little more time. Despite the spontaneous improvement in his state of health yesterday, it was quite possible that he was still a little under the weather and needed to get a good night's sleep. She didn't want to force him to return to full work today, even though she would very much like to use his expertise to investigate the phenomenon of radioactive radiation.

Olofsson put down his coffee cup and cleared his throat. "Dr. Greaves, I must apologize once again for not having had the opportunity to talk to you sooner, but the last few days here have really been unusually turbulent. But it looks like we can make up for it now."

"Yes, I'm also pleased that we're finally getting to know each other," Robert replied.

"I've looked through Nora's reports and support her view that we're dealing with an extremely unusual phenomenon here. But of course, you already know that. Probably much longer than I have, otherwise you would hardly be here." Olofsson paused for a moment.

Nora was already familiar with this quirk. Olofsson did this to let his words sink in and to invite the interviewer to jump on the bandwagon.

But Robert countered with a brief nod, followed by a smile.

So Olofsson continued. "I also don't want to hide the fact that the latest news about the radioactivity of the material found makes me suspicious. And it worries me. Do you know more about it than I do?"

"No, I want to be completely honest. This is a completely new aspect. However, my previous analyses were very limited as I didn't have direct access to the samples. Nevertheless, no such radiation has been observed so far."

"The samples we brought to the station the first time don't give off any radiation," Nora added. "We've also decided not to bring any more material here, but to carry out the analysis at the outpost for the time being. That should minimize any risk as much as possible."

Olofsson glanced at the window, behind which an impenetrable gray wall had formed. "The weather today doesn't look as if a trip to the drilling site is particularly advisable. So much for minimizing risk."

"We'd best wait a while, maybe it'll clear up again," Nora said. "Alex is anyway..."

"Alex should still be resting. When Dr. Keller told me yesterday that he was practically fully recovered, I almost didn't want to believe it. The day before, we were still considering whether he would have to be flown out."

"I think that's off the table now. If he feels well, he should be able to work again. We will need his expertise. Robert and I are biologists, not geologists or physicists," Nora replied.

"Of course, I'm well aware of that. But as station manager, I'm responsible - for you and for him." He looked at Robert. "As for you, well ... In principle, you can do whatever you like. As long as you don't endanger any of my colleagues."

"Nothing is further from my mind. I'm just interested in finding out more about this phenomenon," Robert assured him. "And we're making good ..."

He was interrupted by Ian Macmillan, who rushed into the room and addressed Olofsson directly. "Per, one of the snowmobiles is gone! I was just about to refuel them all when I noticed that number 3 is no longer in the garage."

"Is there nothing in the logbook?" Olofsson asked.

"Would I barge in like this otherwise?" Macmillan asked back.

"That's not possible! Do people think we're doing this for fun? We're surrounded by a desert of ice, every trip has to be registered so that we can react in an emergency!" Olofsson got up and went to an intercom installed next to the door. He pressed a red intercom button. "Good morning everyone, please listen in. I've just been informed that one of our snowmobiles is missing, and there's no entry in the logbook. Anyone who knows anything about it, please let me know immediately. Olofsson out." He returned to the table where Nora and Robert were still sitting. "I guess breakfast is over. Let's hope we don't have to spend the day searching."

"I have a bad feeling," Nora said now. "Alex wanted to have breakfast with us, but ..."

"Do you think he ... All right, let's go and see!" Olofsson interjected, pointing in the direction of the exit.

They left the canteen together and made their way to Alex's quarters.

Olofsson pounded impatiently on the door with his fist. "Alex, is everything all right? Open up, please."

Nothing happened.

"Alex, it's us!" Nora now tried.

They listened for a moment, but everything seemed quiet inside the quarters.

"We're coming in to check on you now, all right? You'd better put your pants on quickly!" Nora shouted.

Olofsson waited a few more seconds, then pulled out his

electronic ID card, which could unlock all the doors on the station like a master key, and held it in front of the reader. It beeped, and an LED on the device lit up green.

Olofsson pressed the handle and opened the door. Followed by Nora, he entered Alex's quarters. Robert and Macmillan stayed in the background.

"Alex, are you in the shower?" Nora asked. But she saw straight away that there was no light on in the bathroom. The rest of the room was also in twilight.

Olofsson flicked on the light switch and they immediately realized that there was no one in the room. The bed was rumpled and there were some clothes scattered on the floor, as if someone had dressed in a hurry.

Olofsson reached under the comforter. "Totally cold. He must have been gone for a while."

Nora frowned worriedly. "That doesn't make any sense. Why would he get up in the middle of the night? And where is he now?"

"I think it's reasonable to suspect that he took the snowmobile," said Robert, who had stepped into the doorway.

"What for? Where could he want to go?" Olofsson asked.

"I can only think of one halfway plausible destination," Nora replied. "The borehole. Yesterday, he said he couldn't wait to get back to work."

"That's no reason at all to take a vehicle without permission. And then all alone and in this weather," Olofsson grumbled.

"We'll go out and look for him," Nora suggested.

But Olofsson shook his head. "First we have to be sure it's him. We'll gather everyone upstairs in the panorama room and do a head count. When the weather gets a bit better, you can check the borehole for all I care. And if you find him there, tell him he's in for a thunderstorm!" Olofsson left the quarters and beckoned Macmillan to follow him.

"It was one hundred percent Alex," Robert insisted. "I can't imagine why he would do something like that, but my gut feeling is that it was. And I can't see any other plausible explanation."

"I'm right there with you. But it's still incredibly stupid," Nora agreed. "It doesn't suit Alex either, he's usually so levelheaded. Something must have happened."

She walked around the room, perhaps trying to pick up another clue as to what could have caused her colleague to leave in such a hurry. But everything seemed normal, relatively untidy, but not unusual. Then, her eyes caught on a piece of paper lying under the desk chair. She went over and picked it up.

Robert approached her and also glanced at the note, which had been written in quick, almost illegible handwriting. "Can you read it?" he asked Nora.

"I think so. If I'm not mistaken, it says: ‚They are inside me' - and further down it says ‚They eat ...'. I can't decipher the last words. Could mean anything."

"What does he mean? Did he write that in a fever?"

"Possibly, yes. But to be honest, I find this note extremely frightening. There seems to be something very wrong with Alex."

Robert nodded. "That's why we should find him."

"That's true, but we can't do it without Olofsson's permission. It's best to wait for the meeting, then we'll know whether we can go on the search."

"I hate this waiting," said Robert, dissatisfied. "I'll go and have a look around."

"Okay, let's meet up later," Nora suggested.

While Robert set off to investigate Alex's disappearance on the base, Nora paid a visit to her lab to study the weather forecast.

Nora had just booted up her laptop when a pop-up appeared on the screen announcing a video call. It was Nora's professor at her university in Munich, Katja Westerhoff. Nora hurriedly sat down and accepted the video call. Westerhoff's face appeared. However, it looked paler and more nervous than usual and showed hardly any of the relaxed friendliness she normally displayed.

"Good morning, nice to talk to you. I wanted to get in touch, but things have come up here. Is there any news?" Nora asked.

"Yes, you could say that. They're pretty worrying developments, to be honest. The material you sent us. It's…" She faltered.

"What about that?" Nora asked.

"Well, strictly speaking, we shouldn't have done anything else without your permission, but we did a few more experiments with it. It was a once-in-a-lifetime opportunity."

"That's all right, it's not a problem!"

"How you take it. There were problems, but they started later. But first things first. At first, it was really fascinating. This material has remarkable properties. It can react both exothermically and endothermically. It even acts as a catalyst. We've never seen anything like it. It can change the chemical and physical properties of the materials around it so that they react in very unusual ways."

"You mean, for example, massively shifting the melting point or boiling point of water?" Nora asked.

"Yes, exactly. That's how it started. We observed this phenomenon and wanted to investigate the effect further. Dietmar, of all people, was the one who pushed this forward, even though he was so skeptical at first. He really wanted to decipher the behavior of the material and come up with a theory."

"Once he throws himself into something, he's unstoppable," Nora agreed with her.

"Right, and I let him do it. Well, we carried out various experiments and discovered enormous potential in this material."

"But that's good!" said Nora.

"Yes, perhaps. At least it's very interesting. But … how should I put it? There are inconsistencies that we haven't been able to clear up. You remember Dietmar's first theory? That it's an artificially produced nanotechnology?"

"Yes, but as I've already explained..." Nora interjected.

"I have to ask," Westerhoff intervened. "Could it be that we're in the middle of a case of industrial espionage or something similar?"

Nora looked at her professor, puzzled. "So ... what do you mean? What makes you think that? The suspicion Dietmar expressed that it could be nanocoating seemed absurd to me from the start. How could such technology get deep into the ice?"

"Yes, I understand your doubts. Dietmar didn't think so recently, but he still wanted to make sure. And it's very worrying what happened next. You know, Dietmar is in hospital."

"Oh no," Nora gasped, "what's happened?" She immediately thought of Steven and Alex, who had recently fallen ill inexplicably. Had something similar happened to the colleague from Munich?

"Don't panic, he's doing comparatively well. Yesterday he wanted to take the material to a specialist laboratory in Garching, where he knows someone personally. The sample was to be further analyzed there. The laboratory has facilities that we don't yet have here at the university and much more experience with high technology. They regularly work for industry, testing nanotechnology and the like. Dietmar simply wanted to know whether this material could be of artificial origin."

"Yes, that was a good idea. What came out of it?" asked Nora.

"Nothing came of it. The samples never got there. Dietmar had a traffic accident on the highway on his way there. He wanted to take the samples there in person, and on the way, someone apparently drove into the back of his car with full force. Nothing bad happened to him, but the car was wrecked. He spent a day in hospital because of his bruises and a slight concussion. I reckon he'll be back to work in a day or two."

"But I can still hear a ‚but'," Nora said.

"That's right. Because the samples are gone. He had them in a transport case in his car. The fire department couldn't recover it. He seems to have disappeared without a trace. Hence my question about industrial espionage. Do you think someone staged this and then stole the material?"

Nora thought for a moment, and the image of Sandra Gillie immediately appeared in her mind. But it couldn't have been her. She was far away from Munich. But who knew if she had hired henchmen there? Nevertheless, she dismissed the idea. "It could be a coincidence or an accident. Maybe someone from the rescue services has misplaced the suitcase and it turns up again?"

"Yes, of course that's possible. But there's more that doesn't fit the picture."

Nora raised her eyebrows. "Like what?"

"There was a major outage on our servers. The hard disks on which the research data is stored were completely destroyed. According to our IT department, most of it is irretrievably lost. And your data was so new that it wasn't even included in the backup. So there's only what I sent you and a few printouts that are here in the lab. I can scan them and email them to you, but I don't think that will be very good. We had high hopes for these new analyses."

"That is indeed curious and no longer sounds like a coincidence," Nora admitted. "I want to get new material anyway. Maybe I can send you more samples that you can analyze. But that's a bit difficult at the moment because some unforeseen things have happened here and the weather isn't playing ball. In any case, I'll be in touch as soon as it's possible to get more samples."

"That would be best, even if I don't know whether we should actually investigate further. The whole thing seems risky."

"You're right. We should think carefully about our next steps. Give Dietmar my best wishes and tell him to recover well. I'm sorry he's been hit like this."

"Don't worry about him, he'll be fine. The guy's tough!" Westerhoff looked at her for a moment, then continued. "Nora, please be careful. This could all be out of your league."

"I'll be careful."

"Also because of this material. I said that it has enormous potential. That may even have been an understatement. I believe that, under the right circumstances, it could act as a kind of super catalyst. It could trigger all kinds of reactions, such as melting large quantities of ice. According to Dietmar's calculations, a few grams are enough to turn tons of solid ice into water, even at sub-zero temperatures. Well, you know best what that could mean in your current environment."

Nora nodded slowly and thoughtfully. "Thank you for your candor. Although this is very disturbing news. The pronounced temperature anomalies in the ice have also given me pause for thought. I just didn't think it could have such drastic consequences. But if your assessment now confirms this ..."

"It certainly looks that way." Westerhoff tilted her head. "You're clever and you'll do the right thing. Let me know if we can support you."

"Thank you, I will. And send Dietmar a box of chocolates from me, please!" Nora asked.

"Wouldn't you prefer a crate of beer?" Westerhoff asked.

"That's not my style," Nora replied with a grin.

"Also true again. Take care."

"Likewise."

Nora ended the video call and sat in front of the silent computer for quite a while. These were indeed very ominous developments and gloomy predictions. Despite all the evidence, she hoped they would be inaccurate - but her gut feeling told her otherwise.

***

The base commander of Pituffik, Gordon Hastings, came storming into Hangar 23 of the base with a grim look on his face. "Gillie!" he shouted angrily. "I think we need to have a talk." His face had taken on a color clearly too red to be healthy.

He headed straight for Sandra Gillie, who gave the commander a quick glance but immediately ignored him again. Unmoved, she gave a troop of soldiers further instructions on what equipment they had to load.

"You obviously think you can do as you please here?" Hastings became agitated. "You're commandeering my men, tying up resources and vast amounts of equipment. What's the point?"

Gillie reached into her jacket pocket and pulled out a sheet of paper, which she unfolded and calmly held under the commander's nose. "You must have gotten a copy, right? If not, I'll ask again."

Hastings snorted contemptuously. "Stop your damned political games. I don't give a damn, nor is this my base! I want to know what's going on, for fuck's sake!"

"It's quite simple. It's all in there. I'm standing in for General Sattler until he arrives here in person. You are instructed to give me your full support in the preparations."

"Preparations for what?" Hastings asked sharply.

"This is beyond your security clearance, I'm sorry."

"Bullshit!" Hastings roared.

Gillie just shrugged her shoulders. "You can get as upset as you like, but you'd better not delay the project. It could have unpleasant consequences for your career."

Hastings narrowed his eyes, but said nothing in reply. He looked at the equipment his soldiers were loading onto three large snowcats. "Will you at least tell me where this stuff is being taken? I hope you know that Greenland is sovereign. We can't do what we like with military equipment. I don't want you to start an international incident."

"You just said that you're not interested in political games. So please leave that to us. Besides, who's going to control this up here? Have you seen any sign of Greenlandic state power out on the ice?"

Hastings did not answer the question. He himself knew very well how things were going on Greenland. "When is General Sattler arriving? I need to speak to him personally as soon as possible."

"In the next few days. I'm sure he'll let you know."

Hastings shook his head and looked at Gillie doubtfully. "I just hope you know what you're doing here." Then he turned and left the hangar with brisk steps.

Outside, Hastings let the icy wind blow in his face and was grateful for the cooling. He knew that his blood pressure was too high, that he got excited too quickly, that he didn't think as rationally as he needed to - especially when it came to someone like Sandra Gillie. She was opaque, played her own game, and had powerful supporters high up in the hierarchy. That went against his grain the most. He should be the unrestricted commander at this base. Pituffik might be in the proverbial ass end of the world, but it was his base, dammit! He was supposed to know everything that was going on here. But it wasn't like that! Hastings realized that his throat was swelling up again, and he was getting caught up in unproductive thoughts.

He shook himself and loosened his limbs, then switched to a run. He would now do a lap around the hangars and cool his head. Then, he could take his time to find out what Gillie and Sattler were doing here.

21

PRIN research station "Amarok II", Greenland
September 17

The meeting of all station staff revealed that the crew - with the exception of Steven Dryer, who was in hospital in London, and Alex Corbinian - was complete. No one had seen Alex get up or go to the vehicle garage that morning. That suggested that he had left very early - possibly even in the middle of the night.

One of the weather cameras installed on the roof of the station confirmed this suspicion. At around 5:10 a.m., it registered a light that could only have come from the garage door opening. As it was pitch black outside at this time, the camera had not been able to track the direction Alex had taken with the snowmobile due to the lack of night vision. The only thing that seemed clear was that he hadn't been back at the station for over three hours and had been driving alone through the icy landscape of Greenland in sub-zero temperatures and windy conditions.

To Nora and Robert's displeasure, Olofsson did not agree to a search operation due to the recent increasingly violent storm. He calmly accepted Nora's protest and promised that they would be allowed to set off as soon as it was safer to do so.

"Great," Nora grumbled as she and Robert made their way to the lab after the meeting. "And now we'll just leave Alex out there on his own."

"I understand that you're unhappy, but Olofsson is right. There's not much point in going out in this driving snow. Visibility is practically zero. We'd probably get lost too."

"Yes, of course I know that. But it still gets me down."

"What exactly?" Robert asked, stopping in front of the lab door. He turned to Nora and looked directly at her.

She swayed her head back and forth. "Oh, I think I might be blaming myself for bringing him into this project. And..." She faltered. "It's probably stupid, but I have a bad feeling that our discovery has something to do with his strange behavior."

Robert raised his eyebrows. "Strange thesis, but not to be refuted. Some strange things have happened."

"Exactly. Including your appearance here. No offense, but it didn't exactly go strictly according to plan. And then there was another thing with my colleague in Munich that I hadn't told you about. He got into a traffic accident, not entirely by chance, when he was on his way to a special laboratory with my samples. I can't prove it, but in my opinion it smells like something Sandra Gillie did."

"That sounds more than worrying. But I don't see how we can deal with it other than to continue pursuing our goal. We have to stay focused and take it one step at a time. So I think the first thing we should do is see if you've heard back about the contact with Erik Jansson," Robert suggested.

"You're right, we don't need any more distractions. Then let's do this. We can't do much else," Nora agreed and entered her lab, followed by Robert.

A reply from Nora's Finnish colleague Ekki Sikanen was indeed waiting for her in her inbox. He was one of the researchers who had done research with Jansson's drill core. Nora opened the message and read it. Unfortunately, the content proved to be less than pleasant.

"Well, that was probably a bit of a dead end," Nora said, showing Robert the contents of the email.

Robert skimmed the lines and made a rather dissatisfied face.

Sikanen wrote that he was not allowed to give out the Dane's contact details. He explained that Jansson had expressly forbidden him to do so. He did not have more than a cryptic e-mail address anyway. Instead, he had forwarded the request to Jansson and asked him to contact Nora directly. The drill core had been transported by a courier service at the time - with a company sender address that certainly did not belong to Jansson.

Now, a "ping" from the computer reported the arrival of another message. It came from the sender c-c-1967@duckmail.com and had the subject "Ice Age".

Nora was taken aback. Either it was a spam message that had accidentally passed through the filter, or Erik Jansson had actually contacted her after Sikanen's request. The sender and subject seemed both appropriate and mysterious.

"I hope it's Jansson and not a hacker," Nora said and clicked on the message. It contained no salutation or other text, just a link that led to a video conferencing platform. "Well, what now?" she asked Robert.

He advised her to move her mouse over the link, and it will show the actual destination without her having to click.

Nora did as she was told and the mail program identified the link. "Seems authentic. The address matches - and I know the provider of the video chat, we use it a lot. So I can hardly imagine that it's a fake."

"Then the colleague obviously wants to talk to us in person, which is a good sign," said Robert.

"I hope it's worth it," Nora replied and clicked on the link.

The video client already installed on the computer was automatically opened via the browser, which immediately started to establish a connection. Nothing happened for a while, then the previously black image came to life.

A man with snow-white, cropped hair in a light blue shirt appeared. Even over the heavily compressed video link, Nora could see that he had countless wrinkles on his face and was probably quite elderly. "Dr. Jansson?" she asked, "Can you hear me?"

The man tilted his head and replied in a sonorous, pleasant voice. "I'm not a doctor, but yes, I can hear you. I assume you are Nora Grimm?"

"Yes, that's right. Nice of you to get in touch right away."
"Who is your colleague?" Jansson wanted to know.
"Robert Greaves," Robert replied. "I'm a biologist - and a specialist in exobiology."
Jansson raised his eyebrows. "And Americans, if my hearing doesn't deceive me."
"That's right. I used to work for NASA, but now I'm working with Nora on a really tricky case here on Greenland."
"So it really is Greenland," Jansson interrupted him. "I had suspected it."
"Sorry to catch you off guard like this," Nora intervened, "but we were really hoping that you could tell us a little more about the origin of the ice core from 1967 that you gave to Ekki Sikanen and his people."
"Why do you want to know about it?" asked Jansson.
Robert took the floor. "Well, we think you may have some important information about the circumstances under which this drilling took place and ..." He paused. "And whether there were any special occurrences. Unusual emissions or ..."
Jansson raised his hands and ordered Robert to remain silent. "Those are rather explosive questions. And the answers would be potentially dangerous."
"So something happened back in 1967 at Camp Century - just before it was evacuated?" Robert asked.
"I've checked you both out," Jansson said calmly. "Miss Grimm's story is true, but you, Dr. Greaves, you've been breeding mustangs in the Idaho wasteland for six years. And suddenly you turn up on Greenland. That's a bit unusual, isn't it? Hadn't you finished your research?"
Robert looked at the old man, puzzled. "Well ... I," he stammered.
"It's all right, I know what's going on. It must have something to do with the US military and very probably also the Secret Service. A profession I happen to know quite well. I worked for the Danish secret service until I retired 17 years ago."

"Then it's as we suspected. You're in deeper than you seemed to be. And it explains how you got the information about us. Nevertheless, as scientists we are interested in much more, for example how you came into possession of the drill core. And since you have decided to contact us directly, I assume that you would also like to tell us something about it," said Robert.

"You're right about that. But it's a long, drawn-out story. I don't want to go into it in detail now, so I think it's enough to tell you that I was there at the time. Fifty-six years ago, when the Americans disbanded Camp Century, I was there as a liaison officer for the Danes. I was young, and that was my first big assignment. I was officially sent on this mission as a scientist because of my background, but secretly, I was working as a kind of spy. I was supposed to keep an eye on what the USA was doing on Greenland, which still belonged entirely to Denmark at that time."

"That's incredible," said Nora in amazement. "You were there yourself? What exactly happened?"

"As I said, it's a long story, and most of it is irrelevant to you. It all got out of hand back then. I still don't know exactly what caused it, but I do know that the whole base was cleared so quickly that only an accident could have been responsible. At first, I thought it might have been the nuclear reactor, which had been causing problems from the start. But it was taken away during the evacuation. They wouldn't have done that if it had caused the problem. There was also this unusual meltdown, which was said to have been caused by the missiles stationed at the base. This caused the underground buildings to sink and buried everything under snow and ice. It was a tragedy because not everyone made it out alive."

"Buried alive under the ice? That's a terrible idea," said Nora, shaking her head. "Didn't they try to save the people?"

"On the contrary. It would have been pretty pointless to try anything. They just poured more ice on it and hoped the world would forget about the place. I also kept quiet for decades, but a few years ago, I happened to receive a message from a former US colleague who was dying. He asked me to have the ice core analyzed. I should have done it long ago, but I never had the courage."

"Why did your colleague want it to be analyzed?" Robert asked.

"Because he - and I too - suspected that answers could be found in it. A cause for what happened there at Camp Century."

"But they didn't find anything?" Nora speculated.

"Only what you undoubtedly read in the study," Jansson replied. "That's why I'm honestly very curious about what you were able to discover. It must have led you to me in the end."

"In short, there's more than just ice under the glacier," Nora said. "And I don't mean the organic remains that have been deposited on the bedrock. The bottom layer of ice contains ... well, what's the best way to put it? They are crystals that exhibit quite unusual behavior."

"Interesting when a biologist uses the words crystals and behavior in the same sentence," Jansson replied.

"I realize that, and I deliberately phrased it that way. But you don't seem particularly surprised. Or is that just your trained secret service coolness?"

Jansson grinned. "Point taken. It's a bit of both, I think. Did you happen to notice a glow? It could have been pink or purple," Jansson asked.

"Yes, when the crystal fragments merged into a larger structure, there was a flash of light that had exactly these colors. After that, however, nothing more happened," Nora explained.

"We recently carried out a second test," Robert added. "And it turned out that not only visible light is emitted, but also electromagnetic signals and - what is particularly worrying - radioactive radiation."

Jansson nodded slowly and deliberately. "That's far more than we could find out with the resources available at the time.

Apart from the fact that we didn't have enough time to investigate the phenomenon in detail before the leaden cloak of silence was spread over everything."

"From whom, if I may ask?" Robert asked.

"What's the saying? From the very top. These decisions were always beyond my pay grade. And in Denmark, we only knew half the truth anyway. Because as far as you Americans were concerned ... You could never really be trusted."

"That may be true as far as the politicians are concerned," Robert replied. "But I'm a researcher and only committed to science."

"You are a tool, a pawn for some of these bigwigs who are pursuing their own interests. Don't be under any illusion that they will let you continue your research for a second if it doesn't suit them."

"Thank you for your frank words," Robert said with audible discomfort in his voice. "I'm aware that there are limits to my independence here. But I want to use every millimeter of leeway!"

"You should be careful," Jansson advised. "Also, for the sake of your young colleague. I'm 82 years old, what do I have to fear? I can venture out of cover. But you, Miss Grimm, are at the beginning of your career."

"I ... I can take care of myself," Nora replied, realizing herself that it didn't sound very convincing.

She suddenly thought of Steven Dryer, who had collapsed and fallen into a coma a few days ago without warning. The talk about secret services and the military gave her a nasty suspicion. What if this Sandra Gillie really had had something to do with it? She had been on the station when it happened. And she hadn't been with them in the lab, but had been traveling alone on the Amarok. She could very well have bumped into Steven and ...

Nora pushed these thoughts aside. It could just as well be paranoia! In Jansson's direction, she asked: "What do you think we should do now?"

"Well, I can't tell you that. You know more about the phenomenon than I do. But I can give you something that tells you more about what happened in 1967."

"What is it?" Robert wanted to know. "A secret file?"

"Not directly. There should certainly be one, but I never got hold of it. But there is something unofficial. I told you about the colleague who has since died. He left me his diary from his time at Camp Century. He also left me a notebook in which he later recorded his own theory about the incident."

"Can we see it?" asked Robert.

"The things are stored in a safe deposit box in Copenhagen. I could get them and take them to Greenland."

"We can't ask you to do that," said Nora.

"You mean to say my age?" Jansson grinned again. "I'm in great shape for my 82 years, I'm perfectly capable of boarding an airplane."

"I'm sorry, I didn't mean to offend you," Nora said.

"That's all right. If you promise to provide me with all the information you have obtained, I will bring you the diary. I'll have to do it personally, because I don't trust a postal service or a courier in this case. And the contents are irreplaceable."

Nora looked at Robert questioningly. "Well, it's not a problem for me, I haven't signed a non-disclosure agreement. Only Robert already has one foot in prison."

"Fuck Sattler and Gillie," Robert blurted out. He was clearly fed up with having his hands tied all the time.

"Did you just say, Sattler?" Jansson asked in surprise.

Robert nodded. "I shouldn't have mentioned his name. But it all goes so much against the grain! Frank Sattler is the general who commissioned me to investigate this phenomenon."

"Well ... then this matter could take on a whole new dimension. If it's the Sattler I'm thinking of, it could very well be that his father was also in Greenland. Or we could be lucky, and it's just a coincidence."

"How likely is that?" Nora asked in an ironic tone. "The way this whole thing has gone so far?"

"I guess that's what we have to find out," said Jansson. "I'll get the records out of the locker today and be on my way. I'll let you know as soon as I know when I can be there, and I wish you both good luck in the meantime."

"Thank you, but please only come if you're absolutely sure," Nora said.

"There can be no absolute security. I have to come. Before I die, I want to be certain."

"Thank you," Robert replied.

Jansson ended the video call, and the screen went black again.

"Well, that was a very interesting conversation," said Nora, looking at Robert.

"You could say that," he agreed. "If Jansson really does have records from that time, it might give us some clues as to how we can avoid such a fatal development as happened in 1967."

"But I also found it quite unsettling," Nora admitted.

"We'll be careful," Robert promised. "But I think it's too late to back out now anyway. We're too deep in the story."

"You can be really encouraging. It's a good thing I'm an optimist by nature!"

"That's commendable. You should keep that."

"Don't worry, I will. Now let me check the weather. Maybe we can head out to the borehole soon and look for Alex." She opened the weather service website and updated the forecast for today.

Robert cleared his throat. "That doesn't look good," he said after glancing at the screen. "That's why I wanted to make another suggestion. But you probably won't like it." He took out his satellite phone and placed it on the table.

"You're right, I don't like it," said Nora.

"Not for me either. But at the US base they have helicopters that can fly even in very bad weather. They're equipped with thermal imaging cameras and other high-resolution sensors. I could ask for help so we can look for Alex. Regardless of Olofsson's authorization."

Nora grimaced. The suggestion made her stomach ache. She was glad that Robert had come to her without Sandra Gillie. And now he wanted them to contact her and go off with a squad of soldiers? Nora was a self-confessed pacifist and had nothing to do with military operations. She detested what so-called superpowers were doing all over the world to supposedly keep the peace. It was always just about power games, resources or getting rid of old stocks of ammunition. But she also realized that the forecast looked too bad to go out on a snowmobile. They could get lost in one of the dreaded whiteouts. In response, she just shook her head silently.

Robert took the floor again. "We should do it. It was just a guess that Alex drove to the borehole. But he could just as easily have lost his bearings somewhere in the middle of the glacier. The circumstances of his disappearance are quite unusual. What if he hadn't recovered and just stormed out in a fever?"

"I know!" Nora agreed. "That scares me too. He could have frozen to death by now."

"Then we shouldn't waste any more time. We'll deal with the consequences later."

"Great attitude."

"Very simple pragmatism. You wouldn't believe how many times I've been offended by that. Many of my conservative colleagues have a problem when you leave the beaten track and do things differently in order to achieve results."

"Yes, I believe that straight away. I've always had to assert myself against the old men who have been stuck in their chairs for ages. Despite all her successes, a young woman is often not trusted to do so much in this profession. You have to constantly prove yourself." She looked Robert in the eye for a moment, then glanced down at the phone. "So let's just try pragmatism. I guess that's absolutely appropriate in a place like this. Give them a call. I'll let Olofsson know."

22

Interrogation room at CIA headquarters, Langley, Virginia, September 17

The door of the windowless, barren room was opened, and an African-American man of about 50 in a black suit came in with two cups of coffee in his hand. He placed one of the cups on the gray Formica table in front of Linda Shoemaker and then sat down on the second chair opposite her.

He smiled at her. "Go ahead and drink it. It's caffè latte with two sugars, just the way you like it."

Linda didn't touch the cup. "You like the role of the know-it-all, don't you?" she asked pointedly.

"I'm CIA; I'm omniscient," the man replied, laughing at his own joke.

Linda ignored the lousy joke as well as the coffee. "What do you want from me? This kidnapping can hardly be legal. I'm sure you know I'm employed by the Air Force. General Sattler won't let such an assault go unchallenged."

"Assault? So please! You're only here for a confidential meeting. As soon as it's over, we'll take you back to D.C. to work."

"A meeting, yes? Then your manners leave a lot to be desired!"

"They ran away, if my agents have informed me correctly. But let's not go there. I haven't even properly introduced myself yet. I'm Luther Bradshaw, head of department at the Agency."

"Head of department for what?"

"Let's call it special internal investigations. Officially, I'm part of the Directorate of Science & Technology."

"You don't exactly look like a scientist."

"I'm not either. But I have enough expertise to evaluate what you have found out."

"What did I find out?" Linda asked.

"How long do we want to play this game? It will get us nowhere if you refuse to cooperate."

"Then start talking plainly," Linda demanded.

"We have intercepted your e-mail to Robert Greaves. He will not receive it."

"What gives you the right to do that?" Linda roared.

"National security."

Linda couldn't suppress a short laugh. "That was obvious! But both Greaves and I signed a strict confidentiality agreement, and General Sattler ..."

"But you didn't inform him!" Bradshaw intervened.

Linda fell silent. The agent was right. She had concealed both the analysis and its results from Sattler.

"You see, that was a good thing," Bradshaw said with a smile. "That's why you're here."

Linda frowned. "That ... I don't understand anything now."

"I want to be completely open. We want you to continue in exactly the same way and work for us."

"You want me to spy on Sattler?"

"I wouldn't call it that, we'd just like you to do us a favor or two."

Linda tilted her head. "Tell me, could it be that Sandra Gillie is also part of your club?"

"You're clever, Miss Shoemaker. Gillie is a very well-trained agent. We've placed her on Sattler's staff to keep track of his activities. There have been concerns for some time about the way Sattler is overstepping his authority. And the latest findings shed a whole new light on the matter. We cannot leave such a discovery to a man like Sattler alone. This is of greater importance."

"Then why did you withhold the message to Greaves? He was supposed to get this information!"

"What do you think?" Bradshaw asked back, smiling.

"You're trying to put pressure on me!"
"Motivation is the magic word."

Linda shook her head. She could hardly believe that she was now apparently in the middle of an intelligence operation and that they wanted to recruit her as an unofficial informant. But that was the case. She doubted that Luther Bradshaw would just let her walk out of here if she refused to cooperate. So what options did she have? She had to make sure Robert got the results of the analysis. Otherwise, he might still be in the dark about what he was really dealing with. And who was to say whether this discovery might not be just as dangerous? The fact that the CIA was so interested in the project spoke volumes.

"I see you're weighing up your options," Bradshaw interrupted her thoughts. "That's a good sign. You'll realize that it's best if we pool our skills."

Linda thought that was an outrageous glossing over of the situation. She was given no real choice in the situation. Could she trust the CIA more than Sattler? All she knew was that she trusted Robert - and that he in turn trusted her. And she could only help him if she got the CIA people to pass on the information to Robert. So the agent was right, she had to cooperate or let Robert down.

Linda sighed heavily. "Okay, what exactly do you want me to do?" she asked grudgingly.

***

A ghostly glow crept up the borehole, pulsating and bathing the area around Alex Corbinian in a surreal twilight. The glow from the ice was the only source of light in the PRIN outpost, where Alex had been motionless for hours. He felt no pain in his fingers, even though he was touching the bare ice directly. On the contrary, he only felt a pleasant warmth and a kind of deep connection in his whole body. But that was as good as anything that could penetrate his foggy mind. Alex didn't know where he was, what he was doing and certainly not why. He couldn't even ask these questions, as if his mind had been folded down to a primitive level where only instincts and emotions existed. It was as if only his cerebellum was responding to stimuli while the rest of his brain was sleeping off a drunken stupor.

Crackling and snapping sounded from the ground beneath Alex's feet. They, too, were bare and stood directly on the icy ground at the edge of the borehole. The pinkish-purple glow from the ice continued seamlessly under Alex's skin. It ran along the veins from head to toe through his body, making it look like he was made of frosted glass.

A roar from the depths of the borehole made the ground tremble, the glow swelled until it almost reached the brightness of a sunny day. Then there was an abrupt roar, like a dozen simultaneous lightning strikes, followed by dead silence. The light disappeared almost completely, only Alex's body continued to glow for a moment before the light from his veins went out.

He finally woke up from his trance. It was dark! Icy. His hands and feet ached as if they were in a hot frying pan. His nervous system was overstimulated, hot and cold blurred, Alex gasped and collapsed to the floor. Where the hell was he? Panic rose up inside him. He couldn't remember anything. He had just been in his soft bed! And now? This was hell. He finally realized that it was freezing cold that threatened to paralyze his body, not heat. He must have frostbite! How could this have happened?

He struggled to get up, got hold of something and pulled on it. It had to be a chair. He bravely heaved himself up and finally escaped the icy ground. He forced himself to calm down and fought down his panic. There was something behind the chair, a work surface. Blindly, he groped around on it. Papers, equipment, pens, tools. Then, finally, a flashlight! With stiff fingers, he tried to press the switch and it took what felt like an eternity. Then he succeeded. The light pushed back the omnipresent darkness.

Alex saw his boots on the floor and pulled them towards him. His feet were as white as snow. Another surge of panic came up. He painfully slipped into the boots. Would he be able to walk? His whole body was trembling.

Now, he limped to the light switch and flicked it on. Further ahead, he saw his hat and gloves lying on the floor. He grabbed these too and put them on. That wouldn't help much if he was already hypothermic and frostbitten, but it was better than nothing.

He remembered the first aid instruction. There was a first aid kit at the back and chemical heating pads that could be activated simply by bending them. That could save his life!

As quickly as he could, he limped to the back corner of the workshop area and tore open the door of the first aid box. Three heating pads! He bent the metal plates inside and within seconds the previously liquid contents solidified into a kind of wax. He took his gloves off again and put his hands around one of the pads. At first, the warmth felt like acid being dripped onto his skin. Alex let out a hoarse cry that echoed off the ice walls. But things gradually got better. He stuffed the remaining two pillows into his boots, gritted his teeth and hoped for the best.

At last he was able to think reasonably clearly. He absolutely had to get help! He would never make it back to the station on his own. Not in this condition!

He didn't know the details of the outpost's technical equipment. Was there a permanently installed radio or just the usual handheld devices that were taken on snowmobile trips?

He looked around carefully, then his gaze lingered on the borehole. Something was wrong here. There was no ordinary circular shaft in the ice, as expected, but rather a funnel that was now almost two meters in diameter at the upper edge. Such a thing was simply impossible. There was no device here that could drive such a large hole in the glacier. It would require a huge drill head like those used in mining. And he knew that Nora's drill was barely more than 15 centimeters in diameter. So how on earth could such a gigantic opening be created?

Alex limped closer and realized that something else was strange. The surface of the funnel was smooth as glass. A borehole should have roughened edges and irregularities, but this looked more like an ice rink melted bare with warm water. But there was nothing here to generate such large quantities of warm water! Who or what had caused this change?

Alex was startled when he suddenly realized that he was the only one who could do this. There was no one else here. And for the life of him, he couldn't remember how he had got here. Was it an extreme form of sleepwalking? He almost laughed out loud, but it stuck in his throat. Because he remembered the eerie glow he had observed in himself that night. He had thought it was a confused dream, but now it was clear: something was wrong with him! Could he still trust himself, were his senses playing tricks on him? Was he so hypothermic that he was hallucinating?

It all had to be a nightmare that he couldn't wake up from. Alex knew it was nonsense, wishful thinking. His pain was too real to have come from a dream. He wanted to slap himself for his childish stupidity. But that wouldn't help at all. He had to grit his teeth and help himself. With difficulty, he reached the airlock that led outside and pulled the zipper of his jacket as far up and his cap as far down as it would go. Then he put his hand on the handle and pulled.

***

The skids of the bulky military helicopter swung violently back and forth in the storm, while the pilot slowly lowered the aircraft further and further towards the icy ground.

"Snowmobile 20 meters in front of us, touchdown in about 10 seconds," the pilot reported over the on-board radio.

"Get ready to get out!" ordered Sandra Gillie.

Robert and Nora were sitting in the crammed helicopter

with half a dozen soldiers and a large load of equipment. They could hardly wait to get out of the noisy, rocking vehicle - even if it meant going out into the storm.

But if everything went smoothly, in less than a minute they would be in the protective surroundings of the outpost where the wanted Alex Corbinian must be. His snowmobile was parked not far from the entrance and was already half covered in fresh snow, which meant that it had been here for some time.

The helicopter touched down with a jolt, and the soldier on the far right immediately opened the sliding side door. The military crew jumped out and immediately began to unload the equipment.

Gillie beckoned Robert and Nora to get out as well.

"Now we'll get some clarity," said Nora, "I hope Alex is okay!"

Robert nodded.

The two of them pulled their hoods up over their faces and followed Gillie's instructions. They ran towards the entrance, crouching. One of the soldiers accompanied them with a rifle over his shoulder.

Nora took the lead and pulled open the outer airlock door. She was startled. Alex was lying motionless on the floor in the airlock, his face almost completely drained of color. She tried to feel his pulse, but could only guess at best. Alex was breathing very shallowly.

"He's far too cold, do you have a medic with you?" she asked in Gillie's direction.

Gillie nodded to the soldier. "Get him, quick!"

"We have to fly him out to the base," Robert said.

"Negative. First, we'll get an overview and secure the facility," Gillie replied.

"But we don't have time for that, just look at Alex!" protested Nora.

"We'll get him inside, the paramedic will find out what's wrong with him and whether he's fit for transport. You don't want to expose him to any unnecessary danger."

Nora bit her lips, but accepted the answer. "Come on then! Everybody lend a hand." She opened the inner airlock door and grabbed Alex's left leg.

Gillie took his right leg and Robert both arms. They dragged him inside. At the same time, the soldier came back with the paramedic and a stretcher. They put it down, and the others put Alex on it.

Now, the paramedic set about examining the unconscious man.

Nora and Robert took a step back and let the man do his work.

"What was he thinking, driving out here alone?" Nora asked, shaking her head. Then she turned around to find a clue as to what Alex had wanted here. Then she froze. Where there had only been a hole as thick as an arm in the ice on her last visit, there was now a gigantic crater. "What..." she began, unable to understand how this could have happened.

Robert stood next to her, as did Gillie. They all stared wordlessly at the large funnel-shaped depression, which only narrowed to its original diameter in an estimated 20 meters.

"Do you see that too?" Nora wanted to know.

"What, the huge hole?" Robert asked.

"Yes ... No..." Nora stammered, "Down there. I think something's glowing."

Robert narrowed his eyes and peered down. "Yes, could be that ..."

Gillie promptly turned on her heel and pulled the radio from her belt. "This is Gillie at the Alpha site. Contact confirmed. Initiate Epsilon protocol and accelerate!"

Robert and Nora stepped up to Gillie. "What does that mean?"

"I won't bore you with the details," Gillie said coolly. "Make your way to the back."

"Excuse me?" Nora became agitated. "After all, this is still our location. You have no instructions to give here."

Gillie made a contemptuous expression. "You're not going to throw us out in this weather, are you?"

"What about Alex?" Robert asked.

Gillie gave the paramedic a questioning look.

He stood up and reported. "He's hypothermic, but as far as I can see, he's not hurt any further. I've given him something to stabilize his circulation. We've wrapped him in blankets and will slowly warm him up in them."

"Right, carry on!"

"Listen, that's not enough! He has to get out of here urgently," Nora demanded.

"No, sorry. From now on this place is sealed off, nobody leaves here," Gillie announced.

"On whose orders?" Robert wanted to know.

"A rather stupid question from a supposedly clever man. From General Sattler, of course. You'd better be glad that you can still be there." She looked at Nora. "And you too. I would have removed you from the project long ago. But now that Dr. Greaves has been so careless as to let you in on classified information, we have to keep an eye on you."

Gillie didn't wait for an answer from Robert or Nora. Instead, she turned and walked to the door, where two soldiers were standing by. "I want the first temporary barracks up in an hour at the latest. Everyone will then gather there. The whole area around the borehole will be declared a restricted zone and can only be entered with permission."

"Understood, we'll assign guards immediately. The helicopter is already on its way to fetch more material."

"Very good!"

Further back, near the workshop table, Nora dropped into a chair. "It was a great idea to call that bitch," she muttered.

Robert sat down next to her and sighed. "I'm sorry, I didn't know anything about it. You'll have to take my word for it."

"Yes, that's all right, at least we found Alex. It probably wouldn't have made any difference whether we contacted her or not anyway. It was obviously all planned beforehand. They would have occupied this facility, with or without us."

"I fear that too. But look on the bright side. We found Alex in time and are still involved. We may be able to influence the further course of events."

Nora gave Robert a skeptical look. "I did say that I'm an optimist by nature, but this ..." She left the sentence unfinished and looked back at the borehole. "I guess we've got other problems, if I'm interpreting the developments over there correctly."

23

Sattler's base near Washington, D.C.,
September 17

General Frank Sattler closed the file with Gillie's last status report and closed his laptop. Tonight, he will set off on the supply flight to Greenland and thus initiate the decisive phase to complete this project. Until then, however, he had to bridge some time, which he was currently finding quite difficult.

He had spent years making plans for this moment, patiently researching and putting together puzzle piece after puzzle piece, meticulously steering his career in the right direction and even delving into the depths of political intrigue to achieve his goals. Now all the preparations were done, there was practically nothing left to do. All that followed was undiscovered country for which there was nothing to prepare.

Sattler looked around his office and wondered whether he should take anything else with him. But nothing really seemed necessary to him. Any equipment he might need had been transported to Pituffik - or was already on its way to the site from there.

Now Sattler opened his desk drawer, where a gold pocket watch lay on top of the secret dossier on Camp Century. It had belonged to his father and was the only sentimental heirloom he had allowed himself to keep. He took out the watch and flipped open the lid. Inside was an engraving that his mother had made.

"Time seems to stand still without you. With love, Eleanor." These words still made Sattler uncomfortable, even though they were meant lovingly. They meant loss, waiting in vain. And they reminded him that his mother had never recovered from the news of her husband's death until she died eight years ago.

Nevertheless, Sattler did not have the heart to have the engraving polished out. The watch had been a gift to his father for their first wedding anniversary. His mother had known that a whole series of foreign assignments were coming up, and Sattler's father was always supposed to remember that the family at home was eagerly awaiting his return. But he had left the watch behind. It had never traveled to Greenland with him, which was the reason it still existed at all. Perhaps he should take it with him and sink it in the ice?

A knock on his office door made Sattler look up. He closed the lid and pocketed the watch. "Come in!" he called out.

The door opened and Linda Shoemaker entered. "Do you have a moment, sir?"

Sattler pointed to the free chairs in front of his desk. "Have a seat."

"I want to ask again: do you have any news from Robert Greaves? I haven't been able to reach him for days."

Sattler frowned and did not answer immediately. He wondered what the question was about. Of course, Shoemaker had been in contact with Greaves. He had even sent her data - which she had secretly analyzed. She just couldn't know that he was aware of it and that he had the results that Shoemaker had obtained.

"Dr. Greaves is doing well. Gillie reports that they're making excellent progress," he said evasively.

Shoemaker nodded. "Yes, that's what I think. He wrote to me, but that was two days ago. And since then..." She fell silent and started again. "General, I have something to tell you."

Sattler raised his eyebrows with interest and leaned forward. "Or would the word confess perhaps be more appropriate? You know, when I was a teenager, I once had the absurd idea of becoming a priest."

"I..." Linda smiled sheepishly. "It's like this: This morning

I had an involuntary conversation with someone from the CIA."

Sattler was actually surprised. Shoemaker didn't want to tell him about Greaves' data. "Go on," he demanded.

"They basically kidnapped me off the street and took me to Langley. There, they interrogated me and put me under pressure. They wanted me to work for them."

"Ha! To do what, please?" Sattler wanted to know.

"It's about you, sir."

"Of course!" Sattler narrowed his eyes. He had made many enemies on his way to the top of this commando. "Who was the agent you spoke to? What exactly did he want you to do?"

"He ... he didn't give his name," said Linda. "I was so perplexed that I didn't ask. They all looked the same: black suits and sunglasses, almost as clichéd as in the movies."

"Yes, take it easy. Now, please tell me what he wanted!"

"The CIA knows we've sent people to Greenland, but apparently they're wondering what we want there. They want me to provide them with internal information and an assessment of your plans."

"Which you haven't done, I hope!" Sattler replied sharply.

Linda winced at the tone of command. "No, of course not. I told the guy he could forget it."

Sattler looked at Linda in silence for a moment and weighed up whether he could trust this statement. "I knew it was a mistake for Gillie to use her old connections."

"Sir?" Linda asked.

"She created cover identities for herself and Greaves with the help of the CIA. That was to convince the PRIN network researchers to let Greaves work with them. She assured me that it was absolutely discreet, but obviously it attracted too much attention from the wrong people. And now that Gillie is far away, you've been snapped up to work as an informant."

"Which I don't! I came straight to you after they took me back to Washington."

"That's commendable, but I see a problem."

"In what way?"

"You have withheld information. Important analysis results." Sattler paused and waited for a reaction from Linda Shoemaker.

"That's not true!" she defended herself.

"Yes, it's true. I have a copy here." Sattler placed his right hand on the closed laptop on the desk.

"But ... if you mean the data Robert sent me, I just analyzed it yesterday, and I wanted to send it to him first so he could validate the results."

"Good try," countered Sattler. "You know it can't be done like that. Why didn't you carry out the analysis here on site, where we can ensure adequate data security? Instead, you did it at your home, where any backyard hacker can get in - not to mention the damn CIA! You'll have to forgive me if that made me very suspicious."

"But sir, I ..."

Sattler waved it off. "Maybe I also contributed to it taking this course."

"You have to understand that it is extremely difficult and unsatisfactory for scientists like Greaves and me if we only get fragments. The natural urge to explore forces us to keep probing. We want to know the truth. And if I'm honest, what the analyses reveal is incredible. You've seen the data, and I assume you know what it means?"

Sattler nodded. "Of course."

"Then let me fly with you, please!"

"Where do you want to go?"

"To Greenland, of course. They're leaving tonight. Megan has already put it in the calendar."

"That wouldn't be a good idea," said Sattler curtly.

"On the contrary. You need people with expertise to investigate this phenomenon. We need to take an interdisciplinary approach. Actually, we should get NASA on board immediately, this discovery is ..."

"Enough already!" Sattler intervened. "We're not going to

involve NASA - or anyone else. It's annoying enough that the CIA is snooping around. This is my project and therefore my decision."

"I didn't mean to question it," Linda defended herself. "But if we do this alone, you'll have one more reason to take me with you."

"I should rather have you placed under arrest after you tried to withhold information from me," Sattler replied unimpressed.

"General, I will be absolutely loyal if you let me..."

"No. I can't have any more variables in my equation. You stay here and deal with the results of the analysis. That's as far as I can accommodate you. Your best bet is to try to decipher the rest of the data from the recording."

"But what about Greaves? I'm sure he needs support."

"I'll make sure he gets everything he needs. Now get out of here before I reconsider the detention." Sattler stood up and pointed to the door.

Linda now stood up as well. "Then have a good journey, sir. I hope everything goes smoothly."

The general nodded silently, and Linda left the office. He stayed behind alone and thought again about Shoemaker's words. He already knew that not everything would go smoothly up there. Something like that seemed completely out of the question on a project like this. But Sattler was still confident that he would steer everything in the right direction when the time came.

***

It was now afternoon on Greenland. Robert and Nora were sitting together at the back of the temporary barracks that the US Air Force had erected just over 20 meters from the entrance to the drilling station. Apart from a guard at the entrance, they were alone after Alex Corbinian had been transferred to a medical barrack that had also been set up about an hour ago - still unconscious at the time.

Through the small window on the side of the barracks, Nora could see that half a dozen more buildings had been erected in a semicircle. There were probably even more on the other side, with no window. As they had been strictly forbidden to leave the building, she was unable to check. She had seen several large snowcats building a meter-high wall around the entire area to keep out the wind and probably also to prevent unauthorized entry into the arbitrarily defined security area. These were certainly preparations for the night that would fall in a few hours.

Nora turned away from the window and looked at Robert, who was leaning against the wall on a cot, deep in thought. "Did you know about these plans?" she asked.

It took Robert a moment to react. Then he looked at her, frowning. "Sorry, what did you ask?"

"Forget it, it wasn't that important. What are you thinking about?"

"Oh, I only have a gripe with myself for being so naive as to get involved with the military. I probably really believed that they would let me investigate this phenomenon in my own way. But it's not going to work out that way!"

"No, certainly not as long as we're stuck in this hut."

"But we're still here. That can only mean that they need us. Otherwise, we would have been taken away by helicopter long ago."

"I don't know if that's such good news," said Nora. "I've been thinking about it for a while now, and I have to say: this change in the borehole worries me. It can only be due to these crystal structures. They have reacted - I don't know to what, but to a much greater extent than before in the laboratory."

Robert nodded. "Yes, and Alex was obviously there. Too bad we can't ask him what happened."

"We'll be lucky if he gets halfway back to health. I could jump down that Sandra Gillie's throat for not letting him fly out!"

"It's no use getting worked up about it. We need to keep a cool head and develop a theory about what exactly is happening here."

"I know. But it's damn hard to ignore this anger."

"Please try."

Nora let out a long, deep sigh and massaged the back of her neck. "All right, then. Let's get the facts together. What do we know?"

"To all appearances, crystals are the cause of the phenomenon - purely inorganic compounds. But their behavior is reminiscent of life forms. They emit radiation, visible light, radioactivity, electromagnetic ..." Robert fell silent.

"What is it?"

"The signal we recorded! I sent it to Linda for analysis. But I didn't get any results. And now we're stuck here and have no way of contacting her. Damn."

"Then we'll just have to ask Gillie to do it," Nora suggested.

Robert lowered his voice. "I didn't tell her about it. Linda was supposed to do the analysis discreetly."

"Phew. You seem to have adapted quickly to this secretive game," Nora commented dryly.

"Unfortunately. But I was afraid that they would want to boot me out or take away my access to the material."

"Which is exactly how it turned out, isn't it?"

Robert made a pained expression, but refrained from replying.

Instead, Nora made another attempt. "Okay, let's assume for a moment that there really is a completely alien life form down there. Then, it's only logical that it has needs. It probably needs certain environmental conditions to exist and has to feed itself in one way or another. It may even want to reproduce. We are at the very beginning of our observations and cannot say what this life form wants."

"That all sounds very plausible," Robert agreed. "At least if you start from what we know as life on Earth. Of course, it's possible that an extraterrestrial life form could exist according to completely different rules, but there should still be certain parallels that we can discover."

"If they let us."

"That's right. We should make sure of that."

"And how?"

"We're gambling. Or bluffing, if that suits you better. We pretend to know more than we actually do. Then Gillie will let us get on with it."

"Very scientific."

"Pragmatic. I told you so."

"And what are we pretending to know?"

"Well, I've been thinking about this funnel and the deviating temperature measurements. It seems to be an exothermic reaction. These crystals give off heat and affect the surrounding ice. Or rather, the ice in which they are encased."

"Wait a minute, I just remembered something ... an experiment we did back in school. An incredible amount of salt was dissolved in a small amount of water by slowly heating the solution over a long period of time. And as soon as the liquid had cooled down, you only added tiny crumbs of the salt and could practically watch the rest crystallize in the solution. I probably memorized it because there were such beautiful star-shaped rays."

"As far as I know, they like to do it with sodium acetate, the salt of acetic acid," said Robert. "And I know what you're getting at. When the salt crystallizes again, it releases the heat it previously absorbed. There could be a similar effect here. We may have provided the trigger that set the process in motion."

"You mean through the drill?" Nora asked.

"I think so. It's probably to do with the state of the water. Before you drilled down there, there was only solid ice, kilometers thick in every direction. But if I understood correctly, your drill failed because it was overloaded. It probably hit something hard and could have generated enough frictional heat to melt a small amount of ice. That acted like the tiny grains of salt in the experiment."

"That's a more than useful theory!" Nora noted with satisfaction. "There was an initial unexplained failure on the drill a few weeks ago. Maybe we triggered something back then."

"But if this theory is correct, I'm also worried."

Nora nodded. "Because of the chain reaction."

"Think of this funnel over by the borehole. The surface was as smooth as glass, as if you'd gone over the ice with an iron."

"With a huge iron," Nora interjected.

"What if this was just the beginning of a larger melting process?"

"So we'll soon be sitting in a lake? Is that what you're saying?"

Robert shrugged his shoulders. "I don't know. No one can say how far these crystalline particles have spread under the ice and how far such a reaction would reach. It still seems fairly limited to me at the moment, but ..."

"... but it would be good if we could find a way to stop them if necessary?" Nora finished the sentence.

"Yes. Think about the history of Camp Century. They may have faced a similar problem."

"That would at least mean that it is theoretically possible to stop the process."

"I would be very interested to know how that was done. Unfortunately, we can no longer get hold of Jansson, who might know," said Robert.

"Because we have to sit around in this hut," Nora added grumpily. "That brings us back to the beginning of the misery. If only we could manage to inform the people on the Amarok. Then they might be able to contact Jansson and your colleague Linda. And they could inform the Greenland authorities about what the Americans are up to here."

"That's probably pretty hopeless. Gillie took the satellite phone from me, as well as the laptop, which she was probably monitoring anyway. She was too well-informed and always one step ahead of us. I should have guessed that."

"Don't blame yourself, you've been screwed just like me and everyone else involved in this," Nora replied angrily.

"Do you think Olofsson will send someone on the search today? It should be noticeable if we don't turn up again."

"Well, that's all right. The storm seems to be slowly abating, but he'll probably still wait until nightfall to see if we come back or get in touch. That also means he probably won't do anything until tomorrow morning."

"And when he comes here, he encounters a massive military presence. Even the Greenlanders have little to counter this. The Air Force has far more resources."

"I can't help thinking of Jansson's disparaging words about you Yanks," Nora said.

"Yes, I know," Robert replied wanly. "Anyway, I guess we're on our own for now. Gillie and Sattler have tried to take the piss out of us, as you put it so nicely just now. Then it's probably high time we screwed them back a little."

"All right, then. We've got nothing to lose anyway."

24

*Not far from the Woodbridge Library, Washington, D.C.,
Afternoon of September 17*

Shortly after General Sattler had left his office and set off for Andrews Air Base, from where he planned to fly to Greenland that evening, Linda Shoemaker had called in sick and disappeared from the base. The previous conversation with Sattler had not been ideal, but it had not been as disastrous as she had secretly feared.

CIA agent Luther Bradshaw's plan, on the other hand, had not worked out. Despite her openness, she hadn't convinced Sattler to take her on the trip. But that wouldn't stop her from getting involved. She had long since decided that she didn't care about the motives of either Sattler or the CIA. What mattered to her was, firstly, that this discovery was not swept under the carpet and, secondly, that Robert came out of this venture, which she had personally persuaded him to undertake, unscathed. She could slap herself for having been so gullible. But that couldn't be changed now.

Linda planned to drive to Washington-Dulles International Airport, from where she would fly to Nuuk in southern Greenland at 5:20 p.m. - on her own and at her own expense. She had already turned off her cell phone at the office and had not packed a laptop. Since her encounter with the CIA, she no longer trusted digital devices. She had already been tracked and intercepted once. She didn't want that to happen a second time. She therefore only used public transport and not her own car, which might also be fitted with a tracking device.

Under normal circumstances, Linda would have found this load of precautions rather absurd and inconvenient, but now they seemed absolutely necessary. Especially since she wanted to stop by the library on her way to the airport and get the backup copy of the analysis results. She had to ensure that Robert received this data in a way neither Sattler nor the CIA could control.

She got off the bus at a bus stop not far from the library in Woodbridge and walked quickly towards the entrance. She entered and looked around searchingly. There was no sign of her boyfriend Mike, not behind the counter, not even by the computers.

Linda went to the counter and approached a young student who was obviously helping out. "Hello, quick question, is Mike still here by any chance?"

"No, sorry. He left half an hour ago, he started very early today."

"Ah, exactly. Um... Never mind. I just wanted to borrow something."

"I can just about manage that," said the student jokingly.

"Yes, of course. Of course you can do it."

Linda turned around and walked the length of the library. From the shelf with the software CDs, she took out the one in which they had hidden the home-burned data CD this morning. With that, she made her way back to the circulation desk. But she stopped halfway there. What if the employee checked the contents and found the CD that didn't belong in there? Linda turned to a shelf and inconspicuously opened the case. She removed the program CD and stopped.

"Shit," she cursed quietly. Her CD was gone.

"Are you looking for something?" asked a vaguely familiar voice. She turned and looked into the mischievously grinning face of Luther Bradshaw. "Or do you actually need a ten-year-old graphics program?"

Linda didn't say anything back, just scowled at the CIA agent.

"Come on! Do you think we'll let you out of our sight for a minute? We're the damn agency. You can turn your cell phone back on now. And then let's make sure we get out of here, we don't want to miss our flight, do we?"

"Ours..." Linda shook her head.

"That's how it is. You and I are flying together. That was plan B from the start, after you failed to initiate plan A."

"That was hopeless. Sattler is suspicious by nature. The chances of him taking me with him were almost zero."

"That's why Plan B. And now come along. There's a car waiting outside. Or do you really want to take the bus to the airport?"

"I'm still thinking about it," Linda replied defiantly.

Bradshaw crossed his arms in front of his chest. "Don't be childish. We both want the same thing: to keep Sattler in check and bring Greaves the data."

"Yes, you say that, but who can guarantee that I can trust you?"

"Nobody," Bradshaw replied curtly and put on his grin again. Then he walked past Linda towards the exit. "And put the CD back. We won't be needing it."

A few minutes later, Linda left the library, where the same black limousine was waiting for her as on her first encounter with the CIA people. She decided that there was no alternative but to put on a good face and get in. But first she wanted to settle one more thing. She opened the door and stuck her head inside the car.

"Okay, Bradshaw, we'll fly together. But only if you give me the CD. You want me to trust you? Then you have to show good faith."

Bradshaw sighed and pulled the data carrier out of the inside pocket of his jacket. "Fine, here it is. But now get in at last."

"Thank you very much," Linda replied, took the CD and got into the limousine.

They spent the journey to the airport largely in silence. After a good 15 minutes, the limousine pulled into an inconspicuous driveway in the airport's perimeter fence, and the driver stopped in front of it. A guard checked the papers he had been given, made enquiries by radio, and then cleared the access road. They finally stopped just 20 meters from a small jet parked in an outside position far from the terminal building. It had to be a CIA aircraft.

"Is that one of the machines you usually use to kidnap people and take them to camps?" Linda asked after they got out of the limousine and walked towards the plane.

Bradshaw twisted the corners of his mouth. "That's not my line of work, so I have no idea. But be glad we were able to find a plane. Otherwise we'd have to fly one way and change planes twice. That would mean we wouldn't arrive at our destination until four or five hours after Sattler. So we should have a chance of landing at the same time or even before him."

As soon as they were on the plane, Bradshaw handed Linda a notebook to work on and then leaned back in his seat. As soon as he closed his eyes, he began to snore softly.

Linda didn't know whether to shake her head or be amazed that some people could sleep at the touch of a button. Perhaps even special training for agents enabled them to do this. For her, that was unthinkable, especially now that she was on a potentially risky mission. So she was almost grateful to be able to throw herself into work during the flight.

As the plane roared up to its cruising altitude, she inserted the CD and began to review the results of the AI analysis in detail.

***

Sandra Gillie knew from the look on the paramedic's face what he was going to say before he had even opened his mouth. "We're not going to take him away," she preempted him.

"I ... Listen, I've exhausted all the options we have here. The man needs a thorough examination. There's something wrong. It's not just the frostbite on his hands and feet, which is less serious than we thought, it's more the fact that he's gone from hypothermia to fever almost seamlessly."

"Then give him antipyretics, you'll have plenty of them here, won't you?"

"Of course. It's just that the medication hasn't worked very well so far. I can try another remedy, but ..."

"Then you do that. You don't need to ask me about it, that's your territory." She returned to the construction work on the new base, which was in its final stages. She noticed that the medic was still standing at her side. "What is it?" she asked impatiently.

The paramedic cleared his throat. "I told you there was something wrong with him. It's more than a fever ... His blood vessels ... I don't know how to describe it. You can see them pulsing through his skin, but he's hardly got high blood pressure. And also ... well, they seem to be glowing."

Gillie looked at the man skeptically. "They're glowing? Are you serious?"

"Like I said, I can't explain it."

Gillie sighed, then waved to a sergeant. "You make sure the perimeter is properly closed!" She then gestured to the medical barracks. "Show me."

The medic went ahead, and Gillie followed him into the makeshift infirmary.

Alex Corbinian squirmed restlessly on the cot to which he had been strapped with three wide belts. His forehead was covered in sweat, and he kept mumbling in incomprehensible sentences.

The paramedic knelt down next to the unconscious patient and rolled up the right sleeve of Alex's shirt. Underneath, the pale skin was revealed, with several veins shimmering in a pinkish-purple hue. "There you see it. Sometimes it gets stronger and sometimes weaker, but it never disappears completely."

Gillie watched the spectacle for a while and couldn't make any sense of what was going on with Corbinian. She knew nothing about medical matters, apart from solid first aid training. But this was suspicious, in that respect she had to agree with the paramedic - even if she didn't say it out loud. Was what was happening to Corbinian potentially dangerous? Should she give in to the paramedic's request and have him flown out? She immediately decided against it. It was better to keep him here in isolation rather than transport him to a fully staffed base if he was a danger. But that would also mean that she would have to provide appropriate security here.

The paramedic cleared his throat. He was obviously waiting for a decision.

"We'll put him in quarantine until further notice, and I'll talk to the general as soon as I reach him."

"All right, on your own responsibility," said the paramedic. "I can't condone this. What if the man dies before then?"

"On my own responsibility, of course!" Gillie snapped at him. "Until General Sattler arrives here, I'll be giving the orders on this mission! And now you take care of the isolation measures."

Gillie turned and quickly left the infirmary.

***

The CIA plane landed at the small regional airport of Qaanaaq in northwest Greenland shortly after 1:00 am. Linda and Bradshaw disembarked and walked towards a low building that had been clad all around with blue-painted sheet metal. It was hardly bigger than a supermarket, but one crucial difference made it clear that this was the terminal. At the top of the roof was a bulky tower for air traffic control. Right next to the terminal was a hangar building with three large roller doors, which presumably housed small aircraft. Apart from that, there was nothing else for miles around except a handful of cars, clearing vehicles, a forklift truck and various freight containers.

It was icy and windy here, so Linda was grateful for the lined jacket and hat Bradshaw gave her on the plane.

"So, what now?" Linda asked as they entered the airport building.

"I have organized a driver. But as everything had to happen very quickly today, he may not be here yet. I deliberately didn't fly to Pituffik so as not to attract any attention. So the logistics are a bit more complicated," explained the agent.

"And don't we have to show our passports somewhere or something?" Linda asked.

"Yes, over there. I have diplomatic passes for both of us, so there shouldn't be any problems."

"What a great career move," said Linda. "I'm sure being a diplomat will look good on my CV."

Bradshaw gave her a disparaging look.

"Yes, I know. It's all a secret," Linda added.

They passed through passport control and made their way to the waiting area, which was virtually deserted at this late hour.

Only an elderly gentleman with snow-white hair was sitting at the far end, leafing through a vintage car magazine.

Linda noticed that Bradshaw kept looking at him suspiciously. "What's the matter? Why do you keep looking at the old man?" she wanted to know.

Bradshaw swayed his head back and forth. "I don't know, he seems suspicious."

"Excuse me? The man must be 80 years old, do you think he's watching us? You must be paranoid by profession?"

"Possibly," Bradshaw replied curtly and picked up his briefcase to look for some documents. Then he pulled out his smartphone and wrote a message.

Linda, meanwhile, watched as the old man got up and went to the toilet. "You see? He's not interested in us," she said to Bradshaw. "What do you think about a coffee? If we have to wait here any longer, I'll fall asleep."

Bradshaw nodded. "That's probably a good suggestion. The driver will need another half hour, there are snowdrifts."

They got up and headed for a small kiosk that was still open. There they ordered two coffees and chocolate chip cookies. The waitress turned away to prepare the coffee on a loudly hissing machine.

Suddenly Linda noticed Bradshaw stiffening next to her. She turned her head a little and saw that the old man was standing right behind him.

"Careful, Grandpa, I don't want to break all your bones!" growled Bradshaw.

"If you twitch too quickly even once, I'll shoot a hole in your spinal cord," the white-haired man replied coolly. "Who are you? Agents?" he asked. "With your complexion, you stand out here like a sore thumb!"

"My concern and the color of my skin are none of your business. Now put the toy away."

"Toys? Surely you know that a gun can be produced on a 3D printer these days. No airport scanner can detect them."

"Listen," said Linda. "Why don't we talk about everything in peace? What do you want from us?"

At that moment, the waitress placed the coffee cups and small paper plates with the chocolate chip cookies on the counter.

"I'm paying," Linda explained and placed her card on the reader.

Meanwhile, the older gentleman had taken a few steps back and put some distance between himself and the two of them.

Linda and Bradshaw turned around.

The white-haired man nodded his head towards a seating area with a table in the far corner of the waiting area. He had his right hand in his amply bulging jacket pocket.

Bradshaw gave him a dark look, but then silently followed the request.

They sat down opposite each other and were silent for a moment.

"Aren't you a bit too old for that sort of thing?" Bradshaw asked. "You could slip very quickly and break your femoral neck," he added sarcastically.

"I have very good bones and a very good condition, don't worry."

"Let's start by introducing ourselves," Linda interjected. "I'm Linda Shoemaker."

Bradshaw remained stubbornly silent.

"Ridiculous. And so typical CIA," the old man commented. "I'm Erik Jansson, pleased to make your acquaintance. What, may I ask, are you doing in the company of such a shady comrade? Because you're not an agent."

"I'm a scientist, formerly with NASA, now working for other government agencies. But you're right, I don't work for the secret service."

"You don't have to tell that guy," Bradshaw said.

Jansson smiled mildly. "You can't get out of your skin either."

"Was that meant to be racist, Grandpa?"

"Not at all. Just a saying."

Linda cleared her throat. "I realize that you two aren't going to be the best of friends, but can we keep it businesslike? What are you doing here, Mr. Jansson? Why are you threatening us with a gun?"

"Because I didn't know if you were after me."

Now Bradshaw raised his eyebrows in astonishment. "I beg your pardon? That's pretty absurd. Why would we want anything from you, we didn't even know who you were."

"Yes? Then why were you looking at me so intensely earlier? I could tell from the trained casualness of your gaze that you were an agent."

"And you too, apparently," Bradshaw replied.

"You don't forget that, even after many years of retirement."

"Okay, to the point," Linda said. "Why would we be after you?"

"Because I wanted to meet someone about a very sensitive matter and your appearance here seemed suspicious to me."

"Who did you want to meet? And now you're not talking about secrecy!" said Bradshaw.

"Two scientists," Jansson replied curtly.

"Their names are Greaves and Grimm, right?" asked Linda.

Jansson nodded. "You know her?"

"Robert - that is, Dr. Greaves - and I are old colleagues. I was the one who hired him for this mission. But I haven't been able to reach him for days."

"Then the military took him in," Jansson replied curtly.

"You're pretty well informed for a pensioner. What is your role in the matter?" Bradshaw wanted to know.

"You still haven't told me your name," Jansson evaded.

"That's silly. But fine. My name is Luther Bradshaw."

"Pleased to meet you, colleague. You know, I've dealt with agents like you before. And with the American military."

"Camp Century!" Linda blurted out.

"Very good!" praised Jansson. "I see you're in the picture."

"Of course we are," said Bradshaw impatiently. "Now tell us what you want here!"

"Finish the job."

"What do you mean? What thing?" Linda asked.

"I've been here before. The first time something was discovered under the ice. But back then they reacted in complete panic and missed the chance to conduct a proper investigation. Instead, everything was abandoned head over heels and filled in. Unfortunately, the fundamental problem was never solved. This phenomenon is still down there, and it's not dead. But apparently they believed it was - or they didn't know any better. Either way, all the information was kept under lock and key and nobody cared for decades."

"Except General Sattler," Bradshaw interjected.

"That's right. Because his father is one of the victims of the incident at Camp Century."

"That explains his secret file!" said Linda. "Bradshaw, do you know what it says?"

The agent shook his head. "Unfortunately not. Most of the data from that time is only available on paper and has never been digitized."

"But I do know. Maybe even more," Jansson replied. He pulled out an old book bound in gray linen.

"What's that again?" Bradshaw wanted to know.

"The diary of Paul Memphis, a colleague who was stationed here with me at the time. I guess we were even friends, because he left me this book. He wrote down everything he experienced in it - even the details he never mentioned to his superiors."

"May I?" Bradshaw asked.

"No," replied Jansson.

"Why not?"

"You first have to prove to me that I can trust you."

"How is that supposed to work? You were an intelligence officer, I am one too. It's impossible for us to really trust each other."

"I'll take it," Linda suggested. "And we'll make an agreement."

Bradshaw and Jansson looked at her with interest.

"We are working together to bring this to the best possible conclusion. Because based on my analysis of this phenomenon, I'm pretty sure it's an intelligence - possibly a completely new life form. And we also know that contact with it has already had serious consequences. This should not happen again."

"Agreed," said Jansson. "You're an intelligent woman."

"Thank you, but you don't need to flatter me." She turned to Bradshaw. "What about you?"

The agent swayed his head back and forth. "What choice do I have, the way things are? But Jansson will have to surrender his weapon if he wants to accompany us."

The white-haired man put on a mischievous grin and then pulled a long, tubular case out of his jacket pocket. "I'm sorry, I can't give you this, it contains my insulin."

25

Provisional US base at the borehole,
Morning of September 18

The morning brought bright sunshine, a meager breakfast of army rations, and the sound of rotor blades. Nora stepped to the window of the barracks she shared with Robert and looked out in eager anticipation. She hoped to see a civilian helicopter out there, searching for them at the behest of station chief Olofsson. But she was immediately disappointed. It was once again one of the bulky military aircraft that had already transported material and soldiers here several times the day before.

Now that the stormy night had given way to a pleasant, almost windless morning, she realized the full extent of the night's work. The soldiers had obviously transformed the area into a small fortress in record time. In the middle of it all, the helicopter touched down on a marked landing pad.

Robert joined her at the window and also followed what was happening outside. After a few seconds, they saw Sandra Gillie come out of another shack and walk over to the landing pad. A few meters away from the helicopter, she waited for the passengers to disembark. The door was pushed open shortly afterwards and a single man got out of the machine.

"That's Sattler," Robert explained, pointing in his direction with his right index finger. "The man who sent me on this mission."

"Well, and now he probably wants to see for himself whether you've done a good job."

"I guess he won't be one hundred percent satisfied. But we should know in a minute. Looks like they're coming straight here."

Less than a minute later, the door opened and General Sattler entered the accommodation together with Sandra Gillie.

"Dr. Greaves, good to see you well," the general greeted him in an almost absurdly friendly manner. Then he looked at Nora. "And you must be Nora Grimm, I'm delighted that we've been able to recruit you as a highly competent partner for this project."

Nora frowned and looked at Robert questioningly. She had expected military rudeness, a lecture on national security, or simply Sattler yelling at them for not cooperating as he had wished. But instead, he buttered them up, which was much more disturbing than any loud rebuke.

"Oh, forgive me! I forgot to introduce myself," Sattler continued. "Frank D. Sattler, General of the US Air Force and Special Assistant to the President for Extraterrestrial Emergency Response." He held out his hand to Nora.

She hesitated for a moment, but then shook the general's hand. "Normally I would probably say something friendlier, but I must insist that you don't keep us here any longer," Nora said firmly.

Sattler tilted his head. "I apologize for the inconvenience. But unfortunately, your expertise is still needed here."

"Let her go, I will cooperate fully," Robert intervened. "There's no reason to expose Nora to any more danger."

Sattler shook his head silently.

"Listen, this is kidnapping," Nora spoke up again. "And what's more, it won't work. You can't just seize a station that doesn't belong to you. My station manager Per Olofsson will be sending a search team here very soon. And then you'll have to answer a lot of questions."

"I don't think so," Gillie replied. "We've sent him a message that Alex Corbinian has been found and taken to Pituffik for medical treatment. So Olofsson is aware that the three of you are safe and well."

"But ... that's not true!" protested Nora.

"Oh no? What do you lack? And now don't say comfort!" said Gillie in a caustic tone.

"It's not about me! How is Alex's condition? He looked anything but well yesterday," Nora asked.

"Gillie refused to take him to a proper hospital," Robert added.

"That was exactly right," replied Sattler. "She was only following my instructions. We must not allow any more information to get out. This should also be said explicitly to you once again, Dr. Greaves. You did not follow orders."

Robert folded his arms demonstratively in front of his chest.

"You knew from the beginning that this was an Air Force operation. Now you're not complaining that there are stricter rules here. But I was willing to accept your unreasonable looseness if it got results. And it obviously has. Now come on, I have some very interesting analyses with me that Ms. Shoemaker has prepared."

"Linda? How is she?"

"Good. She really wanted to come here, but I insisted she stay where it's safe for her."

"And it's not safe here?" Nora asked. "Just out of interest, because you won't let me go."

"You don't want to leave," said Sattler curtly. "I can see that in your face, my dearest Mrs. Grimm. I know this expression from scientists." With that, Sattler turned and headed for the exit.

"Meet me over at the borehole in 30 minutes," Gillie ordered. "The guard will take you there." Then she turned around and followed Sattler out.

***

Base Commander Gordon Hastings sat grudgingly in his Pituffik Air Force Base office, staring at his computer monitor. All his inquiries had been fruitless. Everything he had done to trace Sattler's plan here had failed. Everyone he had contacted seemed to either skillfully stonewall or honestly know nothing at all.

This was highly unsatisfactory, as Hastings increasingly felt that he had been reduced to a spectator on his own base. The impression was deceptive, of course, as he was still in charge of Pituffik, but he could not ignore the fact that something very significant was going on that was almost entirely beyond his control.

There was a knock at his door and Captain Barnes stuck his head in. "Sir, do you have a minute?" he inquired.

"Yes, come in. What's up?"

"About ten minutes ago, the post at the north gate reported that a new CIA agent had arrived at the base with some rather unusual companions. He has duly identified himself. But I still thought you'd want to be informed."

"You thought right, Barnes!" Hastings said loudly, realizing himself that he was taking his burgeoning anger out on the soldier, who was not at all to blame. "He came through the gate?" he continued more calmly.

"Right. Someone from the CIA staff here picked him up in one of our jeeps. His name is Bradshaw, an African-American almost two meters tall. He was accompanied by a certain Linda Shoemaker, who is probably part of Sattler's staff and a ..." The soldier paused briefly. "Yes, there was also a rather elderly Dane called Jansson. To be honest, the man looked like he belonged in an old people's home, sir!"

"I see," Hastings replied with interest. "Where are they now? I want to have a look at them."

"In the CIA building at the antenna array," the soldier explained. "Should I send for them?"

"No, don't do anything. I'll go there myself in a minute."

"Understood, sir."

"You may step away, Captain."

Barnes left the office as ordered, leaving Hastings alone. He couldn't figure out what was going on lately. Why were so many people drawn to Greenland at the moment? What was going on here?

First, it had just been that arrogant Gillie and her civilian advisor, then Sattler himself, who hadn't even bothered to pay him a visit tonight before flying on. And now more CIA people and even foreign civilians were coming to his base.

Hastings hated the fact that there was an area on his base that was not officially under his control. But the listening devices installed were under CIA control.

He would get to the bottom of this new agent. His appearance had one hundred percent to do with Sattler's secret operation, which he still didn't think was entirely kosher. They'd had dozens of soldiers and countless tons of material moved to the middle of nowhere, all by his contingent and his people! This wasn't how things were done in the Air Force, Sattler should know. But he was his superior, his scope for criticizing him was very limited. But that didn't mean he couldn't ask uncomfortable questions. And he would start with this Bradshaw now.

Hastings stood up, tightened his uniform and walked quickly to the door.

***

The CIA's work area on the Pituffik base was quite spartanly equipped. Most of the walls were covered with special evaluation electronics for the antenna stations, digital measurement technology and various servers, all of which were housed in man-sized racks. Normally, only technicians and analysts were on duty here, not field agents.

There were two workstations with computers in this room and two more in the room next door. Bradshaw had sent the men stationed here there shortly after their arrival so that they could discuss the next steps undisturbed.

They had previously delayed their arrival at the base until it was certain that General Sattler had already left. And now

Bradshaw hoped that their work here would go largely unobserved. But he was immediately proven wrong on this point.

No sooner had he, Linda and Jansson sat down at their computers than there was a loud banging on the room door, which was locked with a code lock.

"I was afraid of it," muttered Bradshaw. "The sentry reported us."

"Agent Bradshaw," an irritated voice boomed from outside. "I expect you to open the door immediately."

The agent stood up. "I bet that's the commander," he said to Linda and Jansson and then unlocked the door. "Please, come in. We were just coming to see you."

Hastings entered the room brashly and glared at Bradshaw, who was almost a head taller than he was. "Bullshit! Don't take the piss." He looked around the room and also eyed Linda and Jansson. "So, what's this motley crew that snuck into my base?"

"We have registered properly and are authorized to be here. There can be no question of sneaking in."

"A matter of opinion!" Hastings insisted. "And now tell me why you're here, otherwise this will be a short guest appearance."

"This is..."

"Enough of this! If you want to say that this is secret, I'll have you placed under arrest," Hastings threatened.

"You must have been informed by Sattler and Gillie," said Bradshaw.

"Sattler and Gillie are welcome to ..." Hastings stifled the rest of the sentence and cleared his throat before continuing. "I hate being kept in the dark. I can't do anything about Sattler's secretiveness, but you might be a different story."

At that moment Jansson began to laugh and both Bradshaw and Hastings turned to him in irritation.

"Excuse me, but this is almost like before, Jansson said."

"Who is this guy?" Hastings asked in astonishment.

"Erik Jansson," he replied. "And I was already stationed on Greenland when you were still shitting in your diapers."

"Please sit down, Commander," Bradshaw said calmly and pushed a chair towards Hastings.

After a moment's hesitation, Hastings complied with the request and looked questioningly at the others.

Bradshaw also took his seat again. "Okay, Mr. Jansson has already introduced himself and you obviously know my name. This here is Linda Shoemaker, officially an employee of General Sattler, but recently quite unhappy with her boss's behavior."

Linda gave Hastings a brief smile and explained: "I'm a scientist and a former colleague of Robert Greaves, whom you may have met."

"Fleeting," Hastings replied. "Gillie shielded him most of the time, I couldn't talk to him alone. Speaking of Gillie!" He now turned to Bradshaw. "If I'm not mistaken, that's one of your colleagues. With such a rotten character, she can only be CIA."

"Yes and no," said Bradshaw, without responding to the side blow. "I don't want to explain it in detail, but you should know that Gillie has made some enemies in the agency. They wanted to get rid of her and initiated disciplinary proceedings. I probably should have been more supportive, but I didn't want to give up on her. Unfortunately, I was her instructor at the time."

"You obviously didn't do such a good job," commented Linda.

Bradshaw acknowledged with a sigh and continued. "In the end, I was able to arrange for her to be given one last chance. I sent her on an undercover mission, for which she officially resigned from the CIA. Then I placed her with Sattler, which wasn't easy given his suspicious nature. She was supposed to gain his trust and provide us with information. But apparently Gillie found it more interesting to actually take Sattler's side - or at least leave us hanging. I don't know what Sattler might have promised her. In any case, once again the whole story didn't go as I had planned. But let's leave it at that for now, we have other things to talk about."

"And what would they be?" Hastings asked.

"What is the status of Sattler's activities? How many men has he taken with him? How well armed are they? Where exactly is the location?"

"You're asking a lot of questions. Assuming I give you this information, will you tell me what he's doing there? I don't want to put my people in unnecessary danger or get involved in an international incident. Something like that doesn't look good on the record."

Bradshaw nodded. "Let's play with open cards. I want something from you and you have good reason to doubt Sattler's motives."

"I hope I can trust your word," Hastings said and sighed. "I estimate that Sattler must have dispatched a good two dozen soldiers by now, plus the crew of the helicopter that hasn't returned yet. The men have standard equipment with pistols or rifles. Plus tons of equipment, I don't know what exactly. That's one of the things I couldn't find out because most of it arrived on the last transport flight and was taken straight to a hangar. However, the coordinates of the last flights are all identical. The material was always taken to the same place. That's also where Sattler left three quarters of an hour ago. And now please tell me: What is he doing there, what is this presence all about?"

"Give me the coordinates and we'll take a look together," Bradshaw explained.

Hastings pulled out his smartphone and tapped away on it. After a moment's hesitation, he held it out to Bradshaw, who entered the numbers into the computer in front of him.

He watched the displays for a while before taking the floor again. "We're lucky and can get live satellite images for the next 90 minutes. The weather looks good too."

He pulled open a larger window and requested the image transfer. Then he zoomed into the mostly white-grey area until a small settlement could be seen. A transport helicopter stood in the middle of it.

"That's one of ours," said Hastings. "These barracks are also from our stock. They've built a kind of protective wall around the base."

Linda pointed to a spot away from the barracks. "There seems to be an entrance to an underground facility here, it must be the PRIN people's borehole where Robert was working."

"I can't imagine that this approach was coordinated," said Bradshaw.

"Sattler will have told them a nice tall tale," Jansson intervened. "How do we get there now?"

Bradshaw and Hastings gave the old man a skeptical look. "With respect, but..." Hastings began. "Aren't you a little old for such adventures?"

"Wouldn't you rather say ‚suicide mission'? I'm old enough that it doesn't really matter anymore, but I'm very keen to prevent a catastrophe."

"Disaster?" Hastings repeated. "Who said anything about a catastrophe?"

"Do you want to go first or should I start?" Jansson asked in Bradshaw and Linda's direction.

Without really waiting for an answer from either of them, he pulled Paul Memphis' diary out of his briefcase and placed it on the table.

26

PRIN outpost "Snowbird",
September 18

When Nora and Robert were brought into the room with the borehole a little later that day, it had changed fundamentally. Not only had it been fitted with heating units to warm it up to a temperature of around freezing point, but almost all the technology from the PRIN mission had been removed and replaced with new equipment and superstructures. A steel structure with hanging wire ropes had been installed above the borehole, which appeared to have increased in diameter again. Suspended from these was a kind of elevator cabin that could hold an estimated two to three people. Unlike a normal elevator, the motor was not located at the upper end of the cable suspension, but directly on the roof of the cabin, which could thus move up and down independently, so to speak.

The transport basket contained a robotic vehicle with two rubberized track drives, a mechatronic gripper arm, and various superstructures containing sensors and cameras. Apparently, they were preparing for an exploration.

And something else caught Nora's eye. The edge of the former borehole now seemed to bulge upwards, as if it had grown upwards from the reflective surface and had risen a good 20 centimetres above the actual edge. There was definitely something going on here that had nothing to do with the modifications made by the soldiers. The phenomenon had now developed a momentum of its own that literally sent a shiver down Nora's spine. She looked over at Robert, who was just as critical of the change to the shaft and then gave her a look that was difficult to interpret. Did he have a better idea of what was happening here?

Before Nora could delve deeper into the thought, she heard Sandra Gillie's voice calling her and Sattler over to the area full of equipment not far from the shaft. "Come over here, we have jobs for you!"

"Well, pretty much in the front row," Robert whispered to Nora before he started moving.

Nora knew he had meant it as a joking pep talk, but she still wondered what they would be sitting in the front row for. All of this was increasingly beyond her control and she almost wished she had never started looking into this project. But simultaneously, she couldn't help the irrepressible curiosity that still gnawed at her. They had discovered something big here. The only question was what exactly it might be.

"Please take a seat," said Sattler, pointing to two chairs on his right. "I'll bring you up to date."

Nora and Robert sat down and watched as Sattler loaded some of the results onto the screen in front of him. "I have to admit that I wasn't pleased with Dr. Shoemaker's solo effort, but the analyses are very revealing, there's no denying that."

Robert leaned forward and examined the data displayed. It took a moment, then he let out a surprised gasp. "That's fantastic. Have you spoken to Linda about it? Is there any more? Did she analyze the rest, too?" The questions just poured out of him.

"No. Apparently, only a very small part of the recorded signal could be decoded. So far, at least. Perhaps we'll get the opportunity to generate more data very soon."

"Excuse me for asking such a stupid question," Nora spoke up. "But what exactly are we looking at here?"

"Oh, I'm sorry. I was so surprised by the clarity of the results that I forgot to explain it," Robert replied. "Well, in short, the signal clearly shows that we are dealing with an intelligence. It contains elementary mathematical and physical principles that cannot be a coincidence. The signal must be a form of communication."

"Communication?" Nora asked in astonishment. "I mean, that would mean that we're actually dealing with a life form."

"That would be one of the theories, yes. But we can't completely rule out the possibility that it's a form of technology. In either case, it would be a sensation, because we have to assume that this intelligence does not originate from Earth," Robert continued.

"That's right," agreed Sattler. "And Dr. Greaves here proved years ago that the same structure can also be found on Mars. With the subtle difference that it is inactive there - or in other words: dead."

"We can't say that with any certainty," Robert qualified. "We don't have enough data for that. In any case, the observed behavior is much more pronounced here. On Mars, only residues of the crystals seem to have been found, whereas these structures appear to have spread on Earth."

"Why do you think that is?" asked Sattler.

"Many factors are conceivable because Mars differs from Earth in significant environmental conditions. There are icy temperatures, even much more extreme than here on Greenland. There is also practically no atmosphere. The air pressure is so low that water would evaporate at zero degrees Celsius, for example. So there is still no proof that water exists there - at least on the surface. The composition of the Martian soil is also different. We have no idea under what conditions these crystals can exist or what might kill them. What is clear, however, is that they must have come to the planets somehow - which suggests that the cold and vacuum of space should not affect them in principle."

"So you don't think that this life form, if it is one, evolved here?" Sattler asked.

"I think that's out of the question, it's fundamentally different from anything that exists here on Earth. And the fact that residues can also be found on Mars speaks for an origin from outside. It is possible that a meteorite could have hit it. But that would have to have been at least two or a large one that disintegrated into several fragments within our solar system. Nevertheless, this is all pure speculation."

"What does it want?" asked Gillie.

"What do you mean?" Robert replied.

"If this is a life form, it must have a purpose, a goal, or am I wrong?"

Nora tilted her head and looked at Gillie. "That's a fair question, of course. I didn't expect it from you," she said and smiled fleetingly. "If we go by what biology teaches us, we can at least assume that this life form needs food and energy in some form; that it probably wants to reproduce and evolve." She made a sweeping motion with her right arm. "I strongly suspect that the enormous effort here is intended to test precisely this hypothesis."

Sattler nodded approvingly. "That's right. And we want to find out whether we can use this life form to our advantage or whether it poses a danger."

"What do you mean by ‚use for our benefit'?" Robert wanted to know. "I've just explained that we're dealing with an intelligence. And I mean a highly developed intelligence. To hear you talk like that, I'd think you were talking about cattle breeding."

"You probably have more experience with that than I do," countered Sattler. "Enough words now. We'll start exploring the shaft and then we'll know more. Your job will be to pick up and evaluate potential signals. I've had the program Linda Shoemaker used installed on the computers. See if you can find out more. If it is a form of communication, I want you to find a way to respond."

"That ... I can't possibly ..." Robert broke off and shook his head. "Better not expect miracles! But I'll see what I can do."

"Why not, Dr. Greaves? Miracles are a beautiful thing," said Sattler, nodding at Gillie.

"Get ready to lower the robot!" Gillie shouted to two soldiers posted at the shaft.

The next moment, the elevator with the robot in it began to descend into the depths, whirring.

***

"What kind of book is that?" Gordon Hastings asked in Jansson's direction.

"A diary," he explained. "It belonged to a soldier who was stationed here on Greenland more than 50 years ago, Paul Memphis. We had become friends back then, as we were stationed at the same time at Camp Century, which was later abandoned. You know about this secret facility?"

Hastings nodded. "I roughly know the history, the base was developed and handled from this base. Pituffik was still called Thule back then," replied the commander.

"That's right. When Camp Century was abandoned in 1967, Memphis escaped from the collapsing base at the last second, so to speak. He wrote down his experiences in this book and sent it to me shortly before he died. I promised to look into the matter and prove - or disprove - his theory."

"What theory?" asked Bradshaw.

"I'll get to that in a moment. The last few hours before we left the base were highly dramatic and confused. I was already on my way here with a load of equipment at the time and wasn't there myself. That's why some of the entries in the diary were a real surprise to me. According to them, the last people on the base, apart from Paul Memphis, were his superior research manager, Dr. Stirling, and ..." Jansson paused dramatically before continuing. "... Benjamin Sattler, the father of the man who has now set this obscure mission in motion."

"That sheds a strange light on the matter," said Hastings. "But it doesn't necessarily mean anything."

"Oh yes, it means quite a lot. Sattler's father and Dr. Stirling didn't make it out of the base alive. And it gets even stranger." Jansson flipped through a few pages of the diary. "This is where Memphis writes why that happened. Sattler was previously in the infirmary with a high fever, but then escaped from there and somehow managed to get into the missile silo. Stirling and Memphis tried to subdue him and talk some sense into him, but Sattler was apparently convinced that he was being influenced by an outside force and wanted to blow up the whole base. He detonated half a dozen missiles."

"Wait a minute, I thought it had never gotten to the point where missiles were actually stationed there," Hastings interjected.

"That seems to have been the official version for all outsiders. I was there as a liaison officer for the Danes and can confirm that the missiles had long since been installed. Nuclear-capable long- and medium-range missiles. I don't know exactly how many, but it's even possible that a dozen are still down there in the ice, along with all the other equipment and waste left behind."

"Why did he want to destroy the base?" Linda asked. "Was he delusional or was it because he was ill?"

"That's the exciting point that leads to Memphis' theory," explained Jansson. "Setting off the rockets may sound insane, but apparently Sattler had thought it through very carefully. He saw no other way to avert the catastrophe that had already taken its course a few weeks earlier. This had to do with the deep drilling that had been carried out. In order to make Camp Century's disguise as a scientific mission as perfect as possible, research was actually carried out. And Sattler, Stirling and Memphis himself were part of this team. Something was found in the ice cores that exhibited inexplicable behavior and developed an unpredictable momentum of its own. Sattler came into contact with it and began to change."

"I think I already know what Memphis' theory was," Linda explained. "You discovered the same phenomenon then as Nora Grimm has now. We now know that it appears to be a life form." She paused for a moment and looked at Hastings. Then she added in a deadpan tone: "An alien life form."

Hastings just shook his head and showed the expected incredulous reaction.

"I know how that sounds. But surely you've investigated what Sattler's staff unit, which includes me, is involved in?"

Now Hastings nodded. "It wasn't that easy. But if I've been informed correctly, it's about the possibility of extraterrestrial infiltration."

"Exactly. And we now have evidence that this has already taken place in a latent form. My colleague Dr. Greaves has recorded emissions from these crystals, and there are irrefutable signs of advanced intelligence."

"That's exactly what Memphis believed," Jansson agreed. "He asked me to analyze the only surviving ice core from that time. However, there was nothing in it to support the theory. Nora Grimm found the necessary evidence. Whatever caused this phenomenon, it is still down there. Sattler had only seemingly averted the catastrophe back then - delayed it, so to speak - but now we are potentially back where they left off in 1967."

"So you're saying Sattler is tracking it down?" Hastings wanted to know.

"That's pretty certain," Bradshaw said. "According to our findings, General Sattler is obsessed with finding out what happened to his father at the time."

"If that's true, we have a real problem," Hastings said. "Personal interests drive a man in Sattler's position and with his powers..." He left the sentence unfinished and looked back and forth between Jansson, Bradshaw and Linda. "So, assuming I buy this rather abstruse story, what should we do then?"

"Jansson said it right earlier. We have to get there somehow," Bradshaw explained, pointing to the satellite image. "Can you arrange that?"

Hastings grimaced. "Perhaps. But do I want that? It could very quickly mean the end of my career."

"Or a fabulous career leap," Jansson replied with a wink.

"I'll think about it. I need to make a few inquiries first," Hastings explained and stood up. Before he left, he turned around once more. "I'm sure you'll need quarters. I'll give instructions to assign you your own rooms."

27

Sattler, Gillie, Robert and Nora attentively followed the data transmitted by the probe. The sonar confirmed that the shaft, which had once been a thin borehole, was now more than one meter in diameter, even at a depth of 100 meters. The cabin itself was currently about 35 meters below the surface.

It was also noticeable that the measured temperature in the shaft did not fall, but remained more or less constant at zero degrees.

"There!" Robert suddenly exclaimed. "Can you pull over, please?"

Sattler nodded and gave the soldiers on the winch the appropriate orders. Then he asked in Robert's direction: "Have you discovered anything?"

"I think so." Robert made a few computer entries and brightened the transmitted image. "Now take a closer look!"

"I can see it, a pulsation!" explained Sattler.

A pinkish-purple glow could now be clearly seen under the ice on the transmitted video images, which swelled and then subsided again. It seemed to spread out in irregular ramifications like an organic network of veins.

Robert extracted a few still images from the video transmission and saved them. "You can continue to drain now," he said, and a few seconds later the elevator started moving again. Together with Nora, Robert set about analyzing the footage.

"It kind of reminds me of blood vessels or the structure of leaves," said Nora.

"Yes, at least it looks organic. And the color of the light is the same as we saw in the lab when the crystals fused," Robert agreed.

Gillie cleared her throat and turned to Sattler. "Sir, I have something else to report in this connection."

The general looked at her with interest.

"As I reported earlier, Alex Corbinian, who was found unconscious here, is over at the military hospital. The paramedic informed me late yesterday evening that his condition raises some questions. And after seeing this, I have to point out a potential risk."

"What do you mean?" Sattler asked.

"Something very similar to this glow was observed on Corbinian's arms. We still don't know what he was doing here, but now I think he seems to have come into contact with the alien material - or organism."

"He had already come into contact with the drill core before," Nora confirmed. "That was during his last assignment here, when we obtained the most recent samples. After that, he fell ill and then made a miraculous recovery. But this impression may have been misleading."

Sattler nodded slowly and deliberately. "Now I understand what you're getting at, Gillie. If Corbinian has been infected, there's a risk that we'll be infected too. Am I right about that?"

"It's just a consideration that we shouldn't ignore."

"I think we can take precautions," said Robert. "Alex was the only one who had direct skin contact with the ice - or rather the meltwater. The rest of us always wore gloves when working with it, so we didn't show any of Alex's symptoms."

"I agree," said Nora, "although it would of course be safer to wear completely sealed protective suits."

"Unfortunately, we don't have suits like that here," said Gillie.

"Request some from Pituffik!" ordered Sattler. "Just to be on the safe side, in case we decide to send someone down."

"I'll take care of it," Gillie replied and moved away from the work area.

"Why would we send someone down there?" Robert asked.

Sattler pointed to the computer screens that they had almost forgotten about during the conversation. "That's why." Robert and Nora stared at what was now visible on the video image. Another horizontal corridor seemed to lead off from the vertical shaft. It looked like it was made of glass and had a ghostly purple glow.

"What the ..." Nora started and fell silent again. "On the left wall, is there something written there?"

"Silo C," Robert read out loud.

"How can that be ... I mean..." Nora stammered.

"Camp Century," said Sattler. "It had four missile silos - A and B to the west and C and D to the east of the actual base."

"But the camp was several kilometers away from here," Robert objected.

"Yes, it was there - once upon a time," Sattler clarified.

"Holy shit," Nora gasped, "now it all makes sense!"

"What makes sense?" Robert asked.

"That I hadn't thought of that! Glaciers flow. Sometimes several kilometers per year at the edge. The Jakobshavn glacier, for example, moves 17 kilometers per year towards the sea. Here, further inland, it moves much more slowly, but the ice never stands still. We are obviously directly above the former camp - or more precisely: the silos." Nora looked at Sattler in shock. "A few meters further over, and we might have drilled right into one of those missiles!"

"It probably wouldn't have happened much," said Sattler calmly.

"Presumably?" Nora asked.

"I don't know exactly what types of missiles are in the silos - if any were deposited here at all. Silos A and B were destroyed in 1967, and according to the documents, the other two were still empty. But unfortunately, that's not entirely certain due to some inconsistencies in the files."

Nora sighed. "I'd rather there was reliable information about this. But we can't change that now anyway. What really surprises me is that there are still intact structures there. That should actually be impossible. The pressure that the ice has built up over the decades must have squeezed everything together like an oversized scrap press."

"That's obviously not the case!" said Sattler with a downright joyful expression on his face. "This is an unexpected gift that we should take advantage of. But not until the protective equipment arrives."

At that moment, a slight tremor shook the base. It seemed to come directly from the ice beneath them.

Robert instinctively looked toward the shaft leading into the depths. "Something's going on down there, that much is clear."

"And we'll find out what it is," Sattler emphasized and stood up to walk over to the shaft. "Go ahead with your analyses, Dr. Greaves. We should be as prepared as possible before we go down."

***

Nanouk Bruun put down the binoculars and pondered. From her elevated position on a snowbank, she could clearly see that the outpost of the PRIN network had changed fundamentally since her last visit. It was now not only surrounded by a protective wall, but also equipped with various buildings and vehicles. None of this might have been a cause for concern, but Nanouk had seen several soldiers, and there was also a large US Air Force transport helicopter in the middle of the facility. What were the military doing here? Were they about to make another mess like the abandoned Camp Century, whose toxic waste was still stored under the ice?

She reached for her handheld radio and switched it on. "Hey, Thore? Are you there? This is Nanouk, come in!" Then she released the talk button and waited for an answer. All that came out of the loudspeaker for a while was static. "Thore, come in, please!" she repeated. The range of the device was limited, Nanouk knew that, and it was very possible that the signal would not reach the settlement. On the other hand, Thore had a fairly large antenna on the roof and usually had good reception.

At last she heard a crack and then Thor's creaky voice. "What is it, sweetie?" he asked.

Nanouk hated it when he called her that. And since he was aware of this, he did it again and again. But apart from this annoying quirk, Thore was an absolutely loyal comrade-in-arms in their organization.

"Stop playing games and listen," she said. "I'm here at a site where scientists are actually drilling ice, but now it's swarming with American soldiers. They've cordoned everything off. I can hardly imagine that this is being done properly."

"Where exactly?" Thore asked.

Nanouk read the coordinates from her GPS device and gave them to Thore. "Can you please check with the authorities to see if they have a permit?"

"Well, of course! I just don't know if they'll do anything about it."

"Nevertheless! We can't always just do nothing..." Nanouk fell silent. The sound of accelerating rotor blades reached her ears. "Shit, the helicopter's taking off!" she cursed, knowing at the same moment that she would be easily spotted from the air.

"Thore, I have to go. They've got a helicopter. If you don't hear from me again, raise the alarm."

"Listen, isn't that a bit panicky, even for you?" he asked, but Nanouk didn't answer, instead stuffing the device into her bag, grabbing her rucksack and running down the slope to her snowmobile.

The sound of the rotor blades became louder and more penetrating.

Nanouk stepped on the gas and sped off to the west. But the helicopter flew in exactly the same direction. "Fuck!" she shouted, knowing that she had been tracked down. The Americans had probably even overheard her radio message.

A dark shadow flitted over them as the helicopter overtook them and turned around a few hundred meters ahead. It was now approaching her head-on. It was trying to cut her off. For a brief moment, Nanouk thought hard about whether there was a way to escape them, but there were practically no hiding places here on the wide, open expanse of the glacier.

Then she saw that the side door of the helicopter had been opened, and a soldier was pointing a gun at her. The bastards were obviously serious.

Nanouk slowed down and finally stopped completely. She raised her hands and got off the snowmobile.

The helicopter touched down not far from her position, and two soldiers jumped out. They came running over to her at a rapid pace.

"Are you armed?" one of them shouted at her.

"Of course! I have a rifle. Because of the polar bears," explained Nanouk, pointing to the carrier.

The second soldier approached in an arc from behind, stepped up to the snowmobile and took the weapon.

"Come along!" the first soldier shouted again.

"I'm not even thinking about it, why? You can't just…"

The soldier raised his rifle and took aim at Nanouk.

"You must be out of your minds," Nanouk groaned, shaking her head. "I didn't do anything!"

"I said: come with me!" the soldier repeated, pointing to the helicopter.

Meanwhile, the second man radioed in. "We've got her. What should we do with her?"

"Take her to the base and throw her in the brig. But inconspicuously, please," Nanouk heard a cool female voice.

"Wait, which base? What about my snowmobile?" asked Nanouk.

"We'll take care of it," the soldier replied and grabbed her by the right arm. Then he pushed her towards the helicopter.

"If you think there are no consequences, you're wrong!" Nanouk threatened.

The soldiers just laughed: "Of course! The seal hunters' club will give us hell," said one of them.

"Or even worse: the local Eskimo association!" added the other.

Nanouk gave them a grim look, but decided not to waste another word on these idiots. She climbed into the helicopter with the soldiers, and just a few seconds later they were airborne.

***

Per Olofsson stirred the cup of black tea with his spoon and looked at his counterpart speechlessly for a moment. Then he leaned down, opened a large drawer in the pedestal under his desk and pulled out a bottle of Norwegian Håvaldsen Aquavit. He unscrewed the cap and poured a large sip into the cup. Then he held the bottle out to Dr. Keller, sitting on the other side of the desk.

The ward doctor shook his head. "I'd rather not, I'm on call. But feel free to take one. That's probably an appropriate medicine in this case - as long as you don't overdo it."

"I still can't believe that Steven is supposed to be dead," Olofsson replied. "How did that happen? I thought the doctors thought he was already on the road to recovery?"

"It's puzzling, like everything else about his case. Out of the blue, he suffered a brain haemorrhage that could not be stopped. As he was already weakened, it quickly led to his death. But I haven't even told you the worst part yet."

Olofsson glanced at the bottle of aquavit and wondered whether he should pour another shot into the tea. He decided against it. "And that would be?" he asked.

"This morning, Steven actually woke up from his coma. He couldn't speak and still seemed dazed, but he was at least able to make himself understood enough to be brought a notepad and pen. Somehow, he then managed to scribble something on the page. It was hard to read, but they emailed me a photo of it and I can clearly see a name in it."

Olofsson felt the cozy warmth of schnapps and tea in his stomach on the one hand and an icy chill in his fingers on the other. He gripped the cup even tighter to warm his fingers, "What name?"

"I think it says Gillie, the name of this woman who was here on the ward - interestingly enough, also on the day Steven collapsed."

"I'm almost afraid to ask, but what was the second word?" Olofsson wanted to know.

"Poison," Keller replied curtly.

Olofsson shook his head in horror, reached for the bottle and poured another sip into the cup, which now contained more schnapps than tea. "This is simply unbelievable! And I let this person walk around here ..."

"Nobody could have expected anything like this, it was all legitimate. But I think the evidence is now quite clear. Steven was not the victim of a disease, but was ..." Keller paused. "Well, I can't say it any other way. He was murdered."

"This is a tragedy! Why would anyone do something like that? Steven certainly wasn't the most pleasant of contemporaries, but damn it, murder? I'm going to hunt down that Sandra Gillie!" Olofsson was furious.

"We should stay calm," advised Keller. "We still have no idea what exactly is going on here and who our opponents are. But we should leave no stone unturned to clear up the case completely."

"But Greenland is the worst possible place for it. I don't even know if there are any police here. And if there are, they're hundreds of kilometers away. This Gillie is also American and is on a US base." Olofsson fell silent as a bitter realization hit him. Nora Grimm and Alex Corbinian were on this very base. It was very possible that they were also in serious danger at that moment.

"What is it?" Dr. Keller wanted to know.

"I had to think about Nora. She went with Dr. Greaves in a military helicopter to look for Alex. And supposedly, they're now at the Air Force Base in Pituffik." Olofsson put on a grim expression, picked up his cup and drank it down in one go.

"By the way, that's what I meant by exaggerating," commented Dr. Keller. "What are you up to? What are you drinking yourself into?"

"I will now confront the commander of this base and demand that Nora and Alex be brought here immediately. Otherwise, there will be very unpleasant consequences! What do we have a press distribution list for?"

Dr. Keller raised his eyebrows. "Okay, I can tell this guy better dress warm."

28

Pituffik Space Base, West Greenland,
Evening of September 18

Commander Gordon Hastings had now spent some time weighing up his options. But all the brooding hadn't done him much good, so it would ultimately be a gut decision as to whether he should believe the rather crazy story of the three new arrivals on his base. If it was just a CIA man trying to pull the wool over his eyes, he wouldn't give it a second thought and would send him packing. But there was also the scientist Linda Shoemaker, who seemed quite sincere. She seemed to know very well what she was talking about.

But the strangest thing was the appearance of 82-year-old Erik Jansson, who surely wouldn't take on such an ordeal unless there was a damn good reason for it. Either that or the man was suffering from pronounced senile dementia.

However, it was clear that he could not simply stand by and watch as Sattler and Gillie used his men and equipment to create the basis for an international conflict that would ultimately fall back on him if he did not act decisively. In any case, he had serious doubts that Sattler's actions here were in any way authorized by the highest authorities. Especially after he had had a very unpleasant conversation with the head of the PRIN station, Per Olofsson, and had to explain to him that neither Robert Greaves nor his two scientists were here on the base.

Gillie had flat-out lied to Olofsson and concealed the fact that Nora Grimm and Alex Corbinian were still at the borehole - probably against their will. That alone was a fabulous transgression. Olofsson had also accused Gillie of being responsible for the collapse of another employee at the Amarok station. He had even threatened to go to the press if his people were not brought back immediately. The trouble was, Hastings couldn't guarantee that, because the two were in Sattler's newly created location outside his control.

The phone on the desk rang and pulled Hastings out of his thoughts. He looked briefly at the displayed number and then picked it up. "Captain Barnes, what is it?"

"Sir, the helicopter that Sattler took with him is approaching. We are to provide equipment."

"More equipment? What's he up to now?"

"Sir, I'm afraid I don't know. But among other things, NBC protective clothing is being requested."

"NBC equipment?" Hastings repeated incredulously, unable to make sense of whether Sattler wanted to protect himself from nuclear, biological or chemical dangers. None of the three options particularly appealed to him.

"Correct, sir! But there's something else strange. The pilot reports a crew of four plus a passenger."

"Who is it? Is the general himself coming back?" Hastings asked, hoping it wasn't because it could thwart the plan he had just made.

"Unknown, sir. But the helicopter will land in less than five minutes, then we should know for sure."

"I'll come to the landing site myself! Meet me there with three armed men. But stay out of sight on the edge until I give you a signal."

"Got it!"

Hastings hung up and rose hastily to leave his office. He didn't know exactly why he had ordered an armed squad to the landing site, but his gut feeling told him that he had better be prepared for all eventualities. He certainly wouldn't have General Sattler arrested, but ever since he had heard about the request for NBC protection, all the alarm bells had been ringing. He hoped that they weren't planning to haul any hazardous substances into his base. God knows there were enough of them here already.

After a few minutes, Hastings left the eastern exit of the complex where his office was located and stepped outside. He started walking and soon reached the landing site. The booming sounds of the rotor blades were already clearly audible.

Satisfied, he noticed that Captain Barnes and his men had taken up position next to a hangar. He nodded to him and gave a hand signal that he should wait there.

It took little more than another minute for the helicopter to touch down and the crew to disembark. Hastings was now eagerly awaiting the aforementioned passenger and was taken aback when a young Greenlandic woman stepped out of the machine. One of the soldiers held her by the arm and immediately set about leading her towards the buildings.

Hastings overcame his astonishment. "Stop!" he called after the soldier in a tone of command. "Come to me and report!"

The soldier turned back with the woman in tow. He came over to Hastings and saluted. "Airman Rodriguez, sir!"

"Who is this, Rodriguez? Why are you arresting a civilian?"

"I'd like to know that too!" Nanouk interjected angrily. "Those guys chased me with the helicopter!"

"Is that so?" Hastings asked in a tone as icy as the Greenland wind in winter.

"Sir, we've been ordered. Miss Gillie, I mean, General Sattler has ..."

"Who then?" Hastings snapped at the visibly nervous subordinate.

"Strictly speaking, it was Gillie, sir!"

"I see, and what exactly did this person order?"

"The woman here - Nanouk Bruun according to her ID - we should arrest her, take her to the base and place her under arrest ... Inconspicuously."

Hastings gave a contemptuous snort. He knew that he should not take his pent-up anger out on this simple soldier, as it was directed at other people. But that was beginning to require too much restraint.

"Airman Rodriguez," he said in a laboriously controlled tone. "I have a good mind to place you under arrest instead."

"But, sir, she has ... ... entered a secure area."

"That's a lie!" shouted Nanouk.

Hastings raised his hand and motioned for her to remain silent. "I know nothing of a security area outside this base. So how would this young woman know about it? And where would it even be?"

Rodriguez swallowed hard. "Sir, I really didn't mean to ..."

"Get out of here!" Hastings ordered him, and the airman ran off. Then the commander looked at Nanouk. "I must formally apologize to you. Please, let's talk about everything in my office."

Nanouk gave him a skeptical look, but then nodded.

Hastings turned in the direction where Captain Barnes was standing and waved him over.

Barnes came running up in a hurry. "Sir?"

"Pick out the requested equipment, but don't load it yet. The helicopter will be refueled, but it will stay on the ground for now. If Sattler or anyone else asks on the radio, tell them there's been a malfunction that needs to be repaired first." He looked briefly at Nanouk again. "If they inquire about our guest, report that everything went as planned."

"All right, I'll take care of it. Anything else?"

"Yes, send the CIA man Bradshaw and the other two to my office in fifteen minutes."

***

"General, can we perhaps talk in private?" Robert asked, stepping up to Sattler at the borehole.

The general frowned and looked around the room. His gaze lingered for a moment on Nora Grimm, who was looking at the data collected by the probe. "We know that you are keeping far fewer secrets from your new colleague than would have been appropriate. Why this secrecy all of a sudden? What do you want to talk about?"

Robert also looked around. Gillie had been gone for a while, and he wondered when she would be back. But maybe Sattler was right, it made no difference. "Okay, General. I'd like to ask you to stop the exploration."

Sattler looked at him with genuine astonishment. "You're the last person I would have expected to make such a demand!"

"Look, I think we need to plan this more carefully, bring in more experts, not rush into it, especially when we consider what has happened at this site before."

"Now you're bound to mention NASA," Sattler interrupted him. "I've already had to listen to the same lecture from Shoemaker. That didn't convince me."

"Nevertheless, I have to get it off my chest. I see serious signs of danger here, although I have to admit that I ignored them myself for quite a long time. The radiation, the mysterious cases of illness, the inexplicable rise in temperature, the widening of the shaft, the signal, which we have only been able to decode a small percentage of, but which points to a highly developed intelligence. These could all be the perfect ingredients for a catastrophe if we're not careful."

"Do you think I haven't thought about that? How long do you think I've been working on this project? Do you think I wouldn't do my homework?"

"I don't want us to take avoidable risks too quickly," Robert insisted.

"What do you really want, Dr. Greaves? Do you want to leave? Now that we are on the verge of perhaps the most important discovery in history?"

"It's not the discovery. It's the consequences that worry me," Robert replied.

"He's right," agreed Nora, who had obviously been following the conversation very closely from her seat. "I mean, I don't have anything to say here anyway, but if I did, I would..."

"You recognized that quite correctly," Sattler cut her off. "You have no say here. I make the decisions. And I advise you to cooperate."

Robert needed a moment to realize this, but the last sentence had sounded almost threatening. He refrained from asking what would happen if they didn't. Why was Sattler so obsessed with this? He suddenly thought of the conversation with the Dane Erik Jansson, who had reacted strangely at the mention of Sattler's name and had hinted at a potential link to the events of 1967. Unfortunately, it had been impossible to get in touch with him for days. Should he ask the general directly? What did he have to lose?

"One question has been bothering me for a long time," he continued. "Could it be, General, that you are not only on this quest for purely professional reasons? That the interests of the Air Force are perhaps not the primary ones?"

Sattler's eyes fixed on him. "You are undoubtedly an intelligent man, Dr. Greaves. So I'm surprised that you can ask such stupid questions."

"And you think I don't even deserve an answer?"

At that moment, they heard the heavy access door open and Sandra Gillie entered the room. "The helicopter is on its way. There was a minor incident, but we've sorted everything out."

"An incident?" asked Sattler, turning around.

"As I said, the situation is under control."

"Nevertheless, I want to be informed about everything immediately. Let's go over to the command post." He turned back to Robert and Nora. "I'm just keeping them from their work here anyway."

Without waiting for an answer, he left the room with Gillie.

"You can say what you like, but there's something wrong with this guy," Nora muttered, shaking her head.

"Well, unfortunately, this realization doesn't help us. He has us in the palm of his hand. Even if we were to refuse to cooperate any further ..." He left the sentence unfinished.

"You didn't finish it earlier, but I think you have a theory about what this is by now?" Nora guessed.

"I don't have a really sophisticated thesis, but I do have a suspicion. What's more, we have already been able to gather evidence that the process under the ice has taken on a certain degree of independence. The question now is: to what extent can we influence it?"

**

Commander Gordon Hastings led Nanouk Bruun from the landing pad directly to his office and asked her to take a seat there.

However, she stood in front of the desk with her arms crossed and scowled at him.

"I must formally apologize to you again," Hastings began, trying to keep his tone calm and friendly, although he was seething inside. This blameless young woman was the last person to suffer his wrath. "Unfortunately, we don't have much time to beat about the bush, so I'll keep it short. Normally, I can put my hand in the fire for the behavior of my men, but unfortunately something has gone very wrong in our command structure in the last few days. I'm currently trying to find out how and why this has happened. I would even ask you to help me if you can."

Nanouk looked at him in astonishment and lowered her folded arms. "I beg your pardon? I can hardly contribute anything to this!"

"You can tell me what you saw there before you were illegally apprehended by my men. But first, please sit down."

Nanouk hesitated for a moment, then pulled one of the chairs towards her and sat down on it.

"So? Will you tell me how it went?" Hastings asked.

"You should know what happened. The sign on your door says you're the commander here."

"That is correct. But I also have superiors. And one of them went over my head and made decisions that led to your stay here. I'd love to find out why he did that."

"Okay, fine. I didn't think the US Army was such a pile of shit, but somehow I'm not surprised either. Especially when you consider what you did here decades ago when you buried all the garbage from Camp Century under the ice!"

Hastings leaned forward. "Now I'm hearing the name Camp Century again. That can't be a coincidence."

"I'm an activist, and I'm campaigning for you to take responsibility and dispose of your legacy finally! That's also the reason why I was out on the glacier. Otherwise, nobody would have noticed the massive number of people. But don't be under any illusions, I reported it by radio and my friend will certainly have already informed the authorities. You won't get away with such a mess again!"

"Please, Miss Bruun," Hastings interjected. "I'm really not your enemy. I can't say much about the historical events, nor can I do anything about the current measures. On the contrary, I am trying to prevent a scandal from arising." He noticed that Nanouk looked at him for a while. She was obviously trying to gauge whether she could trust him. "Tell me what you know," he repeated.

"It doesn't matter anyway, either you play it very well and know it anyway, or you actually need help. I couldn't care less. All I know is that your people and your presumably crazy superior have occupied the civilian and completely legally established drilling station of an international research network. They've turned it into a fortified facility. There are at least a dozen armed men running around. And I bet they're holding the scientists I met there last time, too."

Hastings nodded. "Thank you, that confirms my fears. And yes, I also think that there are civilians in the facility - whether voluntarily or not, I can't say."

"Then you should find out. What do you intend to do now?"

As if on cue, there was a knock at the door and Captain Barnes ushered Bradshaw, Shoemaker and Jansson in.

"Please take a seat, we have a lot to discuss," said Hastings. "This is Nanouk Bruun, by the way. General Sattler had her arrested because she was traveling near the borehole."

"Unbelievable, that bastard," said Bradshaw. "Does he even know what he's doing?"

"Take it easy. We will find a sensible solution before the whole thing becomes public. And that might happen sooner than we'd like. Because not only has Miss Bruun rightly asked the authorities for information, Nora Grimm and Alex Corbinian's superior would prefer to tell the press everything."

"That would be super-GAU," grumbled Bradshaw.

"We really have other problems than bad headlines," Jansson interjected. "I'd actually like to hear from Commander Hastings now what he decided. Because I assume that's why he sent for us."

"You're damn right to assume that!" Hastings replied. "So, here's what we're going to do ..."

***

General Sattler stepped up to the stretcher to which Alex Corbinian was tied. A thick strap went across his chest, another across his thighs, and a third secured his head at forehead level. This effectively prevented him from freeing himself. The general looked at the man calmly and tried to fathom his role in the whole affair. Night had fallen, and they were alone in the room; the medic had also withdrawn.

Alex's eyelids were closed, but the eyes underneath were twitching wildly, as if he was living through a dark nightmare. His breathing was fast and frantic. His face was covered in thick beads of sweat that glistened despite the subdued light from the overhead lighting.

Alex's arms were exposed, and Sattler could see that the pinkish-purple glow under his skin was still rhythmically swelling and subsiding. The sight held a fascination for Sattler that he could not escape. It was undoubtedly the same glow they had seen down in the ice shaft. So this man here could very well be the key to further insights.

Suddenly, Alex opened his eyes and let out a raspy gasp.

Sattler almost took a step back, so surprised was he by the sudden awakening. But the general had himself under control and didn't budge.

Alex's eyes continued to dart around, so Sattler wasn't sure whether he was actually conscious or still wandering around in a feverish dream.

Then Alex laboriously turned his head as far as the belt would allow and looked directly at Sattler. They both remained like that for quite a while, staring at each other. The men didn't know each other, had never spoken to each other, but they seemed to have something in common, something that came from deep down in the ice.

Finally, Sattler took a step forward and bent down to Alex. "What's that?" he asked, pointing to Alex's right forearm.

Alex's gaze was still penetrating, but at the same time seemed strangely uncertain.

"Do you know what happened?" Sattler asked.

"Get rid of me," Alex replied in a low voice. It sounded raspy, as if he hadn't spoken for weeks.

Sattler shook his head. "Sorry, I can't do that. You'll have to explain to me what exactly is going on first."

"That..." Alex coughed. "I can't."

"You will have to!" Sattler insisted.

"Who ... are you?" Alex wanted to know, and his voice became almost a whisper.

Sattler stepped a little closer so that he could understand him better. "I'm General Frank Sattler, I'm in charge of this operation."

Alex indicated with a nod. "It..." He coughed again. "Water," he finally gasped.

Now, Sattler took a sippy cup from a small table next to the bed and brought it to Alex's mouth.

He drank greedily from it and closed his eyes.

"You must..." Sattler began and fell silent when Alex's right hand grabbed his forearm and squeezed it with such force that even the tough soldier Sattler wanted to howl in pain. But he

255

gritted his teeth and only let out a growl. He tried to loosen Alex's fingers with his free left hand, but they seemed to be made of steel. His fingernails dug into the now bloody skin.

"Let go!" Sattler now shouted, but Alex didn't even open his eyes.

Then Sattler felt a corrosive burning sensation on his skin, right where Alex had grabbed him. It spread up his arm and was mixed with a tingling sensation that felt as if he had grabbed an anthill. Suddenly he was hit by a violent electric shock and Sattler staggered back. For a moment, he thought he was going to die on the spot, waves of pain running through his whole body. Finally, the discharge robbed him of his senses - and the pain. The world gradually became gray and lifeless. His knees gave way, and he banged the back of his head against the back of a chair. Then he was surrounded by nothing but contourless blackness.

29

PRIN research station "Amarok II", Greenland,
September 19

Per Olofsson had just placed the tray with his breakfast on the table and taken his first sip of tea when Oleg Sakharov came rushing towards him, closely followed by his colleague Chloé Lamarque. The excitement was written all over both of their faces.
Olofsson lowered his teacup and suspected nothing good. Didn't he already have enough unforeseen and seemingly unsolvable problems?
"Boss, we need to talk," Sakharov began.
He always called Olofsson "Chief" or "Boss", even though he had already told him a hundred times that he didn't need to do that because most of the people on the station called each other by their first names anyway. But Sakharov remained stubborn - or he did it on purpose, expressing his special sense of humor.
"What's wrong?" asked Olofsson. He had noticed that Zakharov's hair was sticking out wildly and that he had clear circles under his eyes. "Are you ill?"
"What? No!" replied the scientist, irritated.
"We worked through the night," explained Chloé Lamarque, who explored the local glacier together with Sakharov.
Olofsson raised his eyebrows. "Why is that? You still have two months left on the project."
Sakharov finally took a seat, and Chloé sat down at the table. They both looked mysteriously at Olofsson.
"So?"
"Boss, the glacier. Something's wrong. The temperature is far too high at certain points, and we're also receiving ... Yes, what do we call it?" He looked at Lamarque.

"Let's just say seismic activity. I know that's not entirely correct, but the effect is similar. There seem to be faults inside the glacier, small quakes, cracks on the surface."

"Excuse me?" asked Olofsson in astonishment.

"That's why we were up all night analyzing and validating the results," explained Sakharov. "We compared the data from our glacier sensors throughout northern Greenland with various satellite images and all kinds of other sources. It's more than worrying."

"The whole thing started a few days ago, very gradually at first, so we didn't notice it immediately, but since yesterday the effect has intensified to such an extent that we are seriously worried," added Lamarque.

"Worried about what exactly?" Olofsson wanted to know.

Sakharov and Lamarque looked at each other for a moment and swayed their heads back and forth.

Then Sakharov took the floor again. "Well, if the process continues to accelerate like this, large parts of the glacier will burst, the edges will flow into the sea - and a considerable part will simply melt. And probably at an incredible speed."

"I can hardly believe it," said Olofsson.

Sakharov placed a computer printout on the table and slid it over to Olofsson. "The data doesn't lie," he said curtly.

"Is there some kind of epicenter for these quakes?" asked Olofsson.

Lamarque nodded. "Taking bearings is a bit difficult, as our measuring instruments are not directly designed for this purpose. But as far as it can be narrowed down, the vibrations are coming from very close to us. If I had to guess, I'd say they're strongest where Nora and Dryer were drilling. I mean, of course, it's completely absurd that a small hole could cause such an effect, but it's still a very strange coincidence."

"What does that mean in concrete terms?" asked Olofsson. "If I've understood correctly, we're not just talking about quakes, but also temperature rises."

"Correct, and of course, the whole thing comes at an

inopportune time. The latest climate data clearly show that Greenland's glaciers are now shrinking five times as fast as they were in the 1980s. And if this should now accelerate ..." Sakharov grimaced.

"You may know that the Greenland ice sheet is one of the major tipping elements in the Earth system and is extremely threatened by climate change," added Lamarque. "For some time now, we in the scientific community have been discussing when we will reach a critical threshold at which its melting will accelerate and even intensify. It's like a kind of domino effect. And if the ice sheet melts completely, it would cause the sea level to rise by around seven meters."

"Okay, okay, that's enough. I can imagine what that means. Pretty much all the coastal towns would be swallowed up by the sea," said Olofsson. "And you're sure that something like that could be the result?"

Sakharov nodded vigorously. "Yes, definitely. I mean, these are forecasts with margins of error, but the trend is there anyway. This could act as a catalyst. The consequences would be catastrophic. If more and more freshwater flows out of the glacier into the adjacent seas, it could lead to a significant change in the water composition, which could ultimately even trigger a weakening of the Gulf Stream circulation."

"That sounds horrible. And I don't know whether we should speculate that far. The burning question at the moment is: what do we do with this knowledge? What options do we have?" asked Olofsson.

The two colleagues looked at him sheepishly.

Sakharov cleared his throat. "Well, I don't know what you can do about a phenomenon of this magnitude - except eliminate the cause as quickly as possible and hope for the best. That is, if you can find the exact cause. If it's an accelerated melting process, it would have to be contained before its dynamics get completely out of control."

Olofsson demonstratively pushed his breakfast tray away a little and stood up. He had thoroughly lost his appetite. "Okay, we'll call all the scientists together immediately and discuss the results, then we'll go to the place where the quakes were recorded as quickly as possible. I'm still hoping that it's less dramatic than we now fear. But if things continue to develop as they have so far, we'll probably have to brace ourselves for more bad news."

***

Bradshaw was sweating. Since he had put on the airtight hood a minute ago, it had been almost unbearably stuffy in the dark green NBC protective suit. He looked through the window in front of his face, which was far too narrow for his liking, at Linda, Hastings and Jansson, who were also wearing the same protective clothing as camouflage. Bradshaw imagined how the 80-year-old Jansson must feel in the thing. Hopefully, the old man wouldn't have a heart attack. But he couldn't be dissuaded from accompanying them. Now, he had to suffer just like him.

Hastings had decided that he would not simply send the requested protective equipment, but had ordered a special unit for hazardous materials to be flown to the borehole. Only he had left the real specialists at the base and put himself, Bradshaw and the others in the suits instead. This would allow them to get into the newly built outpost without any difficulty - first to get a picture and then to talk some sense into General Sattler.

Now, the helicopter that had brought them here slowly touched down in the middle of the base. The pilot signaled that it was safe to disembark, and a soldier opened the side door.

Hastings and the others climbed out of the helicopter in their uncomfortable suits and looked around. The atmosphere was obviously tense. Some of the soldiers were running around in a hurry, some were tampering with an access point - presumably the one that led to the borehole. No one was interested in the helicopter, wanted to unload the supplies they had ordered, or even noticed their strange costumes.

They had only taken a few steps when they felt a tremor under their feet. Irritated, Bradshaw looked around. What was going on here? Then he saw Sandra Gillie hurrying across the square. He almost wanted to run after her and confront her, but he just managed to hold back.

He waited until she had disappeared into one of the larger huts, then he turned to Hastings, who was standing behind him.

"Yes, I've seen them too," he said. "But we'd better find Sattler. We have to convince him first and foremost."

"Why are they all so excited?" asked Linda. "Something's not right here. I'd like to know where Robert is."

"Then we'll split up," Hastings said. "You and Jansson look for Dr. Greaves. Bradshaw and I will go after Sattler."

"Agreed," replied Jansson.

Linda also nodded. "The most likely thing is that we'll find Robert at the borehole, I think."

"We'll go over there, that should be the command post," Hastings explained, pointing to a slightly larger building with antennas and a satellite dish on the roof. Gillie had also disappeared into it a few moments ago.

"Do we still need these things?" Bradshaw asked, tugging at his suit.

"Let's at least wait until we're inside and have found what we're looking for," Hastings said.

Then, they split up and headed in their respective directions.

Two guards were posted in front of the command post, blocking Hastings and Bradshaw's way as they approached. "Stop, you're not allowed in without permission," said the man to the right of the door.

"We've been requested because of the radiation," Bradshaw replied. "You should know that."

"Negative. I have explicit instructions not to let anyone in."

Now Hastings pushed back his hood and looked at the soldier with a blush of anger on his face. "Stand aside, man. That's an order from your commanding officer."

The soldier recognized the commander and straightened up. "Yes, sir. I ..."

"Dismissed!" Hastings shouted at him, and the two men obeyed immediately.

Now Hastings and Bradshaw climbed the two steps to the door and opened it.

Bradshaw took off his protective hood and looked around the room. It was unkindly but functionally furnished - tables with equipment and computers, two technicians sitting at them, and further back was a conference table where Gillie sat with her back to them, typing hastily on a laptop.

Bradshaw and Hastings approached and walked slowly around the table.

Now Gillie looked up. She had certainly recognized her immediately, but didn't seem surprised. Or she managed to cover it up perfectly.

"Gillie, what are you doing here?" asked Bradshaw. "Don't you remember what we agreed? You wanted to inform me."

"I don't have time for your ridiculous complaints right now, Bradshaw," she replied curtly.

"That's hardly an appropriate answer. You know there will be repercussions!"

Gillie sighed. "Yes, so everything as usual."

Hastings also looked at the agent for a while, undecided what to make of this person. Then he took a quick look around the room. If this was the control center, why wasn't Sattler here? "Now, Miss Gillie, let's talk straight. There's something wrong here. Where is General Sattler?"

"Ha! Funny you should ask that. I'd like to know myself."

"What do you mean by that?" Hastings asked. "He must be here!"

"Do you see him anywhere?"

"That's why I'm asking you, damn it." Hastings became loud. "Now swallow your innate arrogance and talk!"

"He's not here! I'm currently checking all the video recordings from last night to find out where he went, but at 21:38 on the dot, various cameras failed one after the other, starting in sickbay. Other technical systems were also affected."

"Where was Sattler at the time?" Bradshaw wanted to know.

"In the infirmary with Alex Corbinian."

"What was he doing there?"

"I don't know, we don't have any audio recordings, just video. You can see him standing next to the hospital bed."

"And what happens then?" Hastings probed further.

Gillie turned the laptop and pressed play. The sequence showed a noisy image of Sattler standing next to the cot and looking at Alex Corbinian lying on it. Nothing happened for a while, then suddenly Alex's hand twitched and he grabbed Sattler by the wrist. In the next moment, everything was drowned out by digital interference.

"It stayed like that for quite a while. A usable recording only started again at the borehole shortly before midnight. Sattler is nowhere to be seen. But this instead." Gillie changed the camera view and fast-forwarded. "Take a closer look."

The picture showed the entrance to the borehole. Two unconscious soldiers were lying in front of it.

"What about them?" Hastings wanted to know.

"They're dead. Heart attack, says the paramedic."

"Both of them? Hardly out of the blue!" Bradshaw exclaimed. "It must have been someone else's fault."

"That's why everything is going haywire here," said Gillie. "Nobody can explain it, discipline is suffering, rumors are doing the rounds."

"Then Sattler must have gone to this borehole," Hastings speculated.

"Very probably. I've asked Greaves and Grimm to check the probe's log data and video recordings," explained Gillie.

The next moment, the door to the command post opened and Linda Shoemaker came in with Robert, Nora and Jansson.

"So?" asked Gillie and Hastings, almost as if from the same mouth.

Before anyone could answer, Hastings turned to Gillie. "Just to be clear, I'm taking charge here from now on. If Sattler shows up again, we'll talk about the whole thing, but until then, you do as I say - or you're going to jail! The madness has gone on long enough." Hastings had now clearly sounded threatening.

Gillie waved him off. "Please, if you say so."

Robert and the others now approached the table. Bradshaw began to take off the rest of his protective suit, and the others did the same.

"So, are there any clues as to where Sattler is?" Hastings asked Robert.

"It has gone down into the shaft. The elevator control system logs are fragmented, as are the robot's camera and sensor data, but its position has changed. The robot was picked up and unloaded. Then the transport cage was lowered again and stopped at the level of the missile silos discovered yesterday. Sattler must have done this manually."

"Why the hell is he going down there alone at night?" Bradshaw asked in amazement.

"To be honest, I don't really care why," Hastings replied. "Let him stay down there as long as he likes it. That gives us time to get everything back on track here. We'll disband this base immediately and leave."

"With respect, that's not possible!" Jansson intervened. "Sattler went down there for a reason - and it does play a role! He's under someone else's influence." Jansson pulled out Paul Memphis' diary and placed it on the table. "It repeats itself. Sattler's father was stationed here back in 1967. And he came into contact with this alien organism that took possession of him."

"Are you telling me he's possessed or something?" Hastings asked in a mocking tone.

"This isn't about some religious demon nonsense. I believe that the alien life form has invaded him and taken possession of him."

As if as background music, there was a slight vibration that penetrated from the depths to the surface.

Hastings shook his head. "With respect, this all sounds a lot like science fiction. I can't deny that very strange things are going on here. But no one has yet been able to come up with a halfway credible explanation."

"Yes, we have the explanation," Robert insisted. "I know it's a lot to ask, but you have to believe us."

Again, there was a slight tremor that made the empty coffee cups clink on the table.

"What does this life form want?" Bradshaw asked, trying to suppress the unease that the tremors were causing him.

"I don't know, there's nothing about it in the diary. We'll just have to ask her," said Jansson.

"Questions? Of course! It's as simple as that," said Hastings.

"If this hypothesis is correct - and I think it is - then this does indeed offer a chance to communicate," Linda Shoemaker interjected. "You see, Robert and Nora have studied the behavior of the life form, and I was also able to analyze the signals they picked up. It shows intelligence and certainly has certain goals and needs. We should find out what these are."

Hastings let out an unwilling growl. "You mean the plan to simply fill in this hole won't work?"

"That didn't work over 50 years ago. It's probably high time we tried something new," Jansson replied in a sarcastic tone.

"Sir," one of the technicians intervened from further back. "Sickbay reports that the patient has woken up and wants to talk to someone. He's obviously very agitated."

"Alex!" Nora exclaimed. "We have to go to him."

"Well, maybe that will shed some light on it," Hastings said. He pointed to Nora. "You know the man. So we'll both go over there. Greaves can go with us. The others will stay here for the time being and think of a viable alternative to the backfill! At the moment, I don't see me allowing anyone to go down there, but I can be persuaded otherwise if necessary." Hastings stood up and walked quickly towards the door.

Robert and Nora hurried to follow him.

30

*Not far from the "Snowbird" outpost,
17 kilometers north of the "Amarok II"*

Per Olofsson's back was aching. He hadn't been on a snowmobile for a long time and knew that the trip to the borehole was hell for his ailing spinal discs. But there was no way around it. Two of his employees, for whom he was responsible, were there - most likely against their will and in great danger.

The meeting with all the scientists at the station had surprisingly led to a consensus in assessing the situation, even if the consequences were still difficult to assess. The latest satellite images and the seismographic and thermal evaluations had revealed that the phenomenon was worsening. New deep cracks and faults had appeared in the ice and temperature hotspots in the glacier. Whatever the military was doing there, it had to stop immediately. Olofsson only hoped that he would find someone at the borehole to whom he could explain this.

Together with machine operator Ian Macmillan, station physician Dr. Winfried Keller and glaciologist Oleg Sakharov, Olofsson had set off a few minutes ago and was now heading for the site where Nora Grimm and Alex Corbinian had been working.

Even from a distance, they could see that many things had changed here. The complex had been fortified with a high snow wall, and guard posts and vehicles were visible.

Olofsson slowed down some distance away and turned to Macmillan, who stopped beside him. "Any idea how we can get in there discreetly?"

Macmillan swayed his head back and forth. "Well. We'd best try the Highlander tactic. Two of us drive up to the access road and engage the soldiers in conversation while the other two climb over the rampart at the back."

"Not so stupid," praised Olofsson. "We'll both go to the entrance, my back won't take any climbing." He turned to Keller and Sakharov. "You've got the latest data with you. Try to find some people with expertise and convince them to stop whatever they're doing. Tell them to let Nora and Alex go; otherwise, it'll go public. Lamarque has instructions to send everything out via the press distribution list if we're not back in two hours or come back with new information. Use that as leverage as soon as it becomes necessary."

"All right, we'll kick the Americans' asses," said Sakharov with a grin.

Dr. Keller grimaced skeptically, but remained silent.

"Ready?" Olofsson finally asked and received three nods in confirmation.

Then, they split up and headed for opposite ends of the base.

***

Nora, Robert, and Hastings stepped quickly through the door of the infirmary.

"Calm down!" the paramedic shouted at Alex Corbinian, who was trying to toss and turn on the stretcher, tugging violently at his straps.

"Get rid of the man!" Hastings ordered.

The paramedic looked at him, irritated for a moment, then nodded. "Yes, sir! But I must warn you, the patient is ..."

"Get going!" Hastings repeated, cutting off the medic's words.

Nora and Robert stepped forward, and as soon as Alex recognized them, he calmed down and let the paramedic take off his harness without any difficulty.

"Thank God, familiar faces at last," said Alex.

"Are you all right?" Nora wanted to know.

"I ... think so. What's happened?"

"Alex, we were actually hoping to find out about you," said Robert. "We found you unconscious at the borehole, totally hypothermic."

Alex's face visibly mixed cluelessness with fear. "I thought it was a bad dream. My hands and feet were burning like fire."

"What were you doing here?" Hastings asked.

Alex looked at the commander scrutinizingly, but didn't answer.

"This is the commander of the base in Pituffik, Gordon Hastings," Robert explained. "We tracked you down with the help of the military."

"Then thank you very much," Alex replied.

"We don't have time for pleasantries," Hastings said sharply. "So, what were you doing here? What were you doing at the borehole?"

"I... there was this..." Alex broke off and grimaced, as if the memory was causing him pain. "I made contact somehow. No, that's not true. It made me do it." He groaned and grabbed his head.

"Give him something for the pain," Hastings instructed the paramedic.

"No, I'm fine," Alex rebutted. "It's just so hard to get a clear memory. It's all in a fog, I can only see snippets. And I can feel something. Fear, hunger, confusion - I can't even tell if these are my feelings."

"Alex, we think you've had contact with this alien organism," Nora explained. "It seems to have taken possession of you somehow."

"Organism? I thought..."

"They're not crystals, Alex. At least not only. We're pretty sure now that it's a life form - an alien intelligence," Robert continued.

Alex nodded. "Yes, that could be. I can still feel an echo of that intelligence in me. It's so disconcerting that it scares me."

"Whatever it was, it seems to have left you tonight," Hastings said.

"How?"

"Of course, we would have liked to know that from you, too."

"There is video footage of you waking up in the middle of the night and grabbing General Sattler by the arm. Then, unfortunately, the cameras broke down. Can't you remember?" Nora asked.

"I don't even know who General Sattler is!" Alex replied. "I can hardly remember anything since I left the station. And even that I've only experienced as if in a dream."

"We're not getting anywhere like this," Hastings said with audible displeasure in his voice.

"Listen, commander! I don't know what I was doing here. But I clearly sensed that ... it ... wanted to come here. It wanted to be with its own kind."

"Why?" Robert asked.

A tremor shook the infirmary, this time stronger than the previous ones.

"They ... they turn ... I think," Alex replied hesitantly.

Hastings let out a disgruntled grunt. "What kind of shit have I gotten myself into here?" he grumbled.

"Alex, you must know that this General Sattler went down there. The shaft is now much bigger. The military installed an elevator that Sattler used to lower himself down. And as far as we know, he never came back up," Robert explained. "You can't imagine what he might be doing down there?"

"If this alien intelligence jumped from me to him, it was probably for the purpose of him taking it there. I was strapped down here and couldn't move, which probably prompted it to take this step."

"The belts were a safety measure," said the paramedic, who was standing a little to one side. "If it had been up to me, I wouldn't have done it, but Gillie and Sattler ..."

"It's all right," said Hastings. "You're not being accused of anything."

"So Sattler has gone down there and is under someone else's influence," Robert summarized. "The intelligence is using him to achieve its goals. Alex called it a transformation, but into what? But if we consider these recent tremors, I think it's clear that we're in the middle of this process."

A soldier came in the door of the infirmary and reported. "Commander, two people claiming to be from the PRIN station have been apprehended at the entrance. Two more men have tried to climb over the wall at the back. We have arrested them. One of them claims to be the station manager."

"Olofsson!" said Nora.

"It's getting more and more colorful here," growled Hastings. "Take everyone to the command post," he instructed the soldier, who nodded and promptly disappeared through the door again.

Hastings looked at Alex. "You should rest. But I'm not ordering you to. If you feel fit enough, you may accompany us. And I would like to formally apologize again for the restraint."

"That's all right," Alex replied. "I hardly noticed any of it anyway." He swung his legs off the couch and stood up. "I'm coming with you!"

***

"Get this woman out of here!" demanded Per Olofsson of Commander Hastings, pointing with his outstretched right hand at Sandra Gillie, who was sitting calmly at the conference table. "She poisoned Steven Dryer!"

"Please, this really isn't the time for such arguments. We can't clear this up here and now, but I promise it will be done. As soon as possible and in full."

It had taken Nora a few moments to put Olofsson's words into perspective, but now the realization hit her all the harder. "Are you telling me Steven is dead?" she asked, dumbfounded.

"Yes, I'm so sorry, Nora. But there's no doubt that his condition was artificially induced. Steven left a message saying so himself. What's more, the post-mortem is still pending at the clinic in London, and I'm pretty sure it will confirm the poisoning," explained Olofsson.

"This is a serious allegation and it needs to be investigated," said Robert. "But I can only agree with Hastings, we have to postpone the clarification until later."

"Mr. Olofsson, please send me all the evidence," Bradshaw asked, giving Gillie a disparaging look. "We will fully support the investigation."

Olofsson finally took a seat at the table, as far away from Gillie as possible. The others also sat down, so all the chairs were now occupied.

"Why did you come here?" Hastings wanted to know from Olofsson.

"Firstly, to fetch my people, who fortunately seem to be in good health. And secondly, I must ask you to stop your experiments immediately. They are obviously having an extreme impact on the glacier and the ecosystem."

"That will probably be difficult," said Hastings.

"Listen..." Olofsson roared, but Nora put her hand on his shoulder reassuringly and he fell silent.

"Per, the problem isn't that someone would refuse. But there are no experiments going on here that we could stop. They seem to be the consequences of a process that is being driven by the alien intelligence."

Jansson cleared his throat. "This intelligence has certainly learned to adapt over the last 50 years. In 1967, they still managed to slow them down. But the problem has not been solved. It almost seems to me as if this alien organism has been hibernating for a long time and is now experiencing its spring."

"Very well possible. But is he aware of what it does?" said Robert, turning to Olofsson. "What do you mean by extreme effects?"

Olofsson glanced at Sakharov, and he took the floor. "To summarize briefly: The glacier is becoming unstable, deforming, cracking and heating up very strongly in places. If this continues, large sections could melt away." He pulled a tablet out of his pocket and pushed it over to Robert, Shoemaker and Hastings. "Here, look!"

Robert and Linda examined the data and satellite images.

"That's from today?" Linda asked.

"Yes, from today and the last two days," confirmed Sakharov. "The trend is clearly recognizable. Both the strength of the quakes and the temperatures are rising dramatically."

"That's why we're here," said Olofsson. "We had to let you know and ... Well, the hope was that we could convince you to do something about it."

Hastings shook his head. "I hardly understand what you're trying to tell me. But I know that this is not something that can be solved by military means."

"Then trust the science," Nora interjected. "There are many brilliant minds around this table."

"But time is short," said Sakharov. "If we want to do something, we need to do it now."

"We should go down," Robert said. "I'm going anyway and I could definitely use some help. Still, I know it can be very dangerous, and I'm not going to ask anyone to come with me."

"I'm coming with you," Nora and Linda replied almost in sync.

Alex, Sakharov, Jansson and Bradshaw also volunteered.

Hastings looked back and forth between those present. "I cannot and will not forbid you. But I don't think Jansson and Corbinian are in any condition to go."

"You can forget it," protested Jansson. "I'm going with you, I promised an old friend."

"I'm fine," Alex now said. "I am at least partly to blame for this situation and feel I can contribute to solving the problem."

"All right, but I can't guarantee your safety. I will instruct my men to evacuate this base as quickly as possible. Only I myself will accompany you and bring Sattler back."

"What about me?" asked Gillie, who had been sitting

quietly at the table the whole time. "You could use a well-trained agent. Besides, Sattler seems to trust me, maybe I can convince him."

"You're just trying to get your head out of a noose at the last minute," Bradshaw replied.

"Call it what you like. You know that I can be useful and that I only think in a solution-oriented way."

"Yes, that may be. But you don't know your limits and you're a bloody psychopath," Bradshaw replied.

"You will be taken into custody," Hastings determined, giving Gillie a dark look. "Whatever awaits us down there will be challenge enough. I can't have someone stabbing you in the back at the next opportunity."

"Your bad luck," Gillie said dryly and turned away.

Hastings didn't waste another second on Gillie either. "Okay, I'll arrange for the evacuation of this location. In the meantime, the reconnaissance team will gather over at the entrance," he ordered. "The remaining civilians will leave this location with the first helicopter."

31

The small elevator had now descended for the third time to the same depth in the shaft where General Sattler had presumably exited ten to twelve hours ago. The team of eight gathered at the former missile silos C and D in the east of the abandoned Camp Century.

Robert and Linda had already taken measurements at the surface to determine whether radiation, toxins or other harmful emissions were being emitted from the crystal structure, which was now growing beyond the upper edge of the borehole. As this was not the case, Hastings had finally agreed to the exploration. The second measurement at this depth also revealed no potentially dangerous influences.

At the bottom of the exit, Hastings gave the signal that the team could get rid of the protective suits they had put on as a precaution. It was also too warm here to stay in them any longer.

"Robert, do you have a theory as to how temperatures can be so high down here?" Linda wanted to know. "It must be almost 20 degrees above zero."

"Yes, I guess so too. It can only be the crystals. Look at the walls, everything is covered in them like a protective shell."

"We have already recorded massive temperature fluctuations before," Nora added. "These crystals seem to influence the melting point of water. And pressure also plays a role. In any case, the water is not behaving in the way we are used to."

"You mean this isn't ice?" Bradshaw asked.

"Definitely not," confirmed the glaciologist Sakharov. "Look at the structures." He walked very close to one of the walls and examined it. "And this glow, I have to say, is highly fascinating."

"Hey, you'd better stay away from that!" Hastings ordered, looking at Alex Corbinian. "Or do you want a load of alien crystals in your blood too?"

Sakharov slowly moved away from the wall again. "I wasn't going to touch it, cowboy," he said sullenly. "This can't be ice, otherwise it would all be pressed flat like a flounder. The crystals must be powerful if they've preserved all these tunnels."

"How hard?" asked Linda.

"It's hard to say, you would have to take samples and test it."

"There's no way we're doing that," Hastings replied quickly.

"It's very hard anyway," said Nora. "Our drill almost didn't get through, and it has a diamond coating."

"I'm sure it's all very exciting, but shall we finally go in?" asked Jansson. "I mean, before I die?"

"Yes, we will advance slowly. Everything very gently. And nobody touches anything," Hastings repeated and took the lead together with Robert.

Jansson pushed his way to the front with the diary in his hand. "Here, this might help." He showed Hastings a page with a hand-drawn map of the base. "Memphis made this sketch later from memory. Unlike the officially available plans, it also shows the secret missile silos."

"Okay, very good. According to the scale, it's almost 200 meters to the living and working areas. Where should we look first?" asked Hastings.

"Hard to say," Robert replied. "As it turns out, Sattler has a very personal connection to this place. His father was here. It could be that he's looking for his body. On the other hand, he's probably under the influence of this strange intelligence, which certainly has completely different motives."

"That's what I love about scientists," said Hastings in an ironic tone. "They talk a lot, but ultimately we don't know any more afterwards."

"I was just putting the arguments on the table," Robert replied.

For a while, they walked in silence along the mirror-smooth ice tunnel, which was increasingly illuminated by a pinkish-purple glow. Then it shook briefly and violently. Alex let out a strained gasp that echoed off the walls.

"Alex, what is it?" Nora asked.

Corbinian had sunk to his knees and closed his eyes. Hastings now came running to him. "I knew it was a mistake to take him with me. He's still too exhausted."

"No, that's not it," Alex said and shook himself. He opened his eyes and stood up. "I ... felt something. During the last quake, something ... resonated inside me." Alex let out another gasp and staggered. At the last moment, he caught himself with his hands on the wall, where the ghostly glow immediately intensified.

"Let go of the damn wall!" shouted Hastings.

Robert and Bradshaw rushed forward to pull Alex away from the crystal surface. The glow dimmed again.

"It's all good." Alex tightened up.

Robert and Bradshaw reluctantly let go of his arms.

"Are you sure?" Nora inquired.

"Yes. I can understand it better now," said Alex.

"What exactly?" Hastings asked.

"This intelligence, it may be trying to communicate with me. Apparently, there's still some of her left in me. Or it has somehow changed me so that I can talk to it."

"What does it want? Any idea?" Robert asked, visibly agitated.

"It's complicated. I keep hearing something about an assignment, a mission, they shouldn't be stopped. I can't answer, I just hear these fragments. Maybe it doesn't want to talk to me directly either."

"Wait, what are we not supposed to stop this thing from doing? That it melts the whole glacier? Of course, we're going to stop it!" Bradshaw replied.

"The question is how," grumbled Sakharov.

"Why does it do that?" Linda wanted to know from Alex.

He shook his head. "I can't say. The contact was too brief. I could try again, maybe ..."

"No!" Hastings interrupted him energetically. "We'll go on and find Sattler." He started moving again.

Robert let him and Jansson go first and stayed further back with Linda and Nora this time. "The word mission is very interesting, don't you think?"

"Yes, that means these crystals aren't here by chance," said Linda. "And they probably weren't on Mars by chance either."

"But how did they get there? Where did they come from?" Nora wanted to know.

"That's one of the great mysteries I'd love to solve," Robert replied.

"Do you mean..." Linda faltered. "Maybe it's nonsense, but I was just thinking ... what if this is some kind of terraforming project by an alien civilization?"

Robert nodded slowly. "I was almost thinking the same thing. It's very conceivable that an advanced civilization out there has found a way to bridge vast distances to send some kind of seed of life to other promising planets to colonize them."

"Wait a minute," Bradshaw intervened. "Are you saying this is exactly the crazy scenario Sattler's staff unit was created for? The guy was right all along?"

"It's just a hypothesis, Bradshaw," Linda replied. "That's what scientists do. We collect data and evidence and try to explain what it means in context."

"Still ... Does that make sense?" Nora asked. "Terraforming or the colonization of worlds would be carried out on uninhabited planets, wouldn't it?"

"Sure, you could assume that," Robert replied. "But we don't know whether this alien civilization had detailed knowledge of the individual planets. It's also conceivable that the whole thing was done on a scattergun approach, without knowing where there was a real chance of success."

"This could explain why these crystals were inactive on

Mars. The conditions there were not right. The mission could not be realized," Linda speculated.

"Or it failed," Robert interjected. "Perhaps the current state of Mars has been influenced by it. What is clear, however, is that the conditions here on Earth are different and the crystals are obviously continuing to develop and multiply."

"With highly unpleasant consequences for the climate," Sakharov intervened.

"I didn't sense any malicious intent," Alex said.

"Well, that doesn't necessarily mean anything," Bradshaw said. "The highway to hell is paved with good intentions."

"There's something up ahead," Hastings reported, interrupting the discussion.

"We are approaching the living areas," added Jansson.

The entire outer skin of the underground tunnels and caves was also covered with a softly glowing, mirror-smooth layer of crystal. The buildings and facilities inside almost looked as if they had been abandoned a minute ago - as if time had stood still in this base since the 1960s.

"Unbelievable," Jansson breathed. "Nothing has changed. Everything is perfectly preserved, the ..." The old man shook his head in disbelief.

"That can't really be the case, yes," Hastings confirmed. "But it is."

"We should split up," Robert suggested. "We'll take too long if we all search together. And there are eight of us, so that should make two teams."

"Agreed," Hastings said, turning to Bradshaw. "You have combat training, I presume?"

Bradshaw nodded. "Sure, I have! And I'm happy to lead the second team."

"Well, we'll divide it so that everyone takes one of the weaker and two scientists with them. Jansson, Shoemaker and Sakharov will come with me. Bradshaw will take Greaves, Corbinian and Grimm," Hastings decided and handed out radios to both teams.

"Agreed," confirmed Bradshaw, and the others also seemed satisfied with the division.

"Team 1 will search the residential areas with me from the west," Hastings ordered. "Bradshaw will go directly east through the main tunnel to the other missile silos and begin the search there. Whoever discovers something first will report it. Otherwise, we'll automatically meet in the middle at some point."

Bradshaw briefly pressed the talk button to test the radio connection. The device made loud noises and occasional digital crackling noises, but seemed to work in principle.

Now, he beckoned Greaves and the others to join him. "We'll go this way, the big tunnel seems to go all the way through to the back."

Hastings pulled out his pistol and then disappeared with his team into the foremost hut.

"Come on then," Robert said and set off.

"It feels like I'm in a graveyard," Nora said as they moved deeper into the complex. "I feel like I'm doing something forbidden."

"Strictly speaking, we don't have permission to be here either. This used to be a top secret base," said Bradshaw. "But firstly, nobody knew it still existed, and secondly, who was supposed to check us out?"

"Yes, I know that," Nora replied, "I'm just thinking out loud to distract myself. It's all just too crazy. Just over a week ago, I was mindlessly drilling holes in the ice and dreaming of some excitement."

"The craving should have subsided," said Alex.

"You betcha."

"Shh, we should still be a little quieter," Bradshaw advised. "We don't know where Sattler is. He might be lying in wait for us."

They silently crossed the length of the tunnel and, after a good 15 minutes, reached an underground cave that looked like a gigantic air bubble trapped in the ice. From the end of the tunnel, it suddenly stretched more than 20 meters down and almost as far up.

"What the hell is that?" asked Bradshaw.

Robert looked around with interest and tried to get an overview. But there were no prominent landmarks. The bubble was completely empty and smooth. "We should actually be exactly where the missile silos were," he explained.

"Didn't Jansson say that Sattler's father had set off the rockets?" Nora said.

"But..." Robert paused. "There's no residue here. There should at least be some charred fragments or ..." He shrugged his shoulders helplessly.

"Anyway, this is a dead end. Let's go back and search the other rooms," Bradshaw suggested.

"Wait a minute," Alex said suddenly. "I ..."

"Are you all right?" Nora wanted to know.

"Yes, but there's something here."

"Where?" asked Robert.

Alex closed his eyes and turned very slowly on his own axis. Then he stopped and took a few steps until he reached an inconspicuous crevice in the wall. He stopped in front of it and pointed inside. Back there, a staircase led a few meters into the depths.

Bradshaw stepped forward with his gun drawn. "Is Sattler down there?"

Alex shrugged his shoulders. "I ... I don't think so. But ..."

Bradshaw grimaced, then walked slowly forward and descended the stairs, followed by the others. At the bottom, they were presented with a bizarre sight: two men were standing near a half-demolished control panel, one still with his hand on a switch, the other probably about to rush towards it. Both were frozen in their respective poses, covered in the same clear crystal layer as the entire outer skin of the base. Their bodies were as if preserved, even their skin seemed somehow rosy due to the subtle pink glow of the material.

"Oh my God," Nora breathed.

"What happened to them?" Bradshaw wanted to know.

Robert and Alex also came closer and inspected the two of them.

"That's downright crazy," Robert commented. "They must have been trapped within a fraction of a second."

"Could the same thing happen to us?" asked Bradshaw in alarm.

"I don't think so," said Robert. "It was probably a reaction to the rockets being fired. That big bubble over there might actually have been the site of the former silos. The rockets have burned up completely, but their energy has been absorbed."

"From the crystals?" Nora exclaimed. "They used them as some sort of food, didn't they?"

"Something like that," Robert replied. "In any case, it caused the crystals to solidify and behave like this."

"This coat here says Dr. Stirling," Alex said, pointing at the man who seemed to be running towards the console.

"Jansson mentioned him. One of the scientists who couldn't be evacuated and who was supposedly with Sattler's father when he went crazy," Robert explained.

Bradshaw pointed to the second man at the launcher. "That must be the guy here." He took the radio from his belt and brought it to his mouth.

***

Gordon Hastings and his team had already searched a handful of buildings and found nothing except the strange feeling of having traveled half a century back in time. The house they were currently in had obviously been a private residence. Judging by the mess, it had been abandoned in a hurry, as had the other dwellings they had entered. There was inventory, clothing and pieces of equipment lying around everywhere. There were even two half-eaten plates on the table. The remains had shrunk to a wrinkled, black-brown layer, and it could no longer tell what they had once been.

In another corner of the room, two beige-brown upholstered armchairs stood in front of an old-fashioned tube TV with a wooden cabinet. A bouquet of artificial flowers was placed in a purple, bulbous plastic vase, which was in a color duel with the predominantly orange patterned wallpaper.

"I feel like I'm in an old movie, only the actors are all off," commented Linda.

"We're the actors here," Jansson replied, turning to Hastings. "What are we doing here? Searching the residential buildings individually makes little sense. Sattler is hardly going to sit comfortably in an armchair and watch a quiz show."

"Yes, you're right," Hastings grumbled. "Where would you go?"

"We should try the former reactor area. Various technical systems were located there that could potentially be of interest. This is also supported by the fact that the problems started at the reactor. It's possible that removing the reactor wasn't enough, and something is still going on there."

"Okay, that seems to be the best clue. Where do we have to go?"

"Two main tunnels run more or less through the entire complex. We entered the southern tunnel, where most of the residential areas are located. The technical complex adjoins the northern tunnel, which we can cross over into via one of the connecting passages - if they are still intact."

"I think we can assume that," said Linda Shoemaker. "Everything here is so well preserved, I still can't believe it."

"Okay, let's find out," Hastings said and started moving.

They left the building and walked past the next one on the outside. Further on, an airlock in the tunnel wall came into view.

"How is it actually possible that this base wasn't destroyed? What has happened here in the last few hours?" Linda asked Jansson.

"I don't know first-hand because I wasn't there when the rockets went off. The Memphis diary says that Benjamin Sattler, General Frank Sattler's father, somehow escaped from the infirmary where he had been lying for several days in the turmoil of the evacuation. He gained access to the western silos - and apparently there were also casualties. Paul Memphis, Dr. Stirling and some soldiers are said to have tried to stop him, but in the end Stirling even stayed with him and barricaded himself in there with Sattler."

"Why is that?" asked Shoemaker.

"He must have believed that Sattler's plan had to be completed. That they could stop the process."

"It certainly had an effect," said Sakharov. "The whole base seems to be encased in a high-strength shell made of the alien material, as if it were all a giant crystal."

"Yes, but how could Sattler have guessed what would happen?" Linda wanted to know.

"Memphis writes that the foreign intelligence was in him - just as it was in Alex. Sattler was aware of this and fought to keep the upper hand. He must have sensed what this life form wanted and then looked for a way to prevent it," explained Jansson.

They reached the intermediate tunnel, and Hastings opened the steel gate. Behind it, a low passage appeared, which lay in darkness apart from a very faint purple glow.

They entered the corridor, and Linda turned to Hastings. "Do you happen to know what kind of missiles were stationed here back then?"

"No. Officially, there were never any missiles here. But judging by the state of development and intended use, they were probably LGM-30 Minuteman series I and II missiles. These were three-stage intercontinental ballistic missiles, solid propellant-powered and capable of delivering nuclear weapons."

"Nuclear weapons capability, even the word is terrible," said Sakharov.

Hastings stopped and looked at the Russian skeptically. "That was in the middle of the Cold War, what do you think the aim of this base was? Besides, your people were in no way inferior to us when it came to armament!"

"It's okay, that really doesn't help us," Linda intervened.

"You're right," said Sakharov.

"They were obviously unequipped," Hastings noted. "If a nuclear bomb had been detonated, it would definitely look different here."

"And the matter could hardly have been swept under the carpet," added Jansson.

A short, violent tremor now shook the base, and a new crunching sound could be heard, as if ice was deforming and splintering.

"That's certainly true," Hastings agreed. "Let's move on, I don't particularly like this shaft."

They reached the end of the connecting tunnel and opened the door. They immediately noticed a trail of red blood on the floor. It wasn't fresh, but it was still easily recognizable as such. They followed it slowly and found the body of a soldier about 35 meters down the tunnel. He had been shot, it was clear to see as the body was barely decomposed.

"Strange," said Linda. "He looks like a thin mummy. Shouldn't he be in much worse condition?"

"Not really," replied Sakharov. "That's typical of ice corpses. Because of the permafrost that has prevailed for decades and the lack of decomposing organisms, the decomposition process is extremely slow. But that would mean that the rise in temperature has only taken place recently."

"Nora's drilling," said Linda. "She must have scratched the crystal shell and restarted the process that had been halted."

"That sounds as plausible as it is worrying," said Jansson.

"Where does the tunnel lead to?" Hastings wanted to know.

"The infirmary is just around the corner," Jansson explained. "This is probably one of the soldiers who unfortunately got in Sattler's way." The old man looked around. "Back there is the former reactor area."

"Right, let's have a look at it," Hastings decided and went ahead.

At that moment, the radio he was wearing on his vest crackled and he stopped again.

32

"Hastings, do you read me? This is Team 2, come in," Bradshaw reported over the radio and released the intercom button. The device initially emitted an unpleasant crackling and hissing noise. It took a few seconds for him to receive a response.

"Hastings here, what is it?" he heard the commander say over the background noise.

"We checked the silos in the west - or rather what's left of them. The ignition of the rockets vaporized everything except for some of the control electronics. But the really strange thing is that we found two people."

"Is it General Sattler?"

"No, they're ... dead, I guess. I can't say with one hundred percent certainty, but it appears to be a scientist named Stirling and the father of General Sattler. Both are covered in the same crystalline layer as the entire outer skin of the base. It looks like they've been frozen in mid-motion, really bizarre!"

"Understood. We haven't found anything yet except a soldier who was apparently shot. The body is in unusually good condition, considering its age. It hasn't been covered in the alien material. We are now on our way to the former reactor room and hope to find something there."

"Okay, then we'll come there too. I don't know what else we could do here."

"Do that, but continue to be careful, we still don't know where Sattler is."

"Of course we're careful, we're not idiots, Hastings!" growled Bradshaw, putting the radio back on his belt. Then he added to himself: "What a pompous ass, typical military." He pointed back towards the tunnel. "Okay, let's go carefully to the reactor room."

***

Hastings and the others turned into a side arm of the large supply tunnel and entered the technical area. There were various storage rooms with supplies and equipment to the left and right, as well as a combined vehicle depot and generator room further back, in which there were three large diesel generators and huge tanks with fuel, oil and other operating fluids. The containers were neatly labeled and obviously still well-filled. Here, too, everything seemed to have been left as it was. The driver's door of one of the small snow groomers parked here was even open and a hose was still in the tank filler neck.

Opposite the large depot was the former reactor room, which was separated by a massive, lead-filled door. Bright yellow warning signs with urgent safety instructions pointed out the dangers behind this door. Despite the warnings, it stood half open.

"Don't worry," explained Jansson. "The reactor and the remaining fuel rods were taken away. I saw it myself."

"Do I detect a ‚but'?" Hastings asked. "Your tone doesn't sound so convincing."

"There were problems with the reactor right from the start, leaks and failures. The radioactively contaminated cooling water and waste was pumped into a cavern under this base."

"Sounds like an exemplary solution," said Sakharov mockingly.

"Those were different times," Hastings replied curtly. "We shouldn't presume to judge behavior from our perspective."

"Well, we're clearly struggling with the consequences of the omissions of that time," Linda interjected. She pointed to the safety gate, which was glowing and glowing more intensely than anywhere else so far. "That clearly seems to be the center of activity."

"Yes, Paul Memphis and I already suspected that," Jansson agreed. "The radiation from the reactor somehow stimulated these alien structures - or at least encouraged their development. I was never quite sure how this happened, but I hope that we can now find out."

"We'll see," Hastings qualified. "Scientific findings are not necessarily our priority. We'll go in, get Sattler and get out."

"Of course," said Jansson. "As if it should be that easy."

Hastings let out an unwilling snort. "I'll go ahead. When the coast is clear, I'll give the signal," he said, raising his pistol. With his free hand, he pushed the door open a little further and stepped through the opening.

The others waited tensely outside. Nothing happened for an agonizing eternity, then Hastings stuck his head out again. "I think we can go in. But be prepared for a rather curious sight."

Behind the airlock, something awaited them that had nothing in common with the idea of a reactor room. The whole thing looked more like a cathedral made of crystal, with lights so intense that they no longer needed lamps. Behind a short section of tunnel, there was a sudden drop of a good 15 meters, and it was certainly more than 10 meters to the top as well. Unlike the rest of the base, the walls here were not smooth but, on the contrary, were covered in the finest structures. Everything was covered with six-rayed constructs, reminiscent of gigantic snowflakes, whose patterns were constantly repeated. Several thick struts ran right through this bubble in the ice, which seemed to stabilize the whole thing.

"That ... is ..." Linda continued.

"... unbelievable," Sakharov completed the sentence.

"Like inside a geode or something," Linda said. "Only so much more complex."

"It seems to be a fractal structure. Look at the ramifications, everything repeats itself in ever larger dimensions!" said Sakharov.

"Apparently the reactor chamber has merged with the cavern below, which was filled with radioactive cooling water,"

Jansson stated. "I wonder how far down that branches out?" He looked down and could see a number of openings that led like shafts into the depths.

The pulsating pink-purple glow of the crystals continued from here at rhythmic intervals, traveling up from the floor of the cave in waves. It ran through all the channels to the tips of the finest ramifications, where it concentrated into thousands of tiny, almost white flashes of light and then died out before the spectacle began anew at the bottom. All this was accompanied by a soft, almost singing sound, somewhere between soprano singing and a perfectly played violin, but it was even clearer than any instrument and so penetrating that it seemed to originate directly in the listener's ear.

"That's beautiful," commented Linda. "We have to document it somehow!" She dug out her smartphone and started a video recording.

"That's not our mission," Hastings said gruffly, pointing to a spot on the opposite wall.

Now, the others realized what he meant. General Frank Sattler was up to his waist in one of the crystals, pulsing along to the same rhythm as the rest of the cave. He had his eyes closed and wasn't moving.

"Can he hear us? Can he hear anything at all?" asked Sakharov.

"I don't know, but he hasn't moved since I first came in," Hastings replied.

"And how do we get him out of there now?" Sakharov wanted to know.

"Well, I guess it's up to the scientists to think of something now," said Hastings.

Before Sakharov could answer, there was another tremor that caused the crystal structures around them to clink in dissonant tones.

***

Robert, Nora, Alex, and Bradshaw had crossed over to the other large connecting tunnel via a crossover and were now hurrying to get through it as quickly as possible. After almost 50 meters, they reached a large ramp that led uphill. At the end of it were two massive steel gates wide enough for trucks to drive through. At least they had been able to do so once before thousands of tons of ice and snow had accumulated on top.

Not far from the bottom of the ramp was an abandoned snowmobile with a sled attached, on which all kinds of equipment was piled up. Some of the crates had probably fallen off during the rapid ride and were scattered behind the vehicle.

"It all looks like scientific equipment to me," said Robert, inspecting the load.

"You're right," Nora agreed. "The researchers who were stationed here probably wanted to secure their work and continue it later."

"It looks like no more made it," said Alex. "It must have been really hectic here in the last few hours."

"If you believe Jansson's report, there was a lot of chaos. That's probably why Paul Memphis wanted Jansson to have the only salvaged ice core analyzed. This seems to be the rest of the research." Robert looked at Nora. "Maybe we can salvage some of the data when this is over."

Nora nodded. "That would be great. I mean ..."

It was interrupted by a comparatively violent quake.

"We should get going!" Bradshaw choked off the conversation for good.

"Okay, but if there's still time, I definitely want to come back here," said Robert.

Then the group started moving again.

***

The last tremor had subsided, and the deafening clanging from the crystals had finally stopped.

"If we're going to try something, let's try it now," Linda decided, crouched down, slid backwards over the edge of the narrow ledge and then began to climb down the crystals.

"I could have thought of that without a scientist," Hastings grumbled.

Jansson, meanwhile, took a step forward, but Hastings grabbed him by the arm. "You stay here. Please! I understand your insistence, but a climb like this is too risky."

Jansson gave him a venomous look, but finally nodded. "Yes, I suppose you're right."

"Wait for me!" Hastings called to Linda and then followed her downstairs, while Jansson and Alex stayed behind.

The descent was easier than expected, as the widely branching crystal structures offered many stopping points and ledges that were easy to climb down. They also turned out to be smooth, but not pointed or sharp-edged. And they were unexpectedly warm. The surface felt more like holding a glass cup filled with lukewarm tea.

After a few minutes, they reached the bottom of the cave and worked their way past the various struts running in all directions to the other side. There, they climbed the wall to a small platform on which Sattler stood like a priest in his crystal pulpit.

"How could he have gotten in there?" Hastings puzzled.

"I guess the material has grown around him. Bradshaw reported earlier that the two men found near the silo were completely covered in it. So it must be able to grow relatively quickly if necessary," Linda explained.

"I don't think I particularly like it," Hastings replied and climbed on a little more quickly.

They climbed the platform, which appeared to be much larger than initially thought from close up. There was about three to four meters of space in each direction around Sattler's crystal core before it went into the depths.

Hastings turned around and made eye contact with Sakharov and Jansson at the opposite end of the cave. "Everything's fine with us," he called over.

"Here too!" replied Sakharov.

Then Hastings turned to Linda. "I assume you have a plan by now?" he inquired.

"No. Not really. I just want to try and wake him up. Maybe then he'll manage to free himself and we can get him out of here."

Hastings gave her a skeptical look, took a step backwards, then drew his pistol. He aimed it at Sattler. "Approach him from the right. I'll keep an eye on him, and if he - or the crystal stuff - makes a wrong move, then ..." He left the sentence unfinished, obviously unsure whether he could do much in this case.

"That's clear. I hope you're a good shot," Linda said and approached Sattler. She pulled rubber gloves out of her bag and reached out to touch him on the arm. But before she could get closer than 20 centimetres to him, he suddenly opened his eyes. Linda flinched instinctively.

Sattler's eyes scanned the surroundings, but his gaze jumped around more or less aimlessly.

"General?" asked Linda.

At last, his eyes fixed on her.

"General Sattler?" Linda repeated.

Sattler looked at her, but Linda felt as if he didn't recognize her.

"Can you understand me? General Sattler?"

"He ... is ... here," came a choppy, mechanical reply from Sattler's mouth.

Linda wasn't even sure if it was his usual voice or if she was just irritated by the complete lack of emotion and the indifferent intonation.

"We ... are ... here," Sattler said now.

"I want to know who you are," Linda asked without thinking.

"We are ... the seed. You ... are ... the soil."

"What's he talking about?" Hastings wanted to know.

Linda looked at him helplessly. "I don't know. But it's definitely not Sattler."

"Yes ... it's me. We ... are ... it."

"He seems to be deeply connected to this alien intelligence," Linda said. "There could be problems if we try to sever this connection."

"But we have to take him with us. He doesn't belong here," Hastings replied.

"The one you call Sattler ..." the general's mechanical voice was now more fluent, "... he taught us ... taught us a few things. We owe him the gift of ... Consciousness. He can't walk again."

"I don't like that at all," grumbled Hastings.

"Do you think me?" Linda replied and turned to Sattler again. "What do you want?"

"Growing," came the curt reply.

"But ... you will do a lot of damage."

"We will spread out, we will populate this world."

"This world is already populated, damn it!" shouted Hastings angrily.

A shrill clang and a rumble from the floor came promptly in response.

Linda turned to the commander. "Let me talk, for heaven's sake!"

Now something changed in the expression on Sattler's face. He looked around more alertly, blinked faster and let out a gasp. "What the hell..." he gasped.

"Sattler?" Linda asked hurriedly.

"Yes, what happened?" He tried to move, but the crystal shell was tight against his body, yet he managed to get one hand free. He stretched it out towards Linda.

She instinctively flinched. "I'm sorry, that's so ..."

"You have to help me!" Sattler demanded.

"We'll try that, sir," Hastings intervened. "But how is that supposed to work?"

"Can you influence it?" Linda wanted to know. "If you can somehow distract this creature or ..."

"It's not a creature, it's a machine, a program!" shouted Sattler excitedly. "It has ..."

There was another shrill clink, this time so loud that Linda thought some of the crystals above their heads might break off and rain down on them.

Then Sattler grabbed her by the wrist, and she felt a searing pain.

"Let go, now!" Hastings shouted against the clanging. But nothing happened. "I'll shoot!"

"Don't!" shouted Linda, but Hastings' finger was already twitching on the trigger.

For a brief moment, the shot drowned out the screeching from the structures around them. In a fraction of a second, a wall of crystal formed between Hastings, Sattler and Linda. The bullet ricocheted off it and whizzed through the hall as a ricochet. Hastings had already fired a second time, again without success. This bullet was also deflected and flew on uncontrolled.

Then Hastings heard a scream behind him and turned around.

Over there, Jansson had fallen to his knees. He was holding his shoulder. Alex leaned over him.

"Stop shooting, you idiot!" shouted Alex. "You've hit Jansson."

That couldn't be true! Hastings looked back and forth between the two of them, as well as between Sattler and Linda. The latter was protected behind a bulletproof wall of crystal and, therefore, virtually unreachable.

Linda looked at him with eyes widened in shock. She finally managed to free herself from Sattler's grip and staggered away from him. She bumped into the wall and hit it with her fist.

"Shit, why did you have to shoot?" Hastings heard her voice muffled through the wall.

Hastings had no answer for her. It had been a reflex because he had been trained for dangerous situations like this. "I..." he began and fell silent again. "We'll get you out of there somehow!"

Then he looked over to the other end of the cave again, where Bradshaw, Greaves and the rest of the team had just arrived. The CIA agent immediately set about tending to the wounded Jansson.

Hastings turned to Linda, whose situation was unchanged. He had to realize that he couldn't do anything here for the time being. "I'll go over and we'll figure something out," he promised, then he climbed down. He hurriedly crossed the cave and climbed back up.

"Oh, damn," he cursed when he saw that Jansson's jacket was already wet with blood. "Must have been a ricochet," he said apologetically. "I never thought ..." He left the rest of the sentence unspoken.

"What's happened?" Robert wanted to know.

"Sattler ... or this thing ... it was talking crazy stuff and then grabbed Shoemaker. I fired. But the bullets ricocheted, and one must have hit Jansson."

"The bullet is still in there," said Bradshaw. "There's no exit wound in the back. The energy of the projectile was no longer high enough."

"Or she hit a bone and shattered it," Hastings said.

"It certainly feels like it," Jansson said weakly.

"We must take him away immediately," Hastings determined. "But until Sattler and Shoemaker are free, I can't leave here."

"Of course, you're in charge," Bradshaw teased. "But fine, I'll take care of it. But I still need a helper," he explained, looking at those present one by one.

Sakharov spoke up. "I'm coming with you, all this is far too crazy for me anyway!"

"I'm going too," said Alex. "The three of us will get there faster."

Jansson reached into his jacket and pulled out Paul Memphis' diary. He handed it to Robert. "Here, I don't know if it's much use, but you should keep it here just in case."

Robert took the now bloodstained book and pocketed it. "Thank you! And hang in there!"

Jansson nodded and then closed his eyes.

"Come on, hurry up!" Bradshaw demanded.

Sakharov and Alex lent a hand.

"Take care of yourselves!" Nora called after her two colleagues.

"I'll come back down when he's safe," Bradshaw promised as he left, and the next moment they had already disappeared through the entrance.

33

"The damn stuff put up a wall around Sattler and Shoemaker," Hastings explained. "That must have happened within milliseconds while the bullet was still in the air. Otherwise I would have hit Sattler and it would have been over."

"Yes, but now this alien intelligence has two people in its power," Nora said reproachfully.

"I couldn't have known that, I had to react."

"It's all right," Robert replied calmly. "What else has happened? You communicated with it, right? What did it say?"

"Pretty crazy stuff, if you ask me. It wasn't even entirely clear who was talking. At first, it sounded totally strange and peculiar, kind of choppy. Then suddenly, Sattler himself seemed to be speaking again."

"Please, do you remember what exactly he or she said?" Nora wanted to know. "That could be important!"

"It claimed to be the seed. It would spread and multiply. And then Sattler spoke and wanted us to help him. Just before he grabbed Linda, he said that this wasn't a real life form, it was technology. I don't know how that fits together."

"He must have a mental connection to this being - or this technology," Robert suspected. "It's as if two levels of consciousness are fighting for supremacy in his body."

"Yes, that was strange too. The thing said Sattler had given it consciousness."

"Symbiosis," Nora whispered.

"Excuse me?" Robert asked.

"Sorry, I was thinking out loud. What if the two of them have entered into some kind of symbiotic state? If this ..." She paused for a moment. "I don't know if that even begins to get to the heart of the matter, but I'll just call it crystalline DNA at work here. What if these crystals have evolved and adapted through contact with humans? What if their original task, their coding, has now been modified?"

"Coding?" Hastings asked.

"Yes, something like that," Robert agreed. "We haven't known exactly what it is yet, and we certainly don't have the correct terms for it, but it seems increasingly likely to me that these crystals are part of a colonization mechanism. It must have been a probe whose job it was to do terraforming, possibly even to promote the formation of life. After all, it called itself a seed."

"Stupid that there's already life here," Hastings interjected.

"That's right, of course. And I think this has probably led to a modification. The crystals react to the respective conditions they find and incorporate them. And if Sattler calls it technology, then it's probably programmed. This assumption would fit with the signal we picked up. It contained mathematical laws and the like. That's too abstract in a way to really belong to a life form, isn't it?"

"That's a good point," Nora agreed. "We should have noticed it sooner. But everything happened so quickly."

"And does this insight help us in any way?" Hastings wanted to know.

Robert sighed. "I guess not. As fascinating as it may be from a scientific point of view, it also seems threatening to me."

"We're finally coming together!" praised Hastings. "How do we kick this thing's ass?"

"Well, I think first..."

The rest of Robert's reply was drowned out by the clinking of crystals. But their sound was different this time, it seemed to shift in frequency and modulate in intensity. Gradually, the shrill screech turned into a voice, still a highly unpleasant, shrill voice, but an understandable one.

"Don't put up a fight," she said.

Robert and the other two looked around. The sound seemed to come from everywhere at once.

"These are the crystals themselves," Robert realized.

"We can understand you now. We would like to form a bond. It will be to your advantage," the omnipresent voice said.

"Over my dead body," growled Hastings.

"That could happen sooner than we'd like if we're not careful," Robert whispered to him. Then he raised his voice. "Whoever you are, we're not your enemies!" Robert noticed Hastings giving him a skeptical look, but he remained silent and let Robert continue. "We're researchers, we're curious and we want to get to know you. I'm sure there's a way for us to get on well together. But you have to release the two you have in your power."

"No. No one can go. I need them. I need you. I still have a lot to learn, to study you, then the connection will be perfect," the crystal voice explained.

"Please, we have to be able to trust each other, otherwise ..."

"You will make room and subordinate yourselves. The planet will soon be ours. Follow us on this path, and there will also be a future for you in this symbiosis."

"This is a waste of time," said Hastings, shaking his head. "We have to do something!"

"And what, please?" Nora wanted to know.

At that moment, Agent Bradshaw came rushing through the entrance. "Shit, the shaft's sealed at the top!" he reported.

"What?" Hastings asked incredulously.

Now Alex and Sakharov also stepped through the door.

"It's true," Sakharov confirmed. "This thing has trapped us here, there's a crystal dome over the exit. We couldn't break through it!"

"What about Jansson?" Robert asked.

Bradshaw shook his head. "He's dead. We were just about to load him into the elevator when his circulation gave out. We tried everything, but we couldn't revive him," the agent explained.

An embarrassed silence spread, then the crystal voice sounded again. "I am in control. My power stretches for miles beneath the ice. Soon, I will have gathered enough strength to complete the process."

"Sattler!" Robert shouted as loud as he could. "If you're still in there, don't let it happen!" He pulled out the old diary and held it up. "Your father wouldn't have wanted this. He knew better, he was strong enough to stop it!"

"What's the point?" Bradshaw wanted to know.

"I don't know, what brilliant idea do you have?" Robert asked back.

"Over by the shaft ..." Bradshaw began in a whisper and immediately fell silent again. Then he took the diary from Robert and opened a page. He scribbled a few words in the margin with a pen from his jacket pocket.

Robert looked at the paper and read: "There are still missiles in the silos." Then he looked up again and straight into Bradshaw's eyes. Was he serious? He was going to blow everything up?

The others had also read Bradshaw's note.

Hastings nodded in agreement. "Agreed," he said curtly.

Nora and Alex, on the other hand, stared at the agent in amazement. Sakharov shook his head vigorously.

After a moment, Nora regained her speech. "What about them?" she asked, nodding towards the opposite end of the hall.

Robert felt a lump forming in his throat at the thought of having to decide whether to leave Linda to certain death or to the influence of an alien intelligence. "I..." His voice faltered and he had to swallow.

"We're pulling out now," Hastings decided.

"You can't go," replied the crystal voice, which had been silent for a while.

"We'll see about that!" Hastings insisted, raising his fist threateningly towards the vaulted ceiling.

In response, there was a violent tremor, causing the crystals to rattle and clink.

The whole troop now hurried through the former reactor airlock out into the corridor.

"Who told us this would work?" Sakharov wanted to know. "What if it makes everything worse?"

"Worse?" Hastings repeated in a sarcastic tone. "Don't make me laugh!"

"You heard it yourself, this thing doesn't want to negotiate with us," Alex said. "And I know from personal experience how great its power over a person can be. We shouldn't bet on Sattler or Linda being able to do anything - let alone that there's a way to save them."

"I'm certainly not going to sit here and do nothing!" Hastings announced.

"Me neither," agreed Bradshaw.

"Then let's try it," said Robert. "Maybe it will have an effect, maybe not. Or these ancient parts have long been defective. But one thing is clear: we'll only know if we give it a try. And unfortunately, I'm pretty much at my wit's end regarding alternatives. What is certain, however, is that there will be devastating consequences if we do nothing. These crystals will multiply, cause the glacier to melt, and this meltwater will eventually end up in the sea, from where this seed will spread around the world. Water is the medium it needs, liquid water, I realize that now. The reason the fragments on Mars were inert is because it's bone dry there and liquid water can't exist."

"All the more reason not to waste time!" said Hastings, pointing down the corridor.

The next moment, he had already started moving, and the others followed him. They walked through the large connecting tunnel to the point where they had entered the base just a few hours ago.

Robert could see something golden glittering from a distance. Bradshaw and the others had spread a thin rescue blanket from a first-aid bag over the dead Jansson.

"What an undignified way to die," he commented, shaking his head.

"We have to save what can still be saved," Bradshaw replied. "If that's still possible at all."

He pulled Robert with him to the silos.

"How did you even get in?" Hastings wanted to know.

"Wasn't the entrance secured?"

"Yes, but with a motorized lock that was electronically controlled. Without electricity, you could turn it manually. The technology was probably not that sophisticated back then."

The thick steel door that had once protected the rockets from unauthorized access stood half open. They slipped through. Inside, one floor down, they found a control console similar to the one Robert and the others had already seen in the silo at the western end of the base - except that it wasn't half destroyed, but in pretty good condition.

"Will that work?" Robert wanted to know.

Hastings shrugged his shoulders and pressed a large rotary switch to turn on the console. Nothing happened. "Fuck!" the commander shouted angrily.

"If the motorized lock had run out of juice, how is this console supposed to work?" said Sakharov.

"Stop being a smartass!" Hastings snapped at him.

"I..." Sakharov broke off, stepped back, and crossed his arms in front of his chest.

"Manual ignition?" asked Bradshaw.

Hastings looked at the agent scrutinizingly and thought for a moment. "Maybe ... but someone would have to climb in there and ride the rocket to hell, so to speak."

Everyone looked at Hastings. He sighed. "I knew it would be me," he said calmly.

"You don't have to do that," Nora replied, "we don't even know if it'll do much good."

"Yes, I have to do it. If no one presents me with an ingenious alternative plan within the next minute, then I have to do it. I can't ask that of anyone else, maybe Bradshaw, but he's a CIA coward at heart. I have no problem making the ultimate sacrifice, I'm a soldier."

Bradshaw didn't comment on the point against him, but just looked at Hastings with appreciation.

"Now, I want you to go over to the shaft and wait there," Hastings said. "If it works, the dome above the exit could break. Let's get out and run for your lives if that happens."

"You go first," said Bradshaw. "I'll wait here until the last moment, just in case anyone else has to go down there."

Hastings nodded. "Okay, then we won't waste any time."

The others were still hesitant to leave the room, but Hastings immediately made his way to the nearest silo.

Robert saw him enter through a maintenance hatch and gave him one last look.

"You should be ..." The rest was drowned out by a shrill cry of pain that Hastings suddenly let out.

Robert, Bradshaw and Alex immediately rushed over to him, but could only watch as the commander was covered from bottom to top with a layer of crystal in less than a second. His eyes stared through the hull, wide with terror.

"Oh my God! He's choking!" Robert screamed.

Then Hastings' eyes had lost all sparkle. He was dead.

Meanwhile, the crystals continued to grow. They had already filled the entire silo and were now spreading towards the control console.

"Get out!" Bradshaw shouted, dragging Alex with him, who was still staring paralyzed at the dead Hastings. "Get the hell out!" he repeated, shooing everyone into the corridor.

"That was horrible!" Nora gasped outside and stumbled a few more steps into the corridor before they all stopped there.

"I don't want to end up like this!" Sakharov shouted and began to hyperventilate.

"Calm down, man!" shouted Hastings and tried to grab him by the shoulders, but the Russian swept his hand aside, let out a scream and ran down the corridor as if out of his mind.

Robert wanted to go after him at first, but Bradshaw held him back. "Leave him alone, there's no point."

"Yes, you're right," Robert said wanly and resignedly sat down on the floor. There's no point in any of this anymore, is there?"

34

Robert sat on the tunnel floor for an eternity, staring at the wall behind which the pinkish-purple glow was still pulsating. This ill-considered plan had probably failed. The crystal structures were all over the base - and if what the voice had said earlier was true, then they had already spread tens of kilometers beneath the glacier. What would have been the point of firing the missiles anyway? Hastings had died in vain, just like Jansson, whose body lay less than ten meters away. In the other direction, Bradshaw, Nora and Alex were standing together, talking quietly.

Robert couldn't understand what they were saying, and he didn't have the strength to get up and go. He hated the feeling of inactivity and powerlessness, but what could he do about it? They were trapped here. A handful of people were facing an overpowering enemy that they didn't even really understand.

And now? Should he really sit here and wait for death? Or for this alien intelligence to take possession of them? Would they just go crazy in the end, like Sakharov? It all felt so wrong!

"Shit!" Robert suddenly exclaimed.

Nora came over to him, knelt and put her hand on his shoulder. After a moment of silence, she stood up again and reached out her right hand to help him up.

"I'm not an old man," Robert grumbled grumpily, but then took Nora's hand.

She pulled him to his feet with astonishing strength.

"Thank you," he finally said, following her over to Alex and Bradshaw.

"But there must be something we can use here," said Bradshaw. "Maybe we can break through with one of the snow groomers?"

Alex shook his head. "Where is it? The former driveway is under tons of ice."

"An explosives depot?" Bradshaw asked, then waved it off. "Even if it was, it would hardly be enough."

Robert listened to the discussion for a moment and pondered. These suggestions were all too short-sighted, they were along the same lines as the idea with the rockets, only they seemed even more hopeless.

"Perhaps it should be approached differently," he muttered more to himself than the others. Nevertheless, he caught their attention.

"What do you mean?" Bradshaw wanted to know.

"Oh, sorry. I must have been thinking out loud." Robert took out Paul Memphis' diary and looked at it. "I mean, how did Sattler's father know that the plan with the rockets would work?"

"Well, he could only have guessed that," Bradshaw replied. "He probably just tried it on the off chance."

Robert twisted the corners of his mouth. "No, I don't think so. He killed several people on the way to the silo who tried to stop him. He must have been convinced."

"I think so too," Nora agreed with him. "On the other hand, he was ill before."

"He wasn't ill, he was under the influence of this strange ..." Alex fell silent. "Maybe he could have been ... it's pretty crazy, but ..."

"Would it be possible for you to express yourself more clearly?" Bradshaw asked irritably.

"I think I know what he means," Robert explained. "I just had a crazy idea too."

"That's great. But would you geniuses please enlighten me simple-minded agent?"

"Come on!" Robert demanded and set off. He made his way west towards the other end of the base.

"Where are we going?" Bradshaw wanted to know.

Robert did not answer, but fell into step. After a few minutes, they reached the abandoned snowmobile with the scientific equipment.

"If we're very lucky, we'll find something here that will help us," explained Robert.

"Do you mean something specific? Something like a crystal-destroying laser cannon?" asked Bradshaw in a sarcastic tone.

"Hey, we're just grasping at the last straw here. We'll take what we can get," Robert replied and set about searching through the crates from the 1967 mission.

Alex also rummaged around.

"You're looking for the samples from back then, right?" Nora asked.

"Yes."

"But what do you want with it?" she asked. "We can hardly find a solution that quickly."

"It's more of a hope," Robert said, pulling out an aluminum case labeled "Ice Samples, Series B" and marked "Important!"

"I know that sounds pretty crazy now, but basically it's no worse than trying to set off rockets that are stuck underground."

"I hope you don't want to..." Nora began and looked at Robert, startled.

"Yes, if my assumption is correct, then the original samples from 1967 are in here, the unadulterated material that Sattler's father also came into contact with. I want to inject myself with it."

"Wait a minute," Bradshaw replied in astonishment. "How on earth is that supposed to help us if someone else is walking around here as if remote-controlled?"

"We need influence, we have to stop this crystal structure somehow, adapt its programming once again."

"Now I understand. You think it's only escalated since the coding of this alien seed has changed, but the first version is still here in the samples," Nora said.

"Correct. And Sattler's father managed to gain the upper hand. What's more, he seems to have found out about the program's weaknesses himself and then exploited them. I want to repeat that."

"But who can guarantee that it won't control you?" asked Alex. "I wasn't very lucky when it was inside me. I practically couldn't defend myself at all."

Robert nodded. "That's true. No one guarantees that it will work out. I give myself a fifty-fifty chance at most."

"But even if you succeed, you still have the foreign intelligence against you, who, thanks to Sattler, know more about us than we do about them," Nora pointed out.

"I want to rectify this imbalance. And let's be honest, we don't have time to discuss it. But you also have to do something about it."

"You want us to take care of Sattler? Distract him?" Bradshaw guessed.

"Yes, binds his attention, appeals to his humanity. He's still in there and wants to help us."

"That's totally crazy," Nora realized. "But maybe it's so crazy that it's genius again."

Bradshaw sighed heavily. "Whatever. Our options look like shit anyway. And there might be something to Robert's theory. Sattler's been obsessed with finding out what happened to his father. He's made it a personal thing, and that could work to our advantage. His father is still here. We need to shift his focus to his original intention, clouding the consciousness that gives this crystal being its power."

"Congratulations, Bradshaw!" praised Robert. "You seem to have quite a brain for an agent."

"Yes, and you have more courage than I would have given an egghead credit for. Are we done flattering each other now?"

Robert nodded and opened the sample case. A pale pink liquid was floating in half a dozen plastic containers. "That looks good already." He looked at Alex. "Do you have any idea why it affected you in particular when it didn't affect us?"

"I've already thought about it. It must have been the cut on my finger. When I spilled the sample, it soaked my gloves and the plaster on my index finger. I had injured myself the night before while chopping vegetables. That must have been how the particles got into my bloodstream, where they spread like an infection."

"Sounds plausible," Nora said, "but there was an incubation period, if you can call it that."

"A few hours, yes. It only really started at night," Alex confirmed.

"Maybe because only a few crystal particles got into the wound," Robert speculated.

"Or he was just lucky that it didn't kill him," Nora replied.

"You know we have no alternative. If we don't do anything, we'll probably all be dead anyway."

"All right," Nora conceded defeat.

"Then it's settled," Robert said, turning to Bradshaw. "Go with Nora to Sattler and Linda. Do everything you can to keep his attention."

"I'm staying with you!" protested Nora.

"I can do that," Alex suggested. "Maybe I can influence the process? I can still feel a faint after-effect of the contact with the alien substance. We should use everything we have."

"That's the best solution," Robert confirmed. "If I manage to gain the upper hand, or at least enough influence to do something about it, then I want to try to get Linda and Sattler free and undo the sealing of the shaft. Once that happens, I want you to leave."

"And what about you?" Nora wanted to know.

"I'll catch up with you," Robert said, but he realized himself that it didn't sound very convincing.

Nora gave him a skeptical look, but didn't contradict him.

"Do you have a knife?" Robert asked Bradshaw.

He wordlessly pulled a combat knife from his belt holder and handed it to Robert. "Keep it for now, but I want it back later," the agent said urgently and nodded to him.

"Thank you, I'll try my best."

"Well, let's go to Sattler and see if we can get him awake," Bradshaw decided and rose from his crouch. "Good luck!" he said to Robert and set off.

Nora hesitated for a moment, and Robert realized that she was visibly finding it difficult to leave him.

"Go on, now," said Robert. "You have to succeed, otherwise my plan won't work either - if that's even possible."

"What madness this all is," Nora said, shaking her head, then turned and hurried after Bradshaw.

Robert and Alex were left alone in the tunnel, which was lit only by the subtle glow from the walls and the harsh beams of their two flashlights.

"Then I guess it's getting serious now," said Robert, clasping the blade of the knife in his left hand. "I never thought I'd do something so stupid."

"It's either stupid or simply brilliant - and therefore our salvation," Alex put it into perspective and took one of the sample containers, which had been sealed for over 50 years, out of the suitcase.

Originally, they had once been full to the brim with ice, but the rise in temperature at the base had long since melted it. However, as the material could not react with anything due to the airtight seal, the sample still appeared to be active.

Robert didn't hesitate any longer and quickly drew the blade across his closed hand. It didn't even hurt much, as Bradshaw's knife was extremely sharp. But the wound, which was deeper than Robert had intended, immediately began to bleed profusely.

Alex took a roll of bandages from the small first aid bag that each of them had with them and placed it in Robert's injured hand. "Squeeze it tight," he advised. Then he unscrewed the tubular sample container and looked at Robert questioningly.

"Ready to go," he confirmed.

Alex tipped the container and let the liquid run slowly over Robert's hands.

Robert was immediately overcome by agonizing pain. "Damn it!" he groaned and gasped. "It burns like fire."

"I'm rubbing salt in your wounds, so to speak. I don't like doing that, but we should play it safe," Alex explained and let the rest of the contents run over Robert's hand.

Then the pain finally subsided, and Robert slumped down exhausted. He didn't lose consciousness, but he had to fight against the threat of unconsciousness. At that moment, he felt more than clearly how much the exertions of the last few days and weeks had drained him.

Alex took a water bottle out of his rucksack and handed it to Robert. "Here, have a drink. You look really tired."

"Thank you. Now, let's hope we don't have to wait too long for a response."

Now Alex put his hand on Robert's arm and closed his eyes.

"What are you doing?" Robert wanted to know.

"I don't know, it's just an idea. When I touched the wall earlier, I could also feel the activity of the alien intelligence. Maybe I can tell when something is happening to you."

"Well, I suppose it can't do any harm. And the burning sensation has completely subsided. My left hand feels almost numb. I'd like to see that as a good sign."

***

When Nora and Bradshaw returned to the former reactor hall of the base, the pulsation of the crystal structures had visibly increased in both intensity and speed. The room now looked almost like an inverted, grotesque disco ball, in which thousands of reflections were thrown back into the interior rather than outwards.

"I hope it works somehow," said Nora as the two of them set about climbing down the wall.

"To be honest, I think this plan is a load of crap, but of course I couldn't tell Greaves that," said the agent.

"Shit or no shit ... Still the best option we have."

"That says everything about our situation."

They crossed the hall and climbed up again on the other side.

Linda Shoemaker saw them coming and jumped up. "Thank God!" her voice came muffled through the crystal wall. "I thought you'd forgotten about me!"

"No, but we just had no idea how to get you out of there," Nora explained.

"And now you have one?" she asked. "Where are the others? Are they getting help?"

Nora and Bradshaw shook their heads almost in sync.

"We have to help ourselves," said Bradshaw.

"And how, pray tell?"

"We have to try to get Sattler awake to talk to him," Nora replied.

"Speak up!" the crystal voice rang out.

"Sattler?" asked Bradshaw.

"He's here, we are one."

"Sattler, if you can hear this, give us a signal. We've found your father!"

There was a clang and a slight tremor that lasted a few seconds. The next moment, the general opened his eyes.

"What are you saying?" his own voice asked in strange unison with the crystals.

"Your father!" Bradshaw repeated. "You were looking for him, don't deny it. I know that's the reason for all your involvement."

"Go on," Nora whispered to Bradshaw.

"Sattler, we've found him, he's still here. I saw him with my own eyes, over by the West Silos."

"That ... How can that be?" asked Sattler.

"It was preserved," Nora explained, "by the crystals. Please, we're not lying, it's the truth!"

"General, let me out of here," Linda now asked. "If you remove the wall, I'll help you get there."

Sattler looked at Linda for a while. "I ... I don't know if I can do it." His words were intermingled with dissonant clanking, as if the alien intelligence was anything but in agreement with this plan.

"You have to try," Nora said, "We won't hurt anyone, not you, not..." She paused and looked up at the ceiling, where the crystals had now turned into an unpleasant continuous buzzing. "We won't harm the seed either!" she shouted loudly and received a violent shaking of the cave in response.

"You've got nothing to lose," Bradshaw assured him. "What could we do?"

"Let's go and check on your father," Linda said. "Please, General. We've come so far, we're so close to our destination. Let's get some certainty!"

Sattler let out a strained groan and then closed his eyes.

For a moment, nothing happened and Nora thought that the alien intelligence would take complete possession of Sattler again, but then the crystal wall began to melt and shrink before her eyes. After a few moments, it had almost disappeared, leaving only an ankle-high row sticking out of the ground.

Sattler opened his eyes again. "Go, quickly!" he shouted to Linda. "I can't leave. It won't let me."

"But..."

"Go!" He was almost shouting now. "I can't maintain control for long."

The wall began to build up again - this time as if in slow motion.

Linda hurried away from Sattler and jumped over the pedestal, which was now a meter high again. She joined Nora and Bradshaw, who had stepped to the edge of the pedestal.

"Thank God you're free, but that's not enough," Nora said.

"What are you up to? And where are Robert and the others?"

Before Nora could answer, the crystal voice sounded again. "You have no power here, we will rise."

"I'm sorry!" shouted Sattler. "I can't break the connection."

Then his body jerked, and the general slumped unconscious in his crystal corset.

35

Robert felt his whole body was on fire, as if he had a fever like he had never had in his life. He was hot - from the soles of his feet to the tips of his hair. His senses, too, were being led down confused paths that increasingly resembled a bizarre dream. He could still see Alex, who was staying with him, but he had long since stopped understanding what he was saying to him. He only took dull notice of his worried face and barely realized that it reflected the danger Robert had put himself in.

A thought made its way through the clouds of madness that wafted around in his mind and tried to rob him of control. Had he poisoned himself? Why was he in this state? What had happened?

This heat inside him made Robert unable to find convincing answers to these questions. He felt as if his whole body was fighting against something he didn't understand.

Why did he take this upon himself? Why did he endure this pain?

He no longer knew anything. His familiar world was collapsing, melting as if in a cauldron under which a hellfire was blazing. Soon, there wouldn't be a thing left!

Just when it was threatening to become unbearable and Robert thought he was finally losing his senses, it finally cooled down. It felt like a tiny snowflake crystallizing and growing in his head around a single thought. The feeling swelled, and he felt as refreshed as if he were plunging into ice-cold water after an extended visit to the sauna.

I have to save her, Robert thought. Suddenly, he realized again what he had done - and why. His foggy mind suddenly sobered up. But his perception was no longer the same. Only now did he realize that he had obviously closed his eyes and that he couldn't hear anything, only feel vibrations. This state was extremely strange and fascinating at the same time. Even if he was obviously unable to use his own senses, he was still aware of something. How could that be, and where was he now? Was he still in that unreal place under the ice? It had to be like this!

Then Robert felt his mind expand, stretching out its disembodied feelers in all directions and beyond every physical boundary. In his mind's eye, he recognized the base under the ice with all its passages and branches. Beyond it lay the glacier, in which there was a network of channels and caverns of meltwater stretching for miles, in which the dissolved crystals were concentrated and multiplied. The process had progressed much further than he had thought. Was it even possible to do anything about it?

All these crystal structures almost resembled the mycelium of a mushroom that grew invisibly on the forest floor and that you never got to see because only the fruiting bodies were formed on the surface. It became increasingly clear to him that something very similar was probably happening right here in the ice. This alien seed had waited for the right conditions, adapted, spread and was now about to move on to the next phase, which would have devastating consequences for the Earth's ecosystem.

At the same moment, Robert sensed that he was not alone, that there was something with him that gave him the ability to leave his own body with his consciousness. But he also knew that this feeling was deceptive, that the alien intelligence with which he had entered into a symbiosis could overwhelm him all too quickly. He had to oppose it with his iron will!

Linda Shoemaker's face suddenly appeared in the blackness. The thought of her would give him the strength. He would save her, even if he had to sacrifice himself in the process.

And something else would help him! He had allies. Not only Nora, Bradshaw and Linda, but also Sattler, whose presence he could suddenly feel very clearly in this biological network. The general was desperately looking for a way to get free, to defend himself, to escape the influence of the alien intelligence, but he was too weak on his own. Until now! Together, perhaps they could collapse these structures.

***

Alex Corbinian came rushing into the former reactor hall and looked around for Nora and Bradshaw. He found them over at the other end, where Sattler was locked in. He was relieved to see that they had apparently succeeded in freeing Linda Shoemaker.

"Come quickly!" he shouted over. "We have to try to get out of here!"

The others turned around.

"What is it? Did it work?" Bradshaw wanted to know.

"I don't know. Come over here," he repeated his request. He saw that the three of them were arguing with each other but couldn't understand their words.

Then, the group set off and began to descend the other side of the wall.

As they did so, the vibrations became stronger, and the rumbling was increasingly accompanied by cracking and crunching, which sounded more threatening than all the tremors put together.

Alex helped Nora and Linda over the edge and pulled them up to him. "We should make sure we get out of here!" he said in an urgent tone and pointed to the exit.

"But what about Robert?" Linda asked angrily. "We can't leave him here!"

"He ... I don't know what we can do," said Alex.

"What's happened?" Nora asked.

"We did everything as planned, Robert exposed himself to the sample and soon passed out. His body was glowing, but now it's freezing cold and starting to glow from the inside out. But something is different."

"What do you mean?" Nora asked.

"The color isn't right. With me and Sattler, it was pinkish-purple, like the walls here. But with Robert, everything turns turquoise. And it seems to sink into the floor, as if it's melting into the structure."

"We have to help him!" Linda demanded. "I want to see him."

Alex shook his head vigorously. "I can't do that!"

"Why the hell?" she snapped at him.

"That's why I'm here. The tunnel seems to be collapsing. The ceiling has collapsed further back."

"Did Robert do that?" asked Bradshaw.

"I have no idea. All I know is that we should get out of here before the ceiling falls on our heads."

At that moment, the color of the glow in the floor of the great hall changed. The purple turned blue, then more and more green was mixed in. Finally, everything changed again and the pink returned.

The frequencies emitted by the crystals were also constantly changing. Deafening dissonances swelled, fizzled out and suddenly resounded in perfect harmony, only to drift off into a shrill cacophony again immediately afterwards.

"What is that? Is Robert doing that?" Linda shouted over the noise.

Alex raised his shoulders indecisively and looked at her helplessly.

"We'll get out of here while they're fighting!" Bradshaw shouted, pushing the others purposefully through the entrance.

They had barely stepped into the tunnel when a violent shock almost knocked them to the ground. The entire rear section of the tunnel had been brought down by the masses of ice above. The way to Robert was cut off.

"The whole hull is obviously becoming unstable!" shouted Alex.

"To the elevator!" Bradshaw ordered and ran ahead.

Nothing was holding the others back now either. They ran

as fast as they could through the shivering tunnel, in which the icy cold was now spreading.

They left the access to the missile silos on the left and reached the bottom of the shaft that led to the surface.

"Damn it!" shouted Bradshaw.

"Where is the cabin?" Nora asked in amazement.

Bradshaw stuck his head into the shaft and looked up. "I can't see anything. But I can hear a knocking up there."

"Sakharov," Alex said curtly. "He's probably trying to break through the dome."

"The bastard!" growled Bradshaw and turned back upwards. "Sakharov!" he shouted at the top of his lungs into the shaft. "Go back down, we'll try it together!"

The knocking from above stopped for a moment. "I don't trust you!" the Russian shouted. "You're just trying to lure me down!"

"Sakharov, that's not true!" Bradshaw replied. "Everything is collapsing here, you have to get us up!"

The knocking sounded again from above.

"Shit," cursed Bradshaw. "He's leaving us here to rot."

"We'll never get out of here without an elevator," Nora said. "We can't climb all the way up on slippery steel cables." She stepped forward and tried her luck too. "Sakharov, it's me, Nora. Lower the elevator, please!"

But Sakharov stubbornly continued to knock and did not answer.

There was another violent tremor and more tunnel sections collapsed with a crash. A frosty wind tore at them, and the change in pressure made their ears crack as the chambers collapsed.

"That's it then," said Alex resignedly.

"Sakharov!" Bradshaw shouted again.

A shrill crunch came back from above, then a cracking sound and excited voices.

"Did he manage to break through?" Nora asked incredulously.

"What use is that to us?" said Alex.

"Hey, get us out!" shouted Bradshaw.

Nothing happened for an agonizing second, then they heard the hum of the elevator motor.

"Faster!" Nora called upstairs. "We don't have much time left."

The cabin finally reached its position, and the three of them squeezed in.

"Go!" Bradshaw yelled, and the elevator began to rise again with a jerk.

Just in time, because after a few seconds they felt another tremor and a sharp draught of air coming from below.

They reached the surface and jumped out of the cabin. Sandra Gillie, Per Olofsson and Ian Macmillan, who should have been evacuated long ago, were waiting for them there.

"We're complete, no one else is coming," Bradshaw reported.

Everyone immediately ran towards the exit. As they passed through the airlock, the shaft collapsed with a final big bang, closing itself off.

They got outside and ran across the plain to a helicopter ready to take off, in which two soldiers and Sakharov, who was tied up with cable ties, were already sitting.

As soon as everyone was on board, the pilot took off. Not a moment too soon, as the surface became increasingly deep crevices and cracks that were already swallowing up several barracks and vehicles.

"I think we got the timing right," said Sandra Gillie with a winning smile.

Bradshaw looked at her and didn't know what to say. He was glad to have escaped this icy hell, but the fact that Gillie, of all people, had played a part in his rescue made him angry.

"We're so glad we got you out of there," said Olofsson. "It's thanks to Sandra Gillie, who made sure the helicopter was waiting and we were able to break through."

"How did you manage that?" Nora wanted to know.

"Your drill. We ruined it, but in the end we got a small hole in the crystal dome. And Sakharov hit it like a madman with an axe from below. At some point it cracked and the crystals shattered."

Nora and Linda looked at each other knowingly.

"It wasn't the drill or the axe," Linda said wanly. "Robert saved us. I don't know how he did it, but he did. He did it all." Her voice broke and she burst into tears.

Nora put her arm around her comfortingly.

"It does seem that way," Bradshaw agreed. "I can't explain it all, but fortunately I don't have to." Then he turned to Gillie again. "You may have made some amends, but don't think that makes us even. You'll have to take full responsibility for everything!"

"Of course, colleague," said Gillie dryly. "I was happy to do it."

The helicopter gained altitude and headed for Pituffik Space Base.

Olofsson looked at Nora scrutinizingly. "Are you all right? What happened down there?"

"I ... well, to be honest, I can't even answer the question of how I am, let alone what has really happened in the last few hours," Nora replied.

"It's quite simple," said Alex. "We've saved the world. Superman would be proud of us."

"I think we'll have to be a bit more precise for the investigation, which is sure to take place soon," Bradshaw interjected. "But I can live with that for today."

36

West of the former "Camp Century", Greenland,
September 23

Nanouk Bruun parked her snowmobile and lifted her binoculars to inspect the west side of the site. Two days had passed since the collapse of the underground Camp Century, and the military had cordoned off the entire area. Then, they had started cleaning up with heavy equipment. Or rather, they did what they thought was cleaning up. They tried to smooth everything out, fill in gaps, and make it look as if nothing had ever happened here.

At the urging of the Greenlandic and Danish governments, state and civilian actors from these countries were also involved, but Nanouk's non-profit organization was of course not brought on board.

So, she had no choice but to observe everything from the edge of the exclusion zone and take measurements. She still had no idea exactly what had happened here, and all her attempts to find out more had come to nothing or had been met with hair-raising excuses. The silliest and at the same time most used of all had been the claim that there had been a volcanic eruption under the glacier, which was responsible for the massive distortions. But this was in stark contradiction to all previous geological findings in this region.

The fact was that the situation had obviously calmed down. The seismic activity, the effects of which had been felt far and wide, had abruptly subsided and the temperature rises observed by some scientists had also disappeared. Why this was the case remained a mystery, as did the true cause of the whole thing. Detailed information was only available to the US forces, who were now trying to keep the circle of insiders as small as possible.

Nanouk watched as a large snow groomer was being lifted out of a crevasse by a crane and loaded. As usual, the Americans only did what was absolutely necessary. They removed the all-too-obvious evidence of their actions, but left untouched the legacy that lay dormant further down in the ice. What fabulous folly!

She lowered the binoculars and put them away. Maybe this was just tilting at windmills, after all. She was just about to start her snowmobile and begin the return journey when she spotted something dark on the surface of the ice about 50 meters away. At first glance, it almost looked like a seal, but then Nanouk realized that the object seemed to be more or less flush with the surface of the ice and not protruding above it.

Curious, she dismounted and walked over to take a closer look at the object. It was definitely not a seal, but ...

Nanouk had come to a distance of 20 meters when she stopped as if struck by lightning. There was a human lying there!

The body was in a kind of hollow in the ice that nestled right up against its shape as if it had been frozen inside.

Was that a corpse? A soldier or a scientist who had died in the recent incidents here? She looked over towards the military cordon. Should she call someone immediately?

Nanouk slowly started moving again and approached the man. Now she recognized him and knelt down next to him. His body seemed to be covered in a thin film. A super-thin layer of ice? How could that be possible? And why was he lying here all alone in a perfectly recessed hollow? It made no sense.

Instinctively, she reached out and touched him on the forehead. She immediately flinched. "Holy shit!" she exclaimed. He felt warm to the touch.

Then she heard a fine crackling sound, like an empty chip bag being crumpled up. The sound came from the thin protective layer covering the man and now showing thousands of small cracks.

Nanouk was startled and almost lost her balance in astonishment. She caught herself at the last moment and saw the man open his eyes.

"That..." she gasped and shook her head violently.

The man sat up and stared at her.

For almost a whole minute, Nanouk was unable to say or do anything. The man didn't move either, but just looked at her with an expressionless face.

Nanouk finally came to her senses and bent down to him. "Dr. Greaves?" she asked.

Her counterpart tilted his head slightly, as if he had to think about the meaning of the words.

"Robert, is that you?" she asked, "It's me, Nanouk Bruun!"

"I..." he began. "Robert?" Then he frowned and nodded tentatively. "Yes, maybe that's me," he said cryptically. His gaze became more alert now, as if he was finally shaking off the after-effects of an endless nightmare. "Robert Greaves. That must be me!"

"Man, you really have a talent for weird performances," said Nanouk and helped Robert to his feet.

He looked around the barren icy landscape in irritation. "Where ... why?" he stammered and then flinched violently, as if something terrible had occurred to him.

Nanouk put a hand on his shoulder. "What's wrong?"

"Is it ... I mean, did it work?"

"I'm sorry, I don't know what that means."

"The crystals! The ice, I ..."

"It's all right," Nanouk said, without knowing exactly what Robert meant. "I'll take you back to civilization first. But afterwards, you have to tell me exactly what happened."

She took his arm and led him towards the snowmobile.

Robert tried to smile. "I'll ... I will." He stopped and looked over at the military base that was being dismantled. "Oh man, looks like that wasn't the craziest nightmare of my life after all."

"Whatever it was, it seems to be over," Nanouk affirmed. "Come now, or would you rather be captured by the military?"

Robert shook his head. "Thanks, no need."

They boarded the snowmobile and left the frosty Greenlandic ice desert behind them, which now lay as still and peaceful as it had been for the last 400,000 years.

END

R/N/A - Deadly Sequence

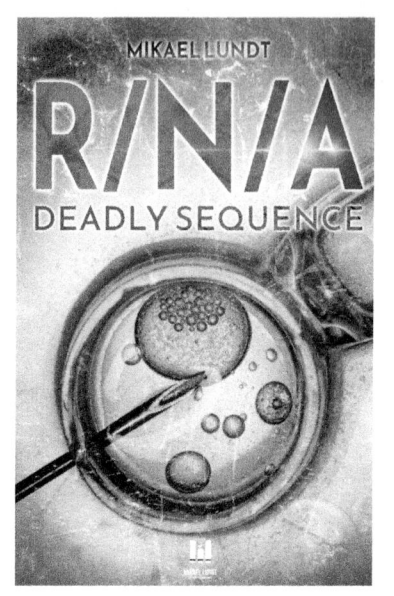

Dr. Laura Delille, a brilliant mind hailed by the World Health Organization, races against time to decipher an escalating crisis. Infertility, miscarriages, and inexplicable deaths sweep across continents, shrouding the world in a cloud of fear. As Dr. Delille uncovers an unsettling connection to a cutting-edge mRNA-based vaccine, initially hailed as a beacon of hope. Yet, the mounting horror defies reason as even the unvaccinated succumb to the devastating symptoms. The chilling truth dawns - the menace runs deeper than anyone could have fathomed.

Amidst the chaos, investigative journalist Hugh Stevens joins the pursuit of truth, revealing the sinister plot of a heartless pharmaceutical giant. With every step, the darkness thickens, leaving Laura and Hugh teetering on the edge of a precipice. Can they expose the malevolent machinations before time runs out? The haunting question echoes: medical scandal or humanity's gravest threat?

Against an electrifying backdrop of global peril, "R/N/A - Deadly Sequence" unfurls a nerve-racking saga that will leave you breathless. Dr. Delille and Hugh Stevens must navigate a labyrinth of secrets, betrayals, and hidden agendas. As the deadly phenomenon spirals toward a crescendo, can they defy the odds and unmask the face of a planned pandemic poised to decimate humanity?

Embark on a journey into the heart of darkness in "R/N/A - Deadly Sequence." Are you prepared to confront the chilling truths that lie beneath the veneer of healing?

NAGLFAR – Ark of the Gods

In the Arctic archipelago of Svalbard miners make an unexpected discovery: a cave with ancient petroglyphs and a giant ship that has a dangerous secret. When one of the men touches it, he goes berserk and kills several workers.

Archaeologist Anika Wahlgren is called out to Svalbard to investigate the ancient ship. Yet she has no idea what she's about to uncover: NAGLFAR! The ship from Norse mythology that heralds the end of the world.

With a team of international researchers she's determined to get to the bottom of the mystery before even more lives are lost. But there is no end to the tragic incidents. It becomes clear that there is far more to the ship than meets the eye. And its inexplicable powers arouse desires. The researchers are no longer the only ones who want to take advantage of this secret.

With a blizzard coming in from the north the team is running out of time...

A breath-taking arctic adventure with a new twist on Norse mythology!

RECURSION – Beyond Time

A mysterious message from the future saves the lives of Dr. Marc Jensen's family. The next morning, however, his entire research material about tachyons is gone – and with it, the proof that these obscure particles even exist.

Ten years later, the past catches up with Dr. Jensen: Fragments of his work suddenly reappear, fellow researchers die, and his daughter is kidnapped.

To save her, he must confront an all-powerful enemy who always seems to be one step ahead of him. Even worse: If Jensen fails, the whole structure of space and time might turn to chaos.

You can't escape your worst enemy – he knows you better than you know yourself.

Printed in Great Britain
by Amazon